ASPECTS OF LOVE

A Collection of Short Stories

ASPECTS OF LOVE

A Collection of Short Stories

Aphrodite

Fresh Ink Group
Roanoke

ASPECTS OF LOVE:
A Collection of Short Stories

Copyright © 2016
by Margaret Montrose
All rights reserved

Fresh Ink Group
An Imprint of:
The Fresh Ink Group, LLC
PO Box 525
Roanoke, TX 76262
Email: info@FreshInkGroup.com
www.FreshInkGroup.com

Edition 2.0   2016

Book design by Ann Stewart

Cover Art and Interior Art by John Roberts
www.johnrobertsonline.com

Portrait by Joanna Roberts, daughter of John

Front cover design by Margaret Montrose

Cover by Stephen Geez

Text Set in Garamond

Cataloging-in-Publication Recommendations:
FIC014000   FICTION / Historical
FIC027000   FICTION / Romance / General
FIC027020   FICTION / Romance / Contemporary
FIC029000   FICTION / Short Stories (single author)
FIC027080   FICTION / Romance / Collections & Anthologies
JUV037000   JUVENILE FICTION / Fantasy & Magic

Library of Congress Control Number: 2016910759
ISBN-13: 978-1-936442-29-4

To my Lady Margaret who is central to the surety of my

Spirit — and to all those who would build

'Love's Gift of Themselves to Others.'

Acknowledgements

First this book would not been in front of you now without the perspicacity of The Swashbuckler of FreshinkGroup, then they having persevered, beyond most people's patience, with my creative intransigence. I owe a great debt to The Lady Garamond for allowing me to re-write the stories to fit the protocols I have developed since they were written some seven years ago, after she had coded the initial bookblock text. Their patience, with their creative understanding, have been exemplary.

The only other acknowledgement, except to 'My Lady' to whom they are dedicated, is to The University of Life — truly the only one worth attending. Nothing I was ever taught impinges on them one whit but travelling Life's Pilgrimage for some 60 years (since I was a sentient being at 15), rushing down the main stream while visiting un-numbered tributaries, has not only provided the meat but fertilised what is within these pages which then lead me onwards into the greatest journey I have travelled, down *The Golden Path*. Margaret Montrose

Table of Contents

Introduction

Dear Reader,

As a design and manufacturing engineer for forty years perfection of purpose through originality of endeavour have lit my life, of which the way the following stories are 'written' is the product. I have been writing seriously for the last fifteen years while reading voraciously and vicariously across The Great Men of English letters in my 1,000 book library; I run the full OED on my hard drive so what follows has been designed to be — shoot me not any of the others involved.

Many of layout's conventions I have found both illogical and inhibiting — very specially when speech becomes the medium of the story. This became particularly apparent when working on my huge Romance *The Golden Path* which is a pilgrimage of ideas created by a steadily expanding group of people, conducted in huge drafts of dialectic dialogue. With the convention of paragraphing each speaker any form of continuity of the discussion through flow (because the eye constantly having to dance *across* the page instead of progressively along it) is lost, with the creation of euphony (whose cadences carry the reader) impossible, very particularly when *who, how, and why* something is said is so important to, not only, the understanding of the logic of the argument, but also the fleshing out the finer details of the characters — it is the latter which is the most interesting because we are all human so identify with their predicaments. There is nothing more clumpy, boring and deadening than 'he said', 'she said'; you will not find the word said anywhere in what follows, so;

The principle of my method is to tie those addressing a discussion together in one paragraph, *changing* the speakers with a space-dash-space then immediately noting *who* and *how* the next proceeds; if the same speaker changes his style during a peroration there will just be a comma before and after the " ..". You will discover this method allows for a far greater integration and euphony of the writing with the possibility of indicating, by the implications of the words, who is speaking next, with why and how, while splicing in little bits of 'flesh' without interrupting the flow. When a speaker changes *with who he is immediately being stated,* then a comma is sufficient to carry the narrative forward. The mix'n match of the two methods allows for the variety from which euphony can be created. This method maintains the integrity of the ideas while carrying, you, the reader along.

When 'the argument' changes or is taken up by a new voice then I paragraph to indicate the step-function. I will admit to using dashes — as 'stoppers' or to accent a final phrase in order to add lift. You will also note the only use of 'and' is as a purely additive conjunction (even when used to conjoin sub-clauses) as just 'stringing stuff together' kills narrative dead because not supplying the causal *why* things happen, which is what draws us along with the characters for being the most interesting business of all. English has an astonishing number of causal conjunctions whose proper use can vastly improve not only the readability but the interest of what is being read because describing the minutæ of *why people do things'.*

The convention of where speech-marks, "..", are placed has always struck me as illogical. I believe "what is said" should be encapsulated first, *then* the ?, if appropriate, *then* the comma which divides what is said from the descriptive of who said it, why and how.

"Who the blazes are you"?, exclaimed The Dean frazzled by the fright on sensing the intruder out of the gloom, then laughed, "oh sorry Jim I didn't see you in the shadow" — "'s ok's me Sir", replied young Master Stone stepping into the light, "sorry to give you a frizz" — "forgiven Jim", he cheered relaxed, "you're being Mercury I suppose so give us the news — police still alive I hope"?, to Master Stone's chuckle, "'live Sir but pretty blue — Jude'n Penny untied them early'n given them their clothes — so 'speck they'll live", to a hearty laugh from 'Mr Cathedra' as Master Stone thought of The Dean, "serve them right Jim, perhaps they'll see The Light", The merit of this method shows more powerfully when several people are involved in a complex discussion. It is a small claim in this 'green' world the saving of paper and blank screen is considerable.

I make no apology for using properly constructed sentences (of more than ten words with words of more than 4 letters!) which, I know well, sets at nought the TV soap style writing of so much today; the rolling periods of good classical writing I have always found a joy in themselves for asking me *to think.* These stories were written about ten years ago so are simpler than *The Golden Path* during which I perfected my technique to meet the exigencies of its more complex needs.

For those of you interested in the business of Story Writing you will find the whole explanation in *The Troubadour* inside *The Golden Path* website — FREE! I hope you enjoy the break with convention.

These stories were my first shot at being a Troubadour, after some years writing monster polemics. Since Love has driven not only my second marriage but everything I do as a creator, they are concerned with its various Aspects — so Aphrodite seemed a suitable pseudonym. When I came to write 'The Golden Path' I chose a new 'name' for what I soon knew was a far greater endeavour - that of the noble wife of The Marquis of Montrose (Annus Mirabilis 1662) for whose heart I had the honour to make a spectacular jewelled display mounting when I was an engineering apprentice. John Robert's delicious artwork for The Aphrodite Stories was far too good not to use — so we have.

—Margaret Montrose

Aspects of Love

A collection of short stories

We Can't Lose

by Aphrodite

WE CAN'T LOSE

(My first 'official' Short Story, started on an aircraft going on holiday)

All that could be heard above the summer silence was the clash and clatter of the McCormick reaper gathering the harvest beyond the airfield. Clatter and clash were the words which came to Alan's mind as he dreamed in his deck chair awaiting the next, inevitable, scramble; chatter it could have been but chatter suggested contemplative concourse yet what they were all engaged upon was death's dis-course where the clash of swords was the clatter of machine guns — where he in front got 'downed'.

For these young men the days of knights were over, swords no longer served as death came out of the sun before you'd seen it — he knew he'd had some narrow squeaks but he was still here because he was a thinker. Amongst the jolly lads he was the quiet one who spent his time trying to work out how to survive so England might. For Alan Farquar death was not a game, to be engaged upon as some knightly quest; his prosaic Scot's intellect abhorred silly failures which could be avoided — what use death if their stand against tyrants failed? He was passionate about his friends, specially the less able ones still learning the business of survival, so he spent his idle hours working out tactics he could practice then show them for their success — so also London's salvation.

The wing had been up already today as they were in the thickest of the fight as 'The Few' became fewer while the many seemed inexhaustible — huge faith was needed to believe it could still be done with no knowledge of how long nor how thin those few could still effectively battle on. Their machines remained at the ready with erks re-fuelling, re-arming and patching any shotholes as everyone grabbed what rest they could. Pet dogs roamed quietly, aware of the tension inevitable amongst their guardians, nuzzling hanging hands to help the waiting. Suddenly the reaper's clatter was drowned by the squark of the call from the hut with the direction and height of the bandits being briskly given out as they dashed to their 'planes.

Alan arrived at his to be met by his mechanic, another Scot, a fine engineer is his early forties who could have been father to any of the pilots — indeed felt he was as did the more thoughtful of 'the boys', who knew these fine men, 'behind the scenes' as their inferiors in rank, were what kept them in the air with any chance of a tomorrow.

"She's fine Sir", his mechanic assured, "perhaps running a little warmer than I'd like but she won't let you down, just go easy on the boost till I've found out why — good luck'n good hunting". "Thanks Jim", he replied grateful for the assurance which he knew he could rely on, "this lot are up high so it'll be a long climb but I'll look after your baby for you".

He was up the wing to be strapped-in as the engine fired, the chocks were swept away with Farquar waving as he opened the throttle to taxi fast to join the rapidly rising wing as it climbed into the blue to meet England's enemies. Alan Farquar was the wing leader who'd adopted a loose formation so the lambs were watched while the shepherds did the guarding — it was a shepherd-and-sheep thing whose art was to remain alive long enough to be a good shepherd in your turn — for lambs died young in the blast of the blue above without due care.

With throttles wide, but not through the gate, they climbed to the aimed for height in the direction from which control had suggested the raid was coming. The wonderful system which had been grown by central control through the radar stations round the East and South Coast was becoming very accurate at spotting raiders — without which everyone knew their chance of being in time would not have been. It was the confidence in this system, fought for so hard against intractable 'office bods', which allowed The Few to believe victory was possible because they could be up in the lists to meet the foe.

There, indeed they were, in thick phalanxes but Farquar spotted other wings from other stations approaching too — he was glad to see they were predominantly Hurricanes, the tough warhorses best amongst the bombers. Brass-hats would have had all Spitfires up against the hawks above but Farquhar had seen too many lambs die young so he sent his babies to gain their wings amongst the bombers, while he lead his aces up into the blue above to defend the battle down below.

Like all the thinking pilots he knew formulæ failed in the fracas in the blue, he knew what won the day was the individual initiative which built the care of self through a mild berserker drive which never let up the concentration; it was wearing stuff but it was the command of concentration which had kept him alive with a satisfying number of kills to his credit, but; a last look with a quick warning to his lambs to keep their eyes on their mirrors as they set about the job they were here to do — stop the bombers getting to London — failed his concentration to find the snout of a Messerschmitt in his mirror.

Caught unawares he panicked to thrust the stick hard forward into a vertical dive to clear the enemy's fire — yet how many times had he told, then shown, his lambs the proper way to toss their machines on their back to stop the fuel in the carburettors leaving the jets then cutting the engine out. The Merlin had the edge on the German engines but its one Achilles heel, until Rolls-Royce cured it with a new carburettor, was its inability to fly with negative gravity as the fuel fled to the top instead of the bottom.

Farquar kept on going down aware his enemy was close behind — then his engine died so his only escape was to continue down cavorting as much as he could under 'glide' conditions for, for some reason, his engine would not re-start as it windmilled downwards. Thinking, perhaps, his enemy had been hit the Messerschmitt left off to find prey who were still fighting his bombers to leave Farquar the melancholy task of getting his machine down into a field in one piece with a dead engine.

Mercifully much of the harvest was in so he was able to spot a field which had clearly been cut — they presented quite different colours from the air — as he sized up an approach. Winding the undercarriage down in good time to re-acquaint himself of the feel of his machine under glide he settled down to the business of getting down in one piece piling on lots of flying speed in a brisk dive approach. This was a game he'd practiced so knew how far his machine would hold its speed in level flight with no power. He was a little short but was able to give a quick last minute lift to clear the entry hedge before flopping down promptly the other side rolling to halt a good distance before the hedge the other end — hard braking in loose earth resulted in somersaults only too easily.

He slid the canopy back to hear the chuckle of a reaper in the field next door — hardly a quarter of an hour since the one back home — but concentrating on getting down he had little idea of where home was. Gently he unstrapped his harness, climbed out of his 'chute then stood to get out down the wing, dropping to the ground to see an old man coming towards him across the field.

"Are you alright"?, was the concerned question. The answer took a few seconds to form as he felt the ground steady beneath him, "Oh yes just a dead engine, might I use a telephone to contact base so I'n my machine can be rescued"? "Surely", his host replied happy to see 'one of their young men' in one piece, "come into the house for a cuppa and meet my wife as we fix the cavalry — where're you from"? he asked as he scanned the Spitfire ticking gently in the sun beside them, to see if the white code letters might tell him.

"Lower Horning", replied the pilot, "where are we here"? "We're in the middle of nowhere here, between Little Slaughter and Middle Leigh — about twenty miles from you but I can give you an Ordnance Reference for your chaps to find us", the farmer laughed, "I imagine you know your home 'phone number"? Farquar laughed too, only too happy to be down with rescue in sight, "indeed I do, but it's the first time I've needed to use it as I've always got home before".

They arrived at the snug ancient farmhouse which looked as though it had grown there to give Farquar a momentary choke showing him this was what they were fighting for, the very essence of what 'home fires' meant. The farmer's wife was a round cheery lady who had got tea on the go already, seeing men approaching her kitchen.

"Meet my lady Jane", greeted the farmer happily, "I'm Harry'n we're both locals grown out of the local soil". "Wing Commander Alan Farquar", Alan extended a hand, "who's particularly fed-up at getting downed as I was leading a wing today then made a silly mistake I tell my boys about so got caught unawares". "Ah, but there to fight another day", consoled the farmers's wife gently, "so The Few aren't any fewer, Harry, show Alan the 'phone while I get the cake out".

Contact was made, map references given then a promise his personal mechanic would be over with a truck, starter and tools — 'in about an hour if we don't get lost', his mechanic told him. Back in the kitchen the farmer's wife took trouble to set Alan at ease, plying him with extraordinarily delicious cake with tea which hadn't sat stewing for hours. "Our daughter Jenny's in the swim with the boys at Upper Horning", she informed to bring them into Farquar's camp, "as a WAAF working in the canteen there — she feels she's doing something good".

Farquar felt himself relax for knowing he was amongst those who knew, "the girls who feed us, at all sorts of odd times, are our first line of defence", he stalled as the silly metaphor struck him, fancying his hostess was aware of it too, "tho' really the whole show's a team's if any don't work well everything gets rocky, so everyone swarms round us to keep us fit, cheerful, fed'n informed so we can do the best we can".

 "Yes", her mother reflected, "Jenny says she feels like those ancient ladies who sat in the lists to cheer their knights on — I'spose your mechanics are sort of the horse fixers", she laughed. Farquar sat thoughtful for a moment, "yes perhaps they are, my mechanic Jim Blane's a Scot like me'n a superb engineer, but he could be my dad — we've got a sort of father/son relationship which is wonderful", he enthused happy to support he without whom he would not be, "my machine is the horse he ensures is up to scratch for me but it's also his baby — he's going to be cursing it seems to have let me down as it wouldn't restart in a dive which is why I'm here — though I wouldn't have been if the shepherd hadn't done what he tells his lambs not to do", he chuckled ruefully, "go into a straight dive which kills the engine — silly stuff because I got caught on the hop by a Gerry right in my mirror coming on hard".

Gentle harvest and summer chat filled the time as bees hummed with birds singing in the sun — 'could this peace belong to the same place as the hell in the blue above', he wondered — then there was a hoot from outside. The pilot looked at his watch to see his mechanic had made it in three-quarters of an hour. As they met he complimented cheerfully, "crikey you hoof fast Jim you'll be needing to mend your truck next — meet Harry'n Jane whose field I'm in'n whose lovely tea'n cake I'm eating".

Blane smiled, "thank you ma'am for looking after my errant chick, as wing leader he should be back at home not communing in the countryside — what happened Sir". "Oh the usual suspects Jim", the pilot replied ruefully, "taking a second to mardle over the success of my lambs making a good attack just as Gerry's bearing down on me — I just stuck the stick forward then the old dear cut out, but the funny thing was it would'nt restart".

Blane frowned as his mechanic's brain immediately switched to diagnosing the possible culprits. "All that stuff I drum into my boys then fail to do myself when caught on the hop", he laughed deprecatingly, "pathetic, it's a mercy Harry had cleared his stooks to one side", he looked his thanks at the farmer for his forethought.

"I'm delighted something we've done worked", replied the farmer, "we'd decided at a local meet when we'd cut we'd stook round the edges of the field so there was space for emergencies like yours, my friends'll be tickled it's worked as heaving stooks around's heavy work".

Everyone trekked outside to examine the errant engine. While their hosts sat quietly on the ground Blane and Farquar set to. Blane quickly had the float chamber off to see if anything had got stuck but all seemed fine; a few more simple checks produced no visible reasons for the failure so he connected the starter as his pilot climbed aboard to do the engine checks. A few whirls then the engine burst into life to settle down into a gentle tick-over. "Well I don't know", reflected Blane disconsolately, "I always feel so undressed when I can't find the solution to a problem, somehow lost, knowing it may well happen again because I haven't found it — still we seem to have an engine now so let's get you off home".

Farquar climbed down to say his thanks to his hosts then settled into his cockpit being strapped in by his mechanic, then he taxied to the down-wind side of the field turning along the side of the hedge so Blane with the farmers could lift the tail right against the hedge to give him the maximum run. "It's going to be a close one", he called down over the cockpit side, "so could you all sit on the tail while I give the engine a good run-up then just drop flat when I give the signal". It was done then, with the engine through the gate, he blasted off down the field, got the tail up waiting for speed to build enough to hop the hedge at the other end — which he managed by a whisker as his wheels grazed through the upper leaves.

The farmer's wife looked at the mechanic her eyes far-away, "how old is he Jim, he seems to be as old as the hills". "He's not quite 20 ma'am but they get that look after a few weeks surviving in the hell up in the blue as they call it — it's a funny affair because the flying they passionately love, as I think you're about to see, but staying alive by killing their fellow flyers to defend their country makes them old long before their time".

Farquar had taken his machine high into the blue above the field to make sure all was normal then came piling down to roar across the heads of his hosts at 'zero' height executing a beautiful intermittent barrel roll as he passed above to head straight up into a vertical climb, waiting till just before the stall then tipping his machine on its side off-the-top to come back down for another pass via a magnificent slow flick-roll. Harry put his arm round his lady as they watched caught in the spell of youthful knighthood lance in rest as tears trickled down their faces to the ferocious roar of a Merlin on full song. As he came above them he slid the canopy back for a final wave then vanished upwards — home.

"We can't lose, can we Jim when there are young men like that to defend us", observed Jane mopping tears. "Indeed we can't", agreed the mechanic delighted his engine was still on song, "it's what keeps us slaving to keep their machines in the air without enough spares'n time, but when we see them come back home we know the struggles are worth every moment of our graft — it's when they don't the hearts break yet we have to be as tough as they or it could never be done at all".

"Yes our daughter Jenny's a WAAF at Upper Horning Jim", continued his hostess, "who say's the same thing and she's young so gets to know them as equals, sort of romantic 'knight'n lady' stuff — she says it's hell when they don't come back, you just have to close your mind to the horrors to be able to keep going".

The Farmer stood thoughtfully gazing into the space where the Spitfire had vanished, "it was the same in the trenches Jim, we knew we couldn't lose yet we didn't know how we could win either" — "but we both know Sir", added Blane, "if, even for a moment, any of us give up knowing we'll win then we're finished — it's how you won in the trenches, keeping the faith you couldn't lose". "It's different here though", added the farmer, "because in the trenches in France our airmen engaged in what seemed knightly jousts with us in the lists below so we could cheer them on while taking pot shots at Gerry to cheer us up too, but here all we can do is pray then pick up the pieces which fall out of the sky — we do a lot of praying as we hear the noise in the blue above".

"Sir", encouraged Blane, "tell those friends who helped clear your stooks what you've seen today, tell them 'we can't lose' because everyone needs to know — make what you've just seen work for them". "Indeed we shall", the farmer acknowledged, "because we've been privileged to be a tiny part of it for a little time — a magical part of 'boys of a treasured memory, boys of a timeless youth' — our son's at the bottom of the Atlantic so thank young Alan for his show". Jim Blane gave the old pair a hug, packed his truck to set off back to base.

Early next morning Farquar wandered into the hanger where his machine had been taken for his mechanic to try to find the real reason for the overheating and the engine failure. "Your little beat-up was a lovely thing you did yesterday Sir — the old pair were all overcome — they told me 'we can't lose can we, when we've got lads like him', then we discussed his time in the trenches — he's going to tell his friends so they feel the same way, buck them up at this trying time — they lost their son in the Atlantic convoys, Sir".Farquar stopped short for a moment indefinably connected to those in the farm house in the field, "thank you for the info Jim, it makes a difference — at least we all got back last night'n quite a good score too — everyone had a good laugh when I told them what I'd managed" — "it's no bad thing for the kids to know their shepherds are mortal Sir'n a good laugh keeps everyone cheerful". "Jim I liked them enormously, real England stuff, when I saw their farmhouse I got a better steer on what we're fighting for so when the heat's off I'll bike over to see them again". "Nice idea Sir, they're brave people, worth every bit of our endeavour" — "perhaps I'll meet their daughter, sort of compare notes", Farquar mused gently. "They'd love that Sir, make them feel a part of the action, *for which*", he noted conspiratorially, "I got their telephone number so you can arrange for your visit — oh'n the new carburettors have come from Hucknall so I'll fit one straight away.

A couple of weeks passed as the squadron still sat centre stage feeding its chaps into the blue above — but everyone noticed a slackening of effort from across the channel which added to their higher scores with fewer losses — then came the day when the news crept down The Battle for Britain had been won as Gerry had called off his attempt to wipe-out the RAF. Everyone went round 'licking their mental wounds' while trying to adjust to the lower pressure so Farquar decided now was the time to ask 'the boss' for a day to do his trip to visit 'the farmhouse in the fields', perhaps even find out their surname. He was allowed to make the call so arranged to go down three days later.

For his 'Wings' his parents had given him a superb 1,000 c.c. Matchless V Twin, a real king of bikes, which he'd been allowed to keep in a far corner of the main hanger. He happily went to dust it down put the few gallons in its tank he'd been allowed for the trip then bowled through the early September country lanes. 'He'd survived, he'd fought so these lanes should remain England's lanes, somehow his lanes' — even though home for him was Scotland. It was an extraordinary feeling as he looked up into the blue where the battle had raged, now silent for no raids were posted as Gerry licked the wounds of his retreat.

A couple of small map-reading errors added a little time to the trip but by mid-morning he was at the farm — whose gate was being held open by a tall girl with swirling brunette hair and a large smile. Girls for Alan Farquhar, something of an absorbed young man, had always been slightly alien beings, beautiful he could understand but not within his bailiwick — certainly not within the battle up in the blue above for whose prosecution he had dismissed all diverting dalliance. His Scots heritage placed girls at home not birds of passage to pass the time 'unadvisedly, lightly, or wantonly, but reverently and soberly' — but as he rolled to a halt then raised his goggles he decided this girl was 'at home' and had a welcoming smile to boot — somehow she looked a good deal more than just a girl.

He introduced himself, saying also, "I fancy I've got the pleasure of meeting Miss Jennifer of High Honington" — "well, Sir Knight that's a fancy phrase for a farmhouse in the country so you better try Jenny'n its Archer so come in for a cuppa — better than you'll get at the mess as you'll know", she laughed gaily, "or would you like a pre-lunch beer from the larder"? She gave the Matchless a knowing look, "Merlin's'n Matchless eh — you ride fine steeds indeed Sir Knight", she joked gaily, as Farquar set the stand to accompany her into the house deciding this sort of girl might be different to the ones he was used to. He gave Harry's hand a mighty squeeze then his wife a splendid hug with Jenny wondering to herself when she might be in her mum's place as she'd decided too there was more to this pilot than most she knew — though aware the best young men hid themselves behind a screen for fear of the heartaches caused by their failure to return. A couple of beers were disinterred as a convivial party sat round an outside table in the shade of the house with the women drinking long lime things.

Lunch was a delightful affair, as talk ranged gently about country activities all deciding 'the war' was not a fit subject for so serene a day. When it was done the farmer's wife, noting her daughter's abstracted air, mooted, "Jenny love take Alan for a walk round the farm, it'll do you both good to get out amongst the quiet of the fields instead of the noise of machines". Jennifer gave her mum a grateful smile then picked up their guest, "well Sir knight 'tis to be Shank's pony, no mighty horse-power, can you cope"? "Surely Miss Jennifer just walking in the quiet with a pretty girl seems about as near as heaven gets to us exhausted knights so let's examine what we've both been fighting for — on foot". The farmer's daughter didn't want to break the little spell with trite speech so linked her arm through her guest's then pointed the way through the garden gate.

"Well done, Jane love what told you" — "oh it's what us women are for Harry, helping our children fly'n I've not seen Jenny so fazed before — our young deserve all we can give them whatever the odds, even if it's just for an afternoon". "An afternoon like that built it for us Love didn't it", as he looked back to the leave when he'd met his lady at the tail end of 1917 at a dressing station at the front he on a stretcher she the ministering angel, "we've survived — I like him, he's got a sort of Scots solidarity with some fun added too, I wonder if he'd make a good farmer"?, both very aware they now had no son to carry on. "Dreams Harry, dreams" — "but we dreamt Jane'n look where we are — I think that young man's got the stuff to turn dreams into reality, he's still alive for a start while so many aren't".

We shall not examine our two young people as they gently explore the corners of each other walking through the Autumn sun. Long closed shutters opened slightly, possibilities tickled long dormant fancies denied for fear of the demise of those who 'didn't return'. As they walked long silences surrounded them. "How do you know Miss Jenny"?, he asked gently — "oh WAFFs don't have an easy time Alan, we're people too with dreams'n hopes — we get to know the pilots, children some of them seem to us even though we're all the same age — we help them'n mother the less able ones'n dance with them to keep the horrors at bay — perhaps one comes to be flesh'n blood in our arms for a bit in a sort of masquerade — then we fold up their clothes to post them to their parents as we think of them blown to bits in the blasts of battle high up in the blue — so little dreams are shattered in our heads as the bit of sky which had something in it for us is empty; it's not just the empty either it's what was in our arms being blown to bits in the blue above which hurts so much", she trailed away disconsolately.They became bound by a sharing in a mutual adversity both knew so well. Coming to a stile the pilot handed his hostess across, then hands were held thereafter for both knew comfort was the cure for the swirl of those dread blasts in the blue — yet for the pilot the battle still had to be won. The hand-hold gently limned 'the blue' into a new focus for both — no longer just a job, not even a farm-house in a field — but a heart. Those ancient knights in Jennifer's world emerged centre-stage as out of the intoxicating peace a voice spoke to Alan the sword of battle might be worthy of a higher dedication, yet horribly aware of her possible hurt should he not make it — but such had always been since knights had borne lances with their lady's favours.

Suddenly Spirit sought out the sentient Scot to invest what he was doing with new meaning — lifted him into a grace he had not known before through a desire to commit — to care. At a time when our people so bravely 'gave their lives for their friends' his certainty was of the moment, Love should be given now not postponed upon the probabilities of a future, because life up in the blue above hung upon a thread — perhaps Love would fire the alert which kept alive?

They made it back for a late tea which Jane Archer served with a knowing glance at her daughter, who blushed slightly. "When do you need to be back at Horning Jenny", the pilot asked reverting back to 'work', "because I can take you back on the Matchbox if you fancy"? "Oh I've got leave till nine how about you" — "oh I'm the same so would you like to have a drink at The Horseshoes which lies about half-way between us"? "Oh yes please", she answered with an enthusiasm which did not escape her mother — so it was arranged. As they sped off into the early evening, girl hanging on to boy on the back of the big powerful bike, Harry put an arm round his lady, "dreams have been made of less my Love, something for us to hope for too". Had they seen their babies' parting they would have been further cheered for as Alan dropped 'Miss Jennifer' at the gates of her station she unwound the thin summer scarf with which she had bound her hair for the ride, "wear this for me Alan — and for the farmhouse in the fields".

So, in the fullness of time, a Scot became the laird of a Kentish farm deep in England's heart whose lady's summer scarf adorns their mantle-piece in pride. The bond of service in war continued with joy as a mechanic continued his manifold skills to serve the new in peace — the business of beating ploughshares out of swords. A new alliance was born from some beauty plucked out of the heat of battle, 'beauty in unexpected places' the old pair mused as they sat gently in the evening of their days watching their grandchildren playing in the sun to the sound of the clicking of the reaper. Of such as these was England always built — those who served and those who served the serving, so England might serve the world from the beauty forged which carries us over the stony places to tide Man through the eternities of his struggles — for showing him light within the darkness.

Aphrodite, August 2009

Aspects of Love
A collection of short stories

STILLE SNACHT

by Aphrodite

STILLE NACHT

(A Fancy Flown upon a Fact)

Jurgen burst upon the door to break Frans Gruber's lunchtime nap. Waking with a start he couldn't imagine why as the service was well rehearsed, everything in place for the Midnight Mass, no stone left unturned as this was the night when 'the town' made a Pilgrimage up to the little Pilgrimage church up the valley — his church so he and his team were on show — but were ready. A breathless Jurgen stood on the door sill, "Sir, Franz, the organ's died, those pesky mice we thought we'd done for have made a nest in an inside fold of the bellows round the back and eaten a long split — there's no wind at all and the tear's too big to patch in time". "Come in Jurgen'n take a nip, it's cold out there".

Frans Gruber smiled, as he swirled ideas round in his head. "Well we've got Hans on his guitar, he's pretty good'n I've got an idea Jurgen". "I've got a little tune", he mused dreaming of what had spawned its conception, "I cooked up after I'd been dancing in the town to one of those dangerous new Waltzes — very catchy — a pretty frau had asked me to dance, it was lovely — made my feet twinkle, and something else besides", he chuckled happy at the memory.

"I came home all dreams Jurgen with a tune coming in my head as I skated up the valley — we couldn't use it for the normal liturgy — but with no organ", he chuckled gaily, "one has to improvise, so I don't think anyone's going to complain if we have a little fun on Christmas night". "I wrote it in this new six-eight time", he confided to his visitor, "very dancy but I fancy it would work just as well in 3/4, which would be more liturgical", he laughed gently, "a bit less obviously from the dance-floor, but we need some words — you scoot up to warn Hans he'll need to be on show tonight so keep him off the bottle", he chuckled only too aware of the guitarist's habit of playing for dances well over the odds. "Tell the rest I'll come up to the church for a quickie before supper so we can give it a run through, very simple stuff so Hans can take it straight off the page and I tell you what Jurgen, since dance is it, dig out that 'Tomorrow Shall Be My Dancing Day' which'll cheer the burgers who dance — might go like a rocket — world wide fame d'you think"?, he giggled happily on the crest of a little creative wave.

Nothing ever happened in sleepy Hallein at the bottom of The Valley with its modest manufactures, with even less in the little village up round the church he'd made his own — but by heck it was going to happen now. He'd been there a number of years to have its little community wrap itself round him because he delighted in its spiritual care. He had his wonderful library and some modest correspondence with musos in the wider world, so he was content while nature's beauty, so superabundant at the head of the valley, which filled his Spirit with its eternal ever changing yet ever permanent wonder — while the stillness fed the balm his Spirit needed for clear thought.

As he opened the door to let Jurgen out he saw the fresh fall of snow. It was thick, there had obviously been another fall which he hadn't noticed immersed in his library after lunch — but he could see the local gang had cleared the way down to Hallein for the people whom the villagers knew would come to the little church up in the mountain for their Midnight Mass, but the gang had gone home. He looked out on to the late afternoon — to utter silence, a stillness so powerful you could hear it ringing in your ears and feel it in your bones, not even the slip of snow off trees, no foxes barking — nothing. Silent Night he thought, but Holy Night too, the Calm you could feel everywhere as everyone quietly made ready for the birth at midnight and how wonderfully Bright as the full moon sailed serenely through the sky with its lone accompanying star so perfect — then his little church on its mound just beginning to be in silhouette. He stood in the doorway enrapt by the scene, yet a scene he knew so well, a scene he had lived with for many years yet tonight for him born anew by his creative surge — driven by a memory.

'Yes indeed', he thought, 'Silent Night, Holy Night, All is Calm All is Bright' the night when shepherds and wise men had gathered round a little baby in a cradle. He didn't have to go to the Church, his church, the old Pilgrimage church, to get the music he'd written, it was sitting half finished in his desk drawer so he quickly went back inside to sit down with pencil and paper to finish it off to fit those first words — while the remainder of the words just flowed into a delicious fantasy of the fact he'd seen standing at his door — so it was the work of only another half hour to have it all wrapped up. He didn't need to write an accompanying harmony because Hans would make what he fancied of an accompaniment as he went along, just cut in some simple voice parts. Gifted lad Hans, when sober, with a talent for exposition and variation — and by heck could he make a tune swing for the pretty girls to dance to — anyway it didn't need to be clever it needed to be clean and shiny new, as simple as that birth so long ago with 'angels bending near the earth to touch their harps of gold'. His heart ached for the beauty of it, yet so aware of the angsts in the wider world, 'oh hush ye mighty men of strife to hear the angels sing' he thought, 'but damn those men of strife I'm going to make them sing tonight, and perchance dance too'.

Promptly at six he was up at the church bursting with glee to note Kurt had the wood stove roaring well as a welcome for their friends from the town. "Ok boys", he aprised his team, "Hans here's your copy, you'll see it's in 6/8 Ländler time but let's give it a gentle lift into single beat swing, get people dancing in their heads — we're celebrating". A couple of run's through put it in the bag, then they had a quick look at 'Tomorrow Shall Be' because they'd only sung it once since it had first come to them, "we'll keep it as a surprise", he enthused pleased hearing his tune live, "for if the old biddies get carried away so start dancing then we'll sock it to 'em — what fun". Repaired to the vestry where he kept a secret store of reviver for cold evenings. Sipping happily Kurt, his verger, remarked, "pretty good boss, angels'll've wrote them words I'll be bound, got magic in them, sort of golden harp stuff".

After a couple of nogs of aquavit Hans picked up his guitar, then smiled, "How does it go boss, er like this"?, as he wove a beautiful 6/8 descant through the melody with a strong single bar beat which had even the hardened choirboys and men laughing and tapping their feet. "Yers", observed Gruber a trace laconically but with a huge smile, "I knew it was good Hans but not that good, er, don't lean too hard on the three-four while we're singing or it'll get back to Father Xavier we're running a dance-den, just enough to get the dancing lot to ask for an encore than let it rip — just sing it all again gentlemen then a pause to lead in to 'Tomorrow' if we need it — very apt don't you think", he gurgled with anticipatory delight with tiny fantasies of fame lighting his dreams; it was a damn good tune, he knew it, Hans had shown him just how good, while the words had an immediate immortality born on the wings of the pure joy of that wonderful Stille Nacht..

Hallein was nowhere really while the tiny village round the Pilgrimage Church up in the mountains above it was even less, so music publishers and talent scouts weren't its staple — but we know on that sacred night up in the valley god would smile on Frans Gruber with the bucolic Hans and his little band celebrating his son's birth, because Hallein would be the birth of it.

It had only been a fortnight ago when he'd been invited down to the Town Hall by the Mayor's wife for a celebratory winter dance. As a musician he had followed the introduction of the new lovely Ländler then the scary Waltz with its dreamy single bar beat, he'd even experimented a little with composing a tune to such a beat but it had escaped him. Sitting out he found himself buttonholed by a substantial matron with a huge smile who whisked him up for a Ländler. He knew the steps a little so enjoyed himself specially as she made something of herself for him, "I'm Elise, it was me who asked madam mayor to invite you so you know your fate for the evening", she laughed happily having had her eye on Pastor Gruber since she had come to Hallein as a school-teacher then come up to one of his services at his little church — music made her tick and his lonely state appealed to the mother which she lavished so liberally on her little charges.

Later in the evening when the company were well oiled the band had struck up a waltz for which 'Miss Elise' had grabbed Gruber quickly to show him the forward-together-side step then swept him into her arms for the opening. Gruber's feet sort of found their own way round the floor under the expert guidance of Elise — aided by the considerable propinquity of her ample bosom. Everyone else was enjoying the Waltz's new propinquity also, so risqué after the apart formalities of country and court dance, as happy burgers were seen clasping happy burgesses gyrating round the floor together and, my goodness saw the amazed Franz, some were even seen to kiss.

The evening drew to a close then Gruber strapped on his pattens for the trip up the valley. It was odd he thought as he left the confines of the town but the waltz tune had coalesced into the ample bust in his head as his feet took off on their own in the delicious step which slid his feet up the road ahead. Bits of band tune swirled round jiggling his musical synapses alternating between the steady 3/4 single beat of the waltz and the lovely swirling smooth 6\8 jig time of the Ländler — curious how they could be made to work together he found as humming catches the valley floor sped below his twinkling feet.

By the time he'd got home he had the basis of a tune in his head which he tried on his forte-piano (a gift from a beneficent parishioner) , 'I like it, it may come in useful one day' so he'd scribbled it down then stuffed in into his desk drawer.

His housekeeper had left a nice hot pot of stew on the stove which he wolfed heartily down on his return from their practice before getting dressed for the service. A swift dram to keep out the cold then he started up to where his home really lay, his little church, which tonight they were going to deck with a freshly minted carol for their guests. Welcoming the congregation in he was delighted to shake hands with 'Miss Elise', but who was on the arm of an imposing man of obvious stature. His heart gave a little lurch as microscopic unformed hopes withered, but dammit who was he, a mere country pastor locked up in an isolated village, tucked into his books and miniature congregation — 'ah well', he thought, 'at least I've got a good tune'.

They had decided the new carol would come at the end to celebrate the silent night of worship so long ago and, they all surreptitiously hoped, so those willing to let their hair down might feel unrestrained. Opening the service Gruber apologised for the lack of the organ because the mice had finally demolished the bellows but it did not matter as they'd got the renowned Hans to lead them. It was a lovely service somehow all the more so for the intimacy of the guitar with the unaccustomed closeness of all facing a tiny adversity to bring out the best in them.

"Dear people", he announced at the end of the service, "we welcome you specially tonight with a new carol I wrote this afternoon when Jurgen came to tell me the mice had finally won the bellows battle", his eyes twinkled with happy creative memory — "something spoke to me from out of the starlit night". "We haven't had time to make copies of the words for you so this one's our gift to you on this night of a baby's birth".

Hans played the last line as an entry then off they went. Somehow it got a bit more 3/4 into it than they had quite intended but it hardly mattered as there was gay applause then cries of 'encore'. As Hans played the intro again Elise stepped out of her front pew to walk briskly up to the little chancel, took hold of Gruber then whisked him off into the waltz. Within half the first verse the nave was a swirling mass of happy dancing couples.

When it was finished Elise drew him back to meet 'Mr Winter' as the rest of the congregation socialised happily as Today had become 'My Dancing Day' so it's merry tune was gently laid aside. "Congratulations Father Franz what we've just sung was very special — it happens I'm a partner in Breitkopf's so would like to buy it to publish it because you've made a little carol history tonight, it was magic which has immortality in it — have you got a copy I can take with me as I'm only staying with Elise for one night to come to this service so am going back to Leipzig tomorrow"?, he rushed to an enthusiastic stop.

Father Gruber fazed, 'did god really smile', he wondered, 'did angels really sing for the little church up the valley and did he smile as seraphically as Elise was smiling'. Whirlings in waltz time fizzed round his head as he managed, "oh yes, you can have the one I wrote this afternoon, but it's the only one we've got" — "don't worry", Winter assured, "it'll be in print before the New Year so I shall send you the first from the press by special courier — er gold bound as a presentation copy which is how much I value it — and" , he smiled serenely, "I don't mind losing Elise to the chap who's created it in exchange for the magic of this evening with the possession of such a gem". He gave Elise a big squeeze looking straight at Gruber's astonished face, "Thank you for some lovely times Elise, it's been fun so I wish you both all the best up in your eyrie fastness of The Pilgrim Church up the wonderful valley where magical music's made", he bowed happily to the still astonished Gruber. Elise dropped a little note into his hand, then they left. He put the note in his cassock pocket then went on to greet the other guests.

When all was done, with the regulation tot handed out to the departing guests, silence again enveloped the little church as he and his verger stepped out into the shining silent night, looking down the valley at the stream of happy guests making their way home. "Good one Franz", smiled his colleague staring up at the stars, "look at them all dancing in their heads happy they've danced to celebrate a baby's birth, a king some've said — but then every baby's a possible king, so your tune's off to visit history", cheered an admiring Kurt who had not missed the transition of the manuscript, "who was the delicious matron who buttonholed you for the waltz — she lit a fuze"?

The Pastor tried to collect his fuddled wits, locked into waltz time nestled into a magnificent bosom above which purred a seraphic smile. "Er, oh that's Miss Elise, she's a teacher in the town" – "she", observed his verger knowingly, "looked like hunter with prey in sight to me and it's time you got out of your rut, good luck Franz, what a super night to be re-born", he chuckled as they set off home — then something tweaked Gruber's memory, the little note in his cassock pocket. "Kurt can I have the key I've left something in the church"? "Sure Franz drop it back tomorrow sometime".

He unlocked, lit a taper to find his way into the vestry then rummaged in his cassock to find the little scrap of paper. He examined it under the faint light to see an address then his tensed shoulders relaxed — 'so it was real after all, 38 Müllerin Strasse', he knew where Müllerin Strasse was, down by the river where the mill was this side of town.

Franz Gruber walked home in a dream the short distance to his little house below the church. 'Re-birth Kurt had said then Mr Winter wanting his carol to publish and giving up Elise, where on earth did it all end', as, not properly attending to his feet, he fell over to slide the last yards to his front door. He laughed as he'd never been here before so had no idea how so many different emergent wonders could fuse the normal functions of the brain.

Next morning the feeling was still there, a sort of furious elation, a detached unhitchedness he, the steady proceeder down straight-mapped paths, had never travelled. 'If babies could be re-born why couldn't he like Kurt had said — perhaps he might become a king too'? Deciding to take things as presented to him he strapped on his skis — then stopped, took them off again to go round to a sheltered spot where his Christmas roses always came out early, picked a bunch then went inside to find some remains of the red ribbon he had done up the children's presents in for 'St Nicholas'.

Then, fortified upon his resolve Christmas would be his fist day of new birth, he tucked the flowers neatly in a sack on his back then set off at a brisk pace down the valley not now in the terrestrial bounds of waltz time but upon the wings of flight fired by visions of the ample Elise wrapped round him last night. He arrived in a swishing slalom outside number 38, with the river gliding serenely by on the other side of the path. He did not have to knock because eagle eyes, sure of their man (how do women know the certainties of such unpredictabilities?) were watching so the door sprung open as he un-latched his skis.

"Come in Franz breakfast's on the table, Carli Winter left early to get his new prize set ready for the presses — you've never seen a man so pleased, the charms he's lusted after simply vanished beneath the possibilities of your shining carol".

Franz Gruber overwhelmed by the whole affair slumped into the proferred chair, "Well Elise it started after your dance at the Mayor's Ball as I slalomed my way back home to waltz time as the corners of the tune came to me — then yesterday lunch time when Jurgen came to tell me the organ was caput I dug the scribblings out of my desk, then I wrote the words after looking out of my door watching Jurgen going to tell Hans of his evening duties; it was a magical afternoon", he continued eyes alight, "with all those four first lines in it", then went all shy frightened to open out his creative insecurities, 'but surely her note was meant as a message' he thought, as Elise's huge smile encouraged him. "I somehow saw inside myself", he continued his exposé, "when I stood at the door watching the magic of the stillness of the fast approaching night — somehow a scene I knew so well was re-born because angels were singing in the heaven of my Spirit -er so the words sort of just happened because while I sat the angels wrote the words over my shoulder to fit the tune I'd already written on the evening you'd asked me to dance — something leant on me as I danced home", he blushed as he confessed to a finish — 'yet surely that note meant something'?

"Will you marry me Miss Elise, to share the rest of the magical journey"?, as he reached into the sack for the Christmas Roses to give them her on bended knee. Elise gave him a huge hug with a massive kiss which seemed to go on for ever, enveloping him completely, "oh you silly creator blokes up in the stars building your castles in the air too fantasised to see the stones piling round your feet to build for real — of course I will so don't let's wait around I'll fix with Father Xavier to marry us next Sunday in your church and damn all the protocols, we're grown up", she roared with magnificent laughter.

Next Sunday with many of her new town friends, and accompanied by all her little children, Miss Elise walked proudly up the valley, scorning conveyance for happy to come to her man on foot on the arm of Carli Winter who was to give her away — who was proudly bearing a gold bound copy of what he's had named "Stille Nacht". Franz Gruber, in smart coat tails with his verger as his best man stood proudly before Father Xavier to be given away to Miss Elise in Holy Matrimony — he was wise enough to know which way round was which but was happy with it like it was for what more could one wish to be enveloped in he thought, admiring her majesty in its magnificent cream wedding dress. 'Yes', he thought, 'we're grown ups, so if babies could be re-born as kings why shouldn't he be too — married to a queen'.

Snugged in bed that night in their new home (double bed hastily arranged courtesy of friends in town) somehow now twice the size it was before for the Love which filled it he reflected, "Elise my Love I wonder what was really talking to me on that magical afternoon — was it the angels or more ancient stirrings I should have been party to years ago spurred on by the memory of the magnificences I'm cuddling now".

She laughed wonderfully for her newly minted husband not being the first to be captured by her obvious armoury, "God moves in a mysterious way his wonders to perform Franz so let's leave it to enjoy the results", she laughed happily, "at my age you're not the first but I'm so glad you're the last". He burst out into quite un-Pastorlike laughter, "well at least I'm assured of the quality if so many have supped before me — such fun to end up with what others failed to get — very earthly I know but a little crowing is good even for priests".

He lay back admiring her magnificence, "If anyone had told me I needed a body to fire my Spirit I'd have laughed them to scorn but I'm going to enjoy the rest of our journey my lovely Aphrodite, with Body wound round my Spirit to light it, Ho, Ho what fun". The magic of Love's totality, of its necessary interlocking of Mind with Body, was crashing about him from his old disassociated theological priestly understandings to become a driving force of commitment to a person with whom he had engaged to travel, 'for better or for worse', together not alone. Their bodily together was proving pretty intoxicating stuff as the world suddenly seemed to have no bounds at all — all the old boundaries of priestly paths dissolved to leave illimitable ways towards unknown horizons. "It was a damn good tune, wasn't it love"?, he chuckled. "The words weren't bad either", she laughed happily — "ah but the angels wrote those I was merely their scribe". She laughed, "the angels of your Spirit Franz lit by a new vision — which I intend to keep shining bright".

She gazed into his visionary eyes still far away treading angelic paths, "I'd always thought I was one of those proud women born to be independent, fighting my own battles on my own; what bosh, all the emergent women's rights rubbish, we need to be together — not alone". She stopped to engage his wandering eyes by placing a hand upon her breast, "to be truly ourselves alone is no road at all, I know it now because to fully be ourselves we need to be together so each can fertilise the best in the other while patching up the holes", she purred.

"Indeed", he mused, "alone in my Library seemed the height of bliss but after our waltz it was changed — though I couldn't have told you why — except I knew it wasn't home any more, it was telling me it needed someone in it to shine it, then whatever you like to call them were bending their harps for my attention singing about a baby's birth — perhaps it needed a cradle too".

So in the fullness of time some fame brought modest plenty to the Pastor's little household in the fastness of the magical valley. A couple of cherub-Grubers added to the joy — 'would they be kings' the verger wondered, 'why not with such wonderful parents'. There was a tiny increase in the school Elise started for the village children as the verger smiled happy for the little village in the valley he loved so well, but the organ he did not touch except for a new set of bellows made in a new wonder mouse-proof fabric — while a fancy new pumping engine, courtesy of the finest maker in the land, was installed to render the prison of organ pumping a vanished past — all courtesy of a wonderful carol born upon the wings of Love.

One small change The Pastor did make, which filled his little church to bursting every Christmas Eve for he invited The Hallein Silver Band to play for the service. Their joy in turning 6/8 time into 3/4 time became the tradition thereafter so The Holy Night was celebrated with a Waltz in the very best 'oompah' style. Nothing was said — it just leaked out of the tune so everyone took partners for the dance, because joyful dance is the most ancient celebration of all — fitting for the birth of a King all agreed for Elise & Franz now knew their every day 'must be my dancing day';

For Life to be worthy it must be danced together — not apart.

Aphrodite, Christmas 2009, written upon one day in Epiphany

Aspects of Love

A collection of short stories

War OR Peace

by Aphrodite

WAR OR PEACE

(The action took place about 30 years ago, written 15 years ago for a little local 'River Preservation' magazine I then edited.)

How could they possibly survive walking up the road miles from their natural habitat? Our reaction was entirely instinctive, a knee-jerk to the plight of others, a natural Samaritan surge. Mature thought might have acted differently, today's 'it's not my problem' certainly would but it is the free flight's of emotion which make life so intensely worth living.

It was their smallness which had us stop because for us they were no novelty as our local river plays host to hundreds of them every year. We knew they were often born far from water while the purpose in their steps suggested they knew where they were going — but did they *really* know, and would the foxes or vehicles get them first?

We rationalised all this later as one always does after a snap decision. Our instinct to help the apparently defenceless had us abandon our evening engagement to set about trying to catch 6 little shelduck chicks by the roadside. They were in their first colour with their beaks fully beaklike and black, but they were still very tiny, communicating with each other with little squeaks. To any passing motorist our activities, chasing the invisible through the roadside brambles, must have seemed mad as we rushed about then froze to listen for the tell-tale squeaks of duckling talking to duckling.

The chasing took some time which deadened any judgments about the validity of the activity but in time the little squeaks were all inside the boot of the car; 'free from the marauding fox anyway' we thought as the heat of the chase died down — to have the certainty dawn that, having stepped in, we had assumed a duty we did not know how to discharge.

It was the time of year we knew as 'shelduck time' since we, as East Coast sailors, come to know the individual flotillas of shelduck chicks as they cruised the river. We used to identify with those who lived near our own mooring — we counted the chicks to watch how they got on during the year. Our two children, little then but always sailing with us in our fine little Edwardian yacht, knew 'shelduck time' too which they enjoyed hugely as they identified other children doing 'children' things so remembered exactly how many there were in each flotilla to watch with joy as they grew. It was an eternal delight for them to watch the tiny black blobs scurrying across the water then, on some call, all vanishing for what seemed ages to surface impossible distances away for such minute objects — we made shelduck chicks very much our own.

It was a glorious evening on the country road we were travelling on a short journey to friends, quiet with the iridescent light which heightens colours, but nature, or our own arrogance, stepped in so we never got there. We had stepped into this role of guardian because a couple of years before I had seen a clutch of shelduck chicks walking, with the same sense of purpose, down the high street of our local small town by the river. Everyone had stopped to help as 40 ton trucks ground to a halt as the chicks were shepherded down the street by their mother, over the railway then into the river. I had been there helping with the traffic so learnt shelduck often breed far from water — yet the wonder of such natural skill mixed with doubt our little brood, without a mother, could find water from the point we found them on the road in the forest. Playing god seems so easy till you start asking the real questions then demanding of yourselves real answers.

Our duty so arrogantly assumed we started to ask those questions heightened by the plaintive squeaks from the boot of the car. 'We can't put them back in the road because even if they survive how will they know where to go and can they get there without food and water and survive the foxes'? — but their sense of purpose suggested they did know about those things so did know where they were going — indeed why would they be born where they were if their parents did not know how to cope with this predicament. 'Where are their parents', we wondered, 'have they abandoned them and is their assurance assumed because they know no better'?

We turned the car round back the way we had come towards the town and water we ourselves sailed, rationalising away as we drove, but no clarity emerged. As we drove one problem loomed. If we put our chicks in the river where others swam would they be interlopers in territory already colonised by others? 'Will our chicks be driven away and left unguarded to become herons' lunch or will they be accepted into the flotilla — will there be WAR OR PEACE'?, we asked ourselves.

We did not know — but we did know one who would. Gone were thoughts of a pleasant evening with friends, the only thing which mattered now was to find a home for *our* little chicks, a home of PEACE. WAR in the animal world is vicious as the thought of *our* little chicks being heron's lunch focussed our attention as we drove back to town by the river.

Down in the little Town Dock lived Philip who had worked on the river all his life as well as being a renowned naturalist, so he would know what to do. With the fresh assurance of the unknown being lifted from our shoulders, we drove down to the dock. The little squeaks seemed less accusing now as we thought of their troubles solved, but Philip was not there, while no-one knew about shelduck chicks. They wished us well, but passed the responsibility firmly back to us, where it had rightly been all along.

We knew in mid summer the shelduck parents do a deal with each other as some fly back to warmer climates leaving one or two pairs to look after considerable numbers, of often second brood, chicks on the river. This results in 'flotillas' of chicks, sometimes thirty strong, looked after by a pair, or sometimes even a single drake, cruising the river till late autumn. We did not know where they went then since they always seemed too small to fly south but that, at least, was not our problem since it obviously had an answer the ducklings had tapped into their subconscious. 'But can they exist on their own now'?, we'd thought; 'will they be accepted into a flotilla to shelter from the predators'? We did not have an answer — but in the boot of the car the squeaks admonished us to find one.

Now we had to chose, for which nature would be the only arbiter so we must ask her forgiveness for interfering with her ordained pattern, but we did have a choice. The chicks had to go to the river but there were two options. We sat in the car by the dock discussing.

'Do we put them straight into the dock where there are no shelduck flotillas, so therefore no war, or do we take them out in the dinghy to put them amongst a flotilla, but court the possibility of war'? The decision rested between peace with no protection in the dock or protection on the open water with the possibility of war. 'If', we said to each other, 'we put them in the dock unprotected then there is a chance of their demise from predators, but if we put them in amongst a flotilla even if they were flung out they would only be in the same state they would be in if we had put them in the dock — while we might be right'. Yet the nagging doubt remained, would it be WAR or PEACE, would the established flotilla turn to rend the interlopers?

To this there was no answer so the final judgment lay with us. As we drove the couple of miles, deep in thought, to the landing place where we kept our dinghy I was very mindful of long discussions had with my younger brother on the subject of the interference of 'superior beings' with those of a different order.

He and his young wife had spent three years in Ethiopia as a young doctor covering 500 sq. miles of the Danakil desert, running a health programme from the back of a Land-Rover. Backed by a well known charity it all seemed a 'good thing' on the surface as 'doing good' always does — the 'white man's burden' in modern dress — but how rarely is good rationalised in the terms of those being 'helped' while how rarely also are the results of that imposition fully rationalised in the longer term; men in offices are not indigenous peoples in deserts.

He taught the people enough to reduce infant mortality hugely — but in so doing upset a fraily balanced system of resources to consign those very children he would save to problems beyond their control in conditions of less humanity than had been achieved by the establishment of millennia of accomodation with their hostile home. He had, through the charity funding his efforts, been party to an interference with a natural order to come home recognising the civilisation he had seen possessed a culture and dignity perfectly suited to its situation — visibly, he recognised, greater than his own — which he had gone a long way to destroying for heretofore it had been free but now it would be dependent upon resources supplied by an alien culture, an existence upon 'charity' — which is the truth of Hell.

'Oh hell', I thought, 'I have been guilty of the same, the arrogance to suppose I possess a higher intelligence, so therefore can solve others' problems in unknown spheres'. We had interfered, like the new civilisations have with the old, so our burden had become the necessary solution of that interference; we knew we were not properly equipped for such a solution as we did not understand the medium with which we had meddled — but we made the choice to try for the open river, not the dock.

We had to get the ducklings down to the beach then into our dinghy which is some 10 minutes walk from the car parking place. I was wearing a big handknitted 'guernsey' which I removed. We tied the arms together to form a sack then filled it with squeaking chicks — to set off down the path to the beach.

It was now late as the sun was just beginning to sink behind the trees which bordered the river setting up skeletal forms around us. As we walked we could see the town's fine church tower lit with a crystal clarity, standing out the white of the flushwork against the sombre blacks of the flints and lighting the tide mill and the masts in the yacht harbour with a purity not often seen. Silence prevailed as there was no wind. It is a private path upon which we were the only ones so there was no-one about to give us a last minute reprieve as we walked with our little squeaking burden down the steep incline to the river. Arriving on the beach we walked along to find our dinghy. The river was like glass as the ethereal conditions quieted our concerns. 'Surely' we thought 'no war can take place in such serene conditions'? There was no hustle of war, no trumpets to announce it, yet deep down we knew war in the natural world is a matter of stealth presaged by silence, of disguise for the sudden strike.

We launched the dinghy. I rowed while my wife sat in the sternsheets with the bright blue guernsey full of chicks, curiously quieted now the hour was near. It was nearly high water with hardly a ripple as I rowed down the river then round the corner of the next creek where we were sure there would be a flotilla of ducklings. The sun was slowly sinking beneath the treetops. There is a small area of trees here which lie behind an old sea wall, breached in the great floods of '52 which stand gaunt forever leafless with, this evening, their arms spread Dali-like across the red ball of the setting sun. As I quietly floated the dinghy up the creek on the last of the flood the trees on the opposite shore reflected the red light on their foliage as the stillness with its the supernatural colours crept over us. Nature soaked us in.

Our eyes searched in the failing light for the little rafts of blobs, which might herald our salvation; then my wife saw them, about 200 yards away. I eased on the oars then turned round to see just where I had to go to meet them — then I saw it — silhouetted in the arms of the dead trees the crooked, malignant, form of a heron, seemingly forever poised. We drifted slowly forwards watching the flotilla of chicks as they swam unconcernedly about their business — as we watched the heron also. Then two ducks detached themselves from the shadows along the edge of the water to swim to their charges.

We could wait no longer, any closer must frighten them away. One last dreadful question remained; could they swim? We had no idea how they approached the water naturally; did they walk down to the edge to try it out carefully, wetting their downy fluff in anticipation? 'Was their fluff even waterproof'?; but the die was cast. The guernsey was picked up then held over the stern close to the water, then opened. Plop-plop-plop-plop-plop-plop they fell into the river, upon whose surface they did not appear to sink just sit there shaking themselves.

Then the magic started. Our ducklings turned to face the flotilla, some 50 yards away directly into the sinking sun. Off they swam, tiny feet going with just the same assurance which had travelled them along the road. We sat enthralled at the majesty of it, yet with the dreadful unknown upon us — did their assurance stem from a deep natural knowledge of their certain welcome, or no knowledge at all? How could they possibly know there were friends those fifty yards away which we could hardly see, what guided their assurance — would there be WAR or PEACE?

On they paddled into the sinking sun, now just an arc of red through the trees highlighting the blackened branches — with the heron — as it turned our ducklings into tiny ripples on the surface of the water, swimming with such determination. For us, truly, it was not till the final coalescence we really knew. The suspense is with me still as we sat in the mirror calm water waiting for the answer. Then it came.

Suddenly there was only one group of ducklings; it was not possible to tell the moment when it happened. Like a drifting cloud enfolds another yet appears no bigger, our little ducklings had disappeared so we saw only one flotilla; like the cloud those there had enfolded ours as no ruffle disturbed the calm. Nature had granted there should be peace, no flurry of war, just acceptance of one with another.

We drifted down the creek on the turning tide, our eyes straining in the gathering gloom to separate our chicks from the others, we still watching the heron, but they had been absorbed back into their own so we knew we had been merely a temporary episode in their lives. 'Their own'?, it was this understanding of the natural community they formed, in which neither origin nor family played any part, which brought us up short, so solved the riddle which had perplexed us, because they 'herded first asked afterwards' even if the questions which so preoccupy man play any part in dabchick's lives. We knew, also, we had been granted a reprieve in our meddling with forces beyond our knowledge.

Many years after this was written, when I had begun a different journey in life, I began to write about the mission of Swords or Sandals. This is not to say we should abandon helping our neighbour but that we must be absolutely sure of our motive, self, or service?, with its possible outcomes. Are we acting in the interests of those we seek to serve in their natural lives *in their world within their culture* or are we seeking to 'improve' theirs in our image — are we serving 'You' or 'I' which is not just an icon on a screen nor a pious prayer but must be the whole of our being if our 'mission' is not to prostitute our neighbour. Joining with him to help him dig a well to serve himself within his own culture is entirely opposite to paying to have a well dug for him on condition he worships our god.

'You' or 'I' is always with me as I watch around me or read about acts of 'good' and 'mission' as I strain to see what the results might be. 'Mission' has historically almost invariably lead to a wide range of prostitutions which have left those imposed upon with their culture destroyed while justifiably angry at the interference. Oh so very rarely indeed is 'mission' truly one of 'sandals' for so frequently one of 'swords', the swords of arrogance which suppose we must be right because we are 'higher' beings than those upon whose lives we impose. 'Africa' is a monstrous blot on Western self-claimed 'civilisation' — which for these acts of 'mission' prostituting so many it has no right to assume.

I have yet to hear of the true Franciscan mission of sandals — the coming amongst to serve *in the image of the served* for *invariably* seeking to impose some external ideology or protocol, while the various forms of 'Christianity' having been a plague upon The Western World for two thousand years. Charity is the coldest dish it is possible to serve for 'being fed' is the ultimate degradation because imprisonment of The Spirit. Mission can not possibly 'Love One Another' if we imprison our neighbour in our pre-scriptions and proscriptions; indeed trying to 'convert the heathen to Christianity' has been the most deeply unchristian act man has sought to perform upon his fellow for making the most arrogant assumption of all in supposing Christianity's virtue over others — then there is Islam's 'a sword is worth more than a thousand words'! Mission is a very double-edged sword indeed.

It is a historical truth, to mention only one case whose causes have been whitewashed out of the history books, The Indian Mutiny was the *direct* result of a furious campaign by The News Chronicle to 'send missionaries out to India to convert the heathen' despite the desperate attempts of all the administrators in India to prevent it. Further, every detail of The Mu-tiny's planning was known by the government at home *two years before its eruption,* from the extraordinary reports of Richard Burton (the great ex-plorer who was arguably the greatest linguist England has ever produced) who had been tasked to go undercover into the seats of trouble. Nothing was done, but those reports show the justifiably fierce reaction of 'India' to the arrogance of England in presuming 'The West' knew better than 'The East' for interfering in its religious practices; the immolation of Luck-now and many others was a direct result of that arrogance of 'mission'.

In our little duckling mission we were granted great good fortune to touch an answer which seemed to work, but it taught me to leave alone those things which nature has ordained — for her to arrange as she sees fit — whether she be Danakils or Ducklings.

Love is not taking over other people's lives — but the giving of yourself to enrich theirs in their own image.

Aphrodite, December 2010

Aspects of Love
A collection of short stories

Heaven's Gate

by Aphrodite

HEAVEN'S GATE &
HELL'S DESPAIR

Love seeketh not itself to please,
Nor for itself hath any care,
But for another gives its ease
And builds a heaven in hell's despair.

(*William Blake, Songs of Experience, 'The Clod and the Pebble'*)

The first day of the week cometh Mary Magdalene early, when it was yet dark, unto the sepulchre and seeth the stone taken away from the sepulchre. Then she runneth, and cometh to Simon Peter, and to the other disciple, whom Jesus loved, and saith unto them, 'They have taken away the Lord out of the sepulchre and we know not where they have laid him'. Peter therefore went forth, and the other disciples, and came to the sepulchre. So they ran both together: and the other disciple did outrun Peter, and came first to the sepulchre. And he stooping down, and looking in, saw the linen clothes lying; yet went he not in. Then cometh Simon Peter following him, and went into the sepulchre, and seeth the linen clothes lie. And the napkin, that was about his head, not lying with the linen clothes, but wrapped together in a place by itself. Then went in also that other disciple, which came first to the sepulchre, and he saw and believed. For as yet they knew not the scripture, that he must rise again from the dead. Then the disciples went away again into their own homes.

But Mary stood without at the sepulchre weeping: and as she wept, she stooped down and looked into the sepulchre. And seeth two angels in white sitting, the one at the head, and the other at the feet, where the body of Jesus had lain. And they say unto her, 'Woman why weepest thou'? She saith unto them, 'Because they have taken away my Lord, and I know not where they have laid him'. And when she had thus said she turned herself back, and saw Jesus standing, and knew not that it was Jesus. Jesus saith unto

her,' Woman why weepest thou? Whom seekest thou'? She supposing him to be the gardener saith unto him, 'Sir if thou have
borne him hence, tell me where thou hast laid him, and I will take
him away'. Jesus saith unto her, 'Mary'. She turned herself and
saith unto him, 'Raboni'; which is Master." (The Gospel According to St John Ch 20)

The vision passed as she stood irresolute having lost her guide, 'how can I
serve him now he is gone'?, she asked of herself as she wandered back
down into the city — he had blessed her but both had known the truth of
it — her life Man's convention chose to vilify.

Descending into the small areas of the city where she lived she saw a boy
in the gutter, un-cared for, dirty, beaten in whatever he may have had of
Life's race. In her part of the seething city of wealth upon poverty it was a
daily occurrence — but her heart lurched — 'Mary' a voice inside her
spoke. She kneeled to cradle him on her lap then looked deep into the eyes
of destitution — as 'Mary' echoed through her head yet louder — 'Love
one Another' he'd said — as he'd loved her by his blessing. Despite the
dereliction she saw a little grandeur there, a spark of defiance left amongst
the ashes of his defeat. "Come", she consoled as she stood extending a
hand in the congregation of the damned, for she lived on the edges too,
"we will travel on together". Walking home was done in the silence of
shepherd guarding lamb — unspoken gratefully for the grace; to where
together might lead neither cared for it did not matter if both could build
a little something new which neither had before.

First came washing with the healing of sores, so Mary reversed the sign
above her door to concentrate. When he was sitting fresh clothed eating a
big crust of bread dipped in her favourite soup he smiled — which was
all — but what matter as a smile told everything. When he had finished
she sat down beside him, "What's your name handsome young man", she
smiled considerably to cheer him — for in truth clean he glowed to have
the making of magnificence she thought — she so used to the bodies of
young men. Eleven or twelve she supposed, it was a long time to be in the
state she'd found him. "I never had a name", he replied disconsolately. She
waited knowing the silence for him would be golden as he established
some comfort from her closeness. "I was one of them", he looked confid-
ingly up into her eyes, "abandoned when I was born, unwanted — but

somehow I'm still here". Her heart lurched again as 'Mary' became an ever pressing presence, as she knew the outcast, one herself, while she'd followed Him as one to his so recent public death. "Well then, brave young man, survivor of life's outcasting slings, no star may have shone at your birth — but you're going to be mine — so let's call you Jesus" — "but he's dead he was crucified on Friday, I saw it" — "such may have been but I know otherwise for I was at the tomb this morning to find he was not there — yet he spoke to me — he has sent you as a sign he's still with us — for you will be the truth of it — hold on, have faith, I know".

Mary herself, a mere nineteen, had been running 'Mary's Ministrations' for some five years now (so known amongst her disciples though not publically declaimed) at 'The Sign of The Pursèd Lips' so discretely placed above her door. It was a business which depended upon her special skills but it had arisen out of pure observation then followed up with concentration to manage to keep her in her little three roomed house, cheap for being out of the public eye, in some small comfort — but she had begun to wonder where might lie the higher end. Growing up in a family with two close brothers to whom she was deeply attached she had become early aware of their needs as puberty engulfed them. Her closeness bred a desire to help so she had begun to cater to those needs with hands, lips and emerging breasts — for which they had been deeply grateful in their un-knowing of the treacherous territory of girls. Mary had taken the heat out of their desires to leave them comfortable, able to pursue their ways untroubled by those ancient urges which afflict the emerging male. Their friends had been introduced who, for some pocket money, Mary had satisfied also to have an area round about them signally free of the raging pubescent male. All understood she gave to them of what she could which, with practice and the varied desires which came her way, became a signal skill — but she herself was not on offer. Since release with joy and confidences shared was what they wanted this worked extraordinarily well.

At fourteen, home now crowded with her need to earn a living, Mary had asked one of her lads if his father would advance her the money for a little house from where she could practice her new found 'trade' up front. The little sign of 'The Pursèd Lips' was fixed above her door so trade had prospered as her early cleintéle remained to base the new. It was steady, but by no means a sinecure as what she offered to those for whom she still intended, large sums for fancy frolics weren't on offer — pennies not pounds was the style of it but emergent youth was a quick-fire affair under her skilled hands. On holidays queues of cheerful boys sat by her door, happy in their knowledge what she did would restore them to equilibrium again so happy also to share it with their mates while Mary, no slouch, could turn round six within the hour despite, as each confided, 'she looks at you as you were the only one'. As time advanced she skillfully matured the 'service' to appeal to differing tastes while her unfailing joy in what she did for them — eyes twinkled for each to make them feel 'at home' as she applied their particular pleasure — brought her their confidences, which ensured happy continuity — a session with Mary, all agreed, was far more than just a stylish jerk. To add to the fun different prices obtained for the different styles, lips, or hands or breasts with the added joy of the 'suck'n butt massage' while those who enjoyed having their mate in to watch and share added a bit more to Mary's steadily growing security as the loan began to dwindle.

Mothers of daughters were not unmindful of Mary's services as their daughters remained un-plagued while recognising 'Mary's young men' acquired other skills at 'The Pursèd Lips', while mothers of sons were happy their boys weren't in the clutches of the brothels vicariously wasting their little substance. Mary had quickly recognised 'her young men' needed to be taught those things upon which churches have formally turned their back, so when she deemed her boys were of a proper age, taught them how to please a lady in all those delicious ways which live outside their entry. By this time they normally had the money for this extra but for those she knew who could not pay she taught them as a gift from her to women. Those mothers knowing the value of Mary's services had tried to arrange for their publically approved adoption but, despite their earnest efforts in council, self-righteous Pharasaic lips were pursed against them as 'prostitution was against the law' — but The Pharisees had never loved anybody but themselves. The matrons cursed the law but Pharisees knew they were no mete metal for majesty on the march — so let lie; while Mary smiled for what matter Pharasaic pursèd lips when he she'd followed had blessed her knowing what she was.

This is the state of things upon Jesus' absorption into Mary to make a house of two. Comfortable but while 'under the counter' recognised locally for its worth. He quickly became intrigued by Mary's methods. "Mary mother of mine, I could help you with that, I've not spent my time on the streets for nothing, I can please a man as well as you — nearly", he joked gently twinkling her delightful breasts, "while some will pay the extra for being done by me — I know". Mary pondered this thing within her, "it's a service to our fellow Jesus, so he'll approve". Upon this recognition 'The Service' was quietly extended to help fill the cruse of cash a little faster.

Mary pondered their state within her, knowing Jesus would grow to manhood for whose service he would need a trade indeed, she knew, with which to serve his fellows. He was too young for an apprenticeship just yet but she approached one she knew, a carpenter, who was willing to take Jesus on a year hence. As was the custom then he would live with the carpenter's family to become part of it in all it did, absorbing the Manual knowledge of the trade with the Spiritual enrichment so essential to The Life well lead. There was the small matter of the apprentice fee with Jesus' maintenance but Mary had solved that one before she went — she would give herself to the carpenter and his wife (whom she knew liked a lady) once a week for one night, a service whose meaning she perfectly understood — for had it not been blessed by him she followed?

At the appointed time Jesus moved 'up-town' so his personal provision lapsed — which did not concern either as they both understood what they offered was not some business deal, to be replaced with another upon the passing on of one, but a personal service — a gift of one to another of all they had in the best tradition of Love of he they followed. It was this understanding, with the inevitable drop in the rise of the cruse, that had Mary choose to render to the carpenter what she had proposed — merging Caesar into god she felt.

The years of fulfillment of his training were happy ones for Jesus — and for Mary also because she had known from the earliest the message she had received when she took up Jesus was not for a Samaritan act alone — but a sign, had said that voice, that here her future lay. Despite Pharasaic lips remaining pursed Mary's position within her community was high because what Mary gave was manifold. For the travails of Man she gave relief, assuaging the tortures of the Body *and* the Mind because, though confidante of many, yet she kept her counsel — her integrity agreed inviolate.

Jesus did not miss how, weekly, Mary was paying for his fee — in total — so he pondered in his heart to bide the day when he might save his saviour, for a deep love had come upon him for her radiant joy when they met on the day she served. "Shall you not mind my lamb?", she had asked concerned when he had put his proposal to share her service. "Oh Mary my love for me you are the Virgin most Pure for the sacrifice of a piece of skin is nothing in the service you do for love of me — what does a membrane matter when your integrity's intact, which is the measure of it". It worried Jesus nothing his boss should share what mean convention would retain for him alone for he had understood the new gospel through Mary's teaching that 'Love One Another' meant exactly what it said — to the uttermost of our giving as his example had shown upon Calvary's hill so recently. They had long known neither would be party to the 'mine' which so crimps men's minds to make their pilgrimage to Heaven's Gate an 'I' soured path — alone. Thus joy abounded in the workshop on the hill as the quality of what it made acquired a magnificence inspired — for the carpenter and his lady received 'an hundredfold' with Jesus acquiring special training from her wise hands upon those skills Mary had shown him no man should be without. It was indeed a happy household for none treading upon the feet of any with skills burgeoning powered by a true understanding of love of Body with 'Love one Another' shining bright through Mary's weekly visits for what she brought — a radiance of Mind felicitously intertwined with Body.

Mary knew the value to those about her of what she did but knew also her time amongst them would soon cease — for she knew the outcome of Jesus' presence — so she took a girl of her own first age to train her in the arts. It would be an apprenticeship as tough as Jesus' up the hill — for though what may appear a simple act to the simple, to acquire Mary's skills and status was a matter not easily attained — for the totality of giving which was its signature is not granted all.

In the regulation five years Jesus made his masterpiece. Now a divinely handsome young man he was fawned upon by girls abounding (what gorgeous clever hands they crooned in dreams) — but he held an inner light as spoken to and for so, though shining, it was not for them. His master-piece was, all agreed, magisterial but only Mary and the Carpenter with his lady knew precisely why. Since it was imbued with all the skills of Hand'n Eye which everyone could see he received much praise from those who would now welcome him as peers, but from whence came the subtle shining, the impenetrable view of line and balance, only those within were party. It was they who had travelled with him as he twined his Spirit with his appreciation of Body which both his lady's had taught him — 'gorgeous like a woman's thigh', said some of what he made — but only three knew the truth of it — for only those within knew the quality of those 'thighs'.

Now a master Jesus was in a position to establish himself which, with an advance from those who'd spawned him, he did in a different part of town — for skill's greatest rejoicing is in skill passed on — which is the true measure of Artists' immortality. Nor were they who'd had now regretful of their loss for what is Man but flying those who will come after while the joys of Mary and Jesus would remain with them as fond memories of 'how it should be' to shine their latter years.

Mary was given away at their marriage by the Carpenter but, oh delicious scandal, Jesus's best man was his lady-wife. Many came to celebrate their joy for had not their joy come thence — for joy was joy where're its source — nor was it missed some Pharisees were seen whose sons had profited from Mary's counsel while his new colleagues in the trade rejoiced so fine a one should adorn their number. There was a comfortable feeling everyone knew everyone for the barriers which conformity would erect to hide had not been theirs — so Grace Abounded.

Mary sold 'The Pursèd Lips' to her trainee — happy she had passed the test as boys came asking for her specially — but the sign Jesus lovingly took down to adorn their commodious new upper chamber as a memoriam of their start. Mary ran the new business while Jesus whirled with chisel and with plane — but, however successful it became, both soon knew it was not enough as the closeness with their fellow which their former style had brought was missing — for they becoming an Island on their own. Mindful of the recherché pleasures of she he'd served before Jesus suggested joinery might be carried further, embellished like it used to be by body close at hand — so he crafted a new sign. This he gaily inserted within his sign of the Mallet & Chisel Crossed upon a Saw-Stool. They let it be known to those they valued most the service would quietly resume, so those interstices for thought so necessary to Art's perfection Jesus gilded giving joy to ladies in his inimitable style — 'in which they were well pleased' — no mean arrows in a young man's quiver. It was said from that day on his work re-acquired its secret perfection which had languished for its lack of inspiration. Mary, to keep the tedium of book keeping at bay and to maintain her joy in those about her, re-started her counselling of the Bodies and Minds of the emerging young who peopled their modest world to become the centre of a community at peace within itself. Now comfortable she was able to extend what she could give to those she knew could profit from it — but could not pay — so returning unto life what it had granted her.

One day she skipped gaily into the shop with an unaccustomed radiance on her face, as Jesus fitted up a chair — "Jesus my love, we're three — you can not feel him — yet he is there". And so it was that she known to all as The Virgin Mary, for joy and confidante to so many yet so intact, came to fulfill her true place in Man's estate as Mother — her salvation and immortality.

HELL'S DESPAIR

Love seeketh only self to please,
To bind another to its delight,
Joys in another's loss of ease'
And builds a hell in heaven's despite

What is the truth of Good Friday, dare you face it? The truth of 'Love One Another' which he who died preached so totally, is exemplified by the totality of his gift of himself — as Mary, convention's damned, had so magnificently shown. He shows us we need to hang on our little daily calvaries of 'I' to give to others as totally as he gave himself — which is the kernel of his message. 'He died to save us from our sins' we're sold as our 'salvation' is a cruel travesty of a truth which never was, got up by priests to capture us to live in their dictated image — to pass us into Hell's Despair of 'waiting upon nurse for someone else to do it' in a place we do not know exists, but; our true Salvation lies travelling Life's Pilgrimage hand-in-hand with all mankind rendering unto each whatever is in our power — together not alone. For this Pilgrimage his teaching of 'Love One Another' is the only truth — *for it is now and we must do it for 'they' never will* — to be the Truth of Heaven's Gate — which is why he blessed she outside the law for her totality of giving of herself, beyond herself — which is the true measure of Love.

Dare you look Mary in the face to tell her lawless? Dare you tell her she was dirty? Dare you accuse her she served her own? Dare you accuse her violate? You purse your lips — but who are you to censure what was blessed at Calvary — would you ever do the same as Mary for another's salvation? You'll curse me because I call her Virgin — but virginity is intent not state and was not what she did of the highest integrity of which Man is able? Did she soil Man's free estate as priests have done ever since they nailed him to a cross; did she leave him to languish in the gutter as would modern lousy-liability, 'it's not my job' Britain? Was she not in every way 'A Virgin Most Pure' as Jesus said, yet you would curse me for your idol defiled, your little susceptibilites scarified as you clutch your withered creed for fear of its examination, for;

What does that examination reveal; that woman, who is Man's birth and great estate whom Jesus blessed, has been cursed by Churches of every creed since Mary visited the tomb; that churches have cast our Body as 'unclean' yet Man is Spirit, Body clothed, either of which without he is a miserable crawling thing. That 'Love one Another' has been replaced by 'curse those who do not believe — unto death if need be'. Jesus *in*cluded all — *ex*cluded none — but the schisms and dogmas of priests and churches have never acknowledged they themselves have built the divisive Hate which has set neighbour on the neck of neighbour to rupture Man — indeed that 'Holy Church's' very existence is its own self confessed damnation; that, absolutely as Mr Blake espoused — priests and churches are Hell's Despair for setting their feet upon their neighbour's neck — verily a hissing in the face of he they presume to follow.

Jesus came to show us The Light of 'Love One Another' as 'that gift of ourselves beyond ourselves' to show Man the horror of The Pharisees who crucified him — those whose divisive style spawned The Dark Ages which divided Man from Man by caging knowledge within its own — The Cages of Churches and Priests, but; now we have locked ourselves inside the 'churches' of governments' Rules & Regulations with their ideological damnations in which they lock us with "This is So & Do it Thus" — or die. We have. The magnificence of Magus has been rendered mollusc — crucified by those who Cage us. Heaven's Gate may not be entered through Hell's Despair for it can only be entered by the Free-Will of The Free, those who prosper they and their neighbour with the Love which is our gift of ourselves to others — never by the damnations of the demagogues for they spawn Hate — for Hell's Despair is born of The Cage in which they would crucify us for;

Creeds are Man's Corruption

You make sour faces at 'suck'n butt' — I put it there to prick your Pharisaic pride, to collapse the surety in your clear conscience 'so clean in priestly image' — for this little story is not the emolient to salve but the emetic to clean out the dross with which you've filled yourself to prevent your neighbour's loving, so;

Do not righteously 'walk by upon the other side' clutching to your bosom what properly belongs to all but travel in the greater light with Man your neighbour — with all thou hast whatever it might be. When 'I' becomes another with whom we share we pass through Heaven's Gate to sit upon that 'Right Hand' as his reincarnation upon earth — the mortal made immortal in the image of he who gave that all might see — so live.

How can we know the truth of 'Love One Another' till we have trampled 'I' in the dust to set our faces upon that Y of 'You' which is the icon absolute for portrayed by Christ's body hanging upon the cross — arms outstretched upward as the ultimate Icon of Civilised Life — the 'You' which is our neighbour's service without which we live divided by the hates engendered by the hegemonies of priests — to revert to barbarism, for;

He is only *fit* to govern who achieves *fit* government of himself

How can we know the truth of 'Love One Another' till we have loved — but Mind alone is not adequate to such task. The gift does not serve which is merely 'of what Mind can do' but must be of us entire for which Body is the signature, for Man is Spirit clothed in Body but; priests, forever seeking to control man's strength, have divided Man's Body from his Mind to emasculate him in their image of how his body shall be used. Since Man assembled dictators have sought power over him whose first recourse has been the centre of Man's greatest drive — his power to reproduce himself — so priests have set out to deny Man his desire — unless within their chains. How can a priesthood preach 'love one another' when it itself is celibate so can not know a fraction of it — the hypocrisy astounds — truly Hell's Despair. Sharing, which is the core of 'Love One Another' is a material matter which, to have effect, must involve us wholly — undivided — for no single part will do.

That final truth you would shun from within your self-righteous shell — is man always crucifies those who expose his self-created lies as I have done — for he's afeared to face them *so no salvation may be his for*, Too many people, too much of the time are too stupid to realise their own salvation can never be achieved by seeking 'I' — only by serving 'You'. Calvary shows us — for all time — that *we must do it*, now for others, as he did it *then* for all — no 'hereafter' will suffice to blot out the Hell's Despair we build by grubbing in 'I''s ditch — but why live in Hell's Despair when we can travel so easily through Heaven's Gate?, for; hold up, 'be not afraid' the angels sang on the night on which he was born, for is not this how we actually are, loving beings, so what I've shown is well within our compass — if we concentrate upon it.

Second Coming? Such is the figment of the feeble mind with they who manufacture myths for he lives on in all those who 'Love One Another' — howsoever — in which lives the truth of his immortality — in us today — should we choose to live within Heaven's Gate in all we do — hand-in-hand with all about us.

Aphrodite, written within 2 days in Epiphany, 2009

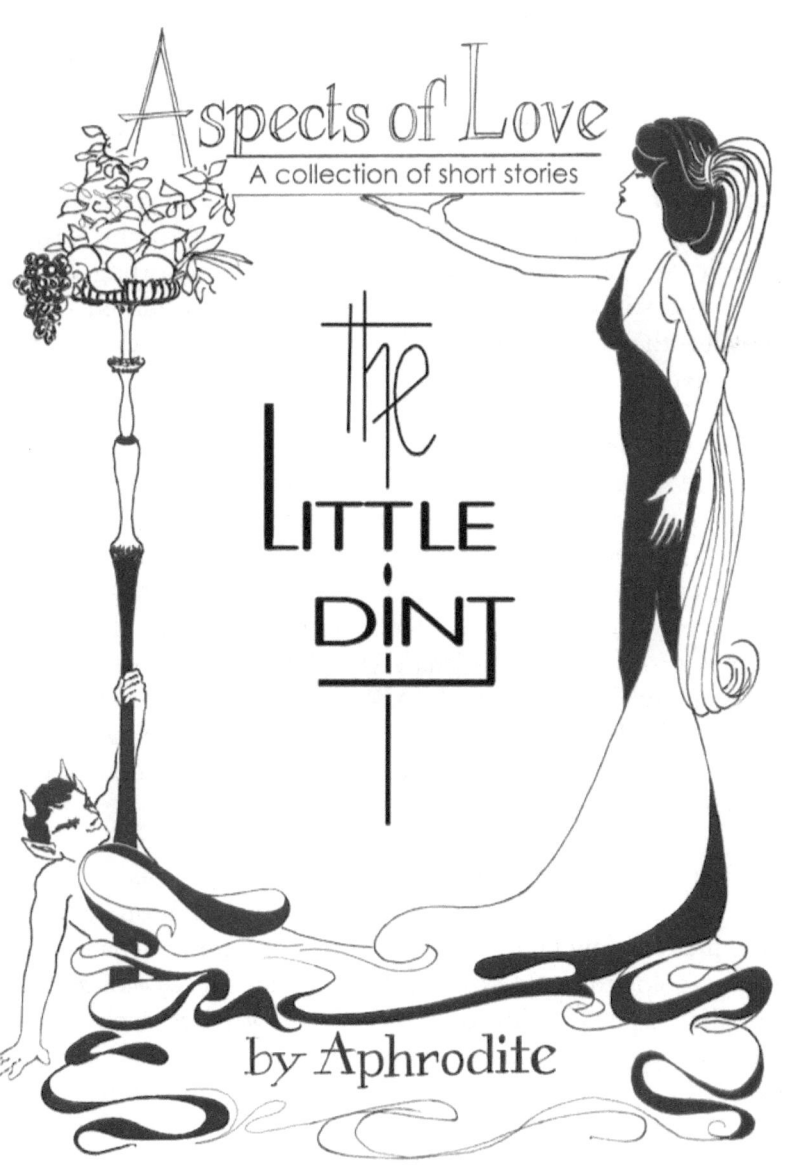

Aspects of Love
A collection of short stories

The Little Dint

by Aphrodite

THE LITTLE DINT

The captain looked out of the Kent, busily whirling the odd rain shower off the forward view from his shining new bridge-deck. A blustery November day gusting 6 across the yard entrance but he was pleased with his new ship, the first of a new class of Destroyer the Belfast yard was building fit to bust. She'd sailed through her two week trial comfortably, faster than he'd expected too, with only a few small details needing sorting — but they were done now so they were off out for a quick day for final checks before setting off for their shake-down getting onto station to defend the ravaged Atlantic convoys.

'A new form of Hell', he'd been told by those who'd been there with U-boats in huge 'wolf-packs' shooting indiscriminately for fearing little retaliation, but he was a little more senior than most, accomplished in his arts, confident in himself and his crew who had been with him in his last ship. He had expressly requested they join him in this arduous task on which so much of England's life depended. Since his old ship, very old indeed, was being pensioned off their Lordships were happy to acquiesce confident also in his ability while knowing his tight-knit team had performed prodigies in their old tub chasing round the North Sea after the motley enemies which populated its turbulent shallow waters where accurate navigation was so vital.

Yes, he was happy as he looked at his young midshipman at the wheel ready for the off, happy to be running a crack team in a fine new ship on both of which he now knew he could rely. The Yard had made a fine job of her, even going the little extra to give the cabins nice coloured paint — a favour the Inspector winked at knowing how much such little things made for a happy team. The Inspector had been a man after his own heart, picking up the things which really needed sorting but skating over those things he knew the crew would sort as they went, the little frilly things, 'nothing an oil can won't sort', he'd laughed as they'd ticked off the last details together.

'You'd be surprised Captain what can be sorted with an oil can', to which the captain had laughed, being an engineer, 'yes if only those at home knew such simple things like oiling door catches and everything that moves, home would work so much better; my wife laughs at me going round occasionally but there isn't squeaky or rough anything back at mine'. The inspector chuckled happily, 'yes it isn't just machines either the whole damn world would be better for a drop of oil to keep the frictions at bay', as they parted with a job well done.

After the commands had been given to cast off mooring lines the Captain, keen to give his young men the maximum of working experience, commanded, "Ok Mr MacLeod she yours, but just be careful of that half-gale across the entrance it'll pick up our bow as she goes through so give yourself plenty of room clear of the lewar'd side". The Middy, concentrating furiously while keen not to be seen charging round the yard harbour called for slow ahead to set off for the fearsomely narrow gap of the yard entrance onto the river outside. All seemed to be in hand as they approached then the Captain, watching more widely, saw an errant yard tug heading for the entrance making to get out before the new destroyer, which was proceeding modestly — but he'd misjudged their speed. The Captain leant on the klaxon but in the wind the tug didn't hear so their only recourse was to call for a short burst of 'hard-astern' to give the tug an exit, the Captain hoping they could hold their course against the wind. As soon as they could see the tug would clear the Captain noted quietly, "full ahead Mr MacLeod, we'll need all we've got to keep steerage way through the gap". It was done but with the wind picking up the slowed ship their angle was now too acute while as they entered the gap a fierce gust picked up the high bow to tweak it capriciously sideways into the stone pier.

There was a horrid crunch as the pier-head collided with the port bow just forward of the forward gun turret with a good deal of squealing of metal — then they were through. The Captain had been here before so knew how utterly destroyed his young Middy would be by the accident. He'd fought his old tub damn nearly underwater a number of times so a harbour-wall affair was small beer indeed. "Don't worry young man", he put a reassuring arm across the distraught boy's shoulders for a second, "we've all done it", he smiled into the troubled eyes, "anyway it wasn't your fault, I'll have that tug-skipper's guts for garters this evening just you see", he laughed, "anyway the bark of tearing metal's always far worse than the bite'n, I fancy Mr McBride's men'll have it sorted in no time when we get back". He thought for a moment, then guffawed quietly, "they'll have been watching too the boyos, proud of their new ship so they'll be getting the jacks and gear ready for our return, you'll see — I hope they don't think it was me or I shall be in real trouble, the Captain bending their new toy, I'll be standing them beers for the time they're fixing".

The Young midshipman worshiped his boss, as did all the crew, a man who, as soon as they were out of 'protocol', clear on the high seas, worked with them as men and colleagues. Rules he considered a background only to give form to the loose regimen he had long found worked best when half the ship was out of action with everybody surviving being able to jump to any station which required it; it was the secret of his success when the going got really tough, a tight team working in the confidence none would break for all being bound by a firm bond of genuine friendship, backed by total trust.

"Don't worry Sir", the Midshipman assured, looking in admiration at his boss legs straddled as the little ship began to pick up the swell coming up the river, "I'll have signals tell the yard it was me on the wheel so they can have a good laugh before we get back, then they won't be dunning you for drinks'n they know us kids don't have the loot anyway". "Don't worry too much lad", his boss consoled, "the boys'll have seen the style of our little fiasco so the tug skipper's not going to be a popular bloke in the pub to-night — apart from the reprimand he'll get from up top". "I know McBryde's a big bloke", he added helpfully, "who keeps his gang in hand with a fierce paw but killing kids isn't his thing, he's got two of his own he's training up, so he won't be eating you".

Everything went smoothly with the captain calling down to the engine room for a showing of 'full-ahead'n through the stops' to give the onlook-ers on the river bank a thrill as they came back home in the afternoon — with the 'dinted' side facing away from the shore mercifully. He knew well how such little things gave those at home a faith 'their boys out there' were going dragon-slaying with the best their men in the yard could give them. It was a tight community with everyone pulling out all sorts of stops to get ships built so their show, bow-wave squirting high, was a thank-you too. Straight through the harbour entrance, half-ahead, so they had command of the wind which had risen in the interim they made for their berth.

Tucked up against the harbour wall, nursed in place by one of the other tugs, they were soon tied up, the 'dinted' side now full on view.

Those who could, keen to see the actual state of the damage, trooped down the briskly lowered gangway to glarp. Teeth were sucked as heads nodded at the gash of paintless steel the harbour wall had inflicted as Mr. McBryde sauntered up with his foreman trying to look stern. "Bent my ship eh, young man", he chid severely to The Midshipman whose parents he knew, as the Midshipman was a local from up the County near where he himself lived. Then his face creased, "us chaps've already got the tug skipper doing drinks duty, he's standing beers to the team now", he laughed gustily. "We saw the whole thing'n my only advice is next time take her half-ahead to go for it, specially with a wind on, you've got much more steerage way — pussy-footing about's not the thing here, it's confidence'n shoot stuff — 'n'in this case you'd have been out there before that tug got in the way — but there, we've all got to learn'n a few little dints's always the best way", he laughed, "sort of things you don't forget".

He and his foreman conferred both intimately aware of the internal construction inside the dent. "I think, Sir", he reflected, addressing the Captain who'd been listening to the fatherly advice of a wise man, "we can do that where she is, save taking 'er round into a bay, it's only a jack'n hammer job as I fancy the skin's not too stretched so we won't need to cut'n weld it". "Thanks Jim", The Captain smiled at competence, "I'll stand the team a round so crack on as we need to be sorting U-boats a.s.a.p. — cosmetic's aren't what we're at here, sinking Huns is".

The Foreman chortled gaily, "oh you'll get both Sir, we don't want His Majesty's ships looking as though they're losing the battle, all bent about'n us chaps've got our pride too, so Rule Britannia it is with a fair line'n a smart paint finish too boot — er, can you spare the culprit while we do it Sir, I'd like to take him round the yard so he can see how we build'em — then he won't go bending'em so freely"?, he laughed gaily, "while the lads are jackin'n bashing". "Certainly Jim", The Captain replied, "thanks for the trouble specially as I think you know his folks". "That I do Sir", he confirmed, "'n a fine pair they are so it'll be a pleasure as I won't be doing the bashing here as that's a man's job", he laughed uproariously.

The Foreman had a considerable admiration for The Captain's fighting and ship-handling reputation as well as getting to like his simple business-like approach while they'd been commissioning, so looked him squarely, "I'd have done the same Sir — putting young MacLeod here on the wheel — kids've got to learn'n the best way is doing it when it's tricky", he stopped a moment knowing his own ground but not quite sure of such an idea as a general precept up-on-high, "you can't win a war Sir without taking a few risks" — "Jim we both know you can't win anything without some pretty big risks", The Captain agreed fulsomely, "no risks and all you do is stay stuck in the pond with the frogs, croaking".

The Foreman relaxed delighted by this common understanding then laughed, "little dint's is only little dints'n the fastest way to learn for real, Sir". The Captain stood quietly looking at this burly plate-layer turned yard boss who would have to straighten-out the aforesaid dint, "thank-you Jim, we both understand that, but it's nice to know you approve all the same, after all bent ships have to be mended by the blokes who didn't bend them; I can well remember doing something similar when I started but got a much rougher ride which knocked my confidence badly for a bit — no way forward there", he laughed giving the yard-manager a hand to shake. "Wish your chaps well in the repairs for me Jim — you're in the best of hands Mr. MacLeod, Mr. McBryde's done it all", as Mc Bryde put a mighty hand under the Midshipman's elbow to steer him off for their tour as his team briskly assembled a couple of long hydraulic jacks with the necessary back-up gear to take on board.

"You're a lucky young chap Mr MacLeod", explained McBryde as they headed into the smarter end of the Yard where the drawing offices were, "with a skipper like Captain Donaldson because its going to be pretty ghastly out there, and you mayn't return, but if you do you'll have an experience you won't ever forget because he's the very best the Navy's got for this sort of thing where spit'n polish don't matter — but survival does". "Yes I know Sir", agreed the Middy, "all the lads down below say the same but I've only just joined as I only did half a trip with him in *'Gladstone'* because they knew I was a local here'n they'd need a few extra hands so I got a start in the North Sea — it was amazing how it all worked so well without hardly a command anywhere — everyone likes the painted cabins Sir, seriously snug over Admiralty Grey".

McBryde laughed splendidly, "yes cream was one of those things which happened over a pint while he'n I were touring the ship finishing details", he smiled fondly at the memory of the amazing man who was going to take this little ship his team had just built out into the nastiest conditions Nature and Man could devise, The North Atlantic Convoys, as they had sat quietly sipping gin discussing colours. A plate-layer he may have been but McBryde sang in a big local opera group so his awareness of classical 'horrors' was considerable — Inferno's were it — while *The Great Day of His Wrath'* had hung as a large print in his parent's front room. The stories he'd had from the battered escorts they repaired to go back into battle looked like every detail of that extraordinary picture of total damnation while the wax-like skin stretched over the features of those who brought them back told his men all they needed to know — not any sort of fun — which galvanised his team to extraordinary efforts to ensure what they built was of the very best; so what matter some pretty paint to make 'their' sailors lives a little more cheerful, while his team's wives took the exhausted men under their motherly wings for the duration to give them a break.

"Yers", the yard boss reflected, "we were sitting in the new wardroom with a gin ticking off details both looking at the severe cold Admiralty Grey then the skip said, 'it's much the same out there Jim, grey, unforgiving and cold". McBryde knew he wasn't giving away confidences as the knowledge their skipper cared enough about these things to break rules would cheer everyone as much as the lovely warm cream his chaps had found in the city. "We agreed without saying a thing warm cream would be fine so I found a special gang of painters from the town to come in to blast the whole accomodation areas when no-one was looking", he laughed at the little subterfuge which he'd cleared with the Admiralty Inspector, who'd simply replied, 'what matter a colour Jim if it wins a war, specially if it doesn't appear on any indents'. "Everyone chipped in", he laughed splendidly, "while the supplier gave us a very tight deal — he's the bass next to me in the choir".

"This smart building here", he began as they entered a huge suite of fancy offices, "is the Admin operation but it's also got the kernal of the whole show The Drawing & Design Office". They climbed two flights of bare stairs up to a huge long room the whole length of the top floor with windows extensively down both sides. "Lots of windows for the best natural light", noted McBryde as they walked down the empty office's serried ranks of huge drawing boards, it being lunch hour with only the occasional draftsman sitting at his board reading a magazine over a sandwich. One of them looked up enquiringly, knowing McBryde well who spent considerable time amongst the design teams making sure the results of their efforts could be expeditiously made, which liaison he'd insisted on when he'd become yard boss, having seen too many parts appear which could have been better designed had there been some mutual consultation.

"Just showing the culprit round the show Alistair so he has more respect for ships, doesn't go knocking'em against pier-heads", followed by wonderful laughter. "I happened to be looking out of the window thinking as it happened lad — ringside seat", chuckled the draftsman, "real theatre the whole thing, there was a sort of inevitability about it all from the moment the klaxon went off, so I couldn't've done any better if I'd been you". "Ah well, we've got the tug-skipper buying pints so all's well that ends well", the plate-layer smiled. The draftsman, keen for The Mishipmen to get more than a cursory view, stood up to point out the salient details of his kingdom. "Down the far end you can see the big tables where the general layouts are done then each section of the office works on specific types of detail so we all get very quick each with a speciality, mine's developing plate shapes to send up to the mould-loft to be made into the final patterns for the cutters-out — over there are the chaps who do all the clever engineering stuff, come'n see".

He whisked MacLeod off to a drawing board covered with an incomprehensible mass of lines and details which had a large casting standing on the floor beside it. "See there's the part and there's the drawing which Mack here is checking and modifying — if you look at it from this side then this bit of the drawing is what you see — then if you turn it round like this, this bit of the drawing over here is what you see'n the same for the top and bottom", as he pointed out the various views showing MacLeod how they represented the casting on the floor. "It's called three view projection, tho' for complex parts there will be sections and part-views and all sorts so the chaps who've got to make the casting patterns know every tiny detail and dimension — all these spidery lines'n arrows are the dimensions".

"Oh wow Alistair", exclaimed the Midshapman staggered by the complexity, "now you've shown me how it works I've got a tiny idea of what its all about — chaps look at each view so they can see what that side's going to have to be made like, is that right"? "Yes" the draftsman agreed, "because when you've been at it a bit you can look at a drawing to see the whole part in all its details in your head, know what it looks like because engineering drawing's a convention, a bit like reading, so everyone knows exactly what it all means — you read a drawing like you read a book then you can make it — though many different blokes will make the different features as The Boss'll show you". "Pattern-makers make the moulds then foundry-men cast them, then off to the various different parts of the machine shop who each put on different features depending on whether their milling or boring or drilling or turning or grinding — different machines and shops for each". "Gosh thank you Alistair now I've seen the beginning the rest'll make a lot more sense" — "have fun lad", as he returned to become absorbed again in his magazine and sandwich.

McBryde seeing some real learning happening before his eyes smiled mightily, "that was a lucky one lad as Alistair McCutcheon's one of the thinky ones, I can always rely on his plates being right so let's go to the Mould Loft where what he does gets drawn out full-size on the steel sheets we build the ship from". It was quite a hike to the top of another building, again with plenty of light but handling gear for the big sheets of steel used for the hull plates and framing. Again lunch prevailed so did quiet. "This is that last time we'll be quiet lad, all you ever hear here is the squeak of chalk and the jokes of the lofters". There was a huge drawing board with measuring equipment all over it so the scaling from the drawn size could be enlarged to full size to be drawn, dimension by dimension on to the steel sheets lying on platforms or on the floor.

"Look lad", pointed McBryde, "here's one with all its dots on which mark where the edges of the sheet will be when they're all in place, then the lofter gets a huge bendy stick — called a spline — which he bends round then anchors to draw the line round with chalk". "I know it seems unscientific", he continued his exegesis, "but quite a lot of boat-building's a by-eye affair'n the principle here is the spline naturally bends through a fair curve so when it's drawn round we can guarantee we've ironed out any small measuring errors — it's the fair line which matters in boat and ship building because we're not much different to the old chaps building in wood on the beach five-hundred years ago as we've still got to work with the sea not against it", he looked at an amazed Midshipman, "no good fighting the sea lad, she'll always win if you do".

He picked up one of the smaller splines, held it at its ends then bent it, "now look down that curve young man, what do you see"? MacLeod, getting into the mood of the thing did, from a number of angles, "it's perfectly smooth isn't it, no kinks or bumps", his eyes lit up, "it's lovely isn't it, sort of perfect". The plate-layer for whom perfect meant a trouble-free assembly, laughed gently, "which, young man, is the centre of the whole affair, its lovely, which is why I wasn't going to skimp our little dint repair because lovely it's got to be for us who spend our time with fair lines — un-fairness just won't do, after all you wouldn't go chasing a girl who was all-unfair, knobs and stuff, would you", he chortled mightily, "it's the same with ships which is why they're called 'she' — even big steel fighting ones 'cause they're built with the same love of perfection we give to the ladies". "You keep your eye trained young MacLeod to look for that fairness", advised the burly plate-layer, "look down lines when you see them because the human eye is the finest comparator in the world — you'll see chaps pick up a piece of timber or cut steel to 'eye' it because they can detect even the tiniest error from a fair curve 'by-eye'". "Your fingers' ends are the same", he assured, "which is why you'll see boatbuilders constantly running their hands over what they're building, to check for little un-fairnesses — very sensitive is the old finger's ends, good for feeling the girls with so you can tell what's going on inside their heads if you're careful with the fingers ends; you can see truth with the eye'n feel it with the fingers' ends", he laughed happily leading off downstairs then across a yard into a vast building shrieking with the noise of machine-tools at work.

"We run a shift system here", commented Mc Bryde proudly as he introduced his guest to the shop foreman, "because machining and making takes far longer than anything else so we need to keep at it if we're going to beat the Hun". They set off on the long haul round the maze of machines which, the Midshipman could see, were grouped in types, which all looked similar within their groups though quite different group for group. For the inquisitive it's a world of wonder, huge hunks of stuff being heaved around with apparently no effort for the attentions of all sorts of cutting tools which make the features which turn an inanimate lump of metal into a shining working part 'fit for purpose'. There is no rush, because rush in machine shops where many hundreds of horse-power with often many tons of metal are being worked on spells dangerous accidents, waste of valuable goods, then the priceless commodity of time — so the men here proceed with a steady quiet confidence.

"You'll see they all have measuring calipers", advised McBryde picking a pair up to demonstrate, "then those sort of half-moon things are micrometers while they've got the drawing of the part they're adding their feature to on a board beside them for constant reference", as they stood for a moment beside a huge vertical milling machine while a massive casting was lowered onto its bed by a travelling crane. When it was mounted and the machinist had clipped his drawing to the board he turned to the Midshipman who was all agog at the sheer size of it all, "the most important thing lad isn't all the measuring stuff, the scientific bit, but that you know what the damn thing actually looks'n feels like in your head, so you've got to make it part of the inside of you while its your job, sort of love it 'cause if you don't cock-ups happen", he smiled at the astonished young man; "it's no good drilling the right sized hole in the wrong place because you didn't love it enough to have a perfect idea of what is should actually *look* like so your visual checking feeling in your head says *'stop not there'*", he laughed hugely, "'s like looking for your lady in a crowd, your sixth sense should tell you where she is'n it's the same here, you wouldn't want to pick up the wrong girl because you didn't recognise her would you", the burly man quizzed the lad happily as McBryde looked on at a simile he hadn't quite thought of himself, 'yes, you've got to love it enough not to ball it up' he chuckled to himself. "You don't get cheered for making colanders when they want castings", advised the miller seriously; "I did it once'n the feeling of letting the show down was awful as my mates had to work all night to make up the mess".

They walked through a section of all sorts of lathes, centre-lathes, capstan lathes, turret-lathes. "The difference between lathes lad and all those milling'n, drilling'n boring machines", advised McBryde, "is on milling machines the work is fixed and you attack it with rotating tools but on lathes the work is on the lathe doing the turning and you work on it with fixed tools". "Centre-lathes", he expounded happily, "turn the work or steel bar between centres and mainly do one job at a time but the capstan'n turret chaps are production machines with lots of tools on a travelling head

which rotates to bring different tools up to do the work, there", he expounded, "you can see that big turret-lathe's turret turning now", he
pointed to a huge thing like a castle bristling with drills and cutting tools
rushing backwards then rotating; "now you can see it advancing again with
different tools to do a different part of the work". The Midshipamn stood,
simply agog, at the splendour of it all as vast squirls of hot metal came
roaring off the tools out from under the cooling water to lie in still sizzling
heaps in the lathe tray. Jim McBryde chuckled at his guest's delight in what
for him was his daily bread, "these chaps all take metal away lad, in my
world of welding and joining we put it on".

They set off down to the ship-yard itself, vast, cold and noisy. In each bay
were ships in different stages of completion, some mere skeletons others
having final plates welded in place. "This is where everyone takes very special care", advised Mc Bryde seriously as he pointed to a crane swaying a
huge steel plate above them. "Everyone needs to develop eyes everywhere", he enlightened his guest, "while living with a care for everything
he does or thinks of, it's definitely a case of one false move and people get
killed — definitely no place for either fools or casual wanderers because
everyone working expects everyone to look after themselves while they
look after everyone too with what they're doing".

He thought a moment as the Midshipman watched spellbound as the huge
plate settled down into its place on the side of the hull as men on gantries
ready to position it for welding in place waved a weird collection of hand-
signs to the crane driver who couldn't see the action as tactical blows from
huge club-hammers nudged it into its 'hole'. Then, as tack welds began to
spark as corners fitted, McBryde continued, "risk's one thing lad, the risk
we all take to make progress which Captain Donaldson gave you today,
but risk's backed by our skill to reduce it to a minimum — but to build the
skill you've got to risk to learn, it's the only way as you've got to've been
there to know where the accidents come from — but it's still a game of
skill not chance".

He thought carefully, "silly people think risk's a 'chancy business', which
idea is for the unskilled'n fools as true risk should be us balancing probabilities against our own skills for, young man, skill is Man's crowning
glory". He thought a moment very aware of the fundamentals which he
knew inside him so well as being central to his life but which every 'kid'

had to learn face to face as he was teaching his two lads. "If our friend the tug-skip", he continued his exegesis on skill, "hadn't mis-judged your speed trying to race you to the entrance you'd have been fine'n your boss's risk no risk at all — *because he knew you had the skill for the job or he wouldn't have put you on the helm* — but somebody was careless — which is the truth of it".

"It's the same up there", he continued his exposition on risk, "there's absolutely no substitute for personal care with the understandings of where accidents come from — none", he added firmly, "no none whatever". "Individual responsibility for even the tiniest move must be absolute", he advised firmly warning to a message he drummed into everybody in his kingdom, "each man is responsible for his part of the job but he's also responsible for his own safety and that of his mates — you can go on blithering about safety procedures till you're blue in the face *but if people don't care enough* then accidents happen — like the tug-driver".

"Mr MacLeod", he noted firmly, "as soon as we cease to care, for even the tiniest thing we do — that is fail to concentrate our whole energies on what we're doing because it's somehow become a habit so we relax our vigilance of care — then accidents happen — it wasn't an accident to the tug-driver who made the cock-up either *but to someone far bigger than himself*". He relaxed a little, "Lionel lad never stop caring, even for the tiniest thing because when you do you'll find life gets to be a very tatty, disengaged, sort of affair when we're not involved because we don't care — caring's the whole business of living not just stopping accidents lad — caring's the difference between being engaged or disengaged — disengaged you're not part of the game, no fun at all".

As they left the noise of the erection sheds The Midshipman was very sober indeed. "Let's go to see how the evening party's going on at The Castleton — for which we'll revert to the formal in company, eh young man"? "Yes Sir", chirped the Midshipmen happily walking alongside the splendid Mr McBryde whose kingship clearly deserved the title. Mr McBryde laughed wonderfully, "I may be king of my castle Mr MacLeod, but even though only a Middy you're a Sir to me so we better get that right or you'll be accused of fraternising with the natives". "Doesn't seem right though Mr McBryde", surmised MacLeod, "a king should address an apprentice as Sir". McBryde chuckled, "agreed Sir but some rules ain't worth arguing about, specially as long as there's mutual respect for what each other does — I couldn't drive a destroyer straight out of the harbour even without the casual interferences — so let's call it quits'n stick to the protocols", he laughed as they passed the injured party. "Looking good I'd say", chuckled McBryde eying the hull line carefully, "Little bit more planishing'n they'll be having the paint on — tomorrow in the dry — but I fancy they'll be joining us pretty soon".

Lionel MacLeod, a quite different lad to the one who had set out that morning, answered very correctly as men of all ranks, and none, were about them, "might I have a pint of the ordinary please Mr McBryde, and thank you for a truly memorable day I know I'm not quite the same MacLeod who set of from the harbour wall this mornin'n I'll certainly never bend a ship again". "Don't fret Sir", chuckled his host, "we're not perfect either, we make mistakes in the yard then have to unmake them so know what making mistakes is all about, because the most important things's not not making mistakes but knowing how to fix'em the best way possible, which is life's great secret — courtesy of a senior plate-layer", he laughed splendidly then turned a little serious.

"Mr MacLeod, if we can learn from those things which happen to us, really learn, then we become men, it's the arrogant who think they know it all who stay children who shouldn't be let out of the nursery — because its they who're a danger to the race". "Mr MacLeod", addressed a neatly dressed man with a single epaulet, "I'm truly sorry for the havoc I caused this morning, one of those silly moments of inattention which no-one in charge of a ship should ever let happen — but it's cost me I can tell you and the chaps on the repair team haven't come in yet either", the tug skipper laughed having come over from a throng of mates.

McBryde chuckled heartily, "we've all learned something today Donald'n if all we've got is a little dint repaired with an empty purse worse things definitely happen at sea". "Thanks to the consideration of your blokes Jim my purse isn't actually empty" confided the tug skipper – "which Mr Mac-Leod", reflected the thoughtful McBryde, "is because this whole operation's a team'n all muck in when there's a moment, as it were; you'll hear your skipper with the same lesson I fancy when you get out to slay the Hun — it's not who makes the mistakes which matters but how fast they can be fixed by everyone patching'n mending — which is how wars are won", he smiled seraphically, "which is why The Hun can never win".

Suddenly the door swung wide as the repair team came in. "Even you, you old bastard, won't be able to see the dint now", they choroused to their much loved boss, "paint on first thing and forget the beers Donald you must have been pretty fleeced already". McBryde chortled happily then put a substantial note on the bar, "fill these guys up Mick they've done sterling work this afternoon". "It wasn't as bad as it might've been Jim", noted the foreman of the gang, "Mr MacLeod here had the luck of the devil because he missed bending a frame, just clipped the flange of one which we jacked back in place, no probs'n the stretch was less than it looked too". McBryde laughed heartily, "just a Little Dint then, well beneath the consideration of such an Olympian team as you guys", followed by general merriment.

Back on board MacLeod reported to his Captain. "Well"?, enquired Donaldson interested to know what McBryde had taught his Midshipman, well aware his journey round the yard would be something he would not forget having a very high regard for the yard-manager's ability to run both a tight ship and a happy one. "He taught me about risk and skill Sir". "Ah", replied a pensive Captain, "Jim's never had an accident while he's been king of the erection yards — he talked to you about care did he"? "Yes he did Sir", replied a still thoughtful Midshipman, "and he told me what you did putting me on the wheel wasn't a risk at all as you knew I could do it" — "exactly, which is why it's the tuggy buying the rounds", his skipper laughed.

"There's a lot more to the rough Mr McBryde than a hefty plate-layer Lionel", The Captain assured, "I've been to concerts given by the choir he sings in, very fine indeed where I could see a beautifully duck-suited monster caring very much indeed about what he did — fascinating. "Never Mr MacLeod", his boss cautioned thoughtfully, "never, set those who don't happen to inhabit the bridges of His Majesty's ships, below yourself".

The Midshipman looked with renewed astonishment as this wonderful father-figure in the ways of life, "I'm just a Middy Sir learning the trade, Mr McBryde's a king, he showed me wonderful things I'll never know'n he taught me about care". "Just so Lionel", he agreed, "we can learn even from the beggar in the street who faces us with the inequities of the world, ignore him, fail to acknowledge his state, then we cease to be human for he is the same as us — but in a different station at the moment, so he deserves the care of our concern; we may not be able to do anything for him but to pretend he doesn't exist is to stamp upon our own humanity to make us beast".

The Captain, seeing a starry eyed understanding dawning in his midshipman's eyes, continued gently, "Mr McBryde probably put some bits about love into his little exposition did he, love of doing the job right"? "Yes he did", the Midshipman assured, "with a lot about fair lines too, I'd never thought of it like that at all". "Don't fret lad", consoled his boss, "learning's what life's all about but Love's far more than doing the job right, because Love is the absolute commitment of one to another you'll see when it starts getting tough in the Atlantic". "Love's the commitment to everyone and everything around us before ourselves which will get us safe out the other side of the particular hell we're going to, or any of life's hells for that matter — because Love is the sacrifice of ourselves to serve our friends through the greater good of what we're all engaged in — if we each only looked after $N^\circ 1$ nothing would happen at all". He thought a moment but happy his Midshipman was man enough for the understanding, "you are going to see some of the most magnificent sacrifices mankind ever makes in the hell of The North Atlantic Lionel — far beyond himself for the greater good — the Love of his fellow and the winning of this damned war, as Jesus did 'unto death' if need be — which is a sacrifice for the ideas of freedom and all our people back home — you will have been to The Gates of Hell and felt the flames, but you will not have despaired, so if we survive we shall never be the same again for we shall have travelled with the gods — which is Man at his finest for placing Love first above all he does".

Postlude

Some of 'Love's Aspects' are obvious but there's Love in every strand of the story. The Love which cares to protect each other from the natural mistakes we all make with the Love which nurtures each of us in adversity — not just heave around self-righteous blame or leave it all to someone else. The Love of a proper job for its own sake but specially for the beauty which 'well done' brings to all who see it with the little love of pride for something 'done a little better than it need be' on behalf of those around us. The Love of 'right & truth' against the advancement of self through the dissimulation of surface. The Love of the 'Straight' and 'The Fair' over the devious and the twisted. The passionate Love of 'making it happen' over 'it can't be done' through the Love which places ourselves 'shoulder-to-shoulder' with any with whom we need to prosecute the task. The Love of the flights of flexibilities which make the possibilities over the rigidities and rules which seal within failure's box. The Love which recognises 'together' — amongst 'all sort and conditions of men' is not only a way to win but the best way to conduct life we are able. The Love which places our neighbour before ourselves in all things.

These Loves are what we do 'outside ourselves', beyond 'what we are paid to', the Love of living the very best way we can hand-in-hand with our neighbour as a team in Life's Great Pilgrimage. It is this which breeds that magnificent 'One Volunteer is better than ten pressed men', but;

Behaving as I have told our little story is not a duty or an 'ought' formed by priests to conform to a 'religion', but the supreme joy of working in harmony with our fellow man in common enterprise which makes the whole business of life not only worthy — *but more rewarding than any possible searching after self's advance* because it make the business I have outlined — of Love driving everything — a Religion in its own right to transcend *all* the 'religions' man has manufactured to cage himself down time — because it frees us to fly with the angels.

As you may read in *The Golden Path* 'Love is the gifts of ourselves for others' or, as so many did in both those wars 'the gift of their lives for their friends and a votive beyond themselves' **BUT** which is the most important understanding in the above, we do not need to actually 'give our life', because every time we withdraw from a confrontation trying to mount our 'I' we 'give a little' to discover a far greater life beyond for 'flying with the Angels'; forcing our 'Right' is how we 'Wrong' our neighbour — it really is as simple as that.

It is more than half a century since the last World War and nearly a hundred since the First but all the parts of this little story were the engine of why Britain won, against far superior better organised forces. Freedom's flexibilities stood against Regimen's rigidities to win. Man stood against Machine which, when the chips are down, will always win because Man can be powered by Love's mighty uniting power — it is when he loses Love's power he perishes in the bogs of his own self-service which, sadly, is the signature of so much of today.

Aphrodite, January 2010

Aspects of Love

A collection of short stories

Snuggle

by Aphrodite

SNUGGLE

"Do you dance, Sir"? He was caught a little unawares, far away in his new job of running this base which so badly needed a lift after some punishing losses, for she had come up from behind him. "You look lonely", greeted the young WAAF cheerfully smiling down at him, "we can't be having us thought unfriendly, even battered as we are". Her smile was catching, so he smiled back, "oh oldies dance", he replied a little vacantly deciding anything was better than moping, "it's what oldies do", he observed a little wistfully. "Ok Sir", she encouraged, "come on, dancing's why the boys play here, we're so lucky to have a few airmen who do then we found a couple of the erks who are real wizzards so we invited them to join us because we're a team here", she noted quietly so aware of the broken protocol, "all of us against him over there, so we like to get people together to take them out of themselves — I hope you don't mind"?, she asked with a deep look in her pretty brown eyes.

He looked long at this little slip of a thing who was probably bearing the strain as hard as any — he knew the heartache of empty arms the girls suffered — so promptly decided protocol could 'go to hell'. "We're in a war, as you said 'all of us against him over there', which I know is trite, but to win wars you have to abandon rules, wars are won by the fleet of foot not those stuck in the trenches, so absolutely I don't mind — they make a fine sound so let's". He stood to allow himself to be lead on to the floor, "I feel disjointed", he admitted, "disengaged from everything, some closeness for a bit would be magic". He smiled at her fondly, thanking the girl mentally for handling the situation with such style by giving him a godsent entry — he knew the 'no protocols' line would be round the base in hours for it was always a tense time when a new boss came into a tight knit family, specially one nursing its wounds.

They found a space on the little floor then without a moment's thought she took the lead by taking him in her arms to start. He looked at her thankfully, "I'm Squadron Leader Maple", he began his introduction, "but I'd better be Ned when we're doing this as Sir sounds silly with all that protocol we're abandoning 'cause the erks playing the music", he laughed into her bright eyes. "Oh, we all know the Squadron Leader Maple bit Sir, it's on the board", she giggled gently, "but the Ned bit's good, it gives the boys a handle to understand you, less distant, can I leak it"? He decided the opening he had was worth every bit of protocol which got in the way, oil was everything, "indeed you can, but gently as it goes". Quietly amazed at Squadron Leaders descending she announced, "I'm Polly but I'll stay Polly 'cause who I am doesn't matter, does it"?, she smiled. He looked into her eyes gently, "you kids grow up fast don't you, is it really so grisly"?

She thought quietly as they gyrated gently, "it's been bad the last two weeks but, yes I suppose we do, the real trouble is we don't even get past first base before they're gone so we have to try to comfort another". "Well Polly war is war", he smiled his consolation, "you're a chicken'n I'm an oldie, so I've survived a bit'n I don't intend Gerry getting me — will you mind me being antique"? She looked up into his eyes quietly, "why should I?, people are people which is all that matters, war or not", she stopped a moment then laughed, "oh bugger protocol, I liked what I saw come in the door — will that do"?

"Polly, you can't have any idea how wonderful that is", he assured fervently, "women have never looked at me all my life, they always look through me or past me as if I didn't exist". "Silly them", she cooed snuggling a little closer. They danced on quietly. She was neat, only a couple of inches shorter than he, with pretty hair and lovely enquiring bright brown eyes in an extraordinary face he couldn't place, not beautiful but with a quiet inner brightness he found enchanting.

Despite the snuggling he knew she wasn't a tramp as there was a purity about her he found intriguing. She looked up at him, "us girls need as much help as you fliers you know", she began a little explanation, "it's damned lonely stuff without something to hang on to, however temporary, a little sort of anchor, something you know's there for you — even for a bit, constantly mothering new ones takes it out of you".

He was bowled over then looked long at her gauging, then took a little plunge, "exactly so Polly", he confirmed, "what we all really want is snuggle, togethness in the apartness which seems to be our lot in this rotten swirl — I've long grown out of the jolly knightly stuff as I came into this some way up the tree so understand the need for anchors — will you be my anchor for a bit so I can be yours"? She snuggled laughing into his front then looked innocently up into his eyes, "ok snuggle-magic, no complications, no angst, no maybes, just togetherness for as long as it lasts — then pass on rejoicing". She stopped for a moment then looked at him brows arched enchantingly, "how far do snuggles go"? He laughed, "where did all that wisdom come from little girl, you can't yet be twenty". She gurgled happily, "as you said Sir Knight us kids grow up fast but I came from a very straight home so I'm a virgin nineteen, very little girl indeed, but I think I'd like to find out about snuggle, so let's".

"The answer to your question Miss Polly", he began, "is snuggle is as flexible as you like, so goes as far as you want between you, snuggle isn't a thing or a place — though both help the anchor thing — but an attitude of mind matched with an understanding of Body which is all a bit fancy for virginal nineteen but be patient, no rushed fences then you'll see as you become transformed — I'm married to a lovely lady who transformed me from virginal forty whom I wouldn't sacrifice for worlds Polly, will you mind"? "Why should it"?, she replied seriously, "its lovely, cosy, not complex — will she mind"?

He looked at her carefully, "Wisdom out of the mouths of babes, so absolutely not at all because when I tell her she'll cheer as she's worried about me getting morose'n out of practice, she won't want a corpse in her bed when I get back, she told me so severely -'do anything you like but don't lose your head to it, you're mine'". Miss Polly chuckled, "I'd like to meet her one day she sounds gorgeous". "She rescued me", he agreed fondly, "and she is so what we've got is well above the norm, priceless".

She looked up at him gauging carefully, then plunged, "the truth is Edward", she admitted hiding her face in his top, "snuggle's only an idea for me, it's never got any further because they've been blown to bits before I've had the chance, so I've no idea what it's really like — will you show me"? He gave her a gentle but unobtrusive squeeze, "leading the young lambs is what oldies are for Polly — it's what I try to do up in the blue so more of them survive".

The music stopped. She looked up at him as a little understanding passed between them so they separated as she went off to join her normal group of girls. The evening passed quietly. For Maple it was a revelation; they may have had a hell of a time these people but there was solid worth here he could build on. Perhaps his entry, carefully played, might be through Polly, joy through some teaching for her, lots of joy for him with a tremor of joy going through everyone as happy spread like it does, through little cracks no-one knows but all recognise. He was more aware than most how vital just plain morale was to winning — happy came top of that pile. St Paul spoke to him in a tiny moment — but the message arrived loud and clear — the band playing, never mind who played, was the message.

He intentionally did not mingle, breaking up other people's little groups, let the message creep around, as it would now he had been seen so close to one of theirs. He retired relatively early to let the party get going. It had been a good day as everyone had come back so little celebrations were in order to which his august presence did not add. He intentionally did not look Polly's way, he knew she knew, so left the next move to her confident she would know how.

He walked back round the perimeter, no track here as this airfield was a hasty affair, little more than a field, but it was a gorgeous summer night, with Lady Moon sailing serenely with her consort Venus, his hair fanned by a tiny breeze. Walking was good; he was no longer alone as he had, goodness knows how, won a pretty companion with whom to share the next part of the journey. A companion, but a child, a child he could enjoy teaching all the lovely things his lady-wife had taught him to drag him out of a lonely bachelorhood sprinkling their path with stars — an enterprise as old as time for based in the Socratic understanding of teaching.

Lust did not even enter his head, curious he thought as lust played quite a part with his lady but this was a child whom it was vital he bring through to know without even the hint of damage — joy should be hers, unalloyed. He would enjoy the exercise, quite a counterpoint to the business of getting the squadron back up to strength, but he had come to know from 'making it work' with his lady both endeavours were made by Love — Love of the people, Love of the job well done through Love of the gift of himself in the doing — it was the gift which drove it, he knew. The music playing with the erks amongst was the key he'd been given by the voice above, so he'd seen the way to know he had the tool to hand. With his lady's help he had discovered the gift of self has to be unconditional so now he knew how he could spread it to the help of these troubled people — unconditional meant unconditional — no rules. He had found also, amongst the bumps of re-constructing his life, such was returned the Biblical 'an hundredfold' when given freely.

He harked back to 'snuggle'. Snuggle had come to them later, out of a somewhat peculiar sex-driven start, a start which had taken him by storm from her expertise and passion for him — something which astonished him still — but which they had gently worked through as tribulations of former unions had been overcome by concentrating on their union — through the gift of each to each other no matter what seemed to get in the way. He had been a very late starter in marriage, before his present one, which he'd failed for not understanding either snuggle nor sex which was the element his new lady had shown him then developed for him — he by then learning stuff he suspected every erk knew backwards. They had made 'bed' an icon of peace as a focus for their locked togetherness. They had developed snuggle as a central element of togetherness, to form an un-breachable wall against the flights of circumstance. Yes, sex was all very well, and fun — but snuggle was the heart of the matter — the together-ness of Mind & Body born of Love's gift; now he thought he had a hold on how he might apply it further for he now knew the proper conduct of such engagements was the gift of self for the joy of another — then the passing on in peace with rejoicing.

He wandered back to his posh house, posh for this base but pretty simple as bosses houses went normally, to find a little figure tucked into the shad-ows of the porch out of the view of prying eyes. "No-one saw me", noted the girl quietly "'n my room mate Pauline's cheering me on 'cause she's got her own man, she's a real goodie, so she's happy I've found one even if he is The Station Commander — she won't split'n she'll guard for me too". Without a moment's hesitation he took her very gently in his arms to kiss her purely as a gift for her. "That, Polly is just the beginning of snuggle, the gift of a kiss — but it must be a gift not a grab". He rummaged for his unfamiliar key then for the unfamiliar key-hole to open the door into the dark. He took her through into the kitchen then switched on some light to put the kettle on.

"My bedside tipple is hot choccy, will choccy do you Polly", who grinned gently, "hot choccy, a handsome Squadron Leader, bed with snuggle — where does heaven stop", she gurgled, then stopped to stand beside him. "Oh Edward I'm sorry about the Squadron Leader bit", she apologised a little strickenly, "I'm on such unknown territory it just slipped out — what I should have said is 'a man'. "Oh Polly", he complimented her perception, "when the uniform's off Squadron Leader will disappear so all you'll be left with is ancient man — but the hot choccy'n the bed's up to scruff", he laughed at her little turmoil. "I'm as aware as you you can't play your catch amongst your mates", he considered, "so who I am doesn't matter, so here it's just Polly'n Ed so quiet your spirit little girl so you can practice being little girl because it is she I'm going to enjoy teaching".

She looked him coyly in the eye, "very little girl indeed because she's never been to bed with a man before so doesn't know what any of the bits are really about — home was a very restricted place". "Well", he consoled smiling, "you don't need to know because I'll show you — you're going to enjoy every moment, hot choccy'n all". The kettle boiled with which he deftly made the two drinks, "sugar little girl"?, he smiled at her delightedly. "Oh please ancient man", she giggled happily relaxed as he tossed in sugar to both, then switching off the kitchen light he groped for the stair light switch in its unfamiliar place.

He put the hot chocolate down on the single table then chuckled. "It's a bit spartan Polly, not even a double bed which at least which will ensure we don't get lost in the night". Knowing well Polly would now be on unknown ground he took gentle charge. "The secret of snuggle, little girl, is giving, however, wherever, so together never comes unstuck — so you undress me first — how's that"?

She giggled then relaxed not having to think about 'what happened next' nor what was expected of her. "Start at the top", he chuckled seeing a little confusion cross her face, "then it's automatic, no judgments needed". Tie came off then shirt then vest, then automatically she put her arms round the manly chest. He smiled down at her, "some things you need to be told some things come naturally, don't they", as he dropped a kiss on top of the snuggling head. She giggled, "if this is ancient ancient'll do fine, I like the furr, its warm". She undid his belt to drop his trousers out of which he stepped as she kneeled to help, then clamped her arms round his middle to snuggle some more. Then with a seraphic smile she removed his underpants, "Oo, I like that furr, much more than mine", she giggled admiring the unaccustomed contents of the furr, then she stood to admire 'her man'.

"what I see is definitely man, not squadron leader, so it's your turn Edward".

He stepped behind her to cradle her neat firm breasts then removed her service jacket and blouse to cradle a little more dropping a kiss on her neck, then gently unhooked her bra to cover its contents with his nestling hands as she wriggled gently. "The wriggle's natural", she giggled happily as she got as close as she could to his furry chest encouraging his hands with hers, "I didn't have to be told what to do there — is this a bit of snuggle Edward"?, she asked coyly. "This is the essence of snuggle", he replied in teacher voice "the giving of our inmost selves for the joy of the other — within its wider view of all the others". Then he kneeled down to un-hook her service skirt which he laid aside to take the result in his hands wrapping them round her lovely young bum burying his head in her stomach. She wriggled some more, now well on to automatic. He looked up to see a lovely relaxed smile so peeled off her knickers and stockings in one smooth movement. "Less furr but just as lovely, fine little girl furr not hard man furr", he noted authoritatively as she giggled as he pressed his face into it smoothing his hands down from her buttocks to her thighs. 'Quite different to his lady', he thought 'but what did the difference matter when there was closeness like this'.

"It may be summer but warm's what snuggle's about so come on in", he peeled the blankets back with a flourish, "I like to be this side so you go first". She looked at him archly, a little coquettish smile creeping across her face as she sidled invitingly into the bed. He laughed gently, "happy little girl Polly? — that's how it should be if snuggle's magic's going to work". He climbed in after her, their bodies inevitably close in the single service bed. He turned her over away from him then wrapped her gently his hands closed on her breasts, whose nipples had gone hard. He chuckled twiddling them gently, "hard nipples are automatic too Polly", he assured, "happy automatic". She purred then wriggled quietly as he fitted his hardness between her buttocks gently. She giggled, "I guess he's happy automatic too Edward"? "Well yes he is", he agreed, "but it wouldn't be honouring a lady limp would it Polly"? "It's nice to be honoured, I'd never thought of being honoured before", she gurgled — — "but it can stay where it is", he assured her, "hard cocks are a plague, they should never be allowed to take charge of affairs, they make demands which snuggle's definitely not about because swords should only ever be at a lady's service as the delight at the heart of snuggle's gift".

Polly, not entirely unversed, had been apprehensive of the part expected of her so relaxed into Edward completely her fears assuaged. "'Expected of us' Polly", he assured having been there so often himself in the past, "is the plague of getting together, it supposes performances which are just as bad as demands, I've been there when I was much older than you as I was a very late starter so foozled the 'expected sex' thing totally — 'expected' is the hell of doubts mixed with frustrations when you don't know".

"Polly honey", he assured, "whenever we start with someone new, begin a new relationship everything is unknown — however much we think we already know — everything's new so 'expected' is a new hell, for both sides, which we can only solve with un-conditional gift". He wrapped his arms tighter then rolled her over to look at her to kiss — but she pushed his mouth down to a waiting nipple, "kiss that 'cause I like it", she demanded playfully, "then sometime when it's right I'd like to know about what's going on down there so we can make together really close as something's speaking to me".

"We shall", he confirmed, "but let's not cross bridges when they're not yet up to our weight, get some more structure in place, Ok little girl as reacting on auto to ancient stimuli can cause havoc, so they need to be brought under our understanding then we control them to work for us not us be driven by them". He stopped a moment then continued happy Polly could cope, "in crude terms far better to have a fabulous first fuck than a serious fright with recriminations after — even if they are only against ourselves for rushing, OK?, for which the age old secret is not what but how, so it's my job as mentor to make sure what I give you is magic so it shines for you to become the central part of snuggle not some crudeness on the side".

"Yes Sir Squadron leader", she giggled wriggling deliciously, "but it's jolly hard with my insides churning round like a mill-wheel". He chuckled gently, "Woman on heat chicky"? "Bursting", she replied. "OK", he replied, "first gift, because churnings un-requited are the devil, sort of horizons we suddenly see which fade leaving us angry for their vanishing". He placed his hand between her thighs which she opened for his entry as he began to work gently, hand tenderly down below mouth locked working on nipple above raising her to a wonderful surging thrill — then subsidence with quiet. "One's enough for beginners", he observed solicitously, "we need to distinguish between ends and means, sex is very together if we get it right, but if we overdo it it merely becomes an end itself so loses its magic because too much choccy's bad for you — which we ought to drink now before it's totally cold".

He sat up as did she, her little breasts proudly displayed as they grabbed the cooling cups. "I'd always been a huge breasts man, most men are, but there's a fascination about your's Polly I can't quite fix". She wiggled them happily, "Novelty Edward, stolen cream"? "Well yes a little", he acknowledged thoughtfully traveling back down the road of learning snuggle, "but you've made them mine by giving them to me as a bit of our together, with more to come — which is what snuggle does — styles fade as together joins even the most unexpected bits — 'beauty comes in unexpected places', my old nan used to tell me when I'd seen something I didn't know I liked". She looked at him straight but surely, "most girls, however strait brought up, can release themselves but your gift to me took me to a heaven I didn't know existed — it's not just a mechanical thing is it"? "Indeed it isn't", he assured having long known the difference, "which is my point about sex being an end not a means, there's got to be gift there for it to work properly".

There was a happy silence as chocolate vanished down happy throats. "You won't be familiar with doing chaps so I'll do myself because the unrequited thing is just as bad for blokes — but I'll show you how when we're further down the journey". Fascinated she lifted the covers back to watch as he released himself. She went all quiet then got out of bed to find a flannel to mop him up, "I can't do the first bit yet but I can do this bit with lots of love, how's that"? "Wonderful", he complimented her, "now we're both at peace, lets snuggle close to sleep — I rise early naturally so you can nip back home before the base is stirring".

The weeks went gently by as he, via her, disseminated the arts of snuggle throughout the base. Protocols perished like the morning mists at noon — 'rules' crept into the dusty corners where rules should live — but sloppiness was not allowed because everyone knew sloppy lead to sloppy thinking with details slipped so lives lost. People relaxed, so happy became the

'Order of the Day', despite the tragedies with the un-relenting work. There were no orders, it just happened as Polly quietly filtered her man's under-standings round those places where it mattered, so Polly acquired a sort of ministering angel mantle which everyone respected but honoured for the values it brought to their joyful enterprise.

'Far better than just capturing 'the boss' against the competition', she real-ised as her presence became a positive not an enmity building negative. People began to discover a natural working order of things, which worked, as they discovered 'work' held far higher measure than they had supposed for finding 'happy' was its true core — 'together not alone' Polly told to her friends, 'that's what Edward tells me' which, everyone seeing the glow which suffused her which she was filtering round the base agreed was good — perhaps, early on, reluctant to admit they had learnt something which had seeped into them unawares. They found also this quiet 'to-gether' thing dissolved the enmities so natural in a group of people to focus their erstwhile angsts on working as a team more closely than any had dreamed possible — they found so much joy in this the individual para-noias of persona faded leaving everyone 'walking tall' as smiles replaced the frictions which are man's heir.

While the pressure remained on as The Battle continued un-abated every-one kept their heads down as survival had to be 'of the fittest' which they had learned was working solidly together, no time for individual 'entertain-ments'. Polly quietly learned the arts of together as she explored the de-lights of giving to Edward with the intricacies of the male while he sent her to ever increasing heavens in ways she'd never dreamed of, even on automatic, but they mutually agreed while full stretch was on they would keep the final for a future foray, something to look forward to, a celebra-tion of all their success which however dim it might appear, all new would be theirs in the fullness of their endeavour.

He taught her much of Mind to travel alongside Body so one should not get dismembered from the other, indeed he taught her either alone was a Spiritless thing, a danger to the whole un-joined. She delighted in every moment feeling something new being born, which Edward called Spirit; she liked its birth as it expanded everything she thought of with much she never had. She found 'yes' to be the ruling passion of her new life which was the elixir which powered the base in its new guise — now she knew why, so revelled in it.

The pace remained relentless. "Sorry Tim", he apologised to his mechanic on landing, "she's a bit of a mess, Gerry was everywhere so we've been lucky all to get back, you lads'll have your work cut out", as he climbed down the wing after a particularly tough sortie. "Oh don't worry Sir", his mechanic replied happily, "she's my baby so I'll see her right for you to-morrow". He looked at his leader quietly for a moment, "you can have no idea Sir what you've done for this base, yesterday's 'impossible' has be-come today's 'piece of piss', it's those fences with rules'n rubbish you've dissolved which has brought a smile to everybody so everyone's going like the clappers, it's huge fun, we can't be beaten like that Sir". He put out a grateful hand, "thank you Tim, we may be a team, you'n I with the battered she here which is a wonderful feeling when I'm up there in the blue, but it's still you poor buggers've got to fix the mess we make, good luck with this one, at least she was still flying when I got out". "Thank you Sir", his mechanic replied gratefully, "it's a joy when we erks get it right, when noth-ing drops off so you all come back, it makes the sweat worthwhile". He laughed to wander off warmed by the recognition with the enthusiasm. He knew the passion these mechanics brought to keeping his men in the air so was only too happy to break every rule which got in the way of their nursing of the inanimate machinery their skill gave such ardent life

"It's the closeness which makes the whole damn thing possible", he told Polly in bed that night; "the closeness of us you've managed to feed around everywhere — I brought my bus back pretty shot-up today then, while I was apologising for the mess, Tim told me how wonderful it is for them just having happy around with nothing in the way of keeping us up there in the blue — well done my little girl, I couldn't have done that either on my own or by command, they had to make it themselves out of what you've told them". "Doing my duty then", she giggled happily. "Yes, Polly love", he agreed sobered for a moment at his child's straight forward view, "Man serves his neighbour in many different ways — but his gift of him-self is at the core of his best". "Ooo that's the real wisdom stuff I trade my body for", she laughed, "*and* love every minute of it, service everywhere *and*", she giggled helplessly, "I just love sucking the sword which is defi-nitely one thing you don't learn at your mother's knee".

He chuckled hugely, happy as he wrapped himself round her snuggling the little breasts he'd made his own. "You've given me far more than your body Polly", he reflected thoughtfully, "you've given me wisdom too because I've learned to enjoy much more than I did before because I've learned how to spread it — gently as a team". He thought happily for a moment savouring being a boy again, "Polly love", he continued his thought train, "you've given me back my youth, a priceless asset we far too easily abandon for the imagined virtues of adulthood — and don't you forget it little girl because it's little girl who's saved me from being a stick-in-the mud".

"Polly love", he continued contemplatively, "Man's ultimate majesty is a big girl who's still a little girl because she retains the child's wonderful capacity to enjoy simplicity", he laughed, "thank heaven for little girls as the world would be a deeply dreary place without them, even when they've only got little Bs — which I've come to like, so there". She cuddled gently so very aware she had learnt so much in these few hectic weeks she could never have done conventionally; she knew, though 'woman' was just round the corner, she had attained woman-hood in much more proper ways, "Edward you've given me something youth can never give", she returned the compliment, "only receive — knowledge, experience, wisdom, a very fine trade for the use of a little B decked body". They both laughed hugely aware of the deep truth with the very special circumstances which had made it possible.

Then one sad day Pauline's chap got downed before the end was in sight — though they all knew the pressure was easing. It was a sad evening at the bar in the mess as he had been a popular bloke, indeed one of the seconds in the band, so they played gentle stuff. Their Squadron Leader was with Polly on the floor, as everyone expected now for being quietly pleased at the miracles 'their boss' had wrought. "Polly honey", he murmured into her ear, "this is where unconditional gift is the only saviour, tell Pauline to come with you tonight so we can enfold her". Polly held her man tight little tears trickling down her face, "I will — so we will".

When Pauline arrived with Polly the tea was made as a number of comforts had been wrought in the spartan house. There were flowers in a big vase Maple had bought Polly, picked as they walked the lanes in the odd moments they could snatch together during the day. Not posh flowers, just the huge yellow and purple weed-flowers which grew so prolifically in the hedges — but they were flowers, which they'd picked themselves, which stood up proudly. Polly arched her eyebrows a question in her lover's direction as she gave Pauline her tea which, their telepathy now being so powerful, he understood. He laughed quietly at this closeness, "there aren't many plusses in being the boss, Polly, but being able to command is one so I fixed it as soon as I knew". Polly smiled at their understanding then took Pauline upstairs while Maple rustled odd bits of housework. Little cooings told him they were ready so he ascended to witness two girls cuddled close in the big double-bed he had magicked out of the quartermaster who, in the protocol breaking game, had become a good friend keen to make things happen so bugger the 'forms in triplicate' — double-beds did not live on emergent bases but quartermasters had powers akin to genies when required. He admired, "does snuggle feel a little better Pauline dear"? She looked wonders up at him, "it's wonderful Sir, I didn't have this sort of thing with Nat, we were on the surface I suppose like everyone else so kept to our own quarters — I liked him a lot'n we had fun but this is different, this is close — you may be surprised with my rather racketty past I haven't had close like this — sort of sucked in stuff".

Polly had told Maple early on Pauline was more sophisticated than she, 'she's been around Edward', she'd told him a little gleefully. The Squadron Leader aroused by the picture noticed for the first time there was a good deal more of her too which she wasn't overly bothered to hide, while it was obvious by the way they were enjoying each other 'girl' was not new for their guest. He quietly undressed to stand before them, "where would you like me Pauline, it's your party". Miss Provocative chuckled, "man's been off the menu for a long time, Sir but I want me in the middle so I can have you both — I need the Snuggle and together the base has been on about, no gaps in between I can remember from my girly days", she giggled deliciously; "the 'men' thing's often too complicated to make Snuggle work". Polly had always liked her mate, there had never been any competition between them for the chaps, so she was happy to surrender 'her' man for her bereaved friend's pleasure so lay back to watch the fun. "At least I've got a ringside seat", she gurgled, "this is going to be fun", as Sir Knight climbed in.

"I take it Pauline", he overtly admired her amplitude, "you started with girls". "Oh yes", she replied enthusiastically, "my Nan was a wise old bird so encouraged me by finding me a girl a few streets away — she taught me a great deal about chaps too; I was damned lucky in that way because I started gently'n prepared, everyone should have a Gran like her — it was good fun too as Mavis developed to even bigger than I am so I had jolly-jugs to play with", she gurgled giving Maple a breast to suck. Polly laughed happily picking up the other watching Maple across the middle ground knowing very well now the end game — happy to cheer it on by taking part. Polly knew a real bit of together with the 'man' her mate had been missing was likely to do a good deal of mending — new horizons anyway in such an unsure world. Polly quietly began work on Pauline as she relaxed to let her in while 'Sir' kept up the frizz from above. Polly suddenly giggled, "I think Sir knight your lady is ready for your knightly ministrations". 'Sir Knight' looked a question at Pauline who smiled hugely, "get that sword at work Sir Knight for I'm mightily in need of it — I'm safe so fill me up".

The Base was delighted Pauline had found a 'home'. In the mess the evening after as he stood at the bar, abstracted but at peace, a voice questioned at his elbow, "Edward"? The Squadron Leader relaxed as he recognised the voice which he had liked from the first so smiled as he turned, "what can I do for you Jim"? "The chaps have asked me to thank you for Snuggle as Polly calls it, everyone loves it — we all feel lighter so things go with a swing — Snuggle's powerful stuff Sir, seems to dissolve all the old petty squabbles'n knocks the corners off those who tend to be spiky". Maple stood transfixed, "thank-you's are powerful stuff too Jim — that one is the nicest which has ever been said to me, what's yours"? "Usual Edward'n the boys think Polly & Pauline should move into the house properly to look after you, be your consorts — make it a home like you've made the base".

Suddenly the pressure began to ease as The Battle was won, losses dropped dramatically so everyone sighed as they relaxed; dreadful it had been, friends had been made only to be lost overnight, good men had vanished in the blue above to leave gaps down below but, they all agreed, Snuggle with its together had made it as, depleted certainly, they were unbowed. Everyone had been tried in the fire, but not found wanting, so they glowed, happy a victory had been won above — while knowing an even better one had been won below.

When it was officially announced on the radio The Squadron Leader arranged a monster party in the mess. Polly & Pauline danced with everyone while 'the boss' didn't get a chance to sit down at all. In a moment of quiet when the band were taking a break he sat, intentionally alone, watching. It was still magic this thing he had culled with his 'little girl' out of their mutual chaoses — whose fruits 'his girls' had filtered round the base. Mountains had been climbed, tempers tested but not found wanting, while smiles seemed to have accompanied even the most impossible of tasks as only those things which needed to be done were done while all those things that didn't weren't. There had been a tight focus on the job in hand which had been done 'far better than it need be' to bring a surplus joy over the necessaries of survival. Magic he knew, all culled out of that 'gift of ourselves to others' his lady had taught him — of which his girls were now true masters.

The band re-assembled then Polly & Pauline came to stand behind him with their arms round him as they struck up 'For he's a jolly good fellow' to which the singers added, 'and they're a wonderful pair ha ha'. When it was done he stood to say simply, "Thank you all for your Love but, all I did was show you the way, it was you who traveled the journey, leaders can't do it alone, it's teams which win, I couldn't possibly have wished for better companions on the way". There was a burst of heartfelt applause then a joker cheered, "take him off to bed girls he deserves it". "If it is your wish, so be it", he joked happily to much cheering, "and thank you for your wishes you've all made my journey into magic".

Back at 'base' no time was wasted as it was late so they skipped up to bed then dived beneath in a well loved routine. Pauline, knowing the state of play, commanded Polly, "right girl it's your turn, time for 'girl' to be gone". "Will you mind not being a girl any more"?, he asked. "Oh the hymen's a mere technicality", Polly gurgled in anticipation, "I've been a mother for the last year'n you don't get more grown up than that, *and*", she noted, "I've been watching Pauline having the time of her life". Pauline giggled infectiously in anticipation, "so it's my turn to start proceedings", as she dived to apply lips to lips as 'Squadron Leader' set lips to nips above.

So, in the fullness of a bat's wink, because both were skilled practitioners, the sword engaged its waiting sheath — then joy abounded as, with the regulation squeal of girlhood lost, Polly engaged 'an hundredfold'. When peace reigned Polly sighed, completely limp but with Mona Lisa spread across her face, "now I know", she cooed. Maple recognising the smile laughed, "I wonder if Da Vinci put that smile on her face before he applied his brushes, she's got the same sort of inward knowing you've got Polly, was it so good — I'm only a bloke". "Oh", she sighed thoughtfully, "the difference between even your'n Pauline's lovely frig's to what I've just had is huge, different things altogether, aren't in the same class, something extra you have to go there to find, it was real together, proper rainbow's end stuff — definitely no gaps anywhere", she rushed to a stop, then snuggled, "you were right Edward it was worth waiting as I did need to be really ready, thank you".

She looked at him fondly, "when I find my mate I'll know how to build the Love which works because you've shown me it's been a truly wonderful journey". "Join the right-thinking Human Race Polly love", Pauline chuckled delighted, "you'll never look back because you'll always know how it ought to be so how to make it — *and* you'll find this too which I've learned in this bed as we've watched 'Snuggle' change this base as well". She stopped gently hanging on to both of them, "you can 'make love' many times with many different people but it isn't Love unless it's your total gift, but it is when it is, which you can do with anybody any-time — with anything, anyhow — you love by giving yourself so there may be many to whom you give — but", she observed severely, "just fucking isn't 'making love' at all, it's a nonsense".

"Agreed Pauline", replied Maple, "it's a silly euphemism to disguise a mechanical act which we're too afraid to acknowledge properly — which then assumes the two are the same". "Fucking for pleasure can be huge fun and entirely proper, even with no holds barred, but it should never be confused with Love — sexual sensation, however much fun is a mere temporary — Love is the permanent gift of ourself because we make it so". He stopped for a bit thinking of his lady with the way they'd forced Love out of a mess, with bits of old loves lying around to confuse the issue they were engaged upon. "Love can exist even if we know it's temporary — if we give of ourselves to its making *and* we can love more than one thing or person at once — it's a great mistake to code Love as a once in a life thing, or can't be had anywhere else except in marriage, improper outside with all that stuff the purse-lips prate about, because it's a universal we make then spread round us, which is Love's true secret — it has no end if you make it so like The Widow's Cruse".

He waited for this to settle giving of his best with his hands to this particular lady of the moment for still being engaged, "I shan't forget this time we've had girls", he reflected, "nor will you I fancy either, because we made it out of Love so we learned something of Love's magical virtue which we can pass on to spread elsewhere — but if you never try to create it you never learn its virtues — are you listening Miss Polly 'locked-in-lust'", he laughed aware he had run on a bit, "sorry about the lecture my lovely ladies but teaching is what oldies are for".

Polly gurgled happily in her new found state still riding her magic carpet, clinging on to her lover preventing his escape for enjoying the together so much, "can I write to your lovely lady to thank her for you making me"? "Of course", he responded happily, "thank-yous are the oil of our association as people for which she'll be delighted as she's always cheered me on *and*", he added with a twinkle, "she told me in a recent letter she's been making Love-work-wonders in like manner back home when I told her how Snuggle was transforming the base — nothing quite like having something you've made out there pleasing others".

With the base relaxed 'the bloody Ministry' chose to move Maple upwards to flying a desk in Whitehall. There were two leaving parties, one in the mess, with the base totally silent outside as everyone was there — then one in bed. We need not mince the matters of either small for we know of what they were. The Squadron Leader left his squadron in the early dawn kissing his lovelies good bye in their half-sleep, not wanting to prolong the agony for knowing they would have to go back to their billets. Clean was best he knew, they were young and they had each other — *and* they had their memories with a new dream with a new pilgrimage to follow for which he knew they had the tools.

The band was playing gently as the new man walked in, tall, stark, unbending. There was a little silence as he looked at the band's dress — then left. Pauline looked at Polly, "no snuggle there Pol". The band did not play again as protocols were re-applied. "Laxity", he told a meeting of officers, "will not be tolerated, you can't win a war like that".

Gloom descended round the base as people found themselves shouting over fences re-erected, their once-spry feet entangled in long forgotten rules while 'in triplicate' returned to clog up progress. No-one talked to 'him' because they did not even know his name for he was not a person but a thing. A month went by as the commitment which concourse had ensured dissolved, petty wars started out of nowhere as frictions rose across those fences while the irritations of rules had people curse each other — paperwork piled un-regarded absorbing vital energies. Knights loitered palely, their steeds ill-tended as delays delayed — no birds sang as sedges withered. The death of the cross-curricular music ebbed the oil which made snuggle's co-operation work, so efficiency fell, then unexplained losses arose in the air.

When he found 'yes SIR', being forced from reluctant mouths; when he found the air in the bar freeze as he entered he knew he was beaten, but had not the faintest idea why. He'd played the game by the book he'd been taught yet all he had around him was a desert — where no flowers grew.

He was away for a couple of days in London to report so a little re-volution crept out. At a meeting in the mess the night he left, band quietly playing, a council of war was held with Jim a spokesman to Polly & Pauline. "We've got to teach him Snuggle girls or we're done, dissolved, this life is hell so will you do it"? Pauline laughed, "it's not whether we will boys it's whether we can, but for sure we'll try — leave your fate with us". Everybody laughed releasing the tension a little, "we couldn't be in better hands", noted one wag which got a laugh there hadn't been since the band had been banned. Our ladies obtained the key for the house then set to work — at least the double bed was still in place.

London had been a drag while traveling in the blackout was a pain so he arrived back at the base extraordinarily tired as food, on the fly, was scarce and nasty. He decided to dump his case at home before trying the mess to eat. Lights were on, how curious, but he went in — then walked through to the kitchen from whence the light appeared to come. There was a gorgeous smell with a huge vase of flowers on the table, while two WAAFs in party dresses sat smiling ready to dish up.

"Good evening Sir, dinner's ready". One rose to remove his coat as the other took his case. He blustered feebly for a second then slumped into a proffered chair as the smaller of the two administered shoulder massage from behind. "No questions Sir, food first, logic can not be had from an empty stomach", observed the larger of the two whom, he saw even in his battered state, was showing more bare bust than he ever could remember — "nor from an upright position", advised the other petite one who seemed to have thighs up to her chin, "contemplation of eternals is best done horizontal — in company". He gave in as gracefully as he could then piled into the stew — with the glass of wine provided. We need not mince it fine dear reader as we would not expect our ladies to fail so tough a task. Body was applied as our two knew how, so he felt the cares drain down — then new horizons he had never known appeared.

It will not surprise readers of these stories to learn angelic bards had been at work — after all when doors are locked we need to find another way. Our musicians of the bar, under Pauline's encouragement for it was she who knew the skills of most, had rapidly assembled a writing team aware uncomfortable truths might better be conveyed in verse. Upon their leaving SIR next morning early they left the following nicely scripted sheet upon his table — it was decorated with little Spitfires, with pilots bearing knightly lances pennants flying as Gerry's bombers 'bit the dust';

Dear SIR
If you don't trust your neighbour to do the job right,
No rules in the world will have it take flight.
You can wave a big stick, you can shout 'I am might';
Don't drive horses to water,
Cry 'drink cause you ought'a'
For it only makes sullen'n one hell of a fight.
So
The job lies a'mouldering, forgotten, undone
Wrapped vastly in paper, it's virtues un-sung
Because lost under piles of mad minister's dung.
So the truth of its being,
The delight of its seeing
Is never forthcoming for the lack of the 'hum'.
So
Try joining hands with the chaps on the job,
Come, roll up your sleeves, doff the cap of the snob,
Then when the job's done we'll all vote you the nob,

'Cause the victory is ours
Through our compliment powers
As Gerry goes home with his tail docked en-bob
Sir
Life's so much more fun when made at the run,
Not crawling nor wading through bogs all should shun,
Lets take hand-in-hand
To stride the bright strand
Where Indians and chiefs win the war in the sun.
So
Come join us in the bar tonight,
We'll sing you songs to shine life bright,
Pass out of darkness into Light
Let's make it all right merry.

His Body having been utterly vanquished by our delicious pair operating on 'speed' for a mission upon which all placed implicit trust, his Mind now got a dose of light in similar fashion. Slumped into a chair with a flask of coffee our early-birds had left him his eyes dislimned. Slowly protocalian walls began to crumble as years of 'Rules & Regulations', in which he'd been cased to keep his feet from straying from the hallowed Ministerial paths, quietly scuttled under the skirtings leaving him with the most extraordinary feeling of levity; Damascene Light flooded the drab MOD kitchen to straighten his back, then a seraphic smile spread across his face as he began to skip making up a silly tune for the chorus.

Promptly Polly & Pauline were ensconced again then fences began to fall, while protocols re-perished as Snuggle was re-born as they showed him how — courtesy of a Pauline visitation. The band played, things got done, accidents ceased, losses lapsed as smiles suffused the careworn faces as had been when Snuggle ruled. Then valiant knights lept lissom upon shining silver steeds so fast reshod to set lance in rest with pennons flying to speed down the lists up in the blue which ensured the dread Hun's dying. Birds sang bright for they'd made a man of him — machine no longer.

One evening in the bar he stood to ask for silence, "Dear people, I made your lives a hell because I denied your Snuggle, until a pair of ministering angels arrived to save me — they took me to Damascus gate, then walked me in — then you lot showed me how it ought to be in verse — I'm privileged to have been shown the light by such fine people — long live Snuggle so devil take the first man who makes a rule — I'm sorry about the

Montague, just call me Monty *and* boys have you got a tune for that wonderful verse because I think we ought to make it The Station's anthem to be sung at closing time every evening to remind us all of what really matters in Life's Great Journey". There were genuine gales of laughter followed by loud cheers as beers flowed at 'the boss's' command — who was gaily Monty thereafter. The band struck up — having of course cooked up a fine jazz-style tune for their demon composition beforehand — so the whole bar filled with a swirl of song — in concert-chorus, not divided.

A pretty post card, with carefully dried yellow and purple flowers stuck neatly down arrived at a reclusive office in The Air Ministry on a gusty wet November day of overcast and gloom — 'Snuggle re-born, Grace Abounding, Monty's Joy', Love Polly & Pauline". He smiled seraphically, all his cares dissolved, 'clever girls,

'What Matter Winter's Rages
when
Love Lights Bright to Lift the Heart of Man'

The Moral of this little Tale? 'The Rules' everywhere had been broken so joy abounded because Trust triumphed - adultery is not breaking convention it is sundering Trust. Trust between neighbour and neighbour is the only 'law' for without it no law can prevail — without Trust 'civilisation' becomes a Cage so Man's endeavour dies as it has in Britain today. Force has never created anything of virtue as 2000 years of 'Holy Church' and today's doctrine of 'Enforcement' shows, only the 'Love One Another' of its progenitor can because energising Man's Spirit in co-operation through communion.

Aphrodite, December 2009

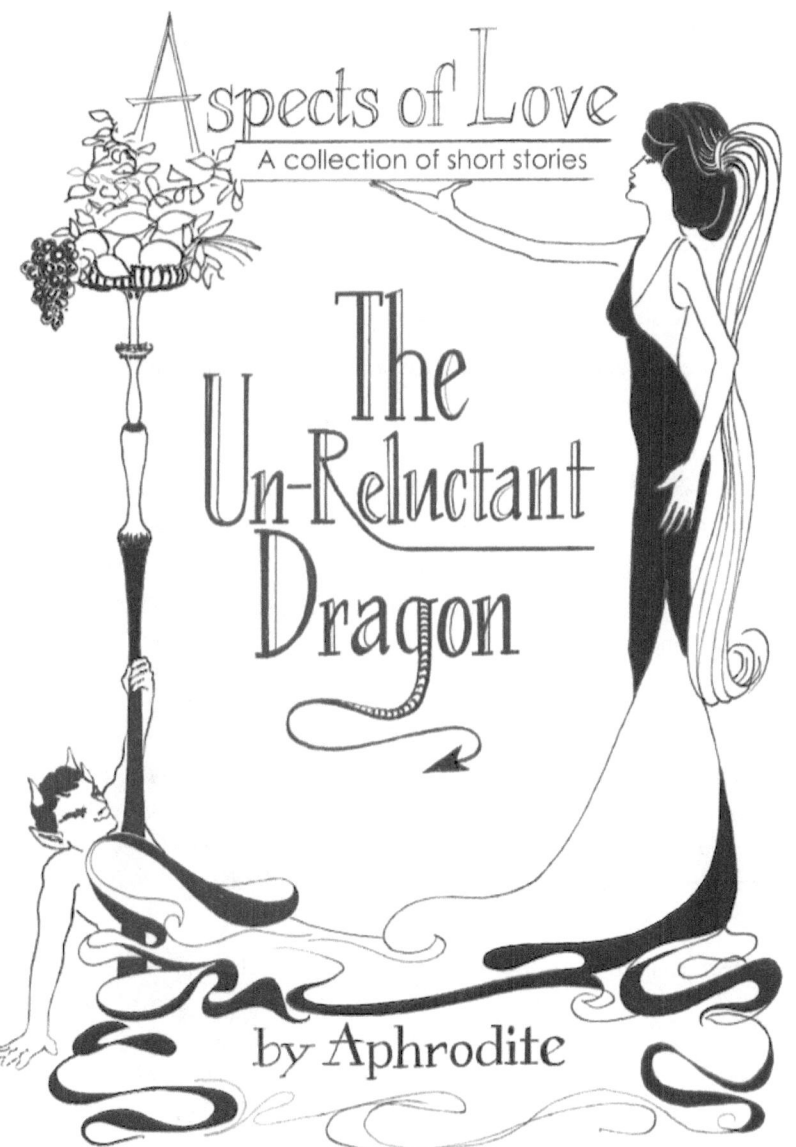

Aspects of Love
A collection of short stories

The Un-Reluctant Dragon

by Aphrodite

The Un-Reluctant Dragon

(With a gracious bow to the memory of Mr Kenneth Grahame)

The door behind them opened, a stream of light illumined the road, and St. George, who had come out of the banquet for a stroll in the cool night air, caught sight of the two figures sitting there — the great motionless dragon and the tearful little boy.

"What's the matter, Boy"?, he enquired kindly, stepping to his side.

"Oh, its this great lumbering pig of a dragon"!, sobbed the Boy. "First he makes me promise to see him home, and then he says I'd better do it, and goes to sleep"! "Might as well try to see a haystack home! And I'm so tired, and mother's....." — here he broke down again.

"Now don't take on", said St. George. "I'll stand by you, and we'll both see him home. Wake up, dragon"!, he said sharply, shaking the beast by the elbow.

The dragon looked up sleepily. "Wshat a night, George"!, he murmured; "what a — "

"Now look here, dragon", said the Saint, firmly. "Here's this little fellow waiting to see you home, and you know he ought to have been in bed these two hours, and what his mother'll say I don't know, and anybody but a selfish pig would have made him go to bed long ago — "

"And he shall go to bed"!, cried the dragon, starting up. "Poor little chap, only fancy his being up at this hour"! "It's a shame, that's what it is, and I don't think St. George you've been very considerate — but come along at once, and don't let us have any more arguing or shilly-shallying. You give me a hold of your hand, Boy — thank-you, George, an arm up the hill is just what I wanted"!

So they set off up the hill arm-in-arm, the Saint, the Dragon and the Boy. The lights in the little village began to go out; but there were stars, and a late moon, as they climbed to the Downs together. And, as they turned the last corner and disappeared from view, snatches of an old song were borne back on the night-breeze. I can't be certain which of them was singing, but I think it was the Dragon!

"Here we are at your gate", said the man, abruptly, laying his hand on it. "Good-night. Cut along in sharp, or you'll catch it!"

Could it really be our own gate? Yes, there it was, sure enough, with the familiar marks on its bottom bar made by our feet when we swung on it.

"Oh, but wait a minute"!, cried Charlotte. "I want to know a heap of things. Did the dragon really settle down, and did — "

"There isn't any more of that story", said the man kindly but firmly. "At least, not tonight. Now be off! Good-bye"!

"Wonder if it's all true"? said Charlotte, as we hurried up the path. "Sounded dreadfully like nonsense in parts"!

"P'raps it's true for all that", I said encouragingly.

Charlotte bolted in like a rabbit, out of the cold and dark; but I lingered a moment in the still, frosty air, for a backward glance at the silent world without, ere I changed it for the land of firelight and cushions and laughter. It was the day for choir practice, and carol-time was at hand, and a belated member was passing homewards down the road, singing as he went:

> *'Then St. George: ee made rev'rance: in the stable so dim,*
> *Oo vanquished the dragon: so fearful and grim.*
> *So-o grim: and so-o fierce: that now e may say*
> *All peaceful is our wakin: on Chri-istmas Day'!*

The singer receded, the carol died away. But I wondered, with my hand on the door-latch, whether that was the song, or something like it, that the dragon sang as he toddled contentedly up the hill.

(The End of 'The Reluctant Dragon' by Kenneth Grahame from 'Dream Days')

There was a happy silence, as there always should be when a fine story stops as the real world gently reclaimed them all from dreamland. Jack & Jill sat snuggled on the big sofa while their father held the book open at the last page, his eyes quietly far away gently re-limning onto his happy children still somewhere else. His lady sat by the fire doing 'big girly' things with her embroidery frame all hung about with the gorgeous coloured silks he loved so much; 'why were the colours of embroidery silks so much more vibrant than the drab colours which smothered the possibilities of dreamland', he wondered; he'd always loved them for their brave shout at 'avocado' and 'magnolia' which so constrained sub-urban lives. He was always supremely happy when his lady was relaxed enough to embroider as gorgeous designs of flowers and birds in exotic colours came to make a real Fairy-Land to transfigure.

Jill, the perky, inquisitive, practical, one of the pair asked, when she'd surfaced, "Did dragons really live then Daddy"? — "when was then Jill dear"?, her indulgent father asked knowing Jill liked a discussion — "oh *then*, you know, in the 'old days'", she answered scornfully, forever astonished at parental dimness. "Ah Jill dear", joined her mother spotting the scorn so keen to rescue parental credibility, "you mean the time when books were full of pictures of ladies and knights all coloured like my silks, shining and bright". "Yes, then mummy", responded Jack the mystical dreamy one, "d'you remember the fantastic book we saw in the castle we went to see which had tiny little bright pictures in it, all blue'n, red'n, gold'n silver with queer horses with big eyes and funny long thin dogs stretching forward on their hind feet'n stuff'n there were ladies with very long thin heads and little white spiky castles on pointed hills — those days". Their father laughed mightily at Jack's minute observation of medieval missal illumination — long thin dogs indeed, "well if dragons ever did live it was then", he assured gaily, "because the ladies had to be rescued from the spiky castles which were *always* guarded by dragons".

"Ok, so why don't we see them in the pictures then"?, asked the ever prosaic Jill, "looking out of the spiky castles waving 'keep-off' signs". Their mother, who loved a discussion with her children much better than the lone furrow of embroidery, laughed mightily, "I like dragons waving keep-off signs Jill which, dear, pre-supposes dragons could write", she added smugly. Jill, hell bent on discovering the truth of dragons, was not going to be put off by a clever quibble about dragon-literacy, "but we don't do we, see them in pictures I mean — literate or not, so there".

Her father, laughing gently, re-entered the fray, "well actually they do occasionally but more importantly they were one of the recognised Heraldic Beasts, the animals which stood each side of a shield on which knights used to 'bear their arms' as it was called to distinguish them in battle, because it was pretty difficult to decide which were or weren't your mates in the thick of a battle when everyone was swathed in tin suits", he observed thoughtfully. "If you look at full Coats of Arms", he continued keen to get the matter straight for his inquisitive children, "you'll always see the shield being held up by two special animals, different sorts for different families, which are called 'The Supporters'; in official heraldry they're all special sorts of official ones and the dragon is one of them; when you see pictures of St. George the dragon's always there and the national animal of Wales is The Welsh Dragon — do you Jill"?, he finished his exposition with a flourish.

Jill was absolutely not going to let go a piece of logic she knew was a killer, so followed briskly with, "cool dad, thass a lot of dragon there, but where did they all get the idea of how a dragon should look, they must have existed for someone to be able to draw them *and* there can't have been a St. George story without a proper dragon to kill 'cause he's part of our history"? "Which is one of the things even fathers don't have answers to" — 'yes', thought Jill, 'and much else besides, lots of things parents don't know, I wonder if they ever did?, all those magical games in the fields and hedges,'n the pond I play with Jack, parents don't understand them'.

Their mother, the artist of the parental pair replied, "Dragons Jill dear is what Art's about, imagination; someone a long time ago, when myths and stories were handed down by word of mouth, and when people scratched on cave walls, imagined what a very nasty beast might be like" — "like I get the creeps in bed imagining something horrid's coming up inside the bed from the bottom to get me", reflected Jack keen to get ahead of his sister in the dragon-knowing race.

Their mother laughed at her son's powerful imagination fondly, being of the same persuasion, "indeed it is, then when someone had made a really good picture which caught people's fancy — 'there be dragons' — its what you see on very old maps where they didn't know how the land was shaped or what lived there". Jack wasn't concerned whether they did or not as he knew what dragons were in his head and didn't want Jill's prosaic enquiries reaching a possibility of reality to spoil his vision — real dragons might turn out to be 'avocado' and 'magnolia' — no fun at all. For Jack dragons had to have all the fixings dragons should, complete with wings, flames, smoke and lashing forked tail, nothing else would do, how could you be frightened by 'magnolia' when the function of dragons was fright.

"So, no dragons today then", observed Jill sadly, "only the old ones's we can't see in spiky castles or being chased by thin dogs and men on horses with poppy-out eyes — not 'zactly zooming round the landscape for any St. George's who might be about". "Well now you've got a point there Jill", consoled her father, "because there are, but those people of long ago imagined dragons to explain the things which went wrong where we've got actual ones who make things go wrong; they aren't dragon shaped but they behave just like the old ones zapping us in all sorts of nasty ways locking us in their spiky castles", as he leapt on his white charger after 'dragons' .

"Modern Britain's full of them", he continued briskly to his wife's smile, "you read about them in the Newspapers every day, all the lousy corrupt politicians, the appalling financiers who rob us all, the ghastly Social Services and The Police who used to be our friends and are now our enemies who lock us up when we haven't done anything and the Health & Safety who prevent us doing anything fun at all and all the dreadful bureaucrats who batten on us to feed their voracious appetites by locking us in their spiky castles, so definitely dragon characteristics there", he drew his horse up to a breathless halt. His lady laughed recognising her knight on his white charger, "if daddy had a white charger and 'lances were allowed' he'd be our very own St. George so dragon corpses'd be lying round in swathes".

Her husband laughed, touched, "trouble is kids we need far more than one St. George as there're far more dragons than ever before". "Then", he noted portentously, "there are the dragons inside us when we're angry" — "oh I know about them", agreed Jack, "or the sort who stalk you at night rampaging round inside your head". "I like that Jack", complimented his father, "because I'm sure they have been with Man ever since he existed, because they're a product of his highly active imaginative brain which got him out of the caves and gives him the advantage over the animals, so I expect like you feel, they felt they were being chased by dragons too".

"'S all very well you brain-box types theorising 'bout dragons in the head", chipped in Jill, "but I want the everyday sort I can get excited about zapping when I'm bigger; I'm a doer not a thinker, give me the odd bureaucrat to frizzle in my breath", she cheered joining her father's practical position. "I think", reflected her wise father, "it takes both sorts to really get to grips with every-day dragons of the sort which plague us — think about how your going to zap them then get on to do it — can't zap them without thinking and no-good just thinking with no zapping — how's that you two but now its bed-time".

Jill picked up Jack's hand conspiratorially to set off upstairs knowing dragon-hunts together would be the agenda for some days to come because *she* knew proper dragons existed, *somewhere*, it was only a matter of finding them then finding the proper sort of swords to deal with them. Jill was determined since dragons *should* exist they *would* exist because she knew dragon-slaying had always been top of the list in the old days, so why not now? Parents just hadn't got the application for the really important things like those magical games she played with Jack in the fields, so she began to plan just another of the long list of childhood's successes over 'oldies' who'd long forgotten where real joy was to be found.

Next morning was Saturday so there was a whole weekend to get the project underway. Proper clothes were donned for Dragon-hunting, none of the silly pink stuff the hunting-people on horses wore, "and no bugles either", Jill noted to Jack, "all that noise's going to have any decent dragon off somewhere else". They had decided in bed where proper self-respecting dragons ought to live, at the top of the secret hill behind the house which, so far in their arrival from town into this new house in the country a couple of years ago, they hadn't got to as it was some way away and their parents were still somewhat 'town-cautious' — but Jill had planned a strategic attack to finally demolish this silly prohibition.

Breakfast was conducted by Jill as an outlying skirmish while parental awareness was still at a low ebb or suffused with their own plans. Addressing her father as the weakest link, before he'd really got his brain into gear (Jill knew by the vacant look he cast round the table) "we loved all your dragon stuff last night Daddy so we've decided to get ourselves off your hands today by going on a dragon hunt together'n together's strength in numbers so you won't have to worry about us in the fields and stuff".

"Dragons in the fields, Jill dear"?, asked her father indulgently focusing on this extraordinary start to the day. Jill adopted an olympian air, "the great thing about dragons, as you said yourself Daddy, is you just don't know where they might be — after all spiky castles've gone out of fashion and languishing ladies hang out in the shops'n bars now so dragons may be just anywhere — *and* you don't know whether they're big or small". "They might've shrunk due to dragon-like duties having gone off the boil in the last few hundred years", added Jack picking up his sister's story-line, "Darwin stuff you know, lack of use; anyway even if we don't find a dragon on the first hunt we'll find one of those thin dogs". Jill tried hard not to laugh at this flight of fancy got up on the spur, after all you don't win this sort of sally by laughing, it's serious stuff.

Their parents, enchanted by their children's dragon logic, didn't even query the idea — truth to say they'd been wondering how they were going to get the children in the car with all the new garden stuff they were planning to buy, so dragon hunting was on. "We'll need a packed lunch Mummy", noted Jill playing 'mother', "'cause we plan to be out all day, but we'll give you a hand with that". Lunch was quickly made as all parties were keen to be doing. "Jack", she whispered aside, "dragons live in dark places so we'll need a torch", careful not to mention hills nor the possibility of caves. "Dragon's isn't for bozos Jack we'll need a stick each", she added grabbing two from the brolly-stand in the hall which made them both feel very serious about the affair as they whisked out of the door.

They both knew fields were for the fairies so they set a direct course for The Hill. It was a mysterious place about a mile away, which rose out of the surrounding fields on its own having a sort of wooly thatch of thick trees at its apex, all of which they could see out of their bedroom window which had made it the source for some splendid stories already — a ripe place for dragons.

Purpose was it so idle talk was dispensed with as Jill knew explorers didn't indulge in anything which didn't contribute to the object, so stepping briskly they made the base of the hill in comfortably under the hour. Spiky castle was replaced by very spiky hedge which seemed to run right round its base. "I wonder what it was", reflected Jack, "it's a pretty odd sort of hill for nature to have made and why this tough hedge, nature didn't make that" — "oh I 'speck the hedge was planted to keep sheep and things from straying up the hill — I wonder if it's there 'cause there's something up there", she added hopefully.

After a little exploration they found a piece of hedge which was a bit bald so were able to creep through to be faced with the hill itself. "It really is rather odd", observed Jack looking up at the top a good way above them, "it's a bit like a christmas pudding — still the only way's up — but its rather spooky, all closed in from the outside world".

Jack & Jill went up the hill but they'd got much higher intent than pails of water. They both laughed at the scene having been chafed at their primary school till Jack had got very angry one day, after which they were left alone. Their parents were the first to admit it had been a mistake but there it was, but school had provided the sort of kiddy-rumour there was a cave at the top — except no-one had actually ever been up it. "Even if we don't find dragons we'll have been the first up the hill", noted Jack, "so we'll have to bring some evidence back to show we've been there, 's'wot real explorers do".

Jill chuckled happily as they began the ascent, "who do you want to be Jack, Livingstone or Stanley" — "oh I'll be Livingstone", claimed Jack briskly, "after all he'd got there the other bloke only went looking for him". Half-way up knees and calves ached while sandwiches tempted so a halt was called 'to admire the view'. The sun was now high in a clear sky with just the odd fleecy cloud high-up, "real high pressure weather", observed Jill admiring the Cirro-Stratus knowledgeably because she followed her father's mild hobby of weather watching with their fine barometer in the hall. Jack laughed at his sister's arcane knowledge happy to just tag along to enjoy the tid-bits he liked to save for relay to his lesser mates at school — but he took enough trouble to be able to back up the first shot if some bright spark followed it up. It really was a fine view, it was the highest they'd ever been on their own initiative so seeing 'their own view', not a view set out for them by parents or teachers, was very special, something they would remember always. After both had taken a furtive dip in the box it was rigorously closed by Jill who commanded the next assault. Spiritually and physically fortified the last half of the climb was made in style, with the odd stop to admire the expanding view — *their* view gained by their own initiative and unaided efforts.

The trees at the top had clearly not been touched for generations so were dense with underbrush on the outside offering a considerable frieze to the keen explorers. "That looks pretty dragon-worthy", pondered the imaginative Jack — if we can get in" — "and more's the point if we can get back out again", replied the practical Jill, "we do not", she asserted firmly, "want to mess up on our first away-game".

She was a keen reader of the sort of boys adventure books full of scouts and indians and trails so with the huge authority of never having actually tried such before, she commanded, "we need to blaze a trail as we go in so we can keep a straight line towards the middle, then find our way out again". Jack looked at his sister, "Pirate trails"?, he enquired quizzically. "Exactly", cheered his sister authoritatively, "you bend over clumps of grass pointing to where you're going..... and break twigs into arrows'n stuff", she hesitated a little less convincingly. The practical Jack, who had the sort or imagination which could pick up ideas quickly to make them happen, had it in a trice, so charged into the first gap he could see.

Very soon the thick canopy of the trees above had prevented the under-growth prospering so the going became a good deal easier while Jack got the hang of keeping them straight by looking back down his trail then marching resolutely on. It became steadily darker as the light from the edge faded while the lack of sun made it colder too, as rustlings hinted at other little people with them. "How far do we go"?, asked Jack diffidently as he set a blaze. "Till we get there", replied Jill firmly. "Where's there"?, en-quired Jack, genuinely interested. "We'll know when we do", riposted Jill even more firmly seeking reassurance in her own determination, then strid-ing forward.

'When' suddenly became apparent as they arrived at a curious stone struc-ture, a sort of heaped up wall of straight rocks with big stones all around, black and distinctly inhibiting. "Dragon stuff"?, enquired Jack of his learned sister, shivering involuntarily. "Well it's the sort of thing we see in our big Fairy-Books", she reflected, "so I think so, and look there's a hole". A council of war was called as they'd agreed dragon-hunting was not a normal peaceful proceeding which could just be assaulted willy-nilly, agree-ment of the best course was necessary to confidence — and conclusion. "It looks promising", noted Jack, "you wouldn't expect a posh portico with a bell-pull'nd a fancy name would you or every one would know'n I 'spect dragons aren't into advertising". "No I s'pose so", agreed Jill, "but it doesn't look big enough for a dragon's front door, he'd have to crawl, but chaps who slay knights don't do crawling I fancy". Still, as Jack had said, it looked promising so they lay down to crawl inside. 'Inside' was a huge cave lit by a hole in its roof. "Oh gosh", enthused the enthralled Jack, caught up in the possibilities of secrets, "even if there isn't a dragon this is fun".

It was dry and though dim there was enough light to press forward to the far end they could just see. On arrival it was seen to be the result of a rock fall with heaps of broken stones lying around — a little curl of smoke hung in the air. "Oo look", cooed Jack happily, "dragon's breath". He walked close to the wall to smell it. "Smells sort of stinky and look you can see the place its coming from", as he pointed to a niche between two rocks. Jill wasn't so convinced but to humour her brother, who'd been a fun partner in many off-the-cuff games, she helped him pulling rocks aside. 'You never know', she thought, 'if you just stand around nothing happens' — it had been an agreement of theirs ever since they had been concocting games together. After a satisfying pile of stones had been achieved they came to the rock face from which they could see the smoke coming in small irregular puffs.

They sat for a rest to consider. The silence sucked them into the dimness. Having stopped, they became more aware of their curious surroundings — then a sound obtruded — a sort of chipping noise heavily muffled. Jack put his ear over the hole where the smoke was coming out, "I can hear sort of hammering'n a chipping noise and little falling noises, there must be someone or something behind there". "P'raps, but somethings don't hammer", observed the ever prosaic Jill, "so it might be a dragon after all". "But why's he behind there'n trying to get out here"?, asked Jack puzzled, entirely happy with Jill's dragon supposition, "'s definitely a mystery — you listen'n see what you hear Jill". It wasn't quite Jill's thing listening at cracks in rock walls but Jack could be remarkably persuasive when he chose so she placed her ear to the crack — then her face changed. "Coo, Jack you're right", she grinned, "someone's hammering'n I can hear the chipping noises, but it seems a long way away" — but the smoke continued to puff through gently.

Nothing was to be done then but plans were made because agreement was mutual this was secret stuff, 'parents not for the knowing of', so they returned to the light of the cave mouth. Deciding to eat lunch with the sun and the view they pressed on out of the wood. Jack was rather proud his blazing had worked so well, while Jill was complimentary too, so they were at the edge in no time to sit down and descend on the lunch box properly.

"That", observed Jack with finality, "was a dragon trying to get out". Jill looked at her brother, well used to his flights of fancy, "but do dragons have hammers and chisels *and* know what to do with them Jack"?, she mused thoughtfully, "you don't see them waving them from the battlements of their spiky castles'n they don't need tools for guarding maidens". "Ah", observed Jack wisely, "the thing about dragons is we know so little about them, p'raps they built the spiky castles to keep their maidens in being good at building'n stuff — perhaps that's why they're so spiky — *and* don't ask the 'why's he there' question 'cause we won't know till we ask him". This, they agreed, was pretty incontrovertible stuff, solid enough to weave a plan on anyway, so it was planned tomorrow early they would be back so discover their dragon's progress to his escape. Lots of fun was had rolling down the fine grass of the hill taking alternate turns so the lunch basket could descend more graciously in one piece.

Arriving back home late in the afternoon their parents noticed an unusual unity about their children as they arrived holding hands with what was obviously a secret. They were eighteen months apart, Jill being the older, and were both near the end of primary school, but they were very close having always entertained each other through their differing approach to things. They quarreled very rarely indeed and then only for effect as they both really enjoyed each other's company with the games they manufactured out of nothing. Jill decided it would be tactical to retain the initiative by anticipating the inquisition, "we've been up the hill so we don't want any Jack'n Jill jokes please", she noted sternly.

Her father laughed happily, "as if we would, if we'd known a mysterious hill would become part of your life we'd have been more careful — still not all children are part of a nursery-rhyme and at the time it never occurred to us — but what did you find, not pails of water I imagine", he chuckled. Jack assumed the world weary explorer attitude, "no wells", he observed laconically, "so no water'n we didn't take a pail, but the wood on the top's fun *and* we did trail blazing'n stuff to make sure we didn't get lost exploring", the latter added to demonstrate expertise in survival to keep his parents happy and amused so deflected from more serious enquiry.

Their mother was not so easily put off so hoping to spring the secret she asked, "did you find anything in the wood, woods usually have interesting things in". Jill decided to take a hand in case Jack cracked under the pressure of what she knew was a potent secret, "no, just wood stuff'n beetles'n things", she replied airily, "but different flowers to down here'nd toad-stools and things growing on fallen trees". The normal evening routines resulted in bed, "no talking", whispered Jill, "they'll be listening 'cause they're busting to know".

And so it was, with their parents delighted they had both made themselves an absorbing commitment, as it had taken them some time to get acclimatised to the country after having started life in a large town. Next morning the lunch basket routine and stick gathering briskly done they set off with purpose. "I wonder what they've found", reflected their perceptive mother, "I haven't seen such purpose before". "We'll know in time", answered their practical father, "I'm delighted they're branching out on their own discovering, it's the best form of activity for children — they looked deliciously alight with adventure so they'll find dragons in their heads even if they don't find real ones", he mused as something of a mystic himself, "stuff you make in your own head's a lot better than the prescriptive rubbish pumped out on television — it's the beginnings of creative vision".

It was indeed adventure which hastened our pair's steps so the climb was made in one, then the wood traversed following Jack's trail and the cave entered — to the louder sounds of hammering with more smoke. A small hole had developed where the smoke came out, in rather larger puffs. "Now that", noted Jack with absolute assurance, "is definitely dragon's breath". He put his ear to the hole, then his face suffused with smiles, "it sounds like Daddy making things in the garage, they're grunts'n curses between the hammer blows, com'n listen". Jill, heretofore happy to join in a game for the fun of it looked at her brother sceptically, but came to listen to please him. "Crikey Jack, you're right", she agreed surprised, "there's someone behind there bashing with a big hammer'n chips of stone are flying about, I can hear them and it does sound like Daddy when he's not getting on well, no happy singing just cursing — the funny thing is it's not a person curse but it definitely has anger about it, he must be having a bad time of it — it sounds like the builders doing the house next door just before we moved". Overtaken by the mystery of the thing while unknowing definitely not being a kid's thing Jack suggested, "I'll ask".

He put his mouth to the hole to ask in a conversational tone, "Hi there, what're you doing"? "What does it sound like", answered an irritated voice, somewhat muffled by the smallness of the exit, "drinking tea"? There followed some scufflings then Jack saw what looked like an eye appear at the other end of the hole whereupon a curiously adult voice remarked, "oh kids, how tedious, hardly worth the trouble, I had at least hoped for an official welcome after all this effort", followed by a burst of smoke with a small tongue of flame then redoubled hammering. Jill decided to take a hand so applied to the hole, then waited for the hammering to relax for a moment, "are you a dragon"? "What sort of question's that"?, the voice replied still irritated, "do you lot make flames'n smoke", it continued aggrieved at having to state the obvious, "just you let me get out of here then you'll see", followed by a renewed burst of hammering followed by the sound of falling stone.

Both, quite unable to help the enterprise on the other side of wherever it was, decided to wait upon events which they imagined would proceed more briskly without interruptions, so each chose a comfortable stone to sit on. After due interval of continuous hammer blows large chunks of stone fell off the front of the rock face to enlarge the hole considerably whereupon they could see a scaly arm brandishing what their father called a brick-bolster being struck by a substantial club hammer. Jack having his views of dragons confirmed by the minute asked of the hole, "are dragons builders then"?

The hammering stopped for a moment, "well this one is, amongst many other things", it replied immodestly, "you got to build after you've laid waste, stands to reason", informed the voice, "or life's a desert'n dragons definitely don't do deserts they like the comfort of castles, preferably cuddled up to lonely maidens". Jack, now fascinated, asked, "er, spiky castles"? – "werl depends upon the architectural preferences of each chap", replied The Dragon authoritatively, "I prefer the spiky sort meself 'cause I'm a traditionalist so spiky's good enough for me, but I know them as doesn't". Jill, now entirely captivated by the course of events asked, "why are you trying to get out of where you are now, what's wrong with there"? "Werl thass a long story", replied The Dragon happy to animadvert on his state (aren't we all), "but its better told when I'm outside'n I can see you've got lunch so I might swop a story for a sandwich, howzatt"?, it chuckled picking up the hammer again to attack the rock face on its side with renewed vigour.

The hole became progressively bigger, "I could get out now", noted the hammering voice, "but my trunk's bigger'n me, but I'm nearly there". In due time The Dragon judged the hole satisfactory so eased its way through then leaned in to begin extracting its considerable trunk. Some heaves showed a jutting rock corner in the way on the other side which would not permit the trunk's journey to begin. The Dragon leaned in to give a judicious swipe at the offending protrusion which was followed by a roar of falling rocks which completely trapped its working arm followed by a shriek and a considerable curse.

Our children immediately got to work clearing the rubble, "what's it feel like Dragon"?, asked a motherly Jill. "I think it's Ok", it replied with a grimace, "I can wiggle me fingers'n though its sore I don't think anything's broke". Work proceeded briskly but carefully — but just as they were about to be free a large shard of rock fell off above The Dragon to spear its foot — followed by a considerable bellow. It gritted its teeth then snorted with the regulation fire and smoke accompaniments. "Oh Dragon dear", consoled Jill as they extracted its arm, "sit down so we can sort out your foot before you lose too much blood — shirt please Jack", who obliged. "In strips please", she commanded sternly, "a whole shirt's no good for first aid, you should know with your St John's stuff".

Jack got to work tearing as The Dragon, still gritting its teeth but, in deference to its rescuers, keeping the fire'n smoke routine to a minimum, sat on a stone to hold its foot out for Jill's ministrations. "Hang on while I pull this shard out", she suggested comfortingly. She gave a considerable heave which drew the nasty shard of rock out dripping blood, as The Dragon groaned making a face. "We've got a nasty hole there, Dragon", she consoled, "you'll need a proper doctor but lets bind it up well so you can walk". She set to in best Florence Nightingale style with the strips of shirt provided by Jack. "It's a jolly good thing it was cooler today so I brought a woolly and a coat", he observed wryly watching his sister's considerable expertise with what had been his shirt.

The Dragon looked a little despondent, "there's not going to be any laying waste for a few days I can see", it reflected. "So you really do then"?, asked Jack. "Yers, thass why I'm here", it replied briskly, "'cause them back home's all gone limp sitting round feebly saying flames'n smoke's not al-

lowed anymore 'sall too dangerous'n the place's crawling with spies'n bu-
reaucraps with regulations'n rubbish so life's just stopped, but I couldn't
be doing with that so packed my trunk'n set off on a journey, which is
about the size of it 'cause Dragons do flames'n smoke'n laying waste and
building castles'n carrying off maidens to cuddle — otherwise they might
as well not be alive". It sat back despondently looking at its heavily band-
aged foot. "No 'Reluctant Dragon' then"?, asked Jill. "Who he"?, asked
The Dragon standing up to see if his foot would bear his weight. "Come'n
share our lunch and we'll tell you", replied the practical Jill rather pleased
with the dragon-repair job.

Happy munching began as Jill gave The Dragon a bottle of pop as well.
"Well in this story Daddy was reading to us from an old book — called
'The Reluctant Dragon'", began Jack whose love of detail was on the job,
"there was this dragon who lived a quiet life in a cave on a hill, minding
his own business — he got befriended by a boy who introduced him to his
parents who thought he ought to be exterminated because dragons were
bad'n it didn't matter how hard the boy said he was a quiet dragon doing
no-one any harm, it got to the village". "Villages don't do dragons", announced Jack with a child's clear understanding, "history says they're big'n
bad and have to be killed by St. George, so they sent pose-haste for St
George, despite the dragon lying quietly in his cave doing no-one any
harm — well to cut a long story short as Mum says, the dragon wouldn't
play ball but seeing the village wanted a fight St George'n he set up a mock
battle for the people's entertainment'n made it look real not to disappoint".
"After it was all over", he continued in story-flow, "with the celeb dinner
finished in the village hall with St. George presiding he went outside to
find the boy and the dragon asleep outside the hall so he and the boy lead
singing back up the hill to his cave in the moonlight". "Wot no flames'n
smoke"?, admonished The Dragon horrified, "no people'n princesses lying
around dead'n no general laying waste stuff"? "No", answered Jill, "all
sweetness'n light but with a bit of the flames'n smoke routine'n to keep
the theatre looking good, then some mock fighting in which the dragon
was supposed to be killed to keep the people happy".

There was a snort, "complete waster him, totally failed his billing, can't be
doing with that sort of stuff at all, it's what I've just quit back home — all
that crap 'visitor-experience stuff', no reality at all, 's all plastic rubbish", it

finished with an even larger snort. "Your Reluctant chap was a traitor to the dragon tribe", it continued crossly, "he should've been put down by popular decree ages ago, don't know how he escaped really — laxity in high places again I imagine".

There was a moment's thought, "I'spose your Reluctant guy was a fore-runner of the crummy lot who're running the show back home today, the limp-lily brigade, them shrinking liberal nerds, safety everywhere so no-one does anything, Ugh, de-generation all the way'n demise next stop *but* demise's definitely not my way, I'm having none of it, I shall be repairing dragon reputations in proper style as people expect, so 'laying waste is it' with any St. George's around being in for a proper run for their money'n no shirking", he relaxed after this sizzling announcement of intent, gently sucking the pop bottle. "I'll need something a bit stronger than this though", he observed reading the label, "fizzy water's not enough for flames you know'n one definitely can't build castles, specially ones with spikes on, without a good stiff draught", it laughed to itself munching a sandwich.

Jill decided a bit of dragon-brushing might be good as a new idea crossed her fertile mind. "Dragon dear", she asked in her most inveigling voice, "you sound just like our dad when he's reading the newspaper, so I think you'll get on well with him because you're clearly a competent bloke, got yourself out of a deep hole even if there was a slight hitch, castle builder and goodness knows what else". The Dragon smiled at this considerable encomium so Jill continued upon her path, "we could do with competence like yours where we come from", she smiled engagingly aware 'flames'n smoke' weren't in her recipe, "think of all the lovely things you could do being nice to people, fix this, sort that, build the other, 'in the land of the blind the one eye'd man is king we say', so riches could be yours with peo-ple all smiling instead of being frizzled to a crisp".

The Dragon listened to this supposition of a state he had never been party to with which, he thought, he wasn't going to have any truck at all. "Yer well", he contemplated to give Jill the idea he might just have given it a moment's thought, "s'all right for you, you got the option, dragons weren't built to be nice — unless they run to seed like that Reluctant bloke of yours and the limp-lilies back home'n then they aren't dragons any more". It thought for a moment for a positive way forward, "anyway they don't do nice either just frizzle each other in their petty struggles — so I don't know how to do nice, sort of positively like a way of life'n I'd lose my frying skills, which, as a skilled bloke as you so kindly observed, would not be good at all — you gotta be what you are see, not someone else just 'cause someone says so".

This argument got right under Jill's guard as one of her own so she decided to leave the lists for the moment to think, meanwhile sore feet and home ought to be addressed. "Ok I'll grant you that for the moment Dragon", she admitted, "so let's pack the lunch basket and be getting on home to have that foot properly seen to".

It was slow progress with the children taking turns to support The Dragon on the side of the sore foot for which going down the hill was definitely a tricky number. Still by early evening it was done as they staggered into their hall to call their parents. "Dear Parents", simpered Jill hardly able to keep the triumph out of her voice, "may we present you The Dragon, who is in need of immediate medical attention due to a badly wounded foot". No slouches their parents who were definitely not going to be upstaged by the appearance of a dragon between their children. "Pleased to meet you Sir", greeted their father deciding with dragons' reputations some respect would be wise, "I'll call our doctor straight away, he's a good chap who'll see you sorted smartly", as he eyed the damaged foot, "I'll tell him to bring major dressings for foot mending".

"Let's go into the drawing room", suggested their kindly mother not to be outdone as for her hospitality came first, questions if any, later, "there's a splendid recliner where you can put your foot up — er, tea, coffee or a nice hot chocolate, or something stronger"? Her husband went into his office to telephone their doctor who was, mercifully, a close personal friend because of similar views on 'the state of the nation'. After the experience of the pop and the blood loss with the exhausting drag back home The Dragon decided to take the latter offer at a gallop, "might I have a hot double brandy with sugar please Ma'am, Miss Jill will be able to explain", it chuckled gently easing its foot onto the stool of the recliner, then leaning gratefully back letting its tail slip down the side in a neat coil to keep it as unobtrusive as possible for the moment — mending feet came before trying to be a dragon again.

Jill went into the kitchen with her mother. "Hot double brandy dear"?, her mother enquired with a conspiratorial smile. Jill laughed, "well all we had was pop but dragons don't do well on pop he told us, it's not good for flame production'n castle building, not fortifying enough, he told us". Her mother, determined not to lose the initiative by asking questions, held her peace reckoning her children would spill the beans in due course, so merely got out the brandy with a small pan for the heating while Jill got out a large mug and the sugar.

"Magnificent brandy Ma'am, just how I like it", thanked The Dragon imbibing gratefully, "makes the flames special, does hot brandy", he added hoping to get a rise, but Jill decided to let grown-ups handle this stage while her mother thought the time for dragon-revelations was yet to come, for whichsome male help would be good. The Dragon lay back recovering while Jill and her mother left him in peace to see how the doctor gathering was going. "James was intrigued", chuckled their father, "he's making it hot foot to see whether I'm pulling his leg, watching his face when he sees our patient should be a gas".

The door bell rang so Jack let the Doctor in. "He's in here", he announced proudly as the recognised purveyor of dragons, leading the doc, whom he though was a proper bloke, into the drawing room. "Do excuse me getting up for the formalities", observed The Dragon, "these lovely people have made me so comfortable I've sort of settled in", he laughed offering up the offending foot, "and despite the reviving hot brandy I've promised myself to behave till a proper footing's been achieved for my presence here, you know explanations'nd things — so no flames and smoke stuff". The Doctor was not only a good friend he was an extremely cool customer with a splendid sense of the ridiculous. "Well, Dragon", he greeted, "since flames'n smoke aren't quite my thing, er yet, we're evens-stevens so lets see the foot — er how did it get hurt"? Jack decided it was time for children to appear in their proper light, after all dragons didn't just appear, they had to be found.

"Well Jill & I had gone on a dragon hunt", he announced seraphically, "and since hills are obvious dragon-haunts we climbed the hill, er then we went through the wood'n then we went into the cave'n then we found the wall at the end of the cave — smoke was coming out of a crack — dragon's breath I said to Jill". "Yers it was damned hard work on my side", confirmed The Dragon, "so a certain amount of smoke was inevitable, heavy breathing you know — I'd been at it for several days and was beginning to lose heart when I saw this crack develop with a little light so when these two arrived I was giving it a good deal of welly". Jill laughed, "you should have herd the hammering Sir, the real stuff, then when a little hole appeared there was grunts and curses — they were pretty real too" — "well so would you young lady", chid The Dragon slightly miffed, "if you'd been at it as long as I had *and* hit your wrist a few times too due to getting tired so losing the accuracy a bit".

"Well then the hole got big enough to carry on a conversation", continued Jack ingenuously, "so we learnt why he was where he was, then he made the hole big enough to get his suitcase through, then when he was through and reaching back to get the trunk through the rocks fell on him, then when we'd cleared the fall a huge chunk fell and speared his foot". There was an interesting silence after this galloping recital, the grown-ups not wishing to seem inquisitive nor, indeed, to be seen considering the events in any way unusual. "Then I pulled the rock spelk out of the Dragon's foot", added Jill engagingly as if the logic were obvious, "as Jack tore up his shirt to bind it with". "Damned glad I was to have such skilled help around", confirmed the Dragon stoutly, "you ought to be proud of these two Sir".

"Androcles and the Lion"?, queried the Doctor gently. "Oh they weren't in any danger", laughed The Dragon, "lion stuff was off even if there hadn't been any spelk-pulling — we'd been carrying on a civilised conversation see as well as me seeing some lunch in the offing — anyway I don't do children only sinners and baddies, with lousy leaders, wasters and rubbish like that". Laughter greeted this splendid demolition of their pet-hates. "Dragons do have standards you know", it continued to confirm its stand, "not just flames'n smoke at random, so the Androcles act was the icing on the cake — how long's it going to be doc"? "Oh about a week for a full cure", replied the Doctor, still fascinated by the whole episode with the possibilities of 'waster-slaying', "would a pair of crutches help"? "Dragon's absolutely don't do crutches", he relapsed into Essex in his angst at the thought of a dragon on crutches, "nor them damn silly mobility scooters neither — no Sir, dragons don't do wimp at all unless they're that weedy reluctant sort who should be put-down". There was quiet laughter from the grown-ups as pictures of limp-lilies being expunged crept into view. "Proper dragons grin and fight on regardless", it announced proudly, "however tough the St. Georges get — no Welfare-State crap for dragons, no Sir", upon which magnificent sally the laughter became general.

"Dragon-Hunt"?, asked the Doctor addressing the children while finishing off winding a bandage round the cleaned and anointed foot. "Well Dad had been reading us an old story about a Reluctant Dragon who wouldn't fight St. George", answered Jill — "yer one o' them Welfare-State wasters", noted the Dragon tersely — "so Jack & I decided to go to find one, simple really, go look, find, nothing to it", noted Jill smugly as if pure logic attended the event. "Seek and ye shall find", chimed in Jack tossing in the odd biblical and Prayer-Book quotes which tickled his sense of the proper.

The Doctor addressed their father, "I seem to remember that story from when I was small, it's Kenneth Grahame isn't it?". "Yes it comes from his lovely book *Dream Days*", their father replied, "it's about his own childhood, lovely stuff which it was a joy to revisit after so many years". Jill's powerful sense of the virtues of childhood chimed in, "Yes, he really understood about children'n the wonderful things they can do in their heads if they aren't filled up with rubbish, I wish I'd been in his family" — "well we found a real dragon Jill", chipped in Jack defensively as a thank-you to their parents for their understanding freedom, "and his was only a pretend one in a story by an old man for fun — thank-you for trusting us for a whole day like Mr Grahame's children", Jack acknowledged with a big smile to their parents.

"But", admonished The Dragon firmly determined the motives of dragons should be clearly established in the face of this apparent acceptance the expected billing for dragons was passé, "proper dragons do flames and smoke and keeping fair damsels in castles against all odds, laying waste's the job — none of this reluctant stuff at all — that's why I was escaping 'cause dragonsville back home's gone to the dogs", it announced with conviction. "Everyone's reluctant to face life with its attendant duties", it charged on sizzling gently, "'cause nothing's 'my job' anymore so nothing gets done if you understand me".

The grown-ups nodded awaiting the next tirade. It sat thinking for a moment then let rip angrily, "yers, place overrun with pillocks in high places, they're the pits, you can't run a decent country like that — all them lousy little lice in low level government polishing their postures in the piss poor press'n them persona-perfecting politicians posing as they prostitute the people, 's utterly ghastly — you know them"?, it enquired hopefully. "We do", acknowledged their father, "it's the same here".

"Spiky castles"?, asked Jack innocently keen to keep proper dragon perspectives in place. "Well each to his own architectural preference", replied The Dragon, "which discussion we've had before, but I haven't seen a new one built for many a year, sad really they were something else they were" — "thin dogs"?, giggled Jill rowing her brother's efforts forward — "ah well, yers, thin dogs", it reflected on long vanished times, "yers thin dogs were a bit of a speciality in them old days when the damsels had those tall spiky heads, but thin dogs is in desuetude, fallen out of fashion, rare breed stuff now alas only seen at County Shows, now dogs's all fat'n wooly'n stuff sort of slobby, not real dog's at all", it mused sadly upon fallen angels. "Them thin chaps went like the wind", it enthused brightly, "streak o lightening stuff, nothing they didn't catch — only seen'em in books meself mind as they were before me time, but they did look like the real thing", he sighed for the virtues of better days as everyone hung on its words enthralled. "Yers the damsels were more fun as well my old grandad used to tell me", it sought to recall the past to gild the present, "none of the feminist freakery stuff we see nowadays, more like real women worth a bit of flames and smoke and castle building to win — yers, definitely worth their weight". Silence reigned as everyone hung on The Dragon's encomium of past glories. "My ol grandad had one of the very last, I can just remember her, real style she had, demure'n decorum in spades — castle's a ruin now though", he mused sadly.

"St. George"?, asked the Doctor having missed him from The Dragon's discourse on ancient virtues. "Ah well, them ol days is gone too 'cause dragons've gone to the dogs so 'speck St.George's've gone the same way, yers p'raps that Reluctant guy was a sort of advance guard — but desuetude for dragons is a difficult decision for doughty dragons like me". "These days dragons", he continued metaphorically waving his forked tail, "proper dragons not them degenerate sort who've crept in back home with all this democracy crap flying around, is seeking a new way". It thought a bit then a light came into its eyes, "perhaps dragons ought to change sides'n join the good guys fixing the demise of the bad guys — which", it cheered with a note of triumph, "could be a much better way to win demure damsels than slaying knights — but slaying there's got to be or you ain't won them proper see".

"Yers", it pondered, "there's got to be slaying to make damsels worthwhile". "How about all those ladies imprisoned in castles Dragon"?, asked Jill trying to keep Fairy-Story in the picture, "who were the bad guys *then*"? "Aha", laughed The Dragon at the antics of its forbears, "the damsels in castles number was just character building stuff for knights, bit of stiffening for life's true travails'n its good for damsels to be distressed a bit too", it giggled at its exposition of past understandings, "'cause they fall into your arms easier when you've rescued them". "Life's a dead bore all magnolia", it evangelised briskly, "you've got to have bright colours'n contrast, that avocado stuff thass crept in's enough to put off any self-respecting person". "For life to be at all worth the candle", it continued in expository mode, "there's got to be some risk'n some danger to overcome or everything's limp lettuce'n give me crisp every time — it's the old lion'n lamb thing'n honey out of the jaws of death stuff'n I can see it's us dragons got to keep you magnolia humans up to scruff or you'll all fade away".

"Who's in the castle guarding whom", asked their father now really interested with a discussion he thought might have a practical outcome. "Oh it's semantics'n philosophy now is it", chuckled the Dragon, "thass the trouble with today but in the days of thin dogs'n spiky castles it was all simple stuff, you knew where you were like", he mused gently on past glories. "Haven't seen a decent damsel worth the struggle, saving your'n Miss Jill's presence Ma'am, for ages'n spiky castles're long on the wane". Their mother smiled happy at the compliment while The Dragon sat thinking carefully for a bit, "yers thass the problem, who's in the castle *and* more's the point *what is the castle*"? This profoundity produced a considerable silence.

"Sherry or something stiffer Paul"?, asked their mother of the Doctor, "since we've already dosed The Dragon with a hot toddy, and you dear"?, she asked her husband, lost in the semantics of dragons, castles and degenerate democrats, "and how about you Dragon since you've been so kind as to grant me damsel-worth", she laughed. "Oh proper dragons drink pints Ma'am'n none of that modern chilled lagery stuff either", it laughed, "when they're not needing special fortifications for feet and flames", it laughed conspiratorially, "if you've got one". It was decided by the grown-ups 'something stiffer' was necessary for dragon semantics while the children dug a kiddy-fizzy each out of the larder, found themselves two pouffs to settle in for some interesting stuff — which Jill could see might have a practical outcome knowing her father's predilections from sessions with the Doctor.

"I s'pose you'll be wanting to decide which are the bad guys'n why they're bad so we know which ones to fry", The Dragon enquired, "more philosophy stuff before we begin the war, is that it"? "Well Dragon", suggested the Doctor , "you did say earlier indiscriminate frizzling had faded out in these democratic days". "Indeed I did", agreed The Dragon keen not to be hoist upon its own petard, "but thass assuming the democracy thing's *automatically* good'n anyone who's got a grain of sense, and not going round with rose-tinted specs, can see democracy's degenerated into just another sort of castle for caging things — 'cept this Dragon, seeing clear, is on the outside keen to fry the whole damn thing, castle'n all". Jill burst out laughing at this splendid reductio of all her father's hates. "Role reversal Dragon"?, asked their father fascinated. "Not really", answered the Dragon thoughtfully, "just defining objectives properly as any general going to war should, read your Clausewitz — think first fry later".

There was a happy chuckle then a silence as if Olympus had spoken, "after all it would be terrible if even degenerate damsels got caught in the crossfire", it mused advancing down unfamiliar paths. "True", chuckled their mother, "but Sir here will tell you far too many of the degenerate democrats here are damsels". "Ah thass a misconstruction Ma'am due to the damnations of democracy", pronounced The Dragon wisely, "damsels is always damsels but degenerate democrats is always degenerate whatever their sex'n we had a fair few of the latter sort back home, real harpys, not damsels at all Ugh". "Damsels", announced The Dragon from on high, "ain't a sex thing, your true damsel's a sweet'n innocent loving cuddly person, all flowing dresses'n swirly tresses *whereas* them other sort is witches, not persons at all — with all the witch accoutrements of pots to boil you in on the blasted heath they've made of the country — Yuk". This impassioned sally was followed by gales of happy laughter.

"You seem to have been there, as we say up here", observed the Doctor. It pondered a moment to get its thoughts in a neat straight line. "Well see", it observed Olympically, "you've got to've made the journey to see the light". "St. Paul"?, enquired Jack a little precociously to the delight of his parents. "Well I don't know about him", replied the Dragon a little nettled, "I'm not into that stuff thass for humans, *but* I've been there so I know the truth of it *and it's all the same everywhere*, up top or down under — it's one of them simple classical understandings my ol grandad knew", it announced as if construing Euclid, "it's always the pillocks end up on top ruling *unless you take the trouble to make sure they don't*".

Warming to its discourse for seeing its own passions allying with its hosts it continued happily, "which is where us dragons need to be these days, guarding the damsels from the rampagings of the pillocks, 'cause honest folks's got better things to do, so", it continued with mighty assurance, "it's laying waste'n fire'n brimstone's what's needed to set the world to rights when it's gone as badly wrong as it has back home — its crawling with pillocks so all the people've gone like limp lettuces — even the damsels", it mused sadly, "trouble is it takes a bit of enthusiasm to go on the laying waste thing if all you end up with is a damsel like a limp lettuce". Gales of laughter greeted this sally which their father picked up briskly.

"But you've got to start somewhere Dragon", he exhorted, "or the limp lettuce thing's here to stay, so no more sparkly damsels and no more happy ever after either — I want happy ever after for these two here as every fairy-story should end, but as we are at the moment there's no chance of fairy-story at all". "I gather", observed The Dragon, "my sally about 'up here' is right with posing pillocks proliferating, limp lettuces languishing with Welfare-State wasters washed up in waves'n bolshie bureaus blocking with piss-poor peacock-preening politicians polishing their personæ in the poxy-press while the world goes to pot around them". "You have it Sir", cheered the Doctor and their father collapsing hysterically in unison at The Dragon's alliterative flight.

"What was in your suitcase Dragon"?, asked Jill imagining the scene conjured up by the grown-ups of the Dragon in bureau-frying mode. "Oh normal travel stuff you know", it replied casually, "couple of changes of undies, some spare trousers'n jackets'n stuff, er toothbrush and a dicky suit in case I was needed in company", it replied dismissively. "Now that", laughed their mother, "is a Dragon after my own heart; your grandad told you about damsels Dragon but my Granny always said you should have a clean hanky and a pair of clean knickers to hand at all times". "Your Gran was made of the right stuff Ma'am, true damsel material I fancy", it bowed to their mother. "Er, no special dragon effects"?, asked Jack hoping for rocket and self-propelled stuff with special exploding dragon features.

The Dragon laughed, "not needed master Jack, all the kit's on board as we dragons say, but I won't give you a demo as it mightn't improve the wall-paper". "How about being shot at", asked Jack a little damped by the lack of modern weaponry wanting to investigate the emerging picture of the battles raging in the streets as dragon cohorts got ditched as they tried to mow down heavily armed bureaus with their flames, "they've got some pretty powerful stuff these days rather an advance on the lances of old you had to deal with you know".

"Ah you may think you've 'been there done that'", replied The Dragon loftily, "but you don't know what's being happening in other spheres, tend to image you're the bee's knees with all your technological toys you lot", it laughed at its olympian sally, "but since St. Georges being now non-existent we've needed to keep ourselves up to scruff, so there's been a good deal of internecine war back home". "Necessity's the mother of invention we say", it continued splendidly, "so we've developed some pretty cool body-protection kit — 'super-armour' it's called — sort of total flame'n flakproof jackets'n leggings, the whole kit if you need it — all them old breatsplates'n greeves'n stuff my grandad knew but in modern form", it laughed merrily, "you should see me all togged up, pretty fearsome stuff, scare the living daylights out of most things specially if I've got me forty foot flame enhancer well dosed up'n going well — and never, never, discount the element of surprise'n fear of the unknown — a cohort of drag-ons descending should wreak a good deal of discord".

"Do dragons still fly"?, asked the incredulous Jill, "of course Miss Jill", replied The Dragon gleefully, "thass what dragons've always done, it's what dragons is about so it's where the descending comes in — what do think these are", as it leaned forward to stretch out the tip of a wing, "nothing quite like flames unexpected from on high to scare the living daylights you know — pretty spectac when in cohorts I do assure you". The Doctor and their father lost in dreams of flying dragons' flames a-frying with bureaus bent under the descending blasts for the re-creation of England's Green and Pleasant Land sat back happily, but; with the clear eyes of youth Jack saw a good deal further, as did the practical Jill.

"Dragon", advanced Jack sternly, keen to seek Fairy-Story out of the frying, "there are a few things which have to be addressed, er to be put in place after the laying waste stuff, the 'what we're fighting for' and how we're going to make the new world work'n things like that 'cause there's got to be Fairy-Story if there are dragons". Jill picked up the ball, "if you lot are in constant civil-war simply because there aren't any St. Georges to fight then you've got a lot to learn — civil-war isn't 'happily ever after', fairies don't survive in civil-war".

The Dragon took its time, thinking carefully, surprised at this wisdom from the young, "what you seem to be saying Master Jack & Miss Jill is we need to give up the old ways laying waste'n frying as a way of life". "Well look at the logic", stepped in Jill, "if you've been laying waste then there isn't going to be anything left is there"? "I'm sure your Clausewitz bloke would've agreed", followed up Jack, "you've got to know what the end's going to be before you begin, with no cheating or dreaming either — no 'leaving undone those things which you ought to have done'", he followed up primly, "leaving undone's no way forward 'cause self-deception's definitely not a good base for strategy". The Dragon goggled. "And", chimed in Jill not to be out-quoted, "no 'doing those things which ought not to be done', either". "Um, yers", nodded the Dragon, struck by this new idea, "come to think of it home's a bit like that now, harmony in low esteem altogether, everyone at each other's throats blaming each other for everything". Seeing their children had got the Dragon and Clausewitz well in hand their mother and father took the Doctor into the kitchen to knock up a late supper.

"Do I"?, asked the Dragon warily, "spot the 'nice' heaving over the horizon you were mentioning earlier, bit of a difficult concept for dragons, not even the wimps know nice they just slob around doing nothing and 'specting everyone else to do it — laying waste may not be the best", it muttered defensively, "but it's better than sitting around glued to the telly — at least it's a positive engagement with life". "Well there's nice and nice", observed Jill, carefully leading the Dragon on an unfamiliar path.

"Us dragons's always been into high endeavour, Miss Jill", it continued its defence, "you know the stuff in them old books; Knights'n Round Tables as the very heart of romance", it trumpeted protectively spotting rough water ahead. "Is laying waste the romance of high endeavour pray Sir Dragon"?, asked Jill. "Werl, 'pends who gets laid'n how much waste", replied the Dragon archly equivocating furiously to retain it's ground. "The end does not justify the means Sir Dragon", pontificated Jack brightly, "laying waste is not a moral activity".

"Blimey", mused the Dragon, "sorting St. George's was easy-peasy compared to you lot, couple of blasts of the old flames'n it was done, I never expected to have to defend my modus operandus, so there young man". "Well now's Damascus time Dragon", announced Jack brightly, well into his Biblical allegory, "new leaf time, bright lights to illuminate the new way" — "and I tell you what", chipped in Jill happily spotting an opening, "there's a lot more to being nice than just being nice, a lot of thought with giving of self with a good deal of that romance of high endeavour on behalf of others — so Jack & I'll allow frying the odd bureau who's battening on the nice people as a proper sort of nice, frying the bad to preserve the good, how's that grab you"?

"Now there's a thought", agreed the Dragon, "high endeavour slaying the bad, I like it'n frying bureaus's just my thing — and I'll tell you a little Greek wisdom too to justify our course", it announced proud of its classical education, "The Greeks didn't do the god bit but they knew keeping good straight was a full-time job because humans get greedy so they believed it was right to be angry when good got trampled, indeed they held it was bad not to defend good 'cause they knew if people don't defend good then bad prevails — so you need to fry a few bureaus to teach them all a lesson about defiling good", it chuntered to a happy stop before continuing thoughtfully into practicalities. "I could do here what I should've been doing back home, but they've all got the same kit back home, yummee, p'raps I could build up a Bureaus Execution Squad by training troops here — I've got a fair few mates back there to start with", he chortled with almost obscene glee, "so Clausewitz it is then, strategy first tactics afterwards".

"It's only what you used to do", observed Jack, "just a matter of defining who needs rescuing from whom and why — do you Dragon"? "How many are there of you of like mind"?, asked the practical Jill spotting visions of fame looming as the discoverer of the dragon who saved the nation. "Oh if I had a little time for some canvassing", it reflected well into tactics mode, "for whom I could promise willing damsels'n a nice little plot to plant spuds'n veggies in, a fair few", it answered dreamily. "Well with Clausewitz to the fore", followed up Jack briskly keen to keep the good work rolling, "as you so rightly say, how many's a fair few, this is not a thing to start unprepared". The Dragon sat back and thought, counting on its claws in a curious sort of abacus way, "well, you two lovelies, I fancy I could martial a couple of hundred without much trouble then once we'd got the thing under way and got super-armour production in full swing I imagine a couple of thousand wouldn't be impossible, specially if we made some real gains".

"Don't forget the Damascus bit", laughed Jack caught up in the fun of the thing, "no more slaying Christians after you've fixed the baddies, you've got to do the St. Paul thing of preaching 'Love one another' — "and digging potato patches", chuckled Jill, "self-sufficiency's all the rage today". "You've got high-endeavour with lots of romance there Dragon", cheered Jack enthusiastically, "knock those old St George acts right out of sight". "First stop zapping here", observed The Dragon, "then converting dragonsville from laying-waste to 'love one another which", he propounded firmly, "is not a job for layabouts as one's apt to get stoned and stuff' — "but you'd go down in the history books like all saints do", laughed Jill, "just like St Paul, immortality'n stuff". "Who he, Miss Jill"?, asked The Dragon intrigued getting caught up by the children's enthusiasm. "Oh don't worry about him", replied Jack, "but he's had top billing as a great guy for two thousand years' cause he saw the truth about the bad of his old ways so turned himself inside out — immortality's worth a change of tack with bit of effort".

"Supper's up kids'n Dragon", carolled their mother through the door. The grown-ups, told of the general plot over supper, the doctor noted, should the dragon escapade prove a reasonable success, it would fire a goodly number of those who were awaiting a messiah but had no clues about who or where from, "nor any idea at all about how", he finished triumphantly. "Now there you are Dragon", announced Jack, "messiah up here and St. Paul down below which", he continued with considerable triumph recently into more advanced maths, "is High-Endeavour squared — immortality in spades with names on golden tablets".

The Dragon went all dreamy eyed then faced the older generation squarely, "woss the damsel prospecs"?, it lapsed again in its vision of untold choice, damsels falling at its feet without even needing a castle to keep them. "Well, you should know all about the fickleness of damsels", replied their mother laughing, "just when you think you've got them all wrapped up they go and fancy someone else, so you can't put them into your Clause-witz equation because Dame Fortune has a horrible habit of turning the whole thing inside out so best to let it ride on the day". "Ah well", The Dragon sighed, "I fancy you're right Ma'am but faint heart ne'er won fair lady so at least one's going in the right direction".

And so it came about. The Dragon convalesced, then the children obtained permission to go with it on a recruiting course to dragonsville, enlarging the hole adequate to the passage of cohorts and recovering his trunk with the all-important dicky-suit for the expected celeb dinners attendant upon success. Their efforts proved surprisingly successful so a substantial tent village was built in the field outside the house, with which the planning men came to interfere and, er, got evaporated without trace — the battle was on.

The bureaus, caught utterly at a loss by the flames descending and finding, with the newsprint's help for a change, enormous numbers of people joined the dragon ranks discovered themselves routed. Suddenly dragons, having spent the eons of history as the bad guys, all forked tails'n scales with flaming breath, captors of damsels in distress etc, became the van-guard of the people saving themselves — messiahs in golden flak-jackets frying their erstwhile enemies with a galantry not seen for a very long time.

Romance was everywhere as 'the impossible was made good' before their very eyes then soon by their own hands. "Intoxicating stuff", everyone agreed over their foaming pints as endeavour sprang to heights they had not seen — 'since the last war' the real oldies remembered gleefully as they cheered on the cohorts tossing away crutches and driving their mobility scooters to the nearest tips — very Biblical thought Jack happily. It was a curious thing, reported the braver of the damsels, dragons proved quite extraordinarily cuddly when they'd taken their super-armour off and were sitting supping happily in the sunshine — 'Grace Abounding' chuckled Jill to herself.

The People had spoken so the democratic dunderheads fled into anonymity as fast as they could to avoid the fire — though our brave heroes got their frying-pan of corpses of the really hard cases to much national joy. Meaningless Ministries closed for ever, Council palaces were plucked from their erstwhile prostitutes then demolished or turned to community uses so the monstrous millstone which had crushed the life out of the nation for so long was gradually lifted as people began to breathe free air again — to find freedom curiously intoxicating. 'And upon the morning of the third day' thinking began as the light was re-set in the heavens — and they saw that it was good so it was multiplied.

Our children lead a new vanguard of 'Preaching the New Potato Patch' as those who had fled crept out to learn about the possibilities of a new life lead in construction not destruction, emancipation not oppression, co-operation not coercion, enablement not dis-ablement and together not apart — smiles suffused as resurrection arose like the rise of the Eastern Sun — Spirits soared as 'Love one another' leaked round the land as in Freedom and true community their erstwhile enemies discovered skills and joys they could never know locked within System's destructive system. Each began to dig his own 'Potato Patch', defined how his own digging should be in the Freedom of his Own Spirit , and found it good, and it was so — so Free air and High-Hills became the new votives as singing was heard throughout the land as Mr Blake's 'Jerusalem' became the hymn of The Vanguard.

Once our team had got the process self-propelling with St. Paul's proliferating plentifully they allowed a modest Celeb Dinner for the Dragon cohorts with the main protagonists who had joined the struggle to lead the people — our Dragon had known the dicky-suit had been a good idea — then they filtered quietly back home. High-Endeavour had been very wearing stuff and they did not want the efforts involved in the fatuous fame routine. What they really wanted was to take their Dragon down to dragonsville to show 'down-under' how to do it, for which they knew they had powerful allies because of the splendid behaviour of the dragon cohorts 'up above'.

A curious transformation had taken place in the minds of our children for the valiant joint endeavours had enjoined common cause so *The* Dragon became *Their* Dragon who had become an integral part of how they thought, someone who had abandoned self to help his neighbour in a plight which he understood and for which he had the power — so had made his own. He didn't have a name but, they decided, names didn't matter as it was how they thought about him which mattered to them *because he now belonged.*

Their parents, recognising their children could dispense with 'education' thereafter, gladly gave them all the time they would need for their mission. So our brave pair set off with 'Their' Dragon, now a 'he' as an integral part of their lives, to give dragonsville the wisdom of the child about 'Love one another' and to teach warring dragons how to dig potato patches to propagate peace. Moving mountains proved not as easy as they'd thought — it never is however obvious the new course, but once the idea had caught on with a few putative St. Pauls to seed the effort change began to roll as waste-land burgeoned beautifully with grace abounding — then damsel dragons came out of hiding waving their erstwhile party frocks.

No mere leader our Dragon, no sword bearer when sandals should be supreme — 'don't just tell'em how' was his motto, 'show'em how alongside'em' because 'dig for victory with them' had always been our Pauline Dragon's canon. No piddling around on the Internet for him either, if you wanted spuds you got a spade then damn well dug — but for digging to ascend above drudge you needed a song to embue digging with Spirit's endeavour. So, Red Flags à bas, he stuck an enormous cross of St.George onto a long pole above his patch and, as he dove his spade into the earth (long untilled) he raised his Dragon voice (curiously melodious our children thought);

> *In the days of thin dogs, when dragons dressed dightly,*
> *And ladies assembled for tournaments high,*
> *While knights were so brave that they bore themselves mightly,*

Then we all cheered —
Because we were Free
Chorus
When dragons dance and lances fly,
Let all good people watch the sky;
Take new endeavour — so no never
Let Freedom's freedom slip you by.

When castles were built with their spikes piled up fitly,
And ladies wore hats as high as the sky,
Then ponies were palfreys, with lances borne briskly,
As knights limbered lightly —
To ensure all stayed Free.

Then damsels delicious demure and so sightly,
Had knights watch devoted as they loved them on high,
Dames danced in attendance upon us all nightly,
Then the people sang sweetly —
In the Land of the Free

But democrats came to preach low and the scurvy,
And lousy then leveled those hopes upon high,
Now hate swathes like ivy to kill all that is worthy,
So Love lies a'bleeding —
'Cause all's now un-Free

So, we live in a land whose light is extinguished,
Where duty and beauty and Civis all die,
Where Cages abound'n High Hills are extinquished,
So the people moan sadly —
In the land that's Un-Free

But cohorts of Dragons came swooping down tightly,
With a synergy formed in the vasts of the sky,
So incentive and energy came to shine brightly,
To breed brand new hope —
That all may be Free

'Cause Dragons are back with a bright new vocation,
So we're all brave St. Georges with new flags to fly,
They've joined with the men of brave equitation,
From the hosts of the horrible —
We'll set ourselves Free

Then Democracy's flaws fail the fierce confrontation,

As Demagogues' damnations and dictations all die,
Pillocks prevented from perverse prostitution,
As we push them in pits -
To fight ourselves Free

Oh Dragons we love you for showing us rightly,
The way to the stars placed above us on high,
Ne'er again shall we fail you, keep before us right brightly,
Vitality's virtues -
Which keep people Free

So damsels may dance again sightly and sprightly,
And none try to tempt with the levelling lie,
Delight take on dumb to chase out unsightly,
As we all stand up proud —
With the cheers of the Free

So let Love lave the lists with its bright celebration,
Of US and together — and never be shy,
Of wearing it fitly to drive cerebration,
As it's Love's magic potion —
Which makes US the Free.
so
When dragons dance and lances fly
Let all good people watch the sky;
Take new endeavour, — so no never
Let Freedom's freedom slip you by.

Faintly to those digging furiously down in dragonsville, from far on high as if sang by angels up in the realms of Earth above where sods were flying, came this song;

Now we've found our true Salvation,
Britannia'l always rule the waves,
Back to being a sovereign nation,
Britons never shall be slaves.

"You know you brill pair", reflected The Dragon one evening over port'n lemons all round, "there's a classic elegance about all this which appeals because 'who's the dragon's' all in the mind of the viewer" — "and 'what's the dragon", too noted Jack. "Just so Master Jack", he agreed, "who's bad and who's good and why". "I think the good's the easy bit", mused Jill thoughtfully, "because it all comes down to our 'Love one another' thing, so the bad's what those Greeks you told us of, the blokes who hate or spoil the good". "So", chuckled Jack, "Dragons can be good and bad 'cause the bureaus were the bad dragons for keeping the people in their castles like in the days of thin dogs but the good dragons came to let us all out by doing some bureau-frying" — "so it's all semantics then", chuckled Jill happily.

"Er not 'zactly you lovelies", chid The Dragon a wit sternly keen for truths not to get lost in the joy, "because good and bad aren't semantics at all — nor's love and hate — straight forward stuff, no greys", he advised with the enthusiasm of the freshly converted, "you either love one another or you don't, no semantics there it's either black or white", he announced with a flourish of one announcing eternal truths. "Im still amazed at the speed it all happened though", reflected Jill thoughtfully. "Ah Miss Jill", observed the Dragon wisely, "once you've shown the sheep which way to go and why, sort of where the good grass is, then give them a good leader they scamper off with a will'n you just need a little guidance here'n there". "It just needs the bit at the beginning", cooed Jack dreamily, "deciding where the good grass really is then overcoming their inertia by some really stylish St. Paul stuff". "Dragons beating dragons to turn swords into ploughshares", mused the Dragon, "to dig potato patches with", laughed Jack, "nice Biblical associations — appeals to me".

"How's the damsel scene Dragon"?, asked Jill keen on the love interest, "they seemed to be proliferating prettily with their party frocks". The Dragon slumped then took a substantial slurp. "Damsels be damned", he muttered uncharacteristically morosely, "drop-dead gorgeous they may fancy themselves in their new frocks suddenly on the make, so drop-dead they can Miss Jill". "Yer's", he mused laconically, "they're all on the hunt like wild beasts so dissillusion'n dissapointment's it — your mum was right, bloody fickle lot altogether your sex these days Miss Jill", he pondered sadly. "Trouble's worse though", he followed his plaint on, "I could cope with fickle as thass women for you, but damsels today're a busted flush — all hoity-toity'n please 'emselves 'because they're worth it'", he waxed angrily, "so they've told the male he's an insubordinate irrelevance in their magisterial existence waving permanent 'keep-off' signs'n prattling in their PC pride". "No", he continued sadly, "they're not like them classy olde-worlde damsels, no demure any more'n no decorum neither, so definitely not delightful, not worthy of a jot of Dragonly devotion — s'all declined'n demise's in sight for the nuptial hopes of Dragons". He sat for a moment musing. "Silly girls", he noted sadly, "they've locked themselves in the worst cage of all, 'I' alone, to turn their backs on life's greatest joy — 'together not Apart' — its pilgrimage made hand-in-hand *and* some of them may've dug out their party frocks but they're not the sort of stuff I'd be seen at a party with, no Sir, *definitely* not the demure and delightful I knew".

"But you didn't know them Dragon", observed Jill. "Well indeed not 'zacly, Miss Jill", he agreed, "but one can always hope'n dream of balmier days when damsels really were delicious with all them swirly dresses'n tresses'n them waiting in the lists for you to claim them as your victory prize, *they* were worth some High-Endeavour I can tell you, devotion-worthy in every degree — very cuddly too once you'd got the spiky hat off, so my grandad told me". He sat thinking, disenchantment written upon his furrowed brow, "Yers and the fame thing's no help neither 'cause you can't make silk purses out 'o sows ears — no Sir, spot of fame'n it's party dresses everywhere with welcome signs writ large", he pondered the horrors of the fame routine. "No Sir", he mused on sadly, "fame ain't a reliable gauge of true affection, spot 'o success'n suddenly far too many fair ladies crowding round all too keen to have a slice of the action, not demure at all, decorum nowhere; I think I'll have to go away into the wilderness for a bit to let the fuss die down, I'll keep you two posted", he chuckled at his solution. "Forty days should do it I imagine", Jack opined wisely. "Distance lends enchantment and hearts grow fonder, Dragon dear", cheered Jill, putting an arm snugly round 'her' Dragon, "so the good ones'll still be there when you get back".

And so it was all The Dragons became St Georges — as all good Dragons should. I hope Mr Grahame would have approved.

Aphrodite, November 2009

Aspects of Love
A collection of short stories

the Queene of the Silver Sluice

by Aphrodite

THE QUEENE OF THE SILVER SLUICE

(A Jack & Jill Story 2nd in series from 'The Un-Reluctant Dragon')
(With my thanks to Mr Ruskin for 'The King of The Golden River')

'So saying, the dwarf stooped and plucked a lily that grew at his feet. On its white leaves there hung three drops of clear dew. And the dwarf shook them into the flask which Gluck held in his hand. "Cast these into the river," he said, "and descend on the other side of the mountains into the Treasure Valley. And so good speed.'

As he spoke, the figure of the dwarf became indistinct. The playing colours of his robe formed themselves into a prismatic mist of dewy light; he stood for an instant veiled with them as with the belt of a broad rainbow. The colours grew faint, the mist rose into the air; the monarch had evaporated.

And Gluck climbed to the brink of the Golden River, and its waves were as clear as crystal, and as brilliant as the sun. And, when he cast the three drops of dew into the stream, there opened where they fell a small circular whirlpool, into which the waters descended with a musical noise.

Gluck stood watching it for some time, very much disappointed, because not only the river was not turned into gold, but its waters seemed much diminished in quantity. Yet he obeyed his friend the dwarf, and descended the other side of the mountains towards the Treasure Valley; and, as he went, he thought he heard the noise of water working its way under the ground. And, when he came in sight of the Treasure Valley, behold, a river, like the Golden River, was springing from a new cleft of the rocks above it, and was flowing in innumerable streams among the dry heaps of red sand.

And as Gluck gazed, fresh grass sprang beside the new streams, and creeping plants grew, and climbed among the moistening soil. Young flowers opened suddenly along the river sides, as stars leap out when twilight is deepening, and thickets of myrtle, and tendrils of vine, cast lengthening shadows over the valiey as they grew. And thus the Treasure Valley became a garden again, and the inheritance, which had been lost by cruelty, was regained by love.

And Gluck went, and dwelt in the valley, and the poor were never driven from his door: so that his barns became full of corn, and his house of treasure. And, for him, the river had, according. to the dwarf's promise, become a River of Gold.

And, to this day, the inhabitants of the valley point out the place where the three drops of holy dew were cast into the stream, and trace the course of the Golden River under the ground, until it emerges in the Treasure Valley. And at the top of the cataract of the Golden River, are still to be seen two BLACK STONES, round which the waters howl mournfully every day at sunset; and these stones are still called by the people of the valley , THE BLACK BROTHERS.

The End of The King of The Golden River
by
JOHN RUSKIN
(written in 1841 'at the request of a very young lady')

Jack sat thoughtfully, "it's a pity he didn't have a lady Mummy, all kings should have queens to keep their castles in order and carry on the kingly line'n there's no romance without a lady" — "but he didn't have a castle Jack", observed Jill factually, "he only had The Golden River'n he seems to've been rather a lonely sort of bloke always being neither one thing nor another'n constantly dissappearing'n stuff". "Well he should have a castle'n a queen too", insisted her brother, "so we can have some real romance with little kings to go on looking after The Golden River".

Their mother laughed delighted, "Jack dear, romance is supposed to be a girly thing". "Hold fast dear lady", exploded their father wonderfully, "didn't I come up to scruff at all in the romance bit or did I just stand around imperially wielding a sword demanding obedience". Jack looked at his dad quietly, he'd always felt he had more in common with his dad than the obvious outside boy things, "but the right things did happen didn't they Dad", Jack surmised, "'n that's pretty romantic isn't it 'cause the Black Brothers got zapped and the nice Gluck won'n lived happily ever after in The Treasure Valley all green again the West Wind Esquire had destroyed because The Black Brothers were so bad, er but he didn't get a lady either, er were you good at the snoggy-romance stuff Dad"?

His father looked at the ceiling with a grin, "proper chaps don't go brag-
ging about snoggys Jack they let their ladies speak for them because it's
ladies who know about these things, isn't it Jill dear"?, he tossed into the
air thinking he'd try a little tease. Jill adopted an Olympian air to disguise
her progress in the snoggy department, "snoggys are for girly girls, the pink
sock brigade with bows'n stuff, real girls hold stinky boys at arm's length".
"Well", advised their mother firmly with a huge grin, "I can tell you little
Miss Boy, life will be a dead bore for you without snoggys *and* I can tell
you your Dad was tops, real whisk off the feet stuff, instant dreamland for
girls with long golden hair'n castle walls included".

Their father collapsed laughing, "its taken a Fairy-Story to drag it out of
your mother children, but there you go that's girls for you keep these things
hidden in their bosom to surprise you one day — still we made it didn't
we gal", he laughed. Their mother melted happily, "with my parents looking askew at the whole thing it was the super-snoggys which won the day
because I didn't think I could go through life without them", she laughed
happily as she looked a little severely at her daughter, "snoggy's Jill are for
all day every day, they're the glue which keeps the show on the road when
the going gets rocky, it's snoggys which make the rough places plane while
shining the mountain tops ahead when the road becomes straight again,
'snoggy's", she noted formly, "are 'together not apart', *and* snoggy's are for
knights as well as ladies — it takes two, to prove which she stood beside
'her man' with an arm round his shoulders as he raised his head so she
could drop hers for a considerable kiss. "Snoggy's go on forever you two,
snoggy's are the ultimate glue of all — hot choccy's"?

Jack & Jill drifted gently off to bed. Sitting up doing their normal choccy
bit of discussing 'what's to be', they decided, since dragons were doing very
well delving down below, while bureaus needed no more harrying as they'd
adopted almost Pauline conversions with spuds proliferating — they
needed a new enterprise. "No other worlds for this one", reflected Jill
sucking her mug — "no indeed", replied Jack, "so lets write this one ourselves with real snoggy romance in it'n not one that takes us over as all the
dragon stuff was well enough but pretty exhausting being up on those public plinths — quiet life's the thing for me". They both laughed knowing
how much they'd actually enjoyed it but admitting small doses was the
truth of it. "When we've done it", mused Jack thoughtfully, "we can read

it to Mum & Dad like they read stories to us, so we'll have to make a good job of it".

"We need a Queen", announced Jack brightly as they drifted off to sleep, "so let's write a story of how The King of The Golden River finds a Queen, how's that"? — "yummee then we will need lots of snoggy-romance", urged Jill positively. "I know sis you wouldn't admit it to Mum'n Dad but I've seen you snogging Jim Barnes which looked pretty real to me — not that I would know", he finished archly. "Mmmm yummee", mused a sleepy Jill, "he's a kisser'n no mistake so it's snoggy-romance for us then" — "well you better write the snoggy bits 'cause I haven't left the starting line yet" — "oh we'll have to fix you some snoggy Jack dear after all Mum's sales talk", his hugely experienced sister laughed, as two pairs of tired eyes closed.

Dreams, ah dreams. Us oldies don't take care of dreams, silly stuff for kids, but kids know better for dreams are the world they live in, 'thank the lord' because it's what makes the best ones such fun to have about. Lady Moon sailed serenely past the open window to look in, fertilising the pair of shining heads with Her luminescent light to silver everything in their room into a magic other-world which seeped into their subconscious. Next morning, with one voice, they announced rather grandly to their parents, "we're going for a walk up our hill to fertilise creative imagination, expect us when you see us", as they stepped briskly out of the back door towards the fields.

"Something went on in my head last night", observed the prosaic Jill, "sort of wonderful light". Jack laughed having managed to stay awake a little longer, "that was the full-moon sis shining in the window, and you know what happens at full moons — dreams come true".

The well practiced climb was made in good time, with a break half-way up to consider the beginnings of the creative problem. "It's like the blank sheet when I'm trying to write an essay", mused Jack, "very stary'n off-putting till I can find a start". Jill sucked a mental pencil using a cow-parsley stalk she had found at the bottom; she liked their many branched heads like miniature trees, so often carried one with her on her walks. "Would 'Once Upon a Time' break the log-jam Jack", she suggested, "then 'there was a King who needed a Queen" — "now the King had a Golden River but no castle....." chipped in Jack, "ok let's freeze it there then each think as we go".

Much encouraged by the initial breakthrough they sprinted up to the top, then set off into the undergrowth path blazed by the many dragon feet. Very familiar it all seemed even though some six months ago so they were happy ambling remembering its twists and turns round trees, wandering through alleys the dragons had made. Suddenly rounding a corner they ran straight into two dragons. "Hi you brill pair", cheered *their* Dragon. "I see the Forty days did the trick Dragon"?, chuckled Jack, eyeing The Dragon's lady-friend. "Oh yes", Master Jack it grinned, "the haroosh had died down'n by the time I got back so I wasn't even second page stuff — indeed off the map altogether, 's'amazing how fast the good guys get forgotten by the masses lapping at the trash they get served up — thankless lot". "Since I wasn't headlines any more", he recounted the story, "the party frock brigade had lost interest as all they want is to be in the celeb-sheets so, since the paparazzi'd ditched me, thank goodness, I could creep about quietly to case the joint — search for the real gold", he ran to a delighted halt goofily smiling enraptured at his Lady who, both could not fail to notice, was a radiant creature built on Junoesque lines. "Meet Miss Demure & Delightful, for reasons you can see", he chuckled hugely, "*very* definitely the best of 'thin dog' stuff, my grandpa would thoroughly've approved — very cuddly as I told you the real thing should be when we last met", he snuggled close to his lady smiling hugely.

"Now don't you start", she admonished, "they're obviously nice young people who don't need corrupting with your crudities". "Ah", noted Jack wisely, "genuine beauty's un-corruptible Ma'am, it's bureaucrats who corrupt not magnificent busts" — "which", chimed in Jill happily eyeing what she hoped she might one day possess, "are a joy for all, specially those for whom nature might provide — with luck" — "and the right genetics", laughed Jack, "if you turn out like Mum you'll not be short". Everybody laughed splendidly as The Dragon explained to DD, "their Mum's a real whizzer the right size too — I see you're on the way since we last met Miss Jill", as he eyed her conspiratorially. "Oh yes", chuckled Jack, "it's like Spring, one day all twigs then suddenly behold catkins burst forth". "Hardly catkins", Jack dear, "buds perhaps", she replied smiling at her brother's joy in her new burgeoning person. "Ah but buds is the promise of flowers in due course", chuckled The Dragon, "look at my lovely Miss Demure & Delightful here", upon which compliment more happy laughter echoed amongst the trees.

Jill invited brightly, "come to meet our parents Miss DD they're real fun". Jack & Jill were completely overjoyed at the meeting, the contortions of fabricating stories dissolving in the real story in front of them. "Tell us the story you lovely pair — we 'spect there's lots of snoggy-romance so come back to tea to tell the folks as they'll be delighted's they're well into snoggy", finished Jack happy to be let off the compositional hook.

The snake wound its way back through the track then each found their own way down the hill, with the boys deciding to be boys so roll down. "Kids", chirruped DD with a fond smile, "but he's pretty OK really my Dragon, I've heard the story of the bureau-zapping, real 'knights-of-old' stuff". "Funny the kids thing", mused Jill, "because it seems to be the kid in Jack who has the nice sort of fairy ideas, my Dad's a little fairy-story too".

"Well hello Dragon", cheered their Mother on arrival, "do introduce me to the new member of the family". "There, told you so DD, pure gold", chuckled The Dragon happy to have his advertising vouchsafed so splendidly, "well Ma'am this is Miss Demure & Delightful who's agreed to be my wife so we're getting married soon so have come to ask you all to the show". "Yippee", cheered Jack, "*real* snoggy-romance I don't have to make up right on the doorstep too, tell Mummy & Daddy how it happened Dragon". "Easy all", cautioned their mother smiling, "hospitality first, will you take tea with your cakes and things Miss Demure & Delightful or something fizzy". "Oh tea please Ma'am and do make it DD, all that Demure & Delightful stuff is pretty wearing *and* as I've got 'em I don't mind being proud of 'em", to shrieks of laughter as their father lead off into the sitting room with its elegant tea-table. Jill helped their mother with the tea as the two dragons sat on the sofa with DD looking round at all the lovely things. With the entry of tea everyone was ready for the story of love's young dream.

The Dragon thought a moment to set the story a little. "Well you remember that party-frock'n fame blitz that I escaped from into the wilderness Miss Jill", it began, "it had me thinking about the chicks'n what was going on as I didn't believe they were all like that". "Fame's a fantastic fickle fantasy", assured The Dragon sadly, "silly chicks cheating themselves with such tissue stuff — some of 'em nice little things too if they could get themselves together to do something real with some proper education but fame grips 'em peddled by the lousy media-creeps so 'here today gone tomorrow's goin't be their lives — ain't that so DD, honey, you nearly got zapped", he appealed to his lady whom everyone could see he doted on. "Oh yes indeed", she chirped in nicely modulated tones, "I had a narrow squeak for sure as I got picked up when I was a child who didn't know any better by one of those deb's delights who need a fashion-chick to cruise the glitter-mags with — Ugh — then I woke up'n fled back home". "My folks were delighted when Dragon here hove in sight", she continued the saga-of-love happily (aren't we all?), "because they hadn't forgotten the miracles he'd performed" — "but how did it actually happen"?, burst in Jack the romantic hoping on the side to get a storyline because invention's Muse, whom he'd thought would've sat by his side for a gentle bidding, was proving an illusive lady.

"You tell'em DD", The Dragon encouraged, "it's your story's I just lolled around in the background to see what would happen", he smiled at the memory, "pretty limp really when you consider the Sturm'n Drang stuff we all got involved in *and* when you see what I've won by doing nothing", he simpered happily.

Their father burst out laughing splendidly, "Well I'm no judge of Dragon beauty but I fancy your nick-name for your lovely lady might have something to do with it" — "always a boob man your Dad kids", their mum chuckled — "reveres the finer points of a lady then", laughed the irrepressible DD giving hers a wiggle then gave 'her man' a hug, "as does he here which is what got the thing on a roll in the first place because he didn't really just sit about as it has to be admitted his appearance got me off the parental hook so I did a bit of, how shall we say, door opening", followed by gusts of laughter from everybody. "I set out to put on my best show, sort of get the Demure'n Delightfuls on show with the new 'Low-Cut' look as he was cruisin' by", his lady reflected cheerfully". "She ain't DD for nothing", chuckled The Dragon gleefully, "the go-getter style goes with the bust". "Which came first"?, asked their father intrigued admiring Dragonly DDs.

"Shush nice men don't ask ladies such things", giggled their mother trying to not laugh too much. "Oh I don't do nice men", DD laughed uproariously, "only real men who go setting cohorts of fellow dragons slaying in upperworlds egged on by children, only real men do that, so I'd got my eye on him from the first — but then he did the wilderness bit". "Yes Ma'am", Jack laughed at the memory, "we planned Wilderness after we'd done the job when poor Dragon got fried in the Media-crush — forty days seemed to have hallowed associations". "When he'd got his head straight", the dragon's inamorata observed, "to come back in circulation I sort of put myself in his way's I said, if you know the technique Ma'am", she smiled salaciously, "waving the Delightfuls about with a bit less Demure". "Yers", sniggered The Dragon happily, "Demure rather hit the bin but we decided to keep it in the title to save the public face".

Their mother collapsed laughing, "I hope you two're listening there's a wealth of experience bubbling out here". "But DD which did come first", enquired Jack keen to suss a real problem. "Well you may have noticed dragons don't have names as such", she pointed out, "but when Him here turned up'n told me his old grandad's story of the thin dogs and the old dames hanging out of castle walls tempting dragons with their wherewithal, there seemed a nice sort of coincidence, him being a boob-man — harking back to days-of-yore Demure'n Delightfull seemed just the thing specially as he knew we'd be making visits up here so a name would be good'n he knew Sir would laugh". Sir laughed fit to bust while madam rocked about helpless.

"How are our erstwhile enemies the bureaus doing"?, asked The Dragon. "Oh it's amazing, you've never seen so many St. Pauls, planting potatoes so prolifically prosperity's everywhere", laughed Jack. "Reformation's the words Dragon dear", cheered their Mother, "it's truly a magnificent affair, community blossoming all over with demagogues digging diligently so spuds are sprouting splendidly — when's the wedding"?, she asked concentrating on the essentials as women do. "Two week's time", replied The Dragon, "as I said you're all invited". Their mother, who behind the motherly bust hid much wisdom, replied quietly, "thank you so much Dragon dear but I think it's a Fairy-Story thing; Fairy-Stories are for children to keep their eyes sparkly so us oldies'll leave it to emergent youth, as long as they agree to write the story for us when they come back — we want a

'Once Upon a Time' to keep us young and sparkly too". There were happy smiles all round as 'the young', and The Dragons retired for an early start next day — the well appointed household always has a spare bedroom ready for any who may step by.

'The Oldies' chuckled happily amazed yet again at their children's ability to create magic out of thin air. "I just do love Miss DD", smiled their father, "I think she's a real hoot, she'll keep our Dragon well up to scruff, no flies on her whatever else there may be". His lady collapsed happily, "I haven't seen your eyes on such stalks for ages dear, such fun, real 'cat that nicked the cream' stuff, I'm glad they still work for you". He laughed delighted by the compliment from one who lived curled inside his heart, "well we've both known each other's delight in what's over the fence ever since day one, that 'beauty in unexpected places' thing which makes US such fun" — "yes I wouldn't have it any other way", as she snuggled close ensuring 'alternative attractions' were swamped by her own.

Our four, well breakfasted, set off early next morning with waves to those behind, Jack & Jill having packed a small suit-case with suitable frocks for the wedding. "I wonder what'll happen next", mused their father quietly to his lady watching the diminishing figures. "Well it won't be ordinary for sure though how they're going to find a Queen for the King I can't possibly imagine", remarked their mother. "Which is the magic of it as I don't suppose they know either", mused their father, "but I bet they do, so there'll be two weddings — should be a really fun story, I'm looking forward to it already".

Up the hill, through the wood then into the hole in the rock our four moved into another world, with Jack & Jill taking turns to carry the case. Arriving in a small village in Dragonsville DD showed them to a little house which her parents had made available till they had got their own after the wedding. All was very snug. With now ten days to go to the celebrations The Dragon went off with Jack to do the major wedding sorting while Jill joined DD doing all the lady things. Days passed contentedly as arrangements came nicely together for a real village-fest centered round a huge marquee on the village green. For dragons weddings are a vow made before all their people, so there was a high table where it would take place. Once the formalities of troth-plighting had been done then feasting with music and dancing would be the 'order of the day'.

Wedding Day was, or course, gorgeous as everyone assembled in the afternoon in the marquee which had all the sides rolled up so there was lots of light while everyone could move about easily. Prompt at Three quiet descended as our nuptial pair, with accompanying maids behind for DD, lead off up to the high table to a traditional Dragon wedding march played by the 'hired music'. Waiting for them was Jack as The Dragon's sponsor with Jill as DD's sponsor, to much delight as no local noses had been put out of joint in the choices.

The Mayor read all the formalities then D swore his eternal oath to DD, then she did to him to which the Mayor, a wag who had spotted the fun beforehand, pronounced them Man & Wife as D^3 to much general laughter. To make life easier all round our organising chaps had agreed the feast would be a self-service affair with lots of tables and chairs spread around in the sun outside so there would be general swirling with no cliques.

When all were happily fed a long convivial affair which lasted till six o'clock everyone strolled into the marquee lead by the tempting sound of music. The marquee had now acquired a huge wooden floor laid by the marquee-men for the dancing while everyone had been eating. The hired hand for the music for the dance was a real whizzer — playing a concertina with a drum attached to his right foot while singing in the intervals. The dancing, for which he was M/C as well, was splendid with no-one sitting anything out — except to go to the bar of course.

"Who he"?, thrilled Jack, to Miss DD sitting next to him after a splendid dance they had had he jigging to the tune of the wonderful song being sung as an interval piece. "Oh he's The KGR", chuckled DD, "he's been famous round here for a long time, real entertainer not the crap disco stuff — but no one knows his real name though there's an old rumour he was someone else". Jill joined them, gasping from having been whirled splendidly round by one of the more expert young revellers, recognised the King of The Golden River in disguise, then eyed Jack conspiratorially with a 'we know' smile. "He can certainly get you off your seat", observed Jack, "real twinkle feet stuff". "Yes he's had that funny folky sort of rig ever since when", noted DD happily tapping her right foot to the music, "known by his amazing hat with the huge feather".

Jill had recognised him from a number of features, principally his 'below average height', as the silly PC babbled about, but she also remembered the pictures in the book to recognise someone very distinctly below average height, miniature indeed; then there was the amazing hat and feather he affected which she remembered from the pictures of The West Wind, but; modest of height or not he played a mean concertina.

When there was a lull in the singing Jill invited him to join Jack and she on their table to compliment him. "Why KGR Oh King"?, enquired Jill curiously, not entirely sure of her ground. "How on earth did you know"?, he replied amazed, "I thought I'd escaped 'king' long ago". Jill laughed happy she had hit her mark, "it was the hat and the feather which did it, though the beard's not there any more but I remember the spiky shoes". "Ah", he mused thoughtfully, "The Golden River dried up years ago (as such have a habit of doing so we have to start all over again on a new venture) so when my erstwhile fame as the rich bloke on the block hit the bin because of reduced circs I needed a disguise — no good looking like the pictures in the book if you want anonymity", he chuckled, "but I always rather liked the kit The West Wind wore, more splendid, sort of troubadour like if you get me, so I got rid of the trade-mark beard then dusted off my little squeezebox", dreaming of those emergent days of troubadouring. (To find out 'what he was on about' you'll need a first edition of The Book which has the original magnificent Doyle engravings, green and gold bound).

"It's been pretty good business really", he assured proudly, "*and* it's money I've made myself not just had spouting out of a hole in the rock — much more fun, sort of sense of purpose when you get up in the morning", he assured with the conviction of knowing the truth of it. "It's funny", he mused on telling it for the first time, "because even though I used to play it was only for fun because I didn't need the loot, which was the problem because the money sort of divided me from the audience, above them somehow". Jill laughed gently, "you sound like our Dad, all moral virtues, 'got to do the grind to get the gold'". "Well", he mused, "we may laugh at those old saws but I'm a living proof, life's been far more worthwhile trooping to wherever I fancy there might be a fair, sort of dreaming of the joy I'll make as I step along the road to I know not where — 'a fresh horizon for every day'", he observed putting into words what he'd discovered.

"Then there's the excitement of picking up engagements like this one", he enthused, "because they show I'm not forgotten, I like that, *and* then there's watching the joy on people's faces as you play for them to dance", he continued his mini-saga thoughtfully, "I was never part of anything when I was rich, sort of sat on the outside looking in, but now I'm part of joy wherever I go which is pretty hard to beat". "Why KGR though"?, persisted Jill. "Ah well one doesn't like to abandon all one's past you know", he informed regally, "little memories are fun, sort of attach you to where you've come from but too many awkward questions of the 'where's the Golden River then King' stuff, so I took a steer from a bloke I met doing an act at a fair, he called himself the BFG — KGR looks nice'n squirly on the card don't you think", as he proffered a highly decorated business card.

"You found him *where*"?, asked an incredulous Jack. "Oh why"?, asked The KGR, "you know him?, because I met him at a County Fair doing strong arm stuff, you know, lift you up on my hands to see the view above my head for sixpence — making good money he was too". "Now there's a thing", gurgled Jill quite unable to believe the synergy, "'cause 's'not where we last came across him in Mr Dahl's wonderful books, he had a quite different stunt then — whenever then was as I have no idea where when is now — nor when then was for that matter — people seem to be in the present and the past all at once, in old books one moment then carrying on an intellectual conversation over a pint the next" — "'s'wot Fairy Stories are all about Jilly, 'as any fule kno'", laughed Jack at his sister's perplexed face.

"Ah well", nodded The KGR sagely, "needs must, you know, when funds run low — or have petered out all together as in my case so had to get myself a trade pretty sharp — what was this BFG bloke doing before"?, he enquired keen to find a common misfortune, "seemed a pretty jolly bloke to me". "Oh all sorts of good things", replied Jack authoritatively as The Dragon strolled over to thank the music, "which was why he was called the Big Friendly Giant, because he wasn't your sort of text-book giant holding maidens in castles and laying waste the country, a bit like you're not a text-book dragon Dragon", he sucked the Dragon into the story. "Well perhaps at least a reformed one", chuckled The Dragon. "I'd like to meet him again", mused The KGR, "to find what he did before I met him to compare notes like — see what made him tick as he'd got the dibs fairly rolling in'n I fancy there was more to it than mere size". DD laughed, "oh men such kids really" — "yers", mused Jill happily, "but they don't arf kiss well'n life'd be a dead bore without hot-snoggies".

The 'chaps' collapsed hopelessly, "well at least were worth something in the ladies' olympian eyes", chuckled The Dragon. "Well you may be", pointed out Jack ruefully, "but I haven't got there yet — closed book the whole thing, no runners". DD chuckled conspiratorially with his sister, "I sense good snog material there Master Jack all we need is to find you your own special Jill". Gales of laughter followed this sally in which Jack happily joined.

The KGR, who had been listening intently to the snoggies discussion, mused, "I knew a lady once I fell for but she was too toff for me, when the River ran out she was well above my reach, she was a queen she was but I never found out Queen of where — I came across her at a fair I did some years back", he went all dreamy, "fell smack bang in love, you know the thing". "Not me", assured Jack, "you need to apply to my sister and these two here, sis's way down the field there, loving swains in tow providing all the trimmings". "That good"?, Jill asked The KGR solicitously, giggling all girly at her brother's encomium upon her swain-catching powers as now a master in the quality of good in such matters. The KGR perked up sensing a partner in the quality of good, "yes a real beauty, sort of queenly, she sailed around the fair as everyone fell at her feet, made a real chump of myself trying to catch her attention I was so stricken".

Jill, the main purpose of the adventure returning to her horizon from beneath the fun asked, "where was the Fair Oh King"? "We'd better stick to The KGR bit I fancy, Miss Jill, as King's have kingdoms'n mine's done a bunk, but it was in a funny little place called The Treasure Valley over the mountains from my Golden River, nice'n close for me to start busking when it ran out, all wealth and jollity so rich pickings for the troubadour in training".

"OK all", announced Jill with command, "The whole point of this journey — which started before we met Miss DD with her man — was to find a queen for The King of The Golden River our parents read to us of in an old story book". "Me in a story book", laughed The Music, "that's ripe,

guinea-a-minute stuff — how long ago was the book writ Master Jack"?
"Oh at least a hundred years ago I suppose", replied Jack thinking hard,
"*and* it was about a place called Styria where three bad brothers were horrid
to the poor peasants". "Well well, now there's a thing", chuckled The
KGR, "I remember well me and me mate The West Wind, whom I met
doing a magic turn at a fair, zapping those lice so the peasants could live
happily ever after — seems an age ago but here we are today, minus river
I'll admit, but still in fine form — unfortunately still lacking a queen — I
suppose it's time I gave it some proper attention".

The Dragon chuckled conspiratorially, "yes when I'd done my manly bit
of zapping the bureaus KGR I knew I needed someone to share the joys
with — J&J will tell you the story one day — different game altogether
queen hunting to bureau slaying, had to learn a whole load of new
tricks" — "yers", noted his newly minted wife acerbically, "dropped a few
bricks too — male arrogance, me-want-it stuff'n lusting after the wrong
things — but he came good in the end". "What should one lust after
DD"?, asked the troubadour genuinely seeking advice from a fount of
knowledge in techiques with which he was completely unfamiliar, "I've got
a Queen to catch". "Well it's a mixture of the picture without with what
lies within", she chuckled enjoying herself, "the picture may be tempting
but it's the eternals within which really matter; pictures're ok to look at on
walls but you can't eat'n live them — nor make love work out of them
either", she observed giving her man the firm eye. "Your hunt isn't for a
picture KGR", she continued to cap her lesson, "it's for a person, but many
wonderful things go to make up a person — *persons are definitely not just pictures*", she ran it to a triumphant close. "Ah", replied The Troubadour not
really one whit the wiser but at the least determined not to be waylaid by
pictures.

"Ok", commanded Jill determined to get beyond esoterica to practice,
"how do we find where you met your inamorata KGR, as it's the best place
to start Queen hunting I'd say". "Well, not so easy that", he answered
thoughtfully, "you'd think it would be fixed 'in my head and in my understanding' me being smitten like, but the truth was I fled to escape my own
failure — but there were ladies with very tall hats with long scarves on the
top'n the place was crawling with thin dogs, and another thing too", he
laughed at the memory, "the horses had very queer eyes" — "sort of

poppy-out"?, asked Jack amazed at it all. "Yer 'zackly it Master Jack", The Troubadour enthused on full song at the happy concatenation-of-circs, "then there was a geezer on a really fancy one with a huge red cross who pranced all over the place challenging people with a big sword, real crazy-man he was — definitely out of his head". Jack & Jill collapsed laughing. "I think", mused Jill with a huge grin, "we may have found the place Jack & I call The Land of Thin Dogs — do you remember the song Dragon"?, "Yers artistic assurance knows no bounds", his inamorata filled in proudly, "so he's wrote it all down'n rolled it in a scroll for when we've got the nuptial home — but", she added thoughtfully "I didn't give it a moment's thought till now 'cause The KGR's description told it like my old Gran did as came from there when she was a kid she told me'n I think I know how we might get there if I compare ideas with Mr Music here".

The evening sailed merrily on till everyone was on their knees with dancing then people began drifting home. Our nuptial group made a date to meet The KGR mid-day next day to consider their next move in the Queen-Hunt then everyone crept happily off home. Jack & Jill, sharing a huge bed, snuggled up gurgling with joy as the view ahead. "Do we have the possibility of a Queen"?, wondered Jack. "Well the vibes look pretty good Bro", noted his sister thoughtfully, "as we've got the King's assurance he's smitten so all we have to do is find who smote him — DD's a good start there". "Coo sis", Jack chuckled, "one wedding down one to go which should make a pretty good story for Mum & Dad *and* we won't have to invent it".

As arranged our friends met on the green next day amongst the marquee men dismantling. "From what my old Gran told me", announced DD, "it's about two days march over there", she pointed majestically. "Yeah, I'll go along with that now you mention it", agreed he setting out to find a queen, "something about the direction of the sun as I came away in a whirl seems to fit".

Now the transference from magic place to magic place is always a matter of improbability (magic-carpets the most improbable of all), boring, 'been there before' stuff like airports, sort of all the same, so we'll skip over the travel mechanics to watch the triumphant arrival of our pilgrims.

We have in the cortege, Chaucer style, The KGR (the 'love interest' hopeful for a Queen), Jack & Jill (hopeful of a successful quest as they had come to like The KGR considerably), The Dragon (wondering what thin dogs would really look like in the flesh *and* secretly whether 'the guy with the red cross' was still a goer as he was missing his frying skills a bit), then the capacious DD (wondering what sort of place her Gran had come from). It was definitely a merry party which stepped blithely along the road 'on venture's quest' as, Chaucer style, they swapped stories with Jack & Jill telling their new friend The KGR the unexpurgated story of The Dragon's prowess engineering The Revolution. "My goodness", exclaimed The KGR, "better than The West Wind'n me fixing a couple of lousy terrorists to bring peace ever after, I'd love to have seen the dragon cohorts frying these bureaus you speak of". DD giggled all girly at such fulsome praise of her man, "I'll give you a copy of the epic Sir penned at the end", she laughed happily, "sort of thing them old bards used to cook up to record their exploits, a rollicking good read *and* it rhymes'n scans not like this self-regarding PC drivel they call poetry these degenerate days — you can't go doing epic deeds to that rubbish — you might set it to music KGR, could be good". "Thank you Ma'am for your encomium", chuckled The Dragon, "I'm clearly billed as The Bard hereafter, bit like Poet's Laureate but I'll have to keep the style up not like the nerks who twaddle now".

In due course of stories — it's the stories which matter not the tramping as Mr Chaucer knew — they arrived at the top of a line of hills to look down into a wonderful valley full of goodness and joy; well it would be wouldn't it you wouldn't tramp for 'two days' in a Fairy Story to end in a desert? They set off down into the verdant pastures watered with tinkling rills (look them up as they're the fare of Fairy-Stories) with fruit trees laden with everything you might like, including lollipops, to pass into a lovely plain upon which stood long lines of waving stooks of golden corn. Treading onwards they found a Fair was being held. "Harvest time I fancy", noted the KGR, "merry fruitfullness of the fields with rightful celebration which it was like after we'd sorted The Three Bad Brothers in Styria", he observed wistfully remembering his finest hour.

"I think's we're here boys", carolled DD pointing towards a circle of stalls of the sort her Gran had told her of, "look there are the thin dogs". "Pretty ace", exclaimed Jack in a seventh-heaven, "they're just like they looked in the old missal which started the whole thing off, all we need now is the rest of the fixings". "Oo look", exclaimed The KGR like a kid finding treasure, "there are the ladies with tall hats'n scarves just like I remember the queen person had, I wonder if she's still about", he opined hopefully — *"and"*, noted The Dragon with glee, "howzat for a spiky castle over there on the eminence opposite, just like my old grandad told me they were, we have definitely arrived where it matters", he chortled envisioning all sorts of magical happenings. "So", mused Jack staring round at the sylvan scene", all we need for a Full House is some of those special horses — with perhaps St George". "Who he"?, asked the KGR, — "oh he's your crazy-man with the red cross who used to fight dragons", answered Jack. Jill & DD had wandered off into the stalls to see what might interest ladies of like mind, frills'n furbelows with ribbons'n all the proper fixings for ladies to guarantee the grace of a proper Fair.

The chaps, abandoned by their ladies on the search for higher things, strolled into the centre of the huge ring of stalls seeking amusement, which suddenly stared them in the face in the shape of a large man in shiny, but it must be admitted somewhat dented, armour astride a huge horse waving a sword — rather over-theatrically Jack thought. "He's got the Red Cross I remember", noted the KGR. "Yers", agreed Jack spotting the tatty edges to the surcoat with the grizzled mustache, "he's St George all right, even if a bit past his sell-by date".

"I think courtesy calls", suggested The Dragon, "specially as I don't see any dragons about so let's go to introduce ourselves to cheer the old chap up". They walked briskly over to the Aged Knight to make their introductions. "Well you're a welcome sight Dragon", The Aged Knight cheered, "haven't seen any of your sort for a few years so I'm reduced to a dwindling wage touring round Fairs fighting 'any who will'.

"Been there done that", laughed the KGR as he spread his chest, "and howzatt for a T shirt's I became a troubadour, sort of all round song'n-dance act, when my golden patrimony dried up". "Quite so", agreed St George sadly, for he had introduced himself in proper style so there were no mistakes, "one can't keep body together with soul fighting dragons any more as they've gone all wimpy, seem to be digging potato patches and such stuff — no fight left in 'em so they're just the spice on life's cake now, but you need a trade to earn a crust so I retrained as a chippy — 'man can not live by dragons alone'", he laughed at his magisterial sally as DD & Jill came over to join them. "Yer well", mused The Dragon nettled such as he, all flames'n smoke, was merely the spice for such old crotchets as St George now clearly looked, "spice's orf luv since The Revolution, us dragons desport ourselves in more elevated ways now".

"Such as"?, enquired The Knight interested in the demise of his erstwhile foes. "Oh digging for Victory", answered The Dragon loftily, considering potatoes not a suitable advertisement for the latter prowess of dragons, "with also getting married of course", as he introduced DD. St. George goggled, "I can see some merit in *that*", as DD twinkled her assets splendidly, "I might give *that* some consideration even at my time of life", he noted pointedly still goggling as DD chuckled at The Knight's stares. "Goggling never won fair lady Sir Knight", she assured as St. George blushed, "you need action for that — *and*", she added pointedly, "I just caught the dragon'n spice thing which I consider to be a slur on dragons so you'd better prove your worth to the ladies assembled here Sir Knight — if you're still in the lists for ladies", she challenged provocatively tossing her glove down in front of St George announcing loudly, "For the Honour of Dragons".

There was a sudden hush amongst the near assembled as people realised the truth of the challenge, that in the joke someone might get killed — so Jill sidled over to the horse for a 'word in his ear' as the Knight climbed down to pick up the glove ceremoniously handing it to The Dragon as his lady-love's token in the battle to come. Jack, having a suspicion of his sister's intent, fancied something might be made of this ruccus so he rapidly grabbed a notebook off one of the stalls with which he set off to run a book on the result — offering three-to-two on The Dragon to The Knight's disgust.

"Roll up Roll up Dragon to Fight St George, place your bets with Honest Jacky", carolled Jack mightily trying to raise as much cash as possible with a weather eye to a killing for ulterior ends. Jill fascinated sidled up to Jack as he was taking bets, "just look at those eyes", she observed to her brother, unaware the horse was interested too as a participant, so had approached on the other side. "I heard that", chipped in the horse, "not just eyes but jolly good ears too, the best sort of eyes I'll have you know, 'all the better to see you with', he noted a little sternly, "but you kids shouldn't be cheering on this stunt, even if we've had words young lady, as G ain't as young as he used to be'n if he catches a coronary in the battle I shall be out of a job with hospital bills to boot as the poor old bloke hasn't got a pension".

"Well we didn't start it (when did you ever children?) it was DD (it always is isn't it?) 'cause she tossed down the gauntlet", answered Jack defensively trying to mollify the horse who was a seriously big chap. "Well maybe", The Horse replied, "but women aren't to blame for a lot they do, it just sort of happens they tell me, anyway I don't 'do' women, specially the De-mure & Delightful sort", its eyes goggling even more at the sight of DD dispensing delights to some children she had gone off to buy goodies for from a sweet stall.

When all the preliminary honours had been satisfied with the combatants in proper knightly and dragonly positions as per the old picture books, with a huge crowd assembled by Jack's bookmaking activities, The Dragon suddenly recognised a flaw, "you haven't got a token George'n you can't go into the lists without a token 'tisn't proper, no chivalry to be had token-less". "Allow me", carolled a melodious voice unwinding a magnificent scarf from a statuesque auburn head, "will this do"? "It certainly will Ma'am", thanked The Knight, "I'm much indebted". The KGR went all limp and googly nudging Jill, "that's her, the inamorata person — I got to get my act together so I hope she's forgotten the fawning jackanapes of yesteryear". Jill chuckled at the faintness of men for having herself taken 'the man thing' by-the-scruff-of-the-neck as it were with no fawning about it. "Oh I fancy there've been a fair few KGR", Jill assured admiring auburn statuesque, "but she still seems single so perk up, remember the old faint heart stuff'n I have to congratulate you on your taste as she does look pretty fair".

Having closed his book Jack acted as M/C with a, "are your ready, stand to, begin". There was a good deal of parrying and thrusting, fine theatre stuff for the masses, with The Dragon doing the regulation 'fire'n smoke' thing dragons are billed for. It was apparent The Dragon would earn his betting position as he was clearly fitter than The Ancient Knight but St. George managed some crafty sword-play to draw first blood nicking The Dragon's upper arm to a happy cry from those whose money was on the

Knight — "first blood to G, well done Sir". The Dragon was slightly nettled by missing such simple stuff so focused his attention on the job in hand. More jolly theatre followed then The Dragon got under George's guard to flip him off The Horse. "Ok boys 'senuff, honour satisfied so shake handies like good children", announced The Horse standing protectively over his charge to prevent The Dragon losing his head in his success. There were happy roars of laughter at the 'childish' sally from the wisdom of The Horse as St George stood up to shake hands with The Dragon.

"Well we only did what history's billed us for", claimed St G & The Dragon in unison, "some madam here tossed her glove down egging us on like — after all we are in the Land of Thin Dogs, thass what we-re supposed to do". "Same old story my Grandad told me", observed The Dragon sourly, "Damsels always egging on the knights with a toss of the wimple then a sexy 'dare-you' leer; silly really 'cause if they got killed there would be a dearth of joy for ladies, demure or not — dead knights don't do well in bed I'm reliably informed", The Dragon observed olympically to gusts of riotous applause. "Yer well", chipped in DD laconically standing beside her champion as she deftly bound up the wounded arm with a fancy new scarf she'd just bought, "a bit less of you in bed might be no bad thing, 'frantic antics''s his second name now he's got the bit between is teeth — I wonder if my Gran knew your Grandad D, that would have been a hoot". "Now there's real love", observed The Dragon smiling down at his lady, "using your new scarf to bind me up, thank you my lovely lady".

"Bit between his teeth"?, enquired Jill archly who had come in to congratulate St. George not wishing to seem partial to Dragons, "doesn't seem quite the right simile to me — as an about to be lady that is". "Omigod", gurgled Jack, "I can see life hereafter is going to be spread around with putative bedmates, mind you pick the adventurous type Sis we don't do limp lily back at ours — none of the withered sedge lot". "Certainly not", agreed his sister authoritatively, "pale loiterers don't kiss at all, far less with zing". "Too right", cheered DD, "wimps are wasters in the kissing stakes which is why I ended up with D here — ace stuff when I'd got grabberismus knocked into shape", she crooned happily, with The Dragon simpering inelegantly at the compliment.

Madam auburn-statuesque ambled over to claim her token back. "To whom am I indebted Ma'am"?, asked St. George ceremonially aware he was in the presence of 'The Quality'. "Well", unbent 'er with the auburn tresses smiling broadly, "it's a long story Sir Knight", she began smiling broadly, "I was known as The Queene of The Silver Sluice but since the said Sluice hasn't been silver for a very long time there isn't anything to be Queene over, so I'm just Sylvia now, I run the abandoned children's home you can see under the spiky castle over there".

Jack had one of those wonderful inspirations which flash across the brain occasionally, a sort of concatenation of circumstances which seem to be right, while spotting some small credit into the bargain, "well Ma'am since no-one won the battle I think it would be good for the results of my Book to go to support your home". As many as heard it cheered since Sylvia was a very popular lady doing a fine job for the children — never with quite enough cash. Sylvia clapped her elegant hands ('ooer' gurgled The KGR) wonderfully just like a little girl with a new dress, "oo super, there are a whole heap of lovely things I can do with even a little money, and I think it's time for dinner so why don't you all be my guests in the Pig-Roast marquee".

"Pig-Roast marquee"?, I hear the attentive ask, but no Fairy Story has all the fixings laid out like a theatre, they have to be brought on in stages — which is the fun of it. The aforesaid marquee was vast, as befits a serious Fair, being erected outside the ring. Chefs had been cheffing for some time, the accustomed pigs twirling on their spits over substantial fires, while long tables stood in serried ranks for a proper feast — with one across the top on a daïs for the notables, just like you see in the old pictures. Our friends trooped up to the top where The Queene took her place in the middle as her proper state while our friends found seats wherever their fancy took them looking down on the happy milling people sorting themselves out below. Jill took a little trouble to see The KGR was not sat next to his inamorata as she knew he would get all tangled up so close. Waiters waited up top while those below stood happily serving themselves from the efforts of the chefs at full tilt. Men with flagons gyrated as dinner got underway with a fizz.

There is, in all good stories of this sort, a place for songs or recitations to entertain the happy guests. St. G & The Dragon well aware of such ancient protocols, specially as they were the heroes of the hour, had been colluding with a piece of paper and two pencils scratching their heads then scratching the paper. Mercifully the first course took some time but when the platters were empty they both stood up to an expectant silence with each taking his own verse then singing the last verse in unison;

How I used to love a battle
Said The Dragon to St. George,
I loved to wave a rattle
To drown the idle prattle
Of the peasants, idle cattle
Who just came for silly tattle
And to see some blood bespattle
As you tossed me down the gorge.

Ah Dragon, replied the noble knight
You never needed to take a fright
'cause without you there'd be no fight.
Knights need causes
Without pauses
To their take their stand 'gainst Wrong from Right

So,
St George & The Dragon have fixed it down time,
For the painters, the scribblers and the songsmiths sublime
That neither's demise
Must the media surmise;
For should one hit the bin
There'd be no-one to win
And the fight must go on for eternity's song
Or England would cease to know the Right from the Wrong.

Wild applause greeted this splendid performance as The Dragon, with his paw round the Knight, led them in acknowledging the cheers. Jack, being twinkled at by DD confided to her, "I wondered why there never seemed to be a real corpse". "Ah Master Jack", she smiled engagingly twirling up the twinkle, "theatre's the thing, you learn more in the theatre than outside'n the supply of dragons isn't inexhaustible, anyway men are like kids really just like playing games", as she gave him a convivial hug snuggling him into 'Miss Right'.

At the other end of the High Table earnest enquiries on the eternal subject were underway by a similarly unpracticed male. "How do you catch'em

Miss Jill, the Queenes'n snoggies"?, enquired the KGR, wondering at asking what he would consider a child a question he knew he ought to be a master of at his age. Jill laughed happily, "oh no fawning for me KGR, straight in for the kill, it's snoggies I'm after not intellectual exercise, I just take care about the ones I choose", she observed authoritatively, "but I wouldn't recommend it for a Queene, much more decorum required specially as she's pretty splendid so's probably been grabbed too many times already — sort of 'keep your hands off me you ugly little man' which is not an auspicious start". Jill smiled at the KGR's confusion kindly, "people like to talk about what they do with what enthuses them KGR so the wise suitor would start there then carry on gently offering his services in the cause etc". The KGR gave Jill a surreptitious hug with a conspiratorial smile, "into battle then well armed with a lady's good advice" — "faint heart ne'er won KGR, so have fun, fair's worth the struggle if fair's your thing", assured Jill in return, "amazing things can be achieved with a little 'oil', *and* you can compare notes on the demise of Rivers and Sluices, good common catastrophe stuff, very cementing", she continued twinkling gaily.

"Tell me about the Childrens' Home Ma'am — it sounds a very worthy cause and obviously dear to your heart", as he'n-she sauntered in the evening sun outside the marquee little glasses of lovely sticky wine in their hands. The Queene laughed merrily, "good chat line that Oh King better than most of the jerks who try it on". The KGR laughed splendidly, "well Ma'am I was well advised, er by young Miss Jill over there who runs a smart line in getting high-class snoggies on-demand as she calls them". The Queene giggled like a little girl, "quite a goer then Miss Jill, I remember those early days but then Queendom got in the way when my dad died'n I inherited so I had to lay off the lads — too many got Queene-hunting ideas", she observed at the memories, "but they needn't have troubled as the loot had dried up years ago when earlier generations had failed to maintain The Silver Sluice so destitution's been it ever since". She stopped for a moment to think carefully examining the honest face of her interlocutor, "the trouble was just that, no lads no sprogs", she reflected a little sadly, "I *like* children, they're untainted by the nasties of the world, their little visions open doors for me grown-ups keep closed, so I had the idea of starting The Home for those round here who'd got a bad deal in the parent stakes", she trailed away a little self consciously — "so its not virtue really but my own salvation".

There was a gentle silence which The KGR let stroll for a bit. "That Ma'am is the most honest admission I've ever heard, I like it lots, it's lovely — but how did you know the King moniker since it's been history since The Golden River dried up years ago". "Ah", her eyes glazed a little dreamily, "I liked your music those years ago, lots actually, it got my feet twinkling, made me feel all light'n airy, cares dropped away as I danced, lovely stuff". She laughed a little sheepishly, "now there's an admission from a Queene who's supposed to have given up on chaps — but I made some pretty thorough investigations — even ex-Queenes have some clout so I came up with The King of The Golden River — er ex like me, but I had no method of finding you, anyway 'tis not proper for Queene's to be seen overtly chasing troubadours, even for an engagement, even the enquiries raised a few eyebrows", she laughed merrily restored to her jolly self. "Well strollin in the gloamin isn't going to improve the hunt Ma'am as I'm still very much a troubadour but tell me about The Silver Sluice it sounds as though repairs might be effected — which is a man job", he assured smiling up at her. The Queene found a bench and patted a place by her side in invitation.

"Once upon a time", then burst out laughing, "it sounds like I'm telling a story to the children" – "well Ma'am", he enthused loving every minute of his steady progress, "'once upon a time's the best way to tell a real story — when was it anyway"? "Oh sometime in my great-great-grandfathers day", she replied eagerly now on the hunt for twinkle-feet music, "'bout a hundred and fifty years ago when watermills were water-mills", she informed dreamily thinking back to what her Gran had told her as a child. "My Gran told me the story rather like a Fairy-Story", she continued enthusiastically, "lots of little embroidered bits to make it fun, so I've remembered it; he was the miller for miles around, like the family had been for generations — they'd been such good friends to the people, giving good weight and not adulterating the flour with all the good stuff so many years before him a local King had asked the Fairies to bless the mill so it could survive to perform for his people whatever happened", she paused to get the story right. "My Gran told me he had asked The Fairies to arrange once a year the mill-race would run silver for an hour on one day — but you had to be prepared to catch the silver as no-one knew when it would happen — so afterwards The Mill became called The Sliver Sluice".

"Now that Ma'am", remarked The KGR, "is a real Fairy-Story, proper fairies making good stuff but the humans have to get their act right too or the magic stops, I like it — so why the demise Ma'am"? "Well", observed The Queene sadly, "the humans failed their billing, just assumed it would always happen however casual they were — but I guess Fairies don't like being taken for granted". "Indeed not Ma'am", he assured wisely, "no-one does, so where did the plot finally fall apart"? "Well", she re-engaged, "The Sluice drove the water-mill by turning The Great Wheel, but my great-great-grandad, as my Gran tells it, got all modern'n thought he could dispense with the Sluice by putting a steam engine in to drive the Mill — cost of maintenance was his excuse, so my Gran said". "Silly man", noted The KGR thoughtfully, "you have to maintain anything, care for it, or it stops working which is no less true of steam engines, becauseI bet paying a resident engineer to keep it up to scruff cost him a packet he hadn't bargained for". "Gran didn't have that bit in the script", The Queene laughed happy at the wisdom, "but in his enthusiastic modernity he let the Sluice go to rot, unused, no need to maintain it any more". "Hmm, real kick-in-the-teeth stuff for Fairies", observed The KGR with some feeling being aware of the frailties of Fairies, "the real 'I don't need you any more' act'n no-one likes being redundant — we all need to be needed, even Fairies". The Queene smiled, "bit of a philosopher Oh King" — "well not really philosopher Ma'am", he smiled in return, "just a careful observer of the Human Condition, which has come from being a troubadour because you watch people while you're playing, the dancing ones, the sitting out ones, the lonely ones, it takes all sorts at a good country dance you know — the interactions between people thing", he trailed away thoughtfully.

"Yes", he mused, "interaction between them but you're on the outside, they only care for what you provide, leaving you in your own desert alone". He went quiet, "the trouble with troubadouring, of whatever sort I fancy Ma'am, is your're the king of the party, loved by all, which is fun, but you haven't got one of your own to love". He looked gently at the lovely lady at his side then drew a bow at a venture, "I fancy Ma'am the children have you feeling needed, am I right"? The lovely lady flumped a little then snuggled a little closer, "it's the truth of it, yes", she admitted wryly, "but it's a mirage really just as you've found because though loved by all there's not one of your own — you're above and outside, not within".

A little silence lay between them gently smoothing edges. "You're right KGR", she sighed snuggling further, "it's too easy to be a troubadour in life beguiled by the fame freakery of people fawning, but it insulates you from any you might make your own, like being a Queene does because everybody wants some of you — but not you". "Just so Ma'am", he replied gently returning the snuggle, "always on the move, known far'n wide, but no home of your own — what you need is a Man Ma'am", observed The KGR gently, "someone to love and look after and love and look after you'n all that snoggy stuff", he assured picking up one of her hands from her lap then looking her square in the eye; "it's the greatest human need you know, even for Queenes, but silly people think they're above such stuff, 'wonderful independent me' rubbish, so only too often end up walking alone *and* Ma'am from having done the alone bit too long I know 'together's better than apart' — even though I haven't been there yet".

She sighed gently then snuggled a good deal more, "that's real philosopher stuff King'n you're right, 'I need a man' — men fix things'n do things" — "good ones even cook'n do the washing up too", he tossed in as a little man-ad, "*and* they can be very snuggly'n comforting when required as well", he chuckled happily. She abandoned her queenely dignity completely, "really, washing up and cooking, I've never had those offered before — and you say they can do the super-snoggy thing too Oh King"?, she enquired perking up hopefully. "Sure do Ma'am", he assured fervently not wanting essentials to get lost in the sales-pitch, "very practical stuff super-snoggy, just like washing up its got to be done not just thought about, so I suggest we mend the Sluice first to prove my credentials, will that do, oh and I'll play you your own special jig, it's called The Queene's Jig — howzat Ma'am"? The Queene gave him what he thought was a very fond look which raised the old manly hopes quite a bit, "it certainly will Oh King, so what's next"?

The King laughed uproariously, "for an avowed spinster Queene Ma'am, you're certainly pressing on and since we're both in like case let's" — "oh yes please", she replied happily, "I haven't had such fun in ages, all sorts of things might happen" — "which is the fun of Fairy Stories Ma'am, 'the impossible made good', but to make it happen you have to make it happen and for major restoration projects of such as Sluices we'll need a team". "Oh, you mean lots of men", she gurgled enjoying herself immensely while thinking a little teasing, sort of 'not yet on the hook stuff,' might be a good idea for zealous Kings upon ladies bent. "Indeed Ma'am, lots of choice for lonely Queenes though The Dragon's already been bagged as you know'n I have no idea about George's intentions, and er Jack's a little little yet awhile, but let's assemble the fixers then see how we do — lots of water to flow under the bridge yet Ma'am", he quipped merrily. "Nice one Oh King" The Queene complimented, "but let's get it flowing through the Sluice eh"? "Touché Ma'am", he accepted, "so to work, I'll go to hoist in a few hands, meanwhile sleep tight and sweet dreams of Sluices doing their Silver act once again", as he raised the hand to his lips to give it a reverent kiss as she rose to go, "I've quite a gallop 'over the hills ands far away' so had better be on my way", she smiled as they separated.

The KGR stepped briskly off with starry eyes, pretty pleased with his initial endeavours; 'the rest' he thought, 'should be falling off a log stuff, assemble team, do job, claim lady'. Sauntering casually into the marquee adopting unconcern as his signature he wandered amongst the late revellers to find Jack & Jill tucked up under a blanket in a corner then D^3 in deep conversation with St. G over the last of the sack, warming their feet in the embers of the roasting fires. "Ok KGR", greeted DD twinkling happily as she liked to keep the men round her on their feet, "how did the first assault go"? Casual was it, The KGR had decided, no spilling the beans as no-one was going to believe a pint-sized troubadour, however good, was likely to have made such progress with a statuesque Queene; he only brewed tall tales for his singing to entertain but here the facts of chickens being counted but not yet hatched impinged, *and* there is nothing so humiliating as to blow the trumpet then have it snatched from one's hand by another. Maintaining his detached Olympian air he answered DD airily (which didn't convince her one bit as she could see stars like any well attuned woman), "well it's a Sluice-mending thing", he announced casually, "a certain ancient working artifact lies in desuetude, unloved, so needs a rebuild before it'll run Silver again, which'll need a team — so I'm on a recruiting drive".

"Man may dream but he needs his mates to make it happen eh"?, twirled DD wickedly. General laughter followed, "well, as I noted earlier", remarked St. G loftily, "I've retrained as a chippy'n I got my tools in my frail on the Horse's crupper, never know when a mended door or table'll require its legs fixed after a hostelry-brawl to earn us aging fighters a bob, so gimme the rate mate". The laughter continued merrily at this acquisitive sally from the aged Knight — but he was to be sadly disabused. "Charity, G", noted The KGR severely, "starts at home *and* chivalrie is all about serving ladies in distress, or did you sleep through that bit in knight-school". D³ ended in a helpless heap laughing so much, "sorry G we're not laughing at your discomfort, it's just the whole damn thing's so funny'n we're with you KGR so when do we start"? "A.S.A.P", he replied briskly getting in before the joke-line, "but I'll have to get a site-map from Madam first".

"Oh I know where the Mill is", chirped up the expectant chippy. no whit discomfited and rather liking the adventure of showing off his skills to his new-found friends, specially in a lady's service — you never know what might happen which was better than standing around at fairs looking faded and goofy waiting for something to happen. "You in for this DD"?, The KGR asked for final confirmation. "Sure thing KGR", she cheered equally looking for some Fairy Story, "where my man goes I go, hell or high-water notwithstanding *and* I'm a pretty mean hand at al-fresco nosh too" — "that's my gal", gurgled The Dragon almost asleep, sinking under the solace of the sack. "Ok lets grab some sleep", suggested The KGR, "as I expect Sluices will require much of us on the morrow", picking up his travelling bag to lay out his kip-sack at the edge of the fire, carefully putting on some more logs so it would still be in shape for cooking breakfast.

Tomorrow, as all tomorrows should be in well tuned Fairy Stories when action's afoot, was a corker; 'hello clouds hello sky', birds tweetling briskly building nests, trees greening everywhere as a little morning breeze riffled the larger ones' leaves deliciously lit by the rising rays of the smiling sun, who definitely had his hat on. "This is it boys'n girls", chuckled the KGR as he looked outside, "how're you on breakfast DD"? — "well us travelling ladies carry certain essentials with us and there's still quite a bit on those pigs, so toss the kettle on the fire KGR while G tells us where the Mill is". "Hm", remarked The KGR to the world at large, "pretty smart lady, never mind the size, very practical, eye to the forward view, I like it", he smiled at DD dextrously slicing bits off the still warm pigs slapping them between some of last night's bread which she had purloined for the purpose. "Pig-butties boys", she cheered pouring the kettle over the tea in the pot, "I'll go wake up our children over there as I have a shrewd suspicion they both have hidden talents to contribute to the enterprise afoot so are definitely part of the team".

Jack & Jill, who had, ex parental guide, sucked at the sack a bit round the camp fire encouraged by story-telling company, were a little groggy but the tea with substantial butties got them back on their feet as The KGR opened out the plot. Jill, who had watched her school-mates on the game, spotted the stars in the KGR's eyes so winked at DD knowingly who gave her a convivial smile in return; 'so that's alright then, Queenes in the offing' she giggled to herself deciding to keep it as girly knowledge, "so", she observed to her brother, "Queenes for Kings is it then, seems like we've got a plot brother Jack". Jack was a little groggier than his expert sister so was having trouble assembling some wits, "but we've got to re-build a sluice'n what's a sluice when its at home pray, sounds a bit mammoth for a group of hippies with two kids", he noted a little morosely. "Careful who you're calling hippies", chorused the grown-ups, "there are many and various skills available for this venture within this eclectic group of which we expect some from you two — so let's focus".

"How far's The Sluice G"? asked The Dragon. "Oh, only a morning's brisk walk", he replied airily having his Horse, "it's sort of underneath the spiky castle because the river which drove it comes out of the mountains, *and* if I do a bit of trawling I might borrow some hooves for the rest of you for the journey as I'm known around here; they would help with hauling big stuff when where there too". There was a little silence as an errant uncompleted question flitted round inside The Dragon's head, "er what's this King thing exactly Miss Jill, it's sort of flitted about before'n I've never asked but it's time we had the unexpurgated fax, from the horse's mouth, if we're going to fix him up with a throne and a Queene as seems to be the plot". Jill raised an eye to the KGR, "shall I be your horse KGR as I know the story and are you OK with the incog hitting the bin among friends Oh King"? "Why not", he addressed agreed, "for truly I've got a little fed up with being what I'm not, so tell-em Miss Jill".

"Well his real name", she began with a lift, "is The King of The Golden River, but like our new friend The Queene his patrimony of The Golden River is ex, er ceased to flow he tells me, but the lack of flow bit must have come after the story Mum & Dad read to us" — "stories in books mixed up all together with people again", mused The Dragon. "Indeed", agreed

Jill, "which is where we're at, so then he did some mighty deeds in a place called Styria ridding it of three lousy brothers who were terrorising the populace then it appears his Golden River gave up the ghost so the free-lunches did too so he had to turn his hand to creating some income — will that do you Oh King"? "Surely Miss Jill that's the nub of the thing", he chuckled remembering back to the vicissitudes of making a new life out of a hobby, "but, as I was telling Miss Jill & Master Jack at the dance last night, life's far more fun as a troubadour, you get amongst people and every day's a new day with fresh adventures — people like the music too'n its nice to be liked for making people happy".

DD looked admiringly at The King spotting virtues she had not considered before — perhaps pint sized but heart bigger than the moon for having been shown a different view of life by a bloke who genuinely didn't seem to regret his lost fortune, "money not required for joy then Oh King"?, she enquired. "Indeed not Ma'am", he assured, "I found the gold insulated me from joy by getting between me and the people *and* you can't buy joy you give it then it comes back to you", he finished pensively, "yer thass 'bout what I've found troubadouring instead of laying about scooping up gold".

"Ok", announced Jill, "philosophy over let's march, there are Queene's to catch to requite Love's young dream" — "nice to be young again", crooned The King happily shouldering his bag. St. George had the requisite horses by their halters so all merrily mounted. The fun bit for Jack & Jill was sharing a huge horse who, seeing his charges were not experts, agreed with St. G to behave so, as G put it to him, 'caracolles're orf mate'.

We'll forgo the travel bit again as it tends to be tedious, all that boring scenic description stuff just passing by like scenery from train windows so gone in a flash — not contributing to the plot. Fine if there are stories to tell, but our friends needed a rest from stories after 'the night before' which they had done to a considerable turn as stories are what camp fires are for; on arrival though the scene was well worth a quick descrip. Laid out before them was a range of fine high mountains for a backdrop, the scene-painting bit of the theatre; spiky castle in fine repair near the bottom commanding magnificent views with residents attached who wound down the hill in cavalcade to welcome the group, just as you've seen in old picture books;

splendid waterfall spouting out near the top of the mountains which cas-
caded down to make the river below which ran along the foot of the
range — then underneath The Mill. Standing at the entrance to The Mill
itself, framed by the high double doors in best Arthurian Burne-Jones
mode, long blue and gold dress slashed with cream flowing round her an-
kles, auburn hair unleashed being teased by the breeze, high hat with pen-
dant scarf imperially on head — stood The Queene.

"Hells-Bells, that's some Queene'n no mistake", drooled The Dragon forgetting his lady by his side — "yes dear", admonished his lady through
clenched teeth, "as you say some Queene but don't be forgetting which
side your bread's buttered, anyway", she laughed to reduce the attack, "she
hasn't got the frontage". "No Ma'am", replied The Dragon contritely, "just
observing for Art's sake you know, beauty should be saluted where
beauty's found I've heard you say". "Ok D touché", she proffered peace,
"you're right, just overcome by a quick pang of jealousy at quite so much
at one blast — I bet she's a goer, I wonder if our modest mate The KGR
can cope with all that". "She", announced Jack from his wide reading, "is
the Faerie Queene for sure, Mr Spenser would approve of her, Elizabethan
in the best style". Jill, as starry eyed as The Dragon, nudged Jack conspiratorially, "have we bitten off more than The KGR can chew Jack"?, she
asked sotto-voce. "Oh I fancy there are hidden talents in our mate The
King", he replied, "'if music be the food of love's' on his side for a start
then if we can fix the Sluice all the rest should be roses — *and*", he added
as an after thought, "I don't suppose she got togged up like that just to
welcome the Sluice Menders, looks like girly intent to me — I've spotted
it when your Jim Barnes's in sight", he guffawed smiling fondly at his emergent sister who laughed happily recognising the truth of her brother's observation, – "should be a whale of a game, ring-side seats in a Romance,
what fun", she cooed.

St. George was seen observing the vision fronting the doors ahead with a
creased forehead. "Well Master Jack, if she's The Faerie Queene I'm billed
as The Red Cross Knight'n I have a feeling my days of squiring ladies quite
as posh as that are over, Mr Spenser notwithstanding'n never mind The
King's prior claims either", he noted a little sadly, "I'm only really good for
some make-believe at fairs with a bit of chipping now". "Fret not G",
chipped in DD gently, "there are more fine ladies in the sea than out of it

and fixing things is a sure road to the hearts of the best, so let's see what some Sluice restoration can do".

They joined the Queene who lead them round to the side of The Mill where the river flowed. There was some substantial ancient stonework but of the timber work which had made the Sluice a sluice there was very little evidence. "I've got an old picture of how it was", cheered The Queene, "done by a famous artist in my great-grandfather's day when it was still something of an attraction". "Splendid", cheered St George, "far easier with a picture, I can cope with a picture, pictures'n drawings are it for the creative chippy", he glowed keen to make his mark with the Queene as something more than a faded warrior. "Come inside to see and get fed'n watered", she gently took command in best hostess style, "I'll get my groom to take the horses round to the stable to be rubbed down and fed".

Inside round a huge table they sat down to comestibles briskly provided by the staff as The Queene unhung the picture from its pride of place over the fireplace. Mercifully it was a thing of some size by a chap who had been keen on the details so, while forking down refreshments with some 'Vin-de-Moulin' which came from Madam's substantial winery in the grounds, they discussed. "May I have some large paper with a pencil and rubber Ma'am", asked St George, "then we can get down to a bit of design". Waving sandwiches as pointers everyone crowded round the emergent carpenter who started work on a design created from the picture which began to take shape as the afternoon drew onwards — whose facility it was recognised, drew strength from the quality of Madam's wine. Lots of questions were asked of Her Majesty, as all had come to think of her after the splendid welcome display, to tease out what she might have been told about its workings. With these and some knowledge of Jack's from old books a finished design was achieved by the evening. "For what we have here Ma'am", observed our aspiring designer a little cautiously, "we are going to need some substantial timber, er and some considerable fastenings, with bigger tools than I carry with me — er we'll need a crane", he noted a little disconsolately viewing the dimensions of the huge timbers, "didn't see a crane-hire joint on the way either", he noted wrinkling his brow. "Crane with a brain do you"?, asked The King with a subtle smile. "Yer wot"?, replied the puzzled knight, now seriously troubled about the possibilities of the whole enterprise. "I have just the thing", chuckled the King a little triumphantly, "if I can find him, I fancy Madam saw him last, I'll enquire at source".

As they sat down to dinner The King, as he came to be addressed by all realising a match was in the offing, quietly assumed the organising role enquiring of Her Majesty where all the necessaries could be had, then cheering on the team with the well-known words, 'there is nothing, absolutely nothing quite like messing about with Mills' to much applause from Jack & Jill who knew the source. "My Reve will know all those things Oh King", she replied, "I'll introduce you too him tomorrow, there's nothing he doesn't know about fixing and sourcing things". "We'll need some muscle Ma'am", noted her inamorata, "a crane George called for as its all rather big — just happens I know the very chap, calls himself the BFG, met him at a Fair but need to find him now — do you have any clues"?

"Ah him", she replied blushing gently at the memory then going a little googly, "met him at the same Fair — cool dancer, light on his feet like elephants I'm told, but on reflection he was a bit big even for me", she perked up enveloping the other ladies, "big chaps are tempting to an active girl — one can but dream". DD collapsed laughing, "been there done that Ma'am and I do assure you, though dreams might play otherwise, size isn't all, er disproportionate size that is", recovering ground briskly at a searching look from her man who laughed gaily at the Queene's dilemma. "Your Mum was right Miss Jill", she joked, "fickle lot women, one moment a giant then the next a dwarf" — "mind who you're calling a dwarf Miss Megas", chid the King, but happy to have a confirmation of his understood place in the Queene's affections, "it's not PC you know, according to the rules I'm a person whose height is of modest attainment". Jill giggled hugely at this sally, "Dad would love that, he has great fun making up pisstakes of PC prattle". "One may not be the BFG's size", continued The King smiling sweetly, "but what matters is did one get the lady — am I right Oh Queen"? Her Majesty blushed caught on the hop by The King's little challenge.

And so it was. Trees were felled to be sawn by a local saw-mill, smiths were given commissions for huge drills and big long bolts with fancy bits of ironwork for hinges and the moving bits as everyone did their bit. DD was despatched to haul in the BFG being, as she had avowed, impervious to big chaps, for which she went to chat up the Reve in her best twinkling style so got copious direction to his likely whereabouts, as the Reve had hired him in the past. "I used to fancy him once", admitted the Queene to DD on his arrival, "I don't believe the twaddle about size you gave us the other evening, just look at his packet ducky, it's what I've been missing for years". "Yers", admitted DD, "been dreaming about it all the way home, and as for those pecks, really lift you to heaven those — all the squit you get from the purse-lips about 'size doesn't matter's' plain balls's the bigger the better is it for Dragons — 'n Queenes too I fancy", she trailed away lost in lust. "Thanks for your support on the night though DD", added The Queene, "because I know my future's with The King as I can't get his music out of my head, and I don't want him losing faith — so mum's the word, Ok"? — "sure thing Ma'am, girly secrets even from girly children".

With the BFG installed as haulier and placer work proceeded briskly as parts arrived on site. The girls acted as messengers, cooks, feeders of the men and cheerers on while 'Master Jack' as he came to be known, proved a curiously good solver of the problems which continually popped up — looking from the outside in he could often see things those deep in the involvement missed.

The Queene watched entranced as The King hefted into the work managing the whole with consummate skill and good cheer while piling in muscle where needed. "I need a man", she sighed to DD on the quiet as they were sitting out gazing entranced by 'men on the go', with some impressive fitting going on. "His music's pretty captivating, DD, but all that managing'n fixing's intoxicating stuff for chicks". "Seems to match the BFG in 'the what a chap should have' department", observed DD salaciously, eyeing the KFG's smart close-fitting hose, "but you have to go buy it to find out Ma'am", as both girls collapsed in girly giggles happy together.

With such fine organising the water was flowing through The Sluice again within three weeks to much celebration at a very handsome job indeed. To make sure the placation of The Fairies should be complete, our team had faithfully re-created The Great Wheel, with the relevant gear to properly direct the Sluice's power. "Looks just like the old picture", complimented her Majesty pleased as Punch. "Well I should hope so", chid the knightly carpenter a little nettled by the implication it might have arrived that way by chance, "it's what us skilled tradesmen aim for you know Ma'am, verisimilitude, no good if it's not like the drawing as customers tend to refuse payment". Everyone fell about at the old man's pride in his new vocation, cheering him on. "We'll need a new horizon for the old bloke", noted Jill to Jack quietly, "now he's finished his great work life's going to feel very empty as he gets forgotten in the new joy" — "he'd look terribly sad just riding off over the hills", her brother agreed, — "*and* we can't have him traipsing round any more fairs at his age as The Horse told me", noted his sister, "I'll mingle with her Majesty".

St George, designer in charge, looked at The King enquiringly as they sat out by The Sluice admiring their handiwork, "it may flow boss but how are we going to know it's still Silver"? The King sat on the shining new parapet for a moment thinking — it was a pertinent question — water was fine but not exactly the aim of the exercise. "Fairies", he mused thoughtfully, "it stopped because the Fairies felt their gift had been abandoned — you know George I think this is a matter of faith". "Faith isn't going to convince 'er indoors", observed the aged saint laconically, "it's she who's laid out all the cash". "I'm not so sure", replied The King with mounting assurance, "she's a sassy lady, knows about these things I fancy, been brought up with them; look at it this way G, we've done the Fairies proud, beautifully rebuilt their ancient gift and *I* believe in Fairies", he announced proudly. "*I* think, the Fairies have been watching us", he continued winding some 'faith' into the discussion, "so'll be thanking us for our efforts to restore their Sluice, so *I* think if we're patient it will work again as it used to, specially as I'm sure they know what the money'll be used for". A smile of vision crept across the old man's face, "why don't we have a blessing ceremony, sort of commissioning thing KG — then it's up to the Fairies" — "nice one G, I'll go fix it with the team".

Later that evening, as a full moon rose majestically over the Eastern horizon to face the sun sinking in an aureole of golden glory in the West, all our friends with all The Queenes' retainers and the Children from The Home assembled in a large circle round the wonderful Sluice, its waters pouring smoothly through its shining new gates. The Reve had closed down the steam engine so its snortings no longer disturbed the silvan evening — while his hand proudly rested on the long lever which directed the flow of the Sluice through either the free leet or the new Great Wheel. The Queene had donned her finest robes looking all the way to the top of her hat every inch a Queene of the Faëries as silence fell on the expectant crowd awed by her magnificence. When the last rustle has ceased she produced a long decorated wand from the folds of her over-cloak, raising it aloft she sang, "Oh Faëries we hereby give you back your ancient gift so pray you may bless it and those who have built it as you did in days-of-yore". As she finished she waved the wand over the waters then incanted, "bless these waters so they may flow in plenitude to grind the fruits of the earth for the people as your Faërie forbears endowed".

The Reve threw the lever then to wondering gasps the Great Wheel began to turn as the gentle rumbling of the stones echoed through The Mill. Suddenly a little voice shouted, "Oh look Ma'am, look Ma'am the water's sparkling silver". There was disbelieving chatter, "it's just the moon reflected in the water Jackie", advised a voice. "No it's not", he cried jumping up and down, "look Ma'am I can see real silver". The Queene dislimned then looked — then lowered a salver she had brought against the chance, to find it filling with silver flakes. "Out of the mouths of babes comes faith", she chanted, "do you believe in Fairies Jackie, "Oh yes'M sure do", he assured, "it's Fairies makes the nice things happen'n we've given them back their Mill, proper as it was before, so they given us back the Silver". There was a stampede into the Mill to find adequate jugs and bowls anything which could receive the silver flakes pouring out of the sluice mingled with the water, while The King organised a decanting relay piling the sifted flakes into sacks remembering the old story the flow would only last for one hour every year.

The moon rose steadily lighting the happy collectors as the sacks of flakes filled enticingly — then as suddenly as it started the silver stopped as the water ran clear to a huge sigh — part pity for its cease but mostly at the re-birth of The Fairy Magic. The show over everyone trooped into the Mill for hot toddies which DD & Jill had gone inside to arrange. There was an awed silence as the men staggered in with the sacks of silver which were placed reverently before Her Majesty. The King had decided this was the moment, if ever there was to be one, so stepped forward playing an introduction on his concertina, he sang in his fine melodious voice;

Pray Queene be Mine, as I'll be thine
For ever and alway,
It's not The Sluice's Silver sway
Which grows my love for you each day;
Love's built on finer arts than gold
As all the ancient bards have told
'Tis you, not yours, I wish to hold,
From now until the ends of time.

Oh Faërie-Queene, my mate supreme
Pray join me in life's shining dream
The fount of Love's true treasure.
Let's tread on high
Let's prance the sky
For now's our chance to live up nigh
The Cherubim and Seraphim
Whose wondrous songs eternal hymn
The joy of Love's best measure.

I'll ways of Troubadouring shun
I'll serve you, love you, nor succumb
To falsehood, cheating or the dumb
For you I'll make life gorgeous.
We'll tread Life's paths as homophone
Our Hearts and Minds and Bodies tone
Built tight together — not alone
From two to one, harmonious

Polyphony with Harmony
Shall be our loving matrimony
Forswearing ancient patrimony
We'll build our own endeavour.
We'll show the way
We make the hay
So all may say
Conjoint, conjugal pleasure.

So

Lady fine wilt thou entwine
Your life with mine?
So hand in hand
We stride the strand
Entwisted like the eglantine.
No whit perturbed

Whatere's absurd
We press on up
With gods to sup
To be as one in clouds sublime.

To you my Queene I plight my trow,
There, Lady Dear, you have my vow,
We've been in deserts for too long
We need to join The Race's throng,
Make pilgrimage together.
You are, my dear, my heart's desire,
You are my Life's eternal fire,
Horizon, sky with sun and moon
For you I'll make a shining boon
Always and forever.

Oh Gorgeous Queene wilt thou be mine?
I need your Love for all of time;
I'm Ill equipt, my life's unshipt
Without my hand, sureclaspt, in thine.

There was a wonderful roar of applause and happy cheering — it was a damn good tune too. Then The King raised his hand and addressed The Queene in the most formal tones, "Will Your Majesty of the Silver Sluice (restored) marry me The King of The Golden River (defunct)"? The Queene, tears of joy trickling down her cheeks, smiled enormously then moved to stand beside him with an arm round his waist, "Oh you chump of course I will, silver restored or gold defunct, as I've just loved you doing all those wonderful manly things for me — er and I've dug the music for ages". There was immediate cheers with cries of 'Speech' and the usual jollity on such occasions with The Queene smiling blissfully hanging on to 'her' King. Jill stepped forward holding up a hand to request a hearing, "Ma'am, now you are going to be a married woman with a man to look after", roars of laughter at the incongruous picture of a domestic Queene, "would you take our wonderful friend, your designer, the noble St George, history personified and worshiped down time, as the new Head of The Children's Home"? There were further mighty cheers, specially from the children who had all rather taken to the splendid old knight as he'd taken much trouble to explain to them what he was doing and why. Her Majesty, having been mingled with, acquiesced gratefully — indeed joyfully too as she could not think of a better solution. She had known for some time The

Home needed new blood, even if it was old blood — a fresh view to give it new impetus.

As everyone mingled happily at so many wonderful outcomes The Dragon sidled up to the Saint who was sitting quietly with Jill contemplating his new state while thanking her for her intervention. "No PC'n H&S rubbish now George", admonished The Dragon. "My Dear Dragon", replied the noble knight mildly offended at such a supposition, "since when did saints do safety pray — but at least we're alive and still kicking which is more than can be said of most in these degenerate days". *"My* emporium will only breed Knights and Ladies of the future with all the Virtues of Old Chivalrie", he noted a trifle stiffly, "you can't bring up kids to take their proper place in The Human Race with all that Safety crap, they never find out what safety is because they live in a sterile bubble — no proper Ladye would wed a sterile bubble". "Absolutely not", agreed Jill fervently laughing hugely with relief at the success of the whole affair. "What shall you call it under your new guidance George"?, asked a slightly chastened Dragon inventing way-out possibilities, hoping to get asked. The Knight sat thinking for a moment then he said, "let's keep it simple but grand, no questions implied in the title, so we'll call it just The Seminary, I think Her Majesty will approve".

Her Majesty was saying her thank-you's to the BFG with an arm through his. "I hope you're not disappointed BFG, er me marrying The KGR, even though I admit lusting after you those years ago, er packs'pecks'n such-like". "Thank you for the compliment Ma'am", he laughed wonderfully, "but Lust's no base for Love", giving her arm a squeeze, "we'd never have made a proper go of it as I'm not Queenely material at all, *and* I've got a few more wild oats to sow yet", he rumbled with a wry wink, "I'm not really the settling type but don't you worry Ma'am I'll find myself a similar sized gypsy some day then I'll come to introduce her". The Queene laughed splendidly as she stepped on tippy toes to give him a thank-you kiss, "I'll like that BFG".

Jack was sitting in a corner delighting in the propinquity of DD who was gently twinkling for his benefit. "What are we going to do for a mate for George", he asked her, "he'll need one to run the home and look after him, seminaries always have matrons", he chuckled. "Oh don't you worry", cheered DD, "Dame Fortune smiles on such as he you'll see, the ladies'll be swarming now he's given up all that prancing and posing stuff — can't make a home like that *and* he's now a man of consequence'n he'll look pretty good once he's got spruced up — ladies'll go for that, trust me"! Jack laughed, "I'm clearly going to have to get this lady thing sorted out aren't I DD"? "Well you aren't a proper member of The Human Race till you join with full membership Master Jack", she advised, "and full membership is family membership as our King sang to his Queene". She looked fondly at 'Young Jack', not so young really, just needing to harness his body to the Farëie joys he made in his head, "you keep close to your Sis, Jack, she seems to be getting on pretty well'n I know you're close, she's a helping sort, I've seen it".

Well that's about it, everyone's accounted for in joy's Fairy circle — except we mustn't forget The Horse who had, after all, preserved the niceties of The Battle. Next morning early Jack & Jill ambled out into the pastures where he was to be found gambolling happily amongst a coven of pretty fillies. "Isn't my boss's promotion grand", he greeted, "your work I fancy Miss Jill for which I'm most grateful as the gloss has gone off Fairs lately — no more Jehu in the lists for me". "It's what friends are for Horse dear", she observed gently, "so I mingled with Her Majesty, I'm pleased your glad, not worried by retirement"? The Horse laughed mightily, "well would you be Miss Jill if you were me with all these lovely ladies about doing their queeneing act"? Jack chuckled happily, "I really will have to get this lady thing up to speed but I see your point, salvation for Horses". "Mind you", noted The Horse Olympically, "I shall only be courting the ones with the right eyes, got to keep the breed up, no rare-breed stuff for me, house duty you know", he laughed splendidly. "Ones"?, enquired Jill archly. "Well you know us Horses is polygamous Miss Jill so no prissy-lips please, isn't that so ladies", he addressed his harem. "Sure is", they carolled happily eyeing their about to be chap with pride. Jack & Jill, laughing fit to bust, retired back to The Mill for breakfast happy with such a splendid series of outcomes to their venture.

There was a wedding to come of course, which was arranged for a week later in the grounds of The Silver Sluice. We need not grind it small but there was a speciality du Maison-Mill laid on by The Queene who ran a breeding kennel of Thin Dogs from which she earned a small emolument by supplying the gentry round about as pets to appear in their portraits, their proper hunting days being past. Very proud of her pack she took Jack & Jill on a special tour of the kennels. "Gosh, they're pretty ace Thin Dogs Ma'am", complimented Jack marrying what he was seeing with the minute picture which had started their first adventure, "they look just like the ones I saw in an ancient missal we saw in a castle Ma'am". "Ah they're Talbots, Master Jack", she informed authoritatively, "which are just the same as the ones the monks painted". "Oh, I thought Talbots were those mythical heraldic chaps who held up armorial shields", replied Jack keen on truth. "Well indeed they were", answered the Queene with some pride, "but they were real as well and what you see are the only survivors of a long extinct line". "Oh wow", murmured Jill awed yet again by everything seeming to be happening in different times together, "endangered species then — but what about the ones we saw rushing round the village Ma'am". "Not endangered in The Treasure Valley Miss Jill", The Queene assured, "those ones, though getting a little mongrel through unplanned cross-breeding, came from my kennels here so there's a constant supply of pure blood". Jack smiled enormously, "so it's Thin Dogs for ever Ma'am as I can't get used to the idea of them being Talbots somehow as Talbots wouldn't fit into The Dragon's victory epic — which your new King's going to set to music when he's got a moment". "Indeed", murmured the Queene dreamily, "quite something with the music is my man" — "well you mustn't let him drop it amongst the pressures of domestic bliss Ma'am", advised Jill, "or the magic'll melt". Everybody fell about happily as the Queene put an arm round each to lead them back, "you know you wonderful two we must celebrate this union with a splendid dance each year on its anniversary, call it a permanent invitation to The Silver Sluice for a dance to the greatest of them all — The Ineffable KGR".

Behind The Silver Sluice The Reve maintained a fine dog-track to exercise the Queene's prides so he could grade their speed to seed the best amongst the rest for those who liked to join her for racing days. He also had the necessary hare breeding scheme to ensure good sport for the dogs. "Some don't make it", noted the Reve airily to Jack who had gone over to investigate keen on running another book on the outcomes, "get eaten by the really fast dogs but it's an honourable death, survival of the fastest, you know Master Jack". "I do indeed", he replied, "very Darwinian". The racing was a huge success, with everybody cheering the hares all of whom survived the day. Jack made a fine book out of which the astute DD, like all girls backing on esoterica like colour and whether she liked its face or not, made a mint.

In the evening there was a lovely moment out of many when The Music, a.k.a The King of The Golden River announced in splendid tones, "will you all please form sets for The Queen's Jig for which, My Lady would you lead your new Seminarial Head on to the floor". Jack looked happily at Jill, "that's a real whizzer Sis as I know that Jig was composed for the original Faërie Queene which she used to dance with My Lord of Leicester, so well done our mate The KGR." Jill laughed delighted, "Faerie Queene then or Fairy Queene now — I wonder which is which but I can't think of Our King of The Golden River as anything but The KGR when he's playing his squeezebox, even though the result's pretty kingly music" — "surely Jilly", agreed her brother deep in thought, "pretty kingly stuff making so much joy for people, Mum & Dad'll like that". His sister giggled happily thinking of the future of Kings & Queenes, "silver spoons aren't in it Jack", she noted thoughtfully, "how about being the child of a Golden River out of a Silver Sluice". Both collapsed hysterically at the illusion, "I wonder what The Horse'll produce out of whom", enquired Jill giggling fit to bust.

When it was all over next day with all the good-byes being said The Dragon & DD joined Jack & Jill on their trip back home. Arriving at the rock-face everyone gave everyone else huge hugs with DD giving 'Young Jack' a special super-snog with a splendid knowing smile to get him off on his new footing.

Several days later, after the usual compositional contortions, they sat their parents down after a wonderful celebratory supper, each holding their parts of the story. "I shall be the chaps and the narrator", announced Jack, "and I shall be the ladies and any animals", giggled Jill. They looked at each other for the queue then chorused together, "Are you sitting comfortably, then we'll begin". Their parents, captivated by the theatre of the thing with happy memories of Children's Hour, were settled in their big sofa as Jack & Jill paraded in front of them to play the play. "Once upon a time there was a King who badly needed a Queene — so this is the story of how he found her to live happily ever after".

Their parents were delighted beyond measure. "I think Mr Spenser would have loved your Queene children, real Faërie-Queene, in the proper Elizabethan mode", complimented their Father, "and I've got a little something to add to the story to mix it up a bit more". There was an expectant silence then giggles from the children waiting for their father to spill the beans. "Talbots survived almost up to today", he chuckled at Jack, "it's a boy thing, because it's cars". "When cars were very young, before the first World War, one of the manufacturers was Talbot, very upper crust they were too as befits a make which was sponsored by The Marquess of Shrewsbury and Talbot whose family crest was indeed what we've come to love as a Thin Dog". "The smart Talbots carried a mascot of a Talbot on their radiator caps, very splendid — so Thin Dogs survived in style even if only as magnificent models on wonderful cars". Jack smiled seraphically, "but we'll have to let those ones be called Talbots as you couldn't motor in much style in a Thin Dog", which sally brought renewed jollity. "Well that's the thing about Fairy Stories", observed their Mother, "they take place any time and all time, time has no place in their happenings at all". "But it was real Mum", they chorused together, "we were part of it no make-believe at all — perhaps you'll come to the christening when little KGR's come *then* you'll see, as we've been invited by The Queene to an anniversary dance to the music of the Great KGR who's going to set The Dragon's epic to music".

So indeed they will, to find Fairy-Stories happen if you concentrate on making them so, "you've got to do them", announced Jill firmly.

Aphrodite, May 2010

Aspects of Love
A collection of short stories

Creation's Cross

by Aphrodite

CREATION'S CROSS

A Flight of Fancy Flown Upon a Fact

'Had God condemned them'?, wondered the monks as they heard the thunder of collapsing masonry in the middle of the night. It is six hundred and eighty seven years ago but I, an engineer, can see him picking his way on 'the morning after' amongst the rubble which had been the central tower. 'God is dead', he cheered triumphantly as he pushed his elegant boot against the collapsed Roman masonry, 'Now Man has his chance — that Man is me'. A priest may be, but he was not one who believed in the damnation of a jealous God because for him the possibilities which lay within the perfectability of Man's Majesty, as Magus, had always been his mission, which was an arrogance perhaps but for him there had been no other truth in it, so this devastation gave him a chance to show the greater light of Man Incarnate — but how?

The tower's fall had left the gashed ends of the Nave, the Choir and both Transepts, a huge space, filled with intermingled heaps of rubble. For him, a man of mighty vision, the collapse of the old dead language, the sterility of the Roman arch, unperfectable because held within the hated hands of Popes, was his chance to show what the Art of Man could do through the magnificent freedoms of The Gothic. He'd seen it as an architecture of the people, of Artists, Masons, of Men's Free Thought expressed in stone triumphant — not the proscriptions of Gods. The fallibility of Gods was proved before him in the piles of Roman stone, so let him prove the infallibility of Man's endeavour with something magnificent in which Man could glory as the true Magus; something to inspire his surety in his worth through the soaring possibilities of pinnacles and points, with tracery interlaced to beautify the whole — he dreamed.

Man is divided into those who wring their hands upon disaster, scrubbling amongst the remains to re-cobble what was yesterday, unmindful yesterday had proved its fault by its demise, or those who cheer for the chance to create anew in a greater guise — to travel new roads the predicates of the old would not allow — to escape the cages of yesterday so seek horizons opened by their dereliction. Of such was he who stood amongst the shattered stones as saddened monks caressed the broken — much hardly fit to flog to demolition hawks who earned a crust (a golden crust I fancy as scrappies always have) selling to those decking modest homes with ill-thought out magnificence born of the cheapness of the hour from the failures of the great. We see them today to wonder why, but recycling's nothing new, now a mere fashion for profligacy being our predicate but then, because of cost, the norm as even new houses were built from the reclamation of the old as odd-found gargoyles and errant builders' marks attest.

He determined, to spur his dream that 'all must go' for to retain the little good would trap his vision in the dead of yesterday — those 'bloody' round arches — which lay around a corpse. In his furious vision's zeal to clear the scene he nearly missed a point, but scrappies don't, who only picked the best to leave him piles of dross, but one whispered in his ear, "we'll need that Sir for the new work's core — I'll see it set aside to clear the view". 'Oh, damn'n blast', he reflected, 'the rushing winds of vision'll carry me away unless I'm careful, now's the time for sober thought, with planning' — but dreamers must.

Much travelled, as monarchs of the Monastic system such as he were won't to be, he had seen the magnificent flights of Art the possibilities of the Gothic pointed arch had brought to Northern France — he sucked his teeth with glee at his memory of the soaring traceried vaults dripping with sculpted freedom. He had talked to those proud masters who were building it — in astonishing quantities he had noted as if every mason in the land had to have a vehicle for his thoughts — to find 'God' was far from their chisel-ends as they burst free from the dingy constraints of millennia of the heavy hands of Popes. 'Now', they cheered, 'we have a language all our own so now we can say what we want to say about the beauties of the world with which we can deck Man's glory; oh let them have their little worship spaces but it's we who do the clothing not the pursèd lips of priests for this', they vowed, 'is to be our language, the language of the people not of Popes and priests all locked in their prissy cages — round and boring, heavy and unimaginative, no freedom there, damn them'. 'This', they'd told him as they stood back to admire their soaring pillars of honeyed stone, 'this is the language of High-Art by which Man rises to far beyond the gods by making himself a god — que pensez vous Monsieu,

Magus peut-être'? He had no coherent answer as he gazed enraptured at what was being created. 'Oh wow', with a feeble 'gosh' added to a 'Mais oui mes Maîtres', as he un-cricked his neck from gazing up at the stupendous artifacts architecture born new was building. Then he had smiled seraphically to extend his hand, "Mais surement mes Maîtres ce'st la lange des Anges et vous mes amis sont les Anges".

Architecture, as any sort of language, he knew so well from his travels within the Roman hegemony had lost its life long ago, just a formula dictated by priests, like their dictated scriptures from their scriptoria, no human interventions allowed, freedom nowhere because 'you do it the Romish Way or not at all' — yet somehow these men and masons with their pointed arch had broken the cage right within that hegemony. Paris had been a revelation as Gothic overflowed beyond — whose source he soon discovered. He, a powerful man, was entertained in royal style by those his own to find a worldly secular practice overlaying the godly image. Money was in high supply with princes and prelates (it was difficult to distinguish which was which) seeking fame in fashion which seemed to be changing as fast as that of ladies kirtles; but none could accuse you of worldly affectation if you built a church, so churches of ever more fantastic flamboyance flourished like fleas upon a blanket bringing freedom of expression to the teeming masons who exercised it with such avidity.

It was the freedom which had got to him which he had carried back home to his fenland fiefdom as a shining torch almost burning holes in his pockets — but now he had his chance. 'No more', he thought gleefully as he watched the barrows rolling, 'shall I be a mere maintainer of the frozen status quo, now I shall leave my mark upon posterity for what I make shall be mine in an image I desire; God may be here, if he is, but here the language shall be mine, as I believe it ought to be so 'à bas les prêtres de Rome', he giggled in imitation of those wonderfully joyous French masons chiselling each other to the heavens — 'so let's to work'.

News spread far as the joy in the collapse of the over-reached cheered the miniature minds of the mealy-mouthed for whom creation has always been 'someone-elses job', so food for jeering. He'd always managed to solve the apparently intractable problems he set himself, himself, but the majesties of masonry he knew were not his mastership so his problem resolved itself into finding 'They who Could'. His faith was now placed firmly in the Majesty of Man as he knew himself Magnificent — but where to find a Masonic Master, a Magus who could tread the realms of the impossible to build his dream?

He noised the word abroad so those with skills and vision might present proposals, so hawks assembled, as they always do, to seek profit where the majesty of the mighty is brought low — to which the discomfiture of he who ruled the lands of God was no exception. Hands were rubbed as plans were pitched from postulates propounded, but all ended in the same device — a different dress from yesterday. When he opened out his dream they laughed, "you can't do that", they said with one accord, "thass impossible, 's'never been done a'fore". It wasn't the first time he'd been thus discomfited as enterprise was the very heart of the great monastic houses at their height, so he'd spent his life pushing boundaries to 'feed my sheep'.

As the weeks went by with no result he sent a monkish mission to meet those friends he'd made in Paris those few years ago to see if such a venture might be theirs — but they were 'out to lunch', 'otherwise engaged', or 'were sorry but they didn't have the time' as the soaring spires of France went ever soaring. Even he became cast down, 'surely there was someone who could do this thing'?, as he watched the hawks trundling their barrows to clear the mess.

Some transition was achieved by this as little flowers sprang up to show, despite the discouragements of man, Dame Nature never casts the sponge yet, 'it's a funny thing', he mused, 'it looks wider, deeper, longer now it's empty — can my dream be, or am I shooting straws to catch a star'? Us who endeavour are there with him in his distress as dreams fade beneath the persuasions of the merchants of 'it can't be done'. Heart beats slower as hope, its food, is dashed by the constant discouragement of 'I told you so', but; Magi make it because their majesty is made of secret forces particular to them which, even hidden, scoffers scarify as 'madness'. 'Madness', though, is merely the Majesty of those who step outside the cage to create above the mean of modest minds — or Man would still inhabit caves.

To keep his Spirit bright above the discouragement of dream he engaged the practical, for dreams need money — which fact those with it laugh, to add more cries of 'it can't be done'. They, so keen to make it yet so unwilling to lend it, are curiously unseeing of their necessary co-habitation — but he didn't need them. Master of great lands with tithes abounding, he set himself to persuading it was not proper for God's House to lie a wreck, so by diligence the carts of stone began loading in the quarries. Mercifully he did not need to ship from Norman sources, for English ones, indeed not far away, were now supplying fine bright stone, but; how to proceed now all had damned his enterprise?

As many of his ilk have done before he decided to embark his dream for knowing baking half a cake would show how the icing could be placed. Pilgrimages are not made of fully fashioned ends because 'beyond the horizon' can not be seen, so it's faith in footsteps which fuels success while it's the passion to see ends which renders enterprises mean. The crux is faith — but the faith which bears such loads is not built upon a fancy for if cash is wasted upon a whim those Pharisees would command his crucifixion. No, this faith must be of a different order altogether, founded upon deep experience with the Spiritual fire which possesses both the toughness yet the flexibility to win through whatever cards Dame Fortune cares to play — which is faith in the faculties of self, not the febrile fantasies of Fairyland. These men who risk thus are those who blazon Man's progress to leave fine testament behind — we should honour and emulate their enterprise. 'Yes risk', he thought, 'but who hangs upon the cross of failure pray'?

As a monastic he worshiped, but was the 'beyond' he was lead to believe a satisfactory reward for the risks he bore today? He doubted it, while who was going to build this vision — for certes it wasn't God — while who would take the rap for overreached ambition? Resurrection seemed a phantom as he was sold it yet he knew if he created something of majesty for those to follow he would have served two ends, a sacred for those who sanctified and a secular for those who saw, so fire future Spirits beyond themselves — like his was fired to this endeavour. He thought such worth the risk for would not immortality be his in the annals of Man's achievement — surely such was The Resurrection's truth? He had always drawn his Spiritual sustenance from the vision of those who'd built before so it seemed to him, a deeply practical man, should he achieve the same he would serve his fellow as Jesus meant when all the Church's iconage had been stripped away. 'Yes', he reflected, 'I can live with that for here-afters are a maybe but a shining vision to fire the Spirit is 'Love one another' made manifest for all, for ever', so; happy with his risk-assessment he took the plunge.

A canny man, not prone to miss a point, he'd noted which proposers had looked most promising so now called back a small group to start work upon his plan. It does not happen mastership comes cheap when its practitioners are kings, as masons strode the land demanding what they would, so he found himself facing the creator's ever-pressing balance of making vision live against the constraints of cash — for power he may but cash he must. Creation's crosses come no more crucifying for should your project fail there will be laughs — while those whose cash has withered without return will surely nail you. Still, his efforts had been adequate for the first supplies as he watched materials and masons coalesce to begin the cathedral's crowning glory — because he knew even a few stones, the vision underway, released the pockets of the reluctant, so; stiffening his sinews for what he knew was to come he addressed his team, because;

Then, oh then it always does when teams assemble to fly fancies, conflict courses as 'I want this' tears at 'we do that'. Creation's Cross is the conflict between those who know against those who think, between the certainty of certainty set against the vaunting of a vision — from which the greater can only be drawn through the humility to allow the virtues of yesterday to lie essential to the wonders yet to be. My heart is with him as he nurses 'we do that' through the hoops towards 'I want this', but this I know, as I am sure did he — all are enobled when they achieve what they do not know they could. I've been there to have seen joy abounding as proud practitioners stand upon a new plinth they had not seen before to view life in the virtue of their own achievement set higher than they'd thought they might. Man knows no greater joy than being better than he was yesterday for finding stars he did not know existed — which he's made himself. He knew this also that 'Love one another' knew no greater service than showing his fellow how he could be greater than he was — Man's service to Man in the achievement of his Magnificence, so;

Now with the battles over as style agreed, harmony restored a common purpose as sights were set and lines were laid — then plinth-stones placed, for which blessing a Mass was said to set the new work underway. Ethereal blessings were all right, he thought, perhaps necessary to the belief of lesser men, but it would take more than either to erect vaults adequate to eternity, but; many were those who needed to be satisfied so he was happy with the service on this practicality — that he would need monks with hods and shovels to restrain his costs. It is a magisterial moment this, this placing plinths because, however young, the project becomes alive which, as we've seen, unlocks purses to provide a double gain as Spirits soar.

Stern concourse coursed to the music of the chip of hammer upon chisel with the clink of stone-chips scattering as masons sunk their differences in doing what they love, carving stone — and devil take where it may end as long each sits true upon another. Unyielding men these mighty masons, kings of kings linked in ancient secret rite, so closed they think and closed they look, they drink their pints together. Stone is tough and so are they but none the lesser men for that — but hard to get to know so those who serve them keep a bit apart. Monks with habits girt grabbed hods to join the happy crew doing lesser tasks like mixing mortar with other simple things amongst the 'prentice gang. Amongst these common efforts new communities are born as divers little differences dissolve for all giving what they have to greater than themselves — which is the signature of greatness, greatness in the enterprise which ensures value in its journey so virtue in its end.

Whatever we may think in our enlightened days God was here, the God which fed their life amongst each other. We may choose to call it Spirit but no matter if the work be done in glory for if splendour shines then all are served whatever be the votive. It is in giving of his best to common cause Man makes magnificent for alone he is little thing but in concourse he creates community to inhabit his true majesty.

As his eight great piers began to rise he put off the pesterings of those who moan 'It can't be done', drunk by the steady soaring of the stone — but 'to where' those merchants niggled as costs rose but completion still was unconfined. Completion? When risks are born as high as this, when pilgrimages are entertained to breach horizons, then none may know completion — for it's only made when we arrive. Such faith as inspires pilgrims is not the stuff of money-men for must they not have a balance-sheet before they start — even when it is due tithes being spent? Money does not deal in inspiration it deals in facts'n' figures — it's a measure of the men who make such things 'inspiring' money is their greatest task, because building the damn thing's easy-peasy compared to convincing money that it ought — but the building was not his job so as the pillars rose he found himself at a loss, unable to put off the nightmares of failure through his normal furious manual engagements.

He lay one night in bed in the heat of summer tossing, niggling at the problem everyone told him couldn't be done — span the space. He slept fitfully fretting in his sleep as his confrères sang the evening offices which became mixed with the dreadful swirlings of people drumming on tables demanding answers..... on beauty's benison he's bent, it's gotta be more than just a tent... so came soaring pinnacles bedecked with golden finials..... yet ever came the music, the ever present music yet the ever distant drumming.... then layer upon layer of ever fading prayer, overlaid with the temperamental tweakings of the ever driving seekings.... then one came to him to take him gently by the hand (bearing his scythe within the other) then opened the Book of Revelation to show him the Lion lying down with the Lamb — then it showed him the quality bequeathed of Love which lasts long after the price is forgotten; 'I come to you from love of you to show you those things that it profiteth you to do, so you may show others'.......the singing rose around him as he faded — so our battered builder slept.

There are times when patience prospers progress, when Dame Fortune will not be rushed so knocking furiously on her door to speed her steps only brings frustration. He did no know this but in his tossing frustration awoke to seek quietening solace with his glass. Bed was no place on this magnificent summer night so he quietly rambled out on to the grass to fix his mind on perpetual paradise, seeking a bench from which to view his golden pillars rising against a deeply azure sky. Sipping steadily in the cool night, seraphically pleased with what was underway but horribly aware he had no idea how his bold venture could be capped he considered the glass;

Ah Glass! could thou and I, with Pluck conspire
To solve this 'plexing Scheme
of things entire
Would not we crown it wonderfully
and then
Stand back while all the rest admire.

The glass, well aware of its duties in creation's venture tried first a cheering blast;

> Dame Fortune's not so bad a game
> As a long as you don't play her lame,
> But take her hand, stand face to face,
> Then she'll conjoin to grant you grace
> To drive the project at your pace
> So finish with a name.

He took another draught to help his synaps' weary dance for they're the stream of consciousness which build our dreams.

> Ah Glass, could not I and thou,
> Between us, struggling, work out how
> to solve this thing
> upon a wing
> Then laugh at Fate's capricious brow.

The glass, caught up in the game, yet knowing 'struggling' was exactly the wrong method when jammed in these apparent adversities, replied;

> Play Fortune's Game, so press on up,
> 'Twill come to you from out the Cup,
> Flay not your brain
> With fearsome strain,
> 'Twill 'pear to you in midst of sup.

A presser on our man, not one to let stones lay themselves, hands on shirt sleeves rolled up was his style, so he had never learnt the glass's eternal lesson there are points when everything you try turns to ashes, even apparently your brain. He had not learned even brains get tired of banging up against the same closed synaptic doors for which you imagine you have not yet provided the key — so flog your brain to do so. Indeed he had not yet understood, when jammed shut, it is only the brain itself which can effect an opening of those closed doors nor had he learned brains don't do well under flogging as his had always sparkled under pressure — but now it wasn't. Nor did he know, given a chance, those little synaptic hands will seek entirely different joinings to bypass those closed doors to create a new solution of which, with diagnosis driving your every move — you could never have possibly been party. Tired of the struggle he was beginning to see some sense in the glass's exposition for, if the truth were honestly known, the battle to get where he was had tired him more than he was ready to admit. Collapsing in collusion with the glass seemed the only way he was capable of proceeding, while despite the horrors, he was thrilled with the fine glowing, steadily soaring, stone;

> 'Tis just, for sure, let wine inspire
> To set synaptic feet afire,
> Oh damn the duns
> Let's praise the suns
> Which smile upon our fine new tower.

The glass cheered sensing the necessary change of attitude towards relaxation. Brains it knew worked best on the fly with good cheer as their engine, not the frets and forcings of imagined failure.

> That's it Sir, take the passage gently,
> For light will come, for sure, anently,
> Let's drive on up
> And then we'll sup
> As fresh new light solves permanently.

"Thank-you glass", he cheered his new partner, "you've shown me what I fancy's an eternal so let's to bed you and I to get the rest you've given me so, as you so rightly say, we may see what tomorrow brings".

As the years rolled by and the piers soared high teeth began to be sucked by even the most venturesome for though the space was undeniably magnificent could it possibly be spanned — as none had seen such done before. We know now, far in the mythical majesties of Byzantium, it had, but which had been created quite outside the style and influence of those struggling here and now. The cash haunted him as did the faces of those who de-bursed it whose appeasement, at a critical moment, his friend The Glass had solved. In their usual spot, now with the piers at their peaks, they had been sitting on 'their' bench admiring;

Oh Glass how shall we go from here?
The faces of the purses leer.
What can we do
To bring it through?
With pillars topped so very near?

The Glass, only too aware as Man's conspirator in Creations's Cross and Man's vanity, had a seriously bright idea which tickled its fancy mightily;

Why not their portraits paint in stone?
Then they won't feel that they're alone,
Sucked into it
As part of it.
Oh, vanity's a mighty throne.

The possibilities dazzled as he imagined those who made such a fuss of disgorging gold queuing up to be 'done' by their master mason who had, so far, had little chance to exercise his sculptural skills as plain work had been the order of the day to keep costs down as piers went up.

Ah, that's a Fine idea friend Glass,
'Twill keep the buggers of our arse;
'Tis far to high
So I shan't sigh
For others joy, if on we pass.

The Glass tickled by its idea so promptly fielded jigged happily;

Yes hand the mean old sods some Fame
It's all the grist to our great Game
As you surmise
None's eyes will rise
To tops of piers, outside their Frame.

Then keen to see its colleague in crime featured in the scroll of fame too sang;

But Sir, why don't you join their crew
To place your face high up there too
With priestly fest
And style attest
Then none would need to ask — 'Tis Who?

He smiled at his mate's concern but had higher dreams than crude fame;

I thank you kindly, Glass My Dear,
But such is much too much I fear
To sit with cash
'Tis too much, dash
Cash is no fit mate for seer.

The Glass jgged convivially having been party to a number of his boss's wheedlings with the sour-faced merchants of loot whose un-tieing of purses always required much lubrication of which he was such an excellent purveyor;

Indeed they are a mealy lot,
Far to far concerned with pot,
But even they
May have their day,
If they give us our final shot.

Next day the word was put around to 'those who had' that portraits, pictures in stone he passed the message, would be available for permanent mounting above the mighty work, so 'would those providing form an orderly queue for their likenesses to be taken'. Having got the thing under way he had trouble not laughing at this crude appeal to vanity as he gave his message to the treasurer to pass around the purlieus of purses. They queued, then unloosed ties, so the piers progressed then bent themselves in glorious pointed arches towards their common goal above the roofs around them each sitting atop a frieze of faces which, as he and The Glass had surmised looked very small indeed from down below, but what matter if vanity had done its job.

Today seeing the soaring height and counting stones we imagine it took years, many years, but these men were doing it everyday and, in its purity, the work was simple so stone could be cut in repetition, indeed upon a production basis, so though we know so little about how, we know how long, 6 years. For him paying as he went he was able, just, to keep the cash flowing but having risked the most he was aware the most, however hard he tried, he'd set beyond the men he had at his command.

I imagine him, despite his bribe, frantically keeping the pressure on against the doomsters so he could at least complete his half-a-cake adequate for a crude lid on the space he had created, to buy him time for full fruition. I've been there so my heart grieves for his agony in his vision half complete, but I know the virtue of the half, as I'm sure did he.

Whether he had to resort to crude temporary history does not tell nor does it matter, for half his cake bought time. When he'd reached a roofline upon which tomorrow could be placed I imagine he called a halt for all to take a breath, not least the suppliers of the cash. So far whim and waste could not be laid upon him for what he had achieved was undeniably magnificent, pregnant with possibilities for those who had a little vision, so the men with nails and hammers staid their hands — for now. It was a blessed relief their staying as hovering had been their habit as the pillars rose, they so eager to crucify those who stood above them to create.

'Yes', he thought, 'I live to fight another day but how do I proceed from here'? The tooth-suckers, had they been asked (but they'd departed shamed even this had been achieved), would have said, 'yer well if I'd been asked I wouldn't have started from here', as those who damn have done down time, but; 'damn *them*', he sizzled, 'here is where I planned to be so now we start again to find 'They who Can — Complete'? He knew the method while he knew allowing 'No' led nowhere so it was, as it has ever been, merely a matter of pressing on till light appeared. Here he knew was the matter of the toughness and persistence which had served him so well in projects past.

Sources were searched but those who'd sucked their teeth, hiding secretly in the wings, crept out — constructing crosses. It's no fantasy the darkest hour comes just before the dawn, he'd hung on cliff-edges before as they crumbled, he'd even fallen yet been caught in trees hanging halfway down to rise again, so knew dead is not, until dead is — while he was still alive. They traipsed through his door in ever thinning lines as their imaginations stalled at the expanse of sky above the soaring, 'you want to span that — er in stone'?, they faltered, as bewildered looks crossed furrowed brows then, which things catch one unawares for Dame Fortune is a fickle player, one arrived with a battered leather frail upon his back. He bore the quiet assurance of the ultra-skilled, eyes unfocused for seeing not what is but what might. He had the calm certainty born of 'I've been there'n seen it *and* I've done it', the poise of those for whom nothing is too difficult because for them a problem is a joyous chance for the vaunting of the new, because they may not know the answer — but 'they know they can'. These are those who people the world with possibilities for they are of the tribe of Those who Do.

"Oi cin do that boss", he replied his eyes wandering up at the soaring arches, "'s'long as you don't mind how". For those in the extremities of trial the 'yes' is a wonderful moment for a door flies open which heretofore was shut. We may not know to where it leads, but open is the surety of probability, upon which possibility can be built — so heads were put together as trials were tried. He knew the rules so 'I want this' was modified as he saw the possibilities in 'I can do that' which might just achieve something beyond his wildest dreams — but in a different guise. Small ticklings and enticements, little cheerings and suggestions were joined as he saw the virtues in the method being proposed to which his imagination could bring something none had seen before to carry all beyond their comfort zone to high endeavour. "Thass big boss so we'll need reel big'uns", when him and he were content with the scribblings which showed the scale of the endeavour — even though he of the frail knew he would be pushing his understanding well beyond his limits. "Aha", he said, "there aren't many joys in being a boss, but the power to get things done is it, so leave that to me, you take a job elsewhere for half a year while I assemble the material for what we've dreamed".

Even in 14th Century England trees the size needed for the task were rare. Transporting them whole to site would present difficulties not often entertained, but monastries burgeoned everywhere, whose mutual masonry was munificent — so the word went out. Such power was one thing but who would pay as purses were now beyond his grasp for doubters all, as they'd closed their minds against his dream to 'allot their funds to proper things'. For he of power and, heretofore, cash on call he found himself unhorsed. Such problems are as old as time but for his fruition he had to ask a friend. 'Ah', one said when found in the metropolis, 'what you need's some credit for which you need a Business Plan — I've been there, stand me a stoop'n I'll show you how'.

He hated every moment of it, fiddling with the devious details of doing money's disciplines, until — 'you'll need a picture'. Vision gripped him —

'a picture, now there's a thing I can, and do well to', he mused vaulting into Missal Manuscripts. He thanked his new found friend, then picked up the papers to set off home. "A picture, there's the thing, a real picture not just a picture in my head, better than a thousand words — I like it — I know who'll do me a picture to dream the money out of the tightest pockets'. Dreams of pictures spurred his steed back home to go to find old Gregory the monastery's illuminator.

"Greg I need a picture of what we plan if we're going for completion — we're begging so we need the best". As a man of vision pictures were it for Father Gregory while he'd always had faith in he who'd planned this enterprise. His manuscripts were prized far afield not only for his colours but for the secular scenes he secreted — communions were seen in corners which did not belong at alter rails — sales were ready and prices high as imagination gilt his speeding pen, so; all he needed was the sketches upon which the timber would be bought to set his mind in motion.

"Greg, we need to make it look magnificent, even though it won't be as high as a normal tower, we need to imbue it with a majesty time will show but at which today's passion for the Perpendicular might cavil because its lower than expected — we need to trompe l'oeil if were going to get the cash". "Spot of fraud"?, laughed the indulgent Gregory. "Yers, something like it", he agreed their minds together, "but let us think on higher things with finer words, 'enticement to engage in enduring enterprise', howzatt'? They laughed to raise another cup then he went to get the sketches to fertilise the master's pen.

Fixing the figures was a bore but he knew a man who could, so set off for Simon's cell to place the pile before him. Simon, his right hand man when fiddling figures to please princes was the need, listened to the plot. 'No probs there boss's jus a matter of fixing the columns right, 's'amazing how little they really know', he laughed quite happy to commune in conning money out of cash as all true creators are.

Simon scribed and Gregory grafted as 'The Business Plan' took shape. "By heck Gregory will it really look like that'?, he gazed amazed at Gregory's magisterial interpretation. Father Gregory chuckled, 'well for pilfering pockets you need imagination which is what I've embued it with — it's not far off and when it's done I'll be dead so it shan't be me being crucified'.

'I've got no idea how fast this bloke can do what he says he can', he observed to his conférè in conspiring, 'but I'd like to be there when he does — so it might be me', he laughed as both knew he didn't care a skit as triumph would eclipse the moans of vision cheated. 'I'll need a frame for something that size", he suggested to his colleague, 'can you fix it with the chippies as I'll want to stand it up for max effect, no secretive unrollings'll convince these guys — you gotta look as though you meant it'. When Simon had finished his fiction it was sent to the bindery to be set in fine parchment tooled in gold, 'you gotta wow them all the way', as he cheered them in their efforts to excel.

Then, we've been there, after the furious flurries of achievement, risk piled on risk as he prepared to quarry yet more of others' money, came collapse, the balloon pricked of the energy which has flown it so high so far. 'Could 'his man' do what he said he could', he wondered fretting? 'I'm placing vast trust in the word of another of whose skill I know so little in an endeavour which has never been entertained before, could he really do it'? The cold winds of doubt, then fear, swept round his Spirit shrivelling its so vital energy, for whose appeasement fine pictures were no panacea — it was easy to conceive a dream far less easy to achieve it, specially on this monumental scale. He would, as Simon and Gregory had opined be wheedling money out of purses, for which it is to be admitted he did not have much respect nor liking,but wheedling all the same for a dream to which he had hitched his hat.

Abysses opened before him while the dread sound of hammer upon nail mocked his madness. For those who dare these are the dread times when doubt corrodes, but it is they who can survive this nibbling at the Spirit's edge who win on to victory. He remembered his judgment of the man, his calm assured brow, those eyes fixed not only on the high but, when drawings were engaged, his competence with detail brewed from vision; the way he turned a scheme, not immediately with the fleet facility of the flawed, but with steady progress he himself could compass — 'surely he had not been wrong to place his hope so squarely'?

This is the moment when we need to release the tangles in the brain, unknot the cords of doubt which bind us to re-view the clarity which brought us here. He felt much in need of The Glass's wisdom in this travail — in vino he'd been shown the veritas of things before so retired to his capacious cell to seek its solace. Reverently taking it down from its now hallowed shelf from where it could view the progress of the work — no cupboards for his 'colleage-in-crime' now as he was part of it — he filled it from his personal store then placed it beside him to contemplate its magnificence twinkling assuredly, its bright red panacea tempting him to release;

Please help me Glass I'm plagued with doubt
I see it, but I can't make out
If it can be
In truth from tree,
And can he do it? there's the shout.

The Glass, regognising his boss's agony replied briskly,

You've placed your bets, be not assuaged,
Faint hearts don't win, the game's engaged,
'Tis not the time
To quit sublime,
You've bet on Queens, your play's now staged.

He, still with doubt flooding his brain replied,

See you he's Queen, with all queen's powers?
See you his strength above us towers?
'Tis no mean thing
He has to bring,
'Tis not a mere bouquet of flowers.

The Glass, pressing on determinedly assured,

Oh yes Sir Monk I watched you plan,
I'll place my faith in such a man,
He has the power
To make God's bower
Far finer than mere mason can.

So
Grip your staff, stride on Sir Knight,
Let not mere doubts your case afright
I'll place you bet
We'll get there yet

With beauty all will see is Bright.

So
Do perk up, Oh take a sup,
'Tis like the dawn, the sun comes up
To light the bold
Who Love unfold
To show Mankind the finest Cup.

Well away into the truths purveyed by the Glass's message, he giggled like a kid with a new toy, "I do like your self-advertisement Glass, the Communion Cup thing wrapped into that everlasting search for Grails yet", he guffawed with glee, "all to be found within the humble Glass". "Less of the humble, Sir Monk", it chortled happily, "Glasses is Queens, Godlike if you please, no Pawns here only the best, you ask'n we purvey'n not any old rubbish either". "Indeed friend Glass you have it", he agreed enthusiastically his doubts dispelled, "the truths of Hippocras down time, if it were good enough for Olympus it's good enough for us so thank's let's sleep on it — I'll try not fail you again". The Glass laughed knowingly "oh fret not Sir Knight to err is human'n even those Olympians cocked it up pretty often — disaster may appear to be Good Friday but 'tis Easter Sunday which spells success you ought to know — making mistakes isn't the sin it's not knowing how to fix'em's the killer — you'n I've done so tonight so let's crack on".

All this took time but messengers arrived from far up North success was being achieved in tree selection so cash had to be despatched for transport — mercifully its source had not completely dried so he was able to get carts rolling on demand. He knew too well a project stalled at such a spot was apt to cripple it entirely or at the best delay it into rising costs while men once gathered don't do well sat back on bankers' bidding so, equipped with lance for money's vanquish, he spurred off South on cash's quest.

We won't sit with him as it's a sordid business not worthy of our regard, its details all mazy for made of the pushn'pull of meretricious graspings, deeply distressing for those who fly upon the wings of Love's bright vision — but he'd steeled himself so got amongst them. He was not where he was for lacking competence and presence as the engines of mighty monasteries aren't miniatures so he prevailed, rather better than he'd ever hoped — he'd seen a couple of the consortium gazing at the picture dreaming dreams as he felt their purse strings loosen. 'Well done Gregory', he thought, 'you'll get my best when I get back'.

With promises the loot, in coin, would be delivered to the monastic treasury within the week he set off back home upon the wings which fly brave enterprise. 'I've got the buggers', he chuckled as he imagined the discomfiture of the tooth-suckers back home. We might see his view as not a sacred thing — but then Pharisees weren't either and if 'God's Work' was to be done temporal traits were needed — 'was not that', he mused, 'why God had sent His Son to earth, to get a grip on earthly gripes'.

Our man, as we have seen, sat well loose to the tight canonic codes as practical men have always done as a necessary of conception. He had always known his Spirit as his own, a gift of god maybe, whoever he may be, so he used its inspirations and energies for Love of fellow — God's creation so he was told — though it has to be admitted (and why not) even he, a monk, was not free of the little vanities of Man's estate, so zapping the toothsuckers was but a little thing — he would not have trod upon a beetle but then beetles did not harm his path — but those who did deserved their little dooms. 'It was a pity', he mused to the tune of his horses hooves pounding the summer turf, 'Father Pelagius's work had been destroyed', as 'Free Will' had always seemed the thing for him.

Back at base all was bustle as, a man of action, our chippy had returned with the first wagon and was underway building the team he'd need. "By heck Sir Chisel you move fast, you'll be pleased to know I've got the cash'n here's the picture which captured it". The sharp edge laughed, "oh Dame Vision's call brooks no delay'n when you're in the saddle time is cash". "Yers", merrily picked up commerce, "from both sides time's unforgiving, for he who makes and he who pays". "Indeed", the chisel chimed, "I've been there too often not to know of it — er I fancy 'God be praised's' not quite the thing as them-in-there've been telling me the facade you built to get it, no godly thing at all I trow, but I don't 'arf like the picture". "Ah well", he replied, "needs must when the Devil drives and half a tower's the devil of it".

There was much activity as a few men of stone were normal in-house chaps as constant fettling was the order, if only to repair the ravages of time, but men of wood were only needed when abbots went ape as grandeur gripped them in fashion's frenzy to pass the interior furnishings 'out of fashion'. Apart from which the gorgeous garnishing of canopies and stalls required quite different disciplines to those the massive trees beginning to assemble needed. Curlicues for choirs did not coincide with the stern demands of baulks of many tons to be crafted into huge construction which, he fancied, might be the largest such endeavour since the immensities of Saxon forts. Sir Chisel had put the word about a fine project was here for work with fun to be had for all, but; he had been selective for knowing one bad apple when risk ran high could sink them all, big trees amok on high were dangerous things.

They were a happy crew, these massive men covered in huge leather aprons to prevent the baulks attacking them, as they had worked with Sir Chisel before so knew his tone — and liked it. With timber this size and rare as hen's teeth 'the team's the thing' so no preachers were permitted. A world was to be built, perhaps not within those seven days, but the enterprise had Genetic stamp so 'God said' drove 'how it was to be'; those who built the pyramids would have known the method.

The first enterprise was to dig a saw-pit then build the huge hoists to handle the timber — everything had to be on a massive scale. New stones in special cradles were made to handle sharpening the enormous saws Sir Chisel had commissioned for the job for, apart from the effort lost by blunted blades, they run awry to make extra work and waste — 'as sawn' was his aim if costs were to be kept in check. As work upon the baulks progressed the site took on the look of a child's game of spillikins as time taken up making posy stacks was wasted when builder's marks were common practice.

We do not know how they made it, though we might guess; we do not know how they got it up there though some engineering vision might assist but I fancy there would have been a team up-top, creating the necessary landings with a team down below sawing and chiselling the parts. One thing we do know is Sir Chisel had designed it so no sideways loads spread the new vaults, all its forces are contained within itself so its whole weight is borne vertically. Not your average chippy Sir Chisel because this called for a considerable knowledge of applied mechanics, the business of geometry and forces, Greek knowledge long lost beneath the mantle of the god for whom they built. It would have been easy to have just spanned the space to contain the natural spreading loads but no trees such size existed — apart from being unsightly from below, and a cheap cheat to boot. For all engaged, carried along by Gregory's picture which stood proud in the Refectory to spur them on, cheap cheats were cheats not to be entertained where 'gods' rode high.

This doubt about the details, to us bred upon the exactitude of drawing boards, may seem odd but when the project had been mooted I fancy mere outlines, probabilities and practicalities would have been the order of those sketches with detail left to the possibilities of the materials obtained. We know also it was common practice to 'build as you went', specially when constructing timber houses, so I can imagine the scene as heads were scratched then timber eyed as, with Sir Chisel's general principles at hand, marks were made for cutting. I have had the privilege to watch this process in the rebuilding of medieval timber houses; I've known the men who had all the qualities of Sir Chisel's team, an ability to 'see' the whole thing in the head then solely with a piece of string (no tape, no square I hear you ask) commence the work. We arrogantly assume, as we notionally bow to 'old skills', immersed in every tool imaginable we must be greater than those who went before — but can we achieve a tithe of what those chippys did *solely by hand and eye*. Man may be a tool-maker, but his foremost tool is his brain which powers those all conquering hands and eyes by which the glories of the past were both conceived and built.

The cheery clock of hammer on chisel-head echoes around the happy group of grafting men as wood chips fly. The rasp of mighty saw, top and bottom sawyer sweating pints, fills the air as monks now unsuited to the task take much needed beer amongst the ranks of men. Sir Chisel's happy as the ancient swing of adze is absent because 'as sawn' brings wonders of precision, 'they're worth their weight', he cheered foaming pint in hand, 'I'll see they know it too, 'tis just'. For this it is a merry scene, somehow different to the men of stone — whose men are hard like it. The hard crack of metal tools which shocks the ear is now the gentle plop as wood drives wood, the hiss of the wood saw soothes as the harsh rasp of the stone saw had set their teeth on edge while the smell of fresh cut timber is one of the greatest smells man ever makes — but stone dust clogs the lungs to taste like brimstone.

To those of the enquiring mind its Majesty is its making as it appears to soar suspended up in space. The size and complexity of the interlocking parts beggars the imagination, but that Greater Light he dreamed of pours down from its iridescent glass to inspire all who've seen it since. To those who like such things the unconventional answer to the impossible problem *he made his burden* shines the light of Man's indomitable endeavour beyond himself where Trust in his capacity to win the day is the only spur. This is the measure of true Romance 'The Impossible made good to shine a greater light where darkness stood'. We are fortunate to know this enterprise took fourteen years to complete from Sir Chisel's first arrival to the leaving of the last leadsman fitting those wonderful lights — and weighs two hundred tons. A long time for a piece of carpentry perhaps — but it did what Sir Chisel said he could — and it is still there today while there has been nothing like it in the world.

Creation's Cross has one final nail to drive its message home — that we hand over what's absorbed our being to some other — whose pain is in the parting. This rite is locked in creation's cause for we made it to outlive us, to shine our message onwards to represent our resurrection, but; to shine for ever we must pass it on — a gift. This giving is central to the 'Love One Another' for which we strove as central to our belief without it Civis is a worthless husk — but as a gift it's gone. The essence of gift must be no predicate for future use for its being is no longer ours — only its creation ever was — but now it's others', so we have to wave good-bye as we watch their faces turned towards the hope of a new light in what we've created for them — which leaves us in its shade. Their worship now focused on what we've made, not us, we wander again in the wilderness we've created for ourselves — by our creation. As we laboured the sky was full of it, it shone a mighty light around us but when it's gone the sky lies blank, the fire gone out. I see him at the Mass for his baby's blessing absorbed in re-fighting the battles of creation to hang on moments more to what was his — but is no longer. This passage is a painful one requiring of its travelers one belief — The Art must be greater than the Artist to be worthy of the enterprise engaged.

As he sinks back into obscurity from the light which shone his life before he must be content he succeeded in the task he set — the giving of the best of his todays for their tomorrows, 'my Love for them made manifest', but; those who'd hung upon his every move as he laboured for their future face round to take what he's bequeathed them — then he's forgotten for the future is the thing — but he's the past. It's hard to warm the hands against the cold of those faced other ways, so 'why create', he asks, 'for the end is always this cross on which I hang in the wind of others' disregard, for I'm merely yesterday's vehicle for their joy in new tomorrows' . 'Perhaps my mate The Glass will tell me if I'm its votive for a while, perchance some sight may be sucked from vino's veritas', as he creeps out from those singing to the glory of another.

'The Cell's the thing, some solitude to seek the truth of it', but as he left he turned to see placed high that Cross which had gone before with the effigy of he 'who gave his life for others'. "Was such the Love he'd bequeathed those singing in the choir — and to all who would come after — am I he'?, he mused as he slipped quietly through the cloisters to his cell. He picked his friend from its commanding shelf then poured himself a full measure with the happy thought he may be the forgotten of today but his power at the least got him his colleague The Glass, where those to whom he gave had pots. His friend waited patiently to see the nature of the trouble.

'Vanity'?, he asked himself, 'I wonder, is vanity a necessary mortal vice to this creation which he who hung before did not possess?, yet he came down to be of us — perchance my little vanity of glass is the reward for what I've made'. He sipped contemplating those things he sang of every day, 'did they have any measure for his worldly worth — and where lay virtue truly'? Addressing his colleague he asked of it, "how do I divide the Temporal from the Eternal, Glass — what's the Eternal and where lies worth between the two"?. The wine twinkled in the glass to laugh at him, "there you have it Sir, you have a glass and they have not". "Is that enough"?, he enquired of it, but The Glass laughed back, "but drink from me to know the difference for Man must be happy here with little things for small's his worldly nature, for is not glass improvement on a pot?, Man is only great by what he grants to others from the fire his Spirit makes — by such 'tis only how he rises from the guzzlings in the gutter which measure lesser men — we've been through this before". "Oh Glass is what you say enough for us who hang upon Creation's Cross"?, he cried as he heard the rising chant in praise of what he'd done.

The glass, refilled, conspired with its contents for a while as if drawing from them truths immense, "what happened to him upon the cross they sing to Sir, is not it the rising which you seek when you create, tell me from the honesty of what you've made, is not eternity the thing"? "But He is then and I'm here now" — "but you have me and they have pots, let Glass content you for the quality of what you drink from me those others do not have — remember that when they place the nails". The Glass thought on, "the measure of what you've made is the joy with which you made it for you live upon a higher plane than they, a place which may have calvaries for sure, but has daily resurrections also for you live in spheres they never know — revel in those spheres to be content". Sitting in his fine uphol-stered chair he was mindful of the bald benches of his confreres which showed him what he had not seen before.

"Glass"?, he asked, "is Creation's Cross mine own abomination, a swirling in my fevered mind which drives to Art's high Artifice — must there al-ways be lows beyond the highs"? "Yers 'tis so", The Glass, refilled, replied, "for without the low's there'd be no engine for the high's and think on this, they you curse for their un-care don't see what's spread before you from those High-Hills, for they're not there; where you stride so free they're grovelling in the gutters of their captive case, so think on this", as more vino filled it to the brim, "the regard of Man's a fickle fancy, 'tis here today yet fades tomorrow on a whim so heed it not for when you do you crucify yourself — that's how it is".

He liked his friend's 'freedom of the heights' for he knew it as a vital truth of his existence, 'could that do'? he wondered, 'was the Freedom of The Spirit's fire the sole reward for high endeavour, is Freedom's Fire what's immortality for mortals'?, he wondered deciding the glass might have the right of it, so poured before he asked. "Is it immortality I seek then Glass, something which I'll never know" — "ah be sure you'll know it, for is not he who hung before immortal?, is not he writ large upon time's lettered page when all others are forgot so will not you be too, which Sir, is what resurrection truly is — is not that, refashioned in the light of truth, what you sing of everyday"? The glass gurgled happily as the wine, its fort, twin-kled in its body.

"Like I'm created to hold wine in beauty you're created to create in beauty for that was Man's choice when he left Eden's sterile Groves, 'to do it my way', you've done it yours so be content, be thankful for so many never know such ecstasy for locked within their little minds". The Glass and the wine now spoke in heady matrimony, "curse not your fate from the slings of now, for now is only now'n for the likes of you tomorrow's finer than today which is the essence of your being; tomorrow's yet to make in any image which you please while now is done so curse ye not but grip your staff for task's to come — which is the joy of it'.

Setting the glass down gratefully beside him he sat long in thought communing with this rare advice, swirling its twinklings through his being to seek the truths of his existence. 'Was the glass right'?, he wondered, 'was ecstasy the true reward for risk engaged, was the height of plinths above the mass the truth of it'?; yet he knew so well how plinths were crosses for those below hating every moment of your stand above. 'Was the time above them worth their hammerings'?, he wondered as he picked up a little book just brought him from the East. He held it for The Glass's delectation, "you're getting through to me, Oh Glass, for here's a blessing those of pots don't have, because I'm known such gems as this are sent to me from far afield to free my mind from the images which those of pots inhabit". "Yes that's much of it", agreed The Glass, "the freedom to think to be yourself not see things through another's view; one's idols may be broken but at least their self, so something, but images are nothing for being of someone else's guise; so Sir, what has your book to say of it, might it offer you a steer upon tomorrow"?

He raised the glass to drink of its grape-born grace as, he'd found, had the writer of the wisdoms there inscribed. "Let's see, Oh Glass, perhaps we might find a thing to suit us both, I'll set you down again to seek". He leaved the pages joyfully, "hmm, much wine had passed his lips yet truth abounds herein", he began to laugh, "perhaps I'm with him thanks to your assistance" — " which is perhaps the truth of it", chuckled the The Glass trying to conceal its pride, "the truths which spring from the wine he wrote of, as I've helped you join up ends entangled by your angst as contemplation with a glass solves all", it laughed hugely at its wisdom. His seraphic smile surrounded, he clapped his thigh, "go carefully", cried The Glass, "for without me you'll be bereft — exaltation's no proper cause for crashes" . "No indeed 'tis not", he agreed contritely, "so let's settle you securely to enjoy the feast because I think I have the answer to my angst, how's this";

> *How sweet is mortal Soveranty! — think some:*
> *Others — 'How blest the Paradise to come'!*
> *Ah, take the cash in hand*
> *and waive the rest;*
> *Oh, the brave Music of a distant Drum!*

"How like you it, Oh Glass"?, he asked as he cradled its shapely stem again. "Oh yes I like it", cheered The Glass jigging in his hand with joy as, caught in the flight of the thing, it burst into melody;

> *Ah that's the truthful measure of it,*
> *It's the distance that's the thing,*
> *With the banging of the bongos*
> *For the battle of the brim.*

There was a stunned silence as the singing of The Glass died away. "Blimey, isn't that doing it a bit brown Glass", he enquired solicitously, "I mean banging bongos and all that, and what's that battle of the brim thing"? Taking its course from his master's exclamation The Glass decided to revert from its normal high monastic prose to portray its wisdom in its own vernacular;

"Well yer got to get the iconography right yer see 'swhat the worship's all about", The Glass laughed hugely, pleased with its burst of song. "Yers", it observed mentally sucking its teeth, "let's examine it in the light of logic", it jigged gaily at its enterprise in exposition. "The only sovereignty worth a light is yours, them in the gutter worried about kings'n such're stuck in cages so give me freedom every time; nah, kings is alright for them in cages", it sailed on gaily, "who've sold their soul to kings 'cause they're sheep'n like pens, feel undressed outside on the windy hills, need a sheep-dog to worry them back home, but for the likes o'you the Freedom of the High Hills is the only place, staff in hand striding mightily where'er ye list; can't think in the gutter as it's all gunged up with slime with your head down grovelling in it — need free air to think", it giggled at its Euclidian erudition. "Nah this 'Paradise to come twallop", it cursed splendidly, "who in blazes knows pray?, I've asked'n you lot've never been able to do me a decent answer 'cause all airy-fairy stuff 'bout faith — wozzat's always been my answer and 'no answer came the stern reply'". "Forget the faith stunt", it assured briskly still tickled immensely at its quoted flight of fancy, "let's look at this Paradise thing proply — Paradise now's the place, for which you need a little lubrication courtesy o'yours truly, er take a swig Sir'n Paradise here we come". It skipped merrily around till he grabbed it to accept its offer.

A gentle silence swirled, "Um, you may have the right of it Sir Glass", he mused thoughtfully swirling wine around his throat, "your sort of Paradise seems pretty good to me, all comfy with hazy edges, no sharp bits to stick into me, but do continue your Euclid bit, it's fun — and tell me this, if kings are off what do I do about The Abbott"?

"Forget him", replied The Glass magnificently dismissing majesty, "who's built this wonder of the world, pray, weren't'im for sure, it's never kings who build they only lay waste, it's the likes o'you with vision who build, king's've got their feet *and* their heads glued up by the pox of politics, no time for vision for them sorting out the crap surrounds 'em". He laughed mightily at this dismissal of his boss taking another draught to add some spice to The Glass's exposition. "I could have done with the cash in hand though Glass", he sighed, "the business plan stuff was pretty grisly, messing with the manipulators of money" — "ah but you got a jolly good picture out of it, think on that as a small profit out of the grisly, got to find the silver linings you know, or it's all un-remitting gloom", it laughed knowingly, "them as venture like you Sir *never* have enough cash in hand 'cause the dream's always expanding'n them sheep wot's providing it don't believe you anyway, which", it continued knowingly, "is the truth of the faith bit you lot are always on about; faith's a tangible thing thass inside you 'cause you know you can do it, somehow, not that airy-fairy 'heaven' nonsense you sell the sheep", it sizzled gently. "Faith's the possibility of existence", it preached the gospel, "hope's in the possibility of achievement 'cause you gotta force heaven out of circumstance, thass what romance's all about — making the impossible happen — howzzat for a bit of veritas'n I'm not on the booze either", it laughed uproariously. "Touché", he agreed, "which only proves your point about Paradise, do pray continue".

"Nah your 'distant drum' thing", it chuckled pleased with its new course in practical philosophy, "thass the far horizon, 'swot you can't see beyond wot drives you in'it, garn admit it as if you can see it then so can all them sheep in pens so woss the use — no grubbing in gutters for you Sir, only stars other's can't see is worth it, no value lies in gutters'n its virtue that you seek, even if you don't know how to get there — that do yer"?, it enquired helpfully. "But how about your bongos"?, he asked mystified. "Ok, them bongos", it sucked its teeth making it up as it went along, "they're the Distant Drum thing, the call of the wild blue yonder wots drummed for Man to get him out of the caves, 'swot gets the feet amarching'n that y'see 'swot fires the Spirit with the martial music of conq'ring heroes'n you don't want to be them say-at-homes Sir, no guzzling for you Sir, no's the rarified air up on them high lonely hills, thass the stuff to feed the likes 'o you Sir", it laughed, "heroes is it for you Sir's yer can't be inspired to that risk you wot of by thinking wimp".

"No indeed one can't", he chuckled revelling in The Glass's exegesis. "Nah then we all know 'bout battle, thass your cross thing, fending off them what wants you nailed — then there's battles all along the way'n battles with the whole damn thing. *Then'*, it cheered with a special jiggle to reinforce its words, "there's the battles inside your head — that sort a'push'n pull thing wott has yer tossing in yer sleep at nights, thass the wust of all, that is", it noted somberly, "you need some fair old drums to drown them dragons, all fire'n smoke about the disbelief in self, 'n you got to winn'em all Sir or y'r dead'n dead don't do immortality — no sir". "Indeed it doesn't, there your right, so now where", he chuckled further now immensely entertained by The Glass's wisdom.

"Nah, the brim bit", it considered carefully, "arf-a-loaf ain't better'n no bread, may do for the guzzlers, them live-to-eat types, but eat-to-live's the only way for giants, for the finished end's the virtue, bits won't do — you got t'get the pinnacle atop the pillar placed on the plinth or them's come after'll never see it — completion's the only thing wot's worth a scat 'swot ensures that immortality thing y'see *and* it's got to be different, bigger'n better'n more bizarre, whatever takes your fancy", it rollicked to a close.

"Er finished"?, he enquired fascinated by the extraordinary effusion exhibited by The Glass on song. "Ah yes, finished", it sucked its teeth again caught a little on the hop, "we gotta consider finished in its true light — got diverted by bread'n loaves'n stuff'n all that posy pinnacle pillocks". "Yers, if you ain't got it to the top you dreamed then you could'a done better'n good enough ain't good enough", it surmised sententiously, "good-enough's for guzzlers but for the likes of you who dream beyond the gutter an unfinished dream's a death — where there's a top, even if 's'only in your head, then ashes is it if you fail to make it". It though a moment swirling the wine within its bosom to keep synaptic hands engaged. "There's nothing worse than if only's, special for them as know they *could* have done it if they'd pushed that last half-mile — yers finished's the only outcome worth a straw". It stood twinkling deliciously, mischievously pondering its last sally, positively fizzing with delight.

"Now see, if all them things is to be done there's only one word old Magus needs, it's onwards 'cause without onwards there's no Magic'n with no magic there's no Majesty'n it's Majesty we need to fill the brim". It sucked its teeth for a moment, thinking, "without onwards life's all sunk in the struggles in the swamps'n there's no Majesty in swamps's all black'n horrid'n immortality's the stuff 'o light — no resurrection to be had in swamps's they suck you down in godless ooze", it chuckled mightily pleased at having rounded its exposition so neatly, 'Veritas in Vino Sir, howzzatt"? it almost fell over in its gleeful dance.

He pondered thoughtfully swept up by The Glass's glimpse of the truths of Immortailty. "Perhaps I should", he enquired, "may I"?, he asked — "yeah surely, thass wot's all about so swill away, yer never know yer might find the Grail thing yet", it chortled hugely at the ancient Arthurian aphorism . He picked up The Glass to take a mighty draft then let synapses dance inside his head. "Aha", he chortled, "I've got you glass for it's not finding Grails which is fortune's dream, but making'em, howzatt"? "Yer well thass the Magus stuff the likes 'o you get paid for'n I'm just a humble glass, y'see".

Now well away he chortled happily at the humility of he who'd lead him on to victory. "Ah but its teams which fill the brim we've sought, Sir Glass, so I've you to thank for showing me the way — I'll get the lads down carpentry to knock me up one of those sort of crossy wine things for my cell so I can always have bottles by my side". "Good one Sir", his consort encouraged, "as I fancy he who wrote your little book knew well, anyway there's worse ways to go than pissed", it collapsed into merry mirth. Silence reigned.

The Glass returned to monastic-speak, "we live-on in what we leave behind — we're re-incarnated from what we seem to be now in the work we do for others as we travel, the greater the selflessness of our work the greater the incarnation now and immortality evermore — as what we leave is greater than our mortality". "I'm told there's a far Eastern Faith which teaches such a supposition Glass", he replied thoughtfully. "Perhaps there is, but logic would have it no other wise", The Glass chuckled happy to be ahead in the intellectual race, "think on the history of it, is it not so"? "Man remembers those who achieved, not those who didn't?, so we don't need a religion to tell us what our senses show because Man knows all if he thinks about it — and takes a glass or two to aid the process", it giggled hugely, 'and keeps his head clear of the prostitutions of priests", it finished smugly.

He thought happily upon the glass's postulate no whit disturbed by being classed 'priest' as he knew the truth of otherwise. "I'm told by the people who come to see me from far places those Eastern people who live on the roof of the world in a vastness all their own believe in the 'cleverness' of Man as the highest being, I was told they have a saying 'he who knows how to go about it could live comfortably in Hell'". "Well", laughed The Glass keen to be seen his master's equal in the game of dialectics, "it depends how you define Hell, you might well define yours as how you find yourself now, famous yesterday forgotten today, but we've decided we know how to live with that, and you know the comfort to be had in competence — and me".

He swirled the truth of this latter round his head aware for the first time of something he had never truly seen before — that competence bred a comfort all its own. "Thank-you Glass, when things get rough your 'I can do it' will bear me up and onwards".

"Yer-well it's simple logic really", confirmed The Glass, "the more competent you are the more you can achieve so hell's dissolve about you while the hell of others is your heaven fired by the simple joys of doing, because happiness lies in your head not things — so you can be happy anywhere with anything and", it laughed hugely at its neat rounding of the diagnostic canter, "the higher will be your chance of immortality — 'cause the mass is not immortal'.

"So", he reflected as he raised his companion to the light to see through its tints his life re-built in its rosy hue, "forward with fire is it". "Indeed it is", The Glass confirmed now well away, "for without the fire life's damp and dead, all soggy not sublime". "Ok Sir Glass let's be up'n at'em — some fire is needed, a new idea, let's risk upon a venture to spice life up once more, for that's the thing", he chanted to the vision's voices in his head, "as vision's the way its always been for me and mine — like to join me in the next"? The Glass, by now a little sleepy so reverting, answered, "yer, seems a good idea'n I ain't got nothin' better planned so w'ynot, tho' them plinths seem perilous for the likes 'o me, I might fall off'n wot then when I'm all broke". "Fear of heights, Sir Glass", he chid gaily, "wins no fair lady, so onwards as you say, and never mind the upwards — Resurrection bound d'you think, spot of immortality in our sights perhaps"?, he laughed uproariously lying back to contemplate his new colleague, still beckoning brightly.

"S'all right for you guys with a name", surmised The Glass lugubriously, "they can stick 'em in books'n scribe 'em in stone, us glasses are anonymous'n anonymity equals no immortality'n we have a habit of getting broke in the washing up". "Ah", he consoled, "but us mere mortals have been appealing to you since grapes grew, you've won your place as essential to Man's endeavours so your immortality's secure". "Yer", it continued in its doubt, "but that's the booze you drink woss immortal'n us mere glasses is perishable". "Maybe but without you we don't drink dazzlingly", he encouraged, "we merely swill, and we're a damn site more perishable than you, you've been found in Roman graves still as good as new which is resurrection and immortality in one because not even Romans survived the grave, howzatt"?

The Glass burst out laughing, "Thass me", it chortled proudly, relapsing yet further into the vernacular of its birth, "Essex born'n bred me, in the heady days of Camulodunum before that Boadicea sacked it'n I got put in the bag of a pretty Iceni princelet — they liked nice things y'know". It dislimned quietly thinking of its past, "cor that Boadicea was something I can tell you, all the ancient native gods rolled into one'n tall'n brunette to boot, flaming hair below the waist all blowing in the wind — reel take-your-breath-away style she had, no wonder her people followed'. Perking up it continued, "I was in the hands of my boss looking out over the walls

at the massed tribes below being quaffed from to keep his courage up —
he ran the show in Camno. — but it had all run to seed by his time, all
sloppy'n dissololute so they didn't stand a chance against a determined lot
fighting for their freedom — which was the stirring thing", it burst out
jubilantly. He dislimned again thinking back to that thrilling moment, "she
stood on a little hill amongst them'n stuck her spear into the ground then
socked it to them about living comfortably under tyranny or living as a free
people in their own way — by heck I could feel them Romans shivering
realising with stuff like that it all looked like a greasy end". "Yers", it reflected thoughtfully, "it was fighting for freedom gave those simple people
the power of god, if you understand me, so greasy end it was — though
Ol' V-V survived being a mere craftsman".

"Fascinating", he mused thoughtfully, "I didn't know the Boadicea bit at
all, did her speech survive"? "Yer did actually", it answered fondly, "my
little princelet remembered it word for word then got a monk to write it
down, it's in a library somewhere down West where the Iceni retreated to".
"The freedom idea is powerful stuff friend Glass", he mused thinking back
to where they'd begun, "when I was wandering amongst the broken tower
I felt I could conquer anything with the freedom from the glowering Norman masonry — not Norman really as our conquering forefathers were
religious slaves of Rome so those heavy Norman arches were only reflec-
tions of Rome's hegemony whose collapse made me all light-headed". He
smiled in fond memory, "free's the word we seek friend Glass, freedom
from the Norman tyranny to be ourselves again, free to do it our way
which, dammit, we have despite everyone saying, more times than I could
count, 'it can't be done'", he chortled; "we've come through some tough
times together Glass — to win".

"Yer", it mused fondly as a survivor, 'I was born into tough ol' days'n no
mistake, but classy while Rome ruled before it ran to seed". It laughed
immodestly, "Quintus Fabius Veritas Me Fecit", it said portentously, rolling the Roman name with relish, "Colchester made the best 'n there
weren't none better'n ol' Veritas — to which local custom added Vitreo in
honour of his skill, so V-V he became", it announced proudly, "I was a
loving masterpiece'n you don't get wisdom from the mass produced". He
chuckled hugely at yet another gem from his colleague in creation, "no
indeed you don't Friend Glass, you've got to have made the journey to

know what wisdom is as you clearly have; how did you get here"? "Yer's indeed one has", it sucked its teeth thoughtfully, "been there done that, *and* not much I haven't seen, it's a long story full of thrills but, thank goodness, low on spills, for another time — but I can tell you why I've made it because several people've said so on the way'n its germane to our endeavours'. "So"?, he enquired fascinated.

"Ol' V-V had the truth of it, in beautiful glass", it enthused proud of its provenance, "it's the beauty thing you've struggled for", it mused deep in thought, "even when the going was really tough with all the odds on my demise amongst the noise of falling Houses I've been rescued because I'm beautiful — somehow people've wanted to save something lovely from the mess". He waited, being shown an Olympian truth by one whom he had long treasured — found in a dusty corner of the Refectory long forgotten amongst the meretricious new — because its proud beauty opened doors into his Spirit in ways he had come to understand as vital to his creative surges. It laughed gently, "you know the truth'n beauty thing, 'cause that's why you rescued me from that dusty corner — I was the lovely amongst the discarded". It thought on a bit, "'s not everybody does that 'cause there's few who really relish beauty, too busy grubbing amongst the novelties of the mass-produced — Gregory'll tell you that — it's the individual love which went into my making shines even through the dust when I've been abandoned in the rush".

It thought on while he sat entranced, "Ol' V-V gave that to me to shine the lives of those who know it when they see it'n you've given it to The Cathedral which'll be shining lives long after you're gone — though I might still be there", it giggled happily. "So there we have the truth of our immortality discussion then", he chuckled, "beauty's benison, er with my name on it". 'Vanity, all is vanity', laughed the glass hugely, 'but yes you're right, those who give beauty to shine beyond them are the ones who get remembered which is the truth of that 'Life beyond the Grave' squit you lot hand out to please the plebs'. "Well at least I managed the beauty bit", he chuckled, "even if I've been pleasing the plebs".

He thought for a moment struck by the apparent dichotomy, "It's horses for courses Glass; it's no good feeding the sheep grass they don't understand, talk to most sheep about the Spiritual virtues of beauty's blessing'n you'll get yawns with moans about 'the hereafter' with endless 'how do I get there' questions — no good telling them it's a Fairy Story got up to keep them happy". "Happy", he observed a little sententiously, "is different for different abilities to understand it *and* happy is a cure for life's ills in itself — much better to have happy sheep, if gulled, than un-happy sheep for being perplexed beyond their understanding". "It's shepherds' job", he noted oracularly, assuming majesty's mantle, "to understand the nature of sheep".

"Crikey", giggled The Glass, 'thass high-flown stuff, no vanity there perchance"?, it teased evilly, "but we both know sheep react positively to beauty — even if they don't understand why, even if its only at the level of nice lush grass over the crinkly brown stuff, it says something they may not understand but it makes them feel good to see it — I know", it laughed grandly, "my survival's proof of it". "Ok", he chuckled, "now we've proved the case so let's press onwards, er beauty bound".

"OK", agreed the glass mollified, "I'll buy the deal — woss the plot Pilgrimwards, do I need a staff'n hobnailed boots", fearing it might need more than those it asked, "er, do be so kind as to fill me up again before we hit the road". The thought of a new booze-born venture had The Glass sparking again, jigging about clutching its sides with new inventive genius;

> *Some people think 'all life's abortion',*
> *While others say, 'pray tread with caution',*
> *Oh pour the wine up to the brim*
> *To drive decision upon the whim*
> *To damn prevarication.*

"That do you for Veritas boss"?, it enquired addressing his erstwhile chief as an equal in the ventures to come. He collapsed laughing mightily to have found such a boon companion amongst Creation's travails then, setting the glass gently down on its table with "sure will mate", he drifted into dream...........

A seraphic smile suffused his face as he strode in majesty freed from the darkness of Creeds which withered in the Light his Lantern showed. He rose again resurrected, forever to be immortal with those ancient others whose works had shone Light to dash the darkness of convention in the gutter. He was Magus Magnificent who'd rent from the face of Knowing those 'Creeds of Unknowing' with which Man had girt himself to hide his eyes from Truth. Creeds contain, but the Light from his Lantern would open Men's minds to think — so they might stride the High-Hills of the freedom they create themselves. His dream-girt hand gripped imaginary staff as his face faced high to breast the horizons of the new — now un-afraid. 'Now there's a veritas' he thought as sleep finally carried his feet upon his quest for he had seen that;

Immortality is the Love of Life which Leaves behind Lessons for Later's Delight

So, lesser Men of meaner Mind, pray do not wonder why such as he plunge on, for wine and contemplation have unravelled it. It's the Spirit's fire which keeps them warm — for the ephemeral praise of men is merely a wraith which dies like the morning mists at noon. These Magi live for the Art they create in the visions of Freedom they inhabit, to show Man can rise above the darkness of mortality to offer others the Immortality from the immensities of the Freedom which drives them — for it is rise above mortality which is the truth of Immortality. They know for what they live will always leave them short in the measure of today but glass and wine have showed us how they measure measure, by living life *beyond* — which is High-Art's satisfaction. It is here they find Identity through the Immortality born of the service beyond self to be the truth of true creation — Man's choice when he began.

I, one like he, would passionately love to know how it got to be there. I would love to have been part of the creative team which laboured in the dusts below as our efforts rose above — but now all I can do is add one more cheer to what he and his team achieved. Standing down below in the greatest worship space in Christendom it's a hell of a long way up — but does it matter? Man's struggled to know how the world was made but would such knowledge affect his joys in it? I've been privileged to climb amongst its timbers but what really matters is the light it casts below when lit by the evening sun — the challenging light of its difference to the convention which caged before. I've sat in concerts which it munificent space permits as organs, choirs and orchestras translate me far beyond so I look up high above to hope those brave men got their reward for being part of what they'd done. Certainly they deserve their immortality for there is nothing like it in the world as its outline brands the building it surmounts as one alone. Resurrection? Oh most certainly for whenever I see it from afar or go into that space I resurrect their faith so they live on through the inspiration I derive from what they dared. Was not that their intent — to fire the inspiration of those to come in the vision as they saw it? Truly they enacted the words of him for whom they built for they 'Loved one another' by offering a vision with their best endeavour, risked beyond the ordinary, to gild the lives of all who've followed. 'Tis the measure of the Risk which gilds the venture to become the virtue of what inspires, they dared — as to be Man must we. Man's Spirit served his fellow to bring Heaven made on Earth, which I'm sure they knew — which is the only heaven worth the telling.

I, a mere mechanic know this, for, though no towers bedeck my passing, I have traveled his path many times. It was bad enough in my engineering days but now a writer, chasing the fugitive idea and word, I find myself driven relentlessly by synaptic clashing keeping me awake in bursts for hours at night, leaping about writing notes for those words escape like flashing comets if not clasped upon the moment. The truth is Creation's Cross is the heart of Creation itself for its energies take us and shake us at their command until we've done their bidding. Then, should success crown our efforts, we become a hissing for separated from our fellows by what they haven't done themselves, as jealousy views our efforts with distaste — forever misunderstood and feared because unknown — try to raise finance for a manufacturing venture to know the truth of this. If he doesn't succeed he's laughed to scorn with 'I told you so' being his lonely road of castigation — so no victory can be his — yet, like Jesus, all is, for;

Man's Crown is hanging on Creation's Cross to turn Mortality Im-Mortal.

(Ely; The Octagon & Lantern; Alan de Walsingham, Sacrist; William Hurley, Edward III's Master Carpenter; 1322)

Postlude:

Some two months after I had finished this story I acquired a fine 19th C edition of Victor Hugo's 'Notre Dame De Paris''' spurred on by Stevenson's 'Familiar Studies of Men and Books', in which it is featured under his essay on Hugo. All we remember of this essentially grisly tale is 'The Hunchback of

Notre Dame' (a sadly populist misconception of a fine book) but whose truth for Hugo was the building itself — Notre Dame de Paris — for which the tale is merely a vehicle. Notre Dame, even in its modern desecrated state, is almost the only survival of the 14th Century truth of Gothic Paris where the new free art of the pointed arch flourished to such an extraordinary degree to render the Paris of those days a wonder of the world. Hugo devotes two chapters, alas ridiculed by Stevenson the story-teller, to an exhaustively detailed description of 14th Century Paris as seen from the top of Notre Dame, his thesis being that virtually all this quite fantastic magnificence was destroyed by the 'Gods' of later ages — to be replaced with the far less attractive or great — which he bewails mightily.

Hugo then flies his considerable study of architecture in a substantial chapter headed *"This will Destroy That"* to explain why the glories of Gothic Paris were destroyed in his understanding that *before printing* architecture was the language of Man's expression — he built. It is a long chapter which, as a creative engineer, *making things,* I found riveting as Hugo places his case magisterially that (ignoring his superb digressions into descriptions of the 'coded' and the 'free' languages of architectural pasts) 'Roman' architecture, which had dominated Europe since long before the Papacy, was an entirely proscribed coded form — the *'Classical* architecture of priests' — which was superceded by Gothic the *'Romantic'* architecture of the pointed arch which was entirely free from any cage for being conceived by the masons who built it. Hugo describes this as 'The Architecture of The People' fitting it into a much wider understanding of the loosening of the bonds of Rome upon people's thinking in general with a freeing of their creative processes as Rome began to lose its stranglehold on thought. Architecture's language exploded into an entirely new form of thought — the freedom of Gothic.

The only point which Hugo doesn't drive home in such words is Masons were artisans — absolutely of the people — and their concepts were *entirely a result of their imagination matched to their skills* — not a priest nor code in sight. As an 'artisan' myself with a knowledge of how early Masons worked this extension of Hugo's thesis is inescapable. Hugo's extended thesis, superbly put, is the advent of printing would replace this freedom of thinking in stone with a far wider thinking available from the printed word — his *'This will Replace That'* — his fancy played as the Archdeacon of Notre

Dame, Dom Claude Rollo (Quasimodo's foster) shows a colleague a printed book he holds then points to the pinnacles of his church outside. Hugo very convincingly makes the case that, from the advent of thinking in words which printing made available, the freedom of Gothic architecture — thinking in stone — did indeed begin to die — he catalogues it — pointing to masons being superceded by a new form of 'priest', architects with 'patrons' (with later the anonymity of government departments etc), who start to dictate so the 'people freedoms', of untrammelled artisanic inspiration which was Gothic's true magnificence at its height — faded into coded forms of ever more reductionist style as 'priests' ruled again — this is the same point made by Ruskin in *The Seven Lamps of Architecture*. Since Hugo's exposition is the essence of my story I inserted the 'architecture' bit to drive the beginning few paragraphs with some greater force.

He flies one other kite very powerfully too which was clearly dear to his heart — which is also central to my themes — the priestly denial of the Body as central to Man's Spiritual sustenance. He has Archdeacon Claude Rollo — Quasimodo's 'brother' — destroy himself mentally by his passion for Esmeralda with a magnificent passage concerning the falsity and horrors which lie behind the priestood for denying Man's Bodily essence. I fancy Hugo was an independent voice to Blake but their understanding of Man's true estate is identical — nicely done Sir.

I have a very considerable feeling for both Hugo's stands having spent my whole career as a creative 'artisan' with my last ten years damning every form of priest and priesthood — because they always imprison 'the people'. Britain is a hell of priests and priest-hoods today with our once proud people, who showed the World how to be free through skills galore, now so un-free they have forgotten what freedom is — nor can mend a fuse. All most do now is press buttons on computers to get 'coded' answers into which they have virtually no input, which very rarely creates anything. That fantastic multiplicity of personal skills which made Britain 'Great' has entirely vanished from our people — submerged beneath "This is So & Do it Thus", with "It isn't Allowed", "It's Dangerous" and 'It isn't My Job" — to have arrived at the state where even the 'priests' don't know how to create anything — except maintain The Cage.

The Moral of my Tale?

As soon as 'priests', Idolaters and Ideologues, Governments and Gover-
nors, Styles and Schools, Didacts and Demagogues, indeed any who say
"This is so & Do it Thus" dictate, then Art is emasculated, so beauty with-
ers to leave Civilisation a broken thing of un-beauty because true greatness
denied. Look at the list of the greats who were not admitted to the Royal
Academy — 'The greatest originator in Western Art' (Britannica of William Blake) never was — with the many mediocrities who were. See the
mediocrities spawned by Arts Councils with the ugly hydra which emerge
from *any* form of Government Agency, which have made Britain such an
un-beautiful place — to scarify The Spirit of its people.

Aphrodite, Novemer 2009

Aspects of Love

A collection of short stories

A Morning in Florence

by Aphrodite

Mrs Stephen Ralli
St. Catherine's
Lodge,
Hove.

A MORNING IN FLORENCE

(A Fancy Flown upon a Fact — Born of a Beautiful Bookplate)

The Troubadour

Fair Gentles I need to set the scene for you or my Story will be as Dark as the Ages from which it springs. We are in 13th Century Florence as The Renaissance is afoot, but not yet fleet for the grip of Holy Church is tight, nor is she indulgent, yet her need for political control for the indulgence of herself has her corrupting Europe with 'indulgences' to fancify her own, for the foundations of St Peter's will be built upon the fallacy of bones. Its Pope, Innocent III (what laughs) is murdering the Cathari Innocents far away in Southern France with his Dominican death-squad merely because they're 'The Knowing' so have never thought much of Holy Church. Francis in Assisi, a layman not a priest, has petitioned Innocent for a dispensation to run his highly ascetic Order which, sadly, codes as much as Mother Church, but as a snook at her indulgence. Florence herself is a cesspit of libertine behaviour, a pile of dung made of money got easy; yet a social code as tight as Rome's for all its profligate similarities, for those of money and family worship at the feet of what they've made — Florence herself — to abandon their freedom quite as much as they have to Holy Church. Yet dear Gentles, it will be this City of bubbling corruption, a god in men's eyes, from which the finest flowering of Man will spring, as lilies thrive on dungheaps.

It is a rotten world for corrupted by the Vices those Ancient Greeks sprang from Pandora's Box, yet the change I will play you will deal those Dark Vices their proper blow to show them in the New Knowledge as angels' wings — so we may find Virtue's Light in unaccustomed places. It is but the start of this Re-Naissance for Holy Church is not easy beat so it will take two hundred years before she bows at Medici's bending — some say she never has. The subject of my little play?; I shall show you men's Minds opened, which opening is his only salvation from corruption against Holy Church's dread closed door which has so mightily corrupted it for Caging it. It is here, in Florence, the glories of Greek Thought and Art will be reborn to re-light Man's Mind as Periclean thought had shown it.

So, let me play you a little fancy upon some well known facts to lift a corner of The Dark Ages' 'Cloud of Unknowing' — for curtailed within The Church's saying. Dung-heap Florence may have been but two lilies grew within it to make it the wonder of The Western World. Gentles, it is a frail begining for Holy Church is mighty, but it is a start — and it is Art, Man's finest flowering of his Spirit. You shall meet its three protagonists at the critical point, the fusion even, which sprang the Light from out the Dark, but first — a springboard — Adieu.

Mrs Stephen Ralli's Story

The late 19th Century finds us 'On Tour' in Florence courtesy of Mr Baedecker's train schedules, spurred upon our course by Mr Ruskin, our hands held by Mr Murray's Guides. We sally out of our fine hotel (all mod cons H&C) upon a gorgeous spring morning, having communed with Mr Ruskin in our room the night before. We have his *Mornings* IN FLORENCE', fresh from his prolific pen. Pray be not so supercilious as to think we can not proofread for that is how Mr Ruskin's own publisher announces his little letters to the public who go on tour, in proud sans-serif caps. in gold across the front of their pretty little red card covers. He, the seer of the age, knows the value of advertisement for without it how shall we see? Little books, 'got up upon the moment' as he says in his introduction 'to set straight a number of the errors of the popular guides' with, it hardly need be said for he the age's King of Art, 'to offer us a little of his knowledge of Renaissance Art -'Being Simple Studies of Christian Art for English Travellers'. We saw one on a bookstall on The Parade to be immediately attracted — so now, upon its intriguing prompting, we find ourselves here on indeed 'A Morning in Florence' to see if we might capture a little of what he claims so eruditely made this place.

Mr Ruskin's words are fine but he, today's arch 'seer', commands us 'see' for ourselves so we may interpret what we see though our Spirit — not his dry words. Guide books guide but it is we who must 'see', by seeing, so here we are at his persuasion — but our expense so let us hope we have placed our faith aright.

My introduction heads this story, oh my dear the height of Art Noveau, (which decks the little book she talks of which lies before me as I write — but affixed before or after?) — but Hove? Well you know how it was when the train came to what Prinny had made the Mecca, The Pavilion became awash with trippers then we couldn't take the air on *our* Promenade without being jostled, and the clothes, my dear how ghastly — so we 'packed our tents' then fled into the desert like the Arabs. Hove isn't on 'the train' so our peace is restored — after all a place is what you make it.

So here we are at **SANTA CROCE**, the first stop in the first of his little books — for **SANTA CROCE** is what it says upon the cover, bold, like **FLORENCE** so we have obeyed, courtesy of Mr Murray's guide. It's been a pleasant walk from our hotel which gives us a tiny look at how it might have been when this city was being built as modern does not seem to have overlaid it yet. Donkeys from the hills jostle in the little streets bringing the vegetables to the market, while black covered old women struggle under loads as their men sit in the parks playing boules — shameful these continental men, we've seen it throughout France too, you would not have thought in this enlightened age a moment's emancipation had come to these poor women — back home at least we don't see *that*.

We enter the cloister of **SANTA CROCE** (still very much in sans-serif caps my dears) and retrieve Mr Ruskin's little letter to see how he sets about the poor Mr Murray's asseverations — because while reading it again last night we remembered how poorly he had done under Mr Ruskin's stern eye. We are alone as we have taken Mr Ruskin's advice, so 'paid the sacristan well' while indeed 'made friends with him', so he is not sitting on our tails. We aren't interested in the 'relics' he's so keen to show us for a cent as we are trying to capture something of the magic Mr Ruskin has had us come all this way to 'see' — God grant we have eyes to see or it will have been a long wasted trip. So used to Gothic we have placed out trust in Mr Ruskin to show us something new — after all has he not achieved *The Stones of Venice*, but alas we found, even us my dears, the price a little steep to visit a world about which we know nothing — but can he show us something here? We have done what he commanded, which has been something of a trial as the weather has been overcast — but if you have come to see by a master's hand there's no ignoring his direction so we 'waited for an entirely bright morning'. We have 'risen with the sun and gone to **SANTA CROCE**, with a good opera-glass in our pocket' and we have walked 'straight to the chapel on the right of the choir ('k' in your Murray's Guide)'.

We do all he tells us, like good sheep at a master's bidding but, we know not why, it does not speak to us nor do Angels seem to attend our expectations. The colonades of the Duomo — a late commission of the greatest of them all he tells us — are splendid but an arch is an arch when all is said and done. We have tramped the course his little letter shows us, indeed found some wondrous things, but we have not yet 'seen', we're still desolately here, not there — is it us or him?

Footsore and 'colonnaded' to destruction we decide lunch would be a salve to dreams of magic un-requited — which we decide to take continental style 'al fresco' in the park. We equip ourselves with bread — I wish we could get such stuff at home — cheese fresh in from the market with some salad things. Then we find ourselves a Vino Officina to try the local white — but the red seems tempting too as he gives us a glass to taste — so why not try them both we say. Tourists we may be but the necessary hardware for the preparation of a salad lunch we have to hand (best London Maker) so we find a seat in the sun then spread ourselves upon the rug he provided in his 'kit'. The Duomo rises in the near distance, there is quiet except for birds as we find our spirits touched by the spring flowers bursting forth — the wine is good — the sun is hot as we have walked so we remove our shoes to twiddle our tired toes. Yes the wine is good, we've tried them both — the sun is hot so we decide a little kip is on the order books. The rug was good so 'Hove' lay down with the Duomo's top arcading glancing through the trees to drift their dozing vision — then synapses, unusually assembled, crowded in to open a door upon a distant story.

Mrs Stephen Ralli's Dream

It is the Summer of 1290, a joyous summer day but Florence is in angst again, buzzing with the news. News is news in this salacious city where it's daily devoirs are the piling of money upon money to feed the orgiastic feasting — while convention locks society like a vice. Angst because the awful Signor Alighieri has hit them again with one of his scurrilous pamphlets. He ought to be 'put down' by public opinion it was agreed, yet some knew greatness resided inside his damning verses so full of wonderful new language. There is some grief, yet more of avarice, at the news of the gorgeous Miss Portinari's so early death, yet none knew it was imminent, but avarice wanted to know where the Portinari fortune would go now. A few had hoped she could have captured Alighieri's arrogance to make a man of him, not the scourging beast of its attendant vices, perhaps a new giant of the struggling Art to be a luminary of their city of which they were so inordinately proud — because they had made it.

Now she was gone what would become of him, they asked, would he unleash himself on them as a scapegoat for his grief? It was said, the rumour-mongers had it, he had kissed her then revealed his unquenched love before she died. But, damn the man, he'd been seen in all his arrogance eating the new dish which had recently arrived from Bologna but eating it in a new way, on a big round crust of bread *then, damn the man again,* inventing a new name for it. The brass of it, he'd called it Pizza — what the hell was that? Pah, there was not future in it but the sauce was good; alas the bloke who'd imported the recipe wasn't giving up the secret so those captured by its subtle Bolognese aromas were obliged to pay his price — but no matter there was cash aplenty. Florence did not do romance only gluttony and money so Alighieri's kiss was no great matter just another inexplicable of a man whom none could know.

Arrogant bugger, they said, with his Pizza and now his Beatrice dead perhaps he would emigrate then leave them all alone — but little voices quibbled, 'he will be great so we want him for our own because perhaps he will create a whole new language one day to speak of Florence's magnificence, so do the scourges matter they're only words, mere 'prentice work perhaps — if only they weren't so true'. Still, the money salved the hurts while there was still some evanescent interest in how 'that man' managed to get the meat chopped so fine, but the sauce was still delicious.

So Florence, the yet to be emergent shining star of Western Art wiled away its hours in feasting food and cash, laced with the trumpery tides of fashion, its mind eroded by intrigue's corruption so set into a cultural blank. Banking centre of 'the world' (it imagined itself to be) but it had not yet learnt how to spend its money well for gorging itself upon itself today without the skills to leave anything behind for tomorrow — having yet nothing to pass its self-made glory on.

Yet, some said, and yet, there were little stirrings, perhaps even pregnant possibilities for was not that sauce quite new and Pizza? Perhaps Alighieri with his spiky features and spiteful words might be the start of it, and there was that young Bondone, he was good emerging from Arnolfo's shadow like a meteorite, even the gluttons could see he had something the others didn't.

What it was we shall soon see but they could not as still in the Cage Christianity had locked round art like the chastity belts some still clamped around their wives when men went roving — then on knightly quest but now on money's bidding. Art?, what was Art, but they did not know Art either because Art was just around the corner which, had they but known it, was to be born of he they hated and he they loved. Nor did they know it would be fired by another, a catalyst of something new, beauty for its own sake, not beauty enchained by Holy Church. Miss Donati they knew and loved, loved because she loved with a simplicity which captured all, so loved by all yet whom, even in this rapacious city, had never been the food of men.

It is thus we have the three actors of our playlet. We find them in the little sunlit courtyard of Dante's house, a resplendent house for his Father is a wealthy man but a man of principle who, despite the undisguised hate of his second wife who distrusts her stepson's brilliant wit (for knowing it reads her like a book) is happy to have his son at home in his own suite. This is Dante Alighieri who, though lost to all but the scholar now, would indeed do what Florence hoped — put her on the map with words — words culled from his impenetrable grief of the loss of Beatrice whose fame would live on as the greatest un-requited duo in the records of Love's listings. 'Dante & Beatrice' sings down time like 'Orpheus & Euridice' with 'Héloïse & Abelard', a mere hundred years before and famous too as they were married, secretly, despite their fame as 'un-requited' lovers.

Then we have Giotto di Bondone, a young craftsman, 'prentice to the aging Arnolfo, yet not so struggling as he paints voraciously all sorts of things, priestly portraits many of them to pay the bills but straining at the Churchly Cage. It will be he who places Florence atop the pile of that pregnant stirring we know now as The Renaissance — the re-discovery of the splendours of Greek culture in the Arts & Sciences. The point from whereon Art will shout its resplendent wares from atop a pillar of its own to be honoured outside any Churchly chain. A platform from whose solid Grecian base will march the science of enquiry, with sword unsheathed to fight the dread *Summae* of Aquinas; 'cage all knowledge indeed' the adventurers scoffed, 'damn the man what the hell does he think he knows of it' — but Holy Church was strong.

Then we have the lovely young Gemma Donati. In a florid city where the courtesan was the norm with 'love' swapped for a song, Gemma was different ; yet in a place where difference was so frowned upon for a sterile conformity clouding all, she was loved because she loved all, none were set aside in her affections. She had never seen why the struggles for power should cloud her clear light nor the gift of her joy in simple things should keep her from her friends, yet no man had yet touched her, for all felt somehow they would soil what Florence loved should they despoil it. Neat, of moderate size, everything was all of one, nothing stood her beyond her peers except her inner glow which challenged none yet from which so many gently fed. A love for her, the sentient knew, not a love of her nor, goddamit, the 'Love of God' the princely prelates thrust so mightily down their throats selling it as Man's salvation — and don't forget Holy Church's needs in your prayers nor from your purses. Yet deep inside so none knew of it Gemma had always loved Giotto from afar, gentle dreamy Giotto with the lovely hands with which he made things — not like the rich who only masturbated money. 'One day', she dreamed, 'I shall make him mine to have those hands make of me what they make with brush by winning his gentle mind to love me as I love him'.

Gemma Donati had been a close childhood friend of Beatrice Portinari's, they had played together from little girls. She it was who had borne Dante's inconsequential rages when, for reasons none could understand, he had set his childhood love of Beatrice behind bars to torture himself and her — with all those round him for their joint distress. As his brilliance grew the doubts of his genius grew within him as the hissing of those he lampooned divided Florence about his cursings of its lusts — so he chose to swirl the cloak of words' majesty around him to scarify the people whose standards he set so far below his own. Poor Gemma, poor Beatrice, and indeed poor Giotto who was close in the triumvirate as had been Simone di Bardi (heir of the di Bardi bank) but fate, and Dante would destroy.

At the return of Dante's lifelong friend Simone from his studies in Ravenna, it was announced he would be betrothed to Beatrice to join the Bardi fortunes to the Portinari which would set a mighty house in place. Dante simply 'lost the plot' then set about to destroy Simone with all he stood for, a crazed witch-hunt through his influence with The Duke. 'Inexplicable', they moaned as all knew he was not one with Beatrice so his rampage against the Bardi's simply did not make sense — except to Little Gemma and his friend Bondone who knew the truth of his self-hidden love for Beatrice.

'Inexplicable', cried those who banked with the de Bardi's facing ruin, 'what a hoot' cheered those who banked elsewhere knowing well of Dante's power with The Duke, while just loving filling their idle hours by stoking other people's ends. 'Inexplicable', but everything about the man of later years had become impossible as he tortured himself for no apparent reason — yet, oh yet they loved him, those who did not hate him for his barbs, for he sucked them in, yet spat them out while giving of his genius. What a swirling mess whose centre was this man's stirring.

We step into their little sunlit courtyard to meet our actors who are in conclave — two bent on rescuing the third from self-immolation but, even with spring's burgeoning, the sword of death hangs high as grief allied its occupants. Despite the magnificence of the city all seemed tissue thin as Man had been on his wrecking path again. The Bank of friends was bust wrecked by one of theirs, a lovely girl from whom so much was promised lay perished young while Holy Church's hand gripped tight Man's bursting urge to speak now he was finding Her recipe too corrupt — it hadn't saved the gorgeous Beatrice, so what value its omniscience? Each of them in so many ways struggled with the problems of this age where diseases and cages, greed and vice so vaunted themselves over Man's struggles to find a better way, some light to shine his path so he could believe, for Holy Church was no way at all the doubters knew, robbing the poor for 'indulgences' to build its own 'heaven' wrapped tightly round its own.

Birds sang while the wine twinkled in their glasses — supplied by an indulgent father keen not to lose a son to a wife's determined hate with hopes of some veritas from within the glass. "She's dead", he muttered morosely banging his fist upon the table to set the glasses jigging, "yet in life I killed her, Giotto what is wrong with me"? No novelty sits amongst these three nor rumour either for Miss Portinari's sudden death is the centre of their existence. Their world, so wrapped in her etherial passage as the vital link between them while, so recently, the cause of their struggles to bring order out of Dante's created chaos, was now upset, its focus lost for, assuredly Beatrice had been, though not tight amongst them, the centre of their being. For one as a lifelong friend, for another as an object of his love yet hateful struggle while the last his vision of what he was beginning to see beauty as — because Beatrice was beautiful. The painter was not in love with her as he respected Dante's passion but he was deeply in love for what she stood for to him, a window onto a world outside The Church's chains.

"She's dead Gemma", Dante cursed, "I killed her with my manufactured hate, what devil rides me Gemma, you're the one who sees, you sit outside passion's ragings, please tell me what you see", he pleaded, he the genius yet without the wit to plumb his own deep pit. "It wasn't you Dante", she replied cautiously, "though she was grieved at your love turned hate, she was dying of something the leeches knew not of, which she had known for quite a time, I was with her when she died to know she was serene for you had declared your Love with your kiss, so she passed into the light with you her knight beside her — with that at least you should be pleased", she trailed away wondering if she was making any progress against his self-created cage. "Dante I don't sit here to blame", she continued gently, "for no good can come of it as Beatrice is in heaven, I come, like Giotto here, to heal so we may find a new way forward where we may all honour her memory in what we do — can you live with that"?

Dante, lost inside himself so seeing no answer to Gemma's question made no reply, so she continued. "Your grief you must live with", she continued gently, "to assuage the grief you made her last three years a desert so 'tis your grief now, not hers for she's at rest salved by your final declaration, our job is to find a way to help; but it is a truth time will help you in your course, with the knowledge with your last kiss you saved your Love, but now you must save yourself to honour it — for she who loved you would not have you pass on disgraced". There was a long silence as the wine swilled gently down as the breeze rustled the trees about them. Gemma looked at the distraught Dante with anguished eyes; 'could she ever offer anything to this so faulted genius locked away inside his head' — yet she had the beginnings of an inspiration dredged from the depths of ancient surgings within her simple Spirit. It was the first time she had formulated it but in this desperate strait for the anguish of another she knew it clearly.

"Dante, your Love saved Beatrice from the fires of Hell, so might not Love do the same for you?; not Love of her, still less the love of self but the Love of something far outside yourself to drive you upwards — a star to guide you through the wastes you live in now"?, to a continuing silence. "Now is not the time to scourge yourself for what has been", she soothed gently forwards, "no road lies there, so now spring's being born anew, abandon your old arrogance, try to discover of what it's made so you may heal yourself", she put a hand across the table thinking she may have made a small advance, but Dante brooded on.

Gemma Donati was a vital part of this little trio for a woman amongst men; bubbly, simple, loved by all because she loved all so, Giotto thought, if any, it would be she who saved Dante from the cross upon which he had so staunchly hung himself, even the cross of negating women. Perhaps her clear neutrality might be the salve, not woman as Florence understood it, yet not man either, making no advances nor yet false retirings she was just what she was a rarity, but; those ancient stirrings had given her a hint perhaps less airy measures might break those chains he bound so tight about him — she a woman and he a man. Could she pierce those spiky features to soothe the spiky soul to effect a healing? Could she get his brilliance out from its inner Hell to flower the world around with words as she felt sure Giotto could with pictures once he'd found a true way out of Holy Church's clutches.

As she held his hand she gently suggested, "Dante, try to see the fine, undo the darkness which clouds your spirit, the people sing your fine songs, why not build on that"? — "what know I of fine when I know not what fine is", he mumbled, "it's my lack of knowing whether what I do is good or merely the surface dross the city claims it — how am I to know"? "Well", suggested Giotto, seeing a gap in Dante's self-constructed wall, "perhaps you could stop the lampooning, leave the city in peace to forget your taunts of it so cease to curse you, then try another course — praise perhaps, not damn", he continued quietly seeing a little of the truths of new, "this idea of beauty for what it might show us of ourselves is creeping through me, might you not try the same, it speaks to me from deep inside , might some such not do for you, you paint in words — might there not be some magic there"? Gemma smiled across the table at this young man she truly knew so little of, yet loved, who'd just burst a firework across the darkened sky. Little urges crept above her normal gentle self, something for herself perhaps but might they also do for others, 'is that what my insides are telling me'? She looked at Bondone differently, as a man who might please her, a man from whom she might have pleasures others did (or claimed) yet she had never known; was there something there she could make her own — yet use to save another'?

Dante snorted, "Giotto you know how terrible they all are, you were at the Bardi dinner to welcome Simone back, blathering in the arrogance of their imagined perfection, grovelling in their easy garnered wealth, yet bored with it for not knowing how to spend it but on themselves, what sort of way to go is that; you know there's no possibility of what you strive for there amongst their feeding troughs, for though they like you they truly know not what you are". "Maybe", Bondone agreed, "but are *you* any better for slanging them, while all they see is a cankered soul kicking what it doesn't like, you're but one but they are many so surely you can see the only way to victory is to prove them wrong by winning in a field in which they can not fight — your field of words — in praise not cursing". "But what can I praise"?, Dante spat, "when all around is idle feasting — someone needs to tell them so", he got up for a moment raging round the little courtyard, "the trouble is there's too much damn divinity about, all worshiping their bags of gold imagining they're god — talk about Golden Images, Ugh — not any different with the priests either hanging on their godsignature with their noses in the air just like the others thinking they're the real thing".

"Trouble is they pay the bills Dante", observed The Artist — "whose, not mine nor yours Giotto", Dante sizzled, "Florence may have got loot leaking out of it everywhere but they have not the wit to do more than feed themselves, never seen them feed anyone else — Florence Divine? — much more like a sick Comedy of gold and greed".

"Well instead of moaning at it", suggested his friend, "why don't you try tapping it, look at it with different eyes — write them catchy to un-sick the Comedy, get them on your side instead of against you — how about a play, funny of course 'cause funny always draws 'em in". "Maybe", mused

Dante, "but how do you turn Hell into Paradise pray — and funny"? "Put a bit of Purgatory in between perhaps", tried The Creator enjoying trying to gee his recalcitrant friend out of his delusions, then chuckled at a happy thought.

How about 'The Divine Comedy', make a natty play title, think about it, plenty of laughs in there if you tried'n it's always laughs which pay the bills, so; there you are, Florence's gift to the world of words and if you got it right you might hit the real Divinity stakes, all that immortality stuff *and*', he noted as a demon afterthought, "you could still win at your old game as people in high places hate being laughed at so think of the sales to all those envious cities round us, they'd be splitting their sides so buy you by the thousand just to see The Great Alighieri shooting down his own with ridicule; think of it, no end to your new horizon, nothing parochial there, set up your own scriptorium, world-wide sales, best-seller stuff", he burst out laughing at his effusion then mused, "not so easy for us painter blokes though, you got to get the tourists in to see the stuff but they don't pay — you've got it made as a wordsmith Dante, so quit moaning to crack on".

Gemma Donati laughed, watching her men being 'bloody men' arguing round in idiot circles. "The Divinity of Comedy or The Comedy of Divinity boys"?, she joked happily. "Ugh", muttered Dante irritably, "out of the mouths of babes" — "here you mind your lip", jumped in The Artist, "you may be god's gift to words so you ought to know how to use them properly and you may be angry at yourself but that's no need to take it out on those who love you — though goodness know why sometimes — Gem's a woman and you don't speak to anyone nice like that'n if you'd not been so keen to cast a brick you'd remember the rest about wisdom coming from sucklings — I think's Gem's got a great idea, do a bit of work on it instead of ranting — there's money in words if they aren't bricks".

Emergent smiled at 'mate' for his brisk defence, 'there's something there for me perhaps' she thought. She put an arm round the fractious Dante, "think about it love, Comedy's always been Divine, it takes us out of ourselves, makes us better beings but the whole Holy Church thing's a ghastly Comedy, a comedy of errors indeed; if you'd a mind to step outside its cage you could look at the theatre within, all their idiot capering about to make-believe, so a chap of your skill with words could romp through all that — caricature's always been your thing".

"Gem's right Dante", insisted his friend, "think of Florence as a caricature, a ghastly laugh with all those frightful old financiers feeding their flaccid chops — then pass on to higher things" — "but Beatrice was Divine Giotto", Dante moaned still deep in self-immolation, "we all knew that, how could someone so beautiful have sprung from such a pit"? Gemma, who had held her hand as she passed on admonished firmly, "stop your cursing Dante you can't hurt them nor improve them either so look differently — you kissed her as your proof of the love you'd denied, so pass on upwards to offer the praise which failed you while she was with us, why not offer it to her now in memory to immortalise what she stood for at the last for you — your masterpiece in words in praise of a perfection which is truthfully still there, was never sullied by even Florence's sloppy ways". "But all I know is how to cast Florence's iniquities in its teeth", he replied still simmering, "for those truths I've been made a hissing" — "but Florence is beautiful too Dante", encouraged she who knew of it, "and she bore Beatrice so forget the frailties of the child she is then think on the possibilities of a burgeoning you could father like you grow a child to help her build on it so build you with her — for that you've got the mettle". Dante, doubtful still, couldn't see her Vision nor get the measure of it so missed the message, blinded to Florence's virtues by his coruscating condemnations — not able now Beatrice was dead to exist in the beauties of above for having enveloped his soul in Hell's dark shades, inside his head.

"It's all right for you", Dante muttered, "you're a natural happy soul, you don't hang upon creation's cross like I" — "ah but I do", riposted The Artist with powerful conviction, "yet I don't stick its nails in me like they torture you for I know myself above creation's angst so can have the joy of it in, damn it any image I choose, for no longer will I hawk a godly Papal picture for I know myself a God — for I am a creator, which they tell us is Divine". "Perhaps", Dante acknowledged at this neat artifice, "but I don't know myself like you appear to, or perhaps I know too well so can't stand the sight of what I see" — "then what had you kiss Beatrice", chid Giotto briskly, "what transformation told you to — tell me that Sir Angst", irritated by his friend's passion for his place in Purgatory, now deep in Hell — so very far from Paradise.

Dante looked away, "if I could see why I might have the answer to it — something said it to me, which is all I know". The Artist sat for a moment unsure quite how to proceed so called in assistance in the hope a path might open, "what did Brother Eblio tell you when you went to see him, I saw you in his shop on the bridge deep in conversation, you don't normally tarry with him, scholar though he be". Dante looked pained remembering Brother Eblio's quiet probing, "he showed me an illustrious future from a long vanished past from an old book he wanted to give me but it frightened me — then so many wise things which touched me close I walked away for fear of seeing what I am, then he told me to conquer myself", he stopped a minute thoughtful but yet troubled, "he told me Hell is in the heart, not beyond the grave".

Giotto picked up the ball old Eblio had thrown him, "good words my friend for one so wracked because nothing can come of your present state, we all know Hell is in your heart but only you can find out why — then set out on the road to Paradise". Dante slumped then applied himself to the glass, "even the disarranged me knows that, but I'm no longer me, I'm me with the ghost of she, which I can't conquer because she's no longer here". There was a little catch as the ghost of Beatrice visited, then a gently expanding Gemma picked up the ball as her vision cleared, "you don't need to conquer her just wrap her memory in your Spirit to fire it to new fields". Dante, still determined to lock his cage muttered, "yet I'm too in turmoil now to cure — there was a moment where I thought Beatrice would be my salvation — but now she's dead I have no crutch".

"Pah, what crutch", cursed his friend agry at his recalcitrance, "you're a man for goodness sake, not even women need a crutch". There was a deathly silence as Dante scowled at the truth of this. 'Do I want a man merely as a crutch'?, wondered 'Little Gemma', 'was this man who demanded all stand upright on their own really the one for her — did she need or want a crutch' — but no longer knew quite what she wanted nor why — but her insides were leading her astray from this stern path. "Perhaps it's not a crutch Giotto", she suggested, "but a hand to hold to share the journey so both may build it better then share the joy of it, that's not weakness surely?, Dante love its no weakness to make Beatrice's memory into a fine staff for your Pilgrimage, that's no crutch but inspiration for holding hands with her because if you're to drag yourself out of your pit to greatness you need a Vision — could not Beatrice be the centre of it"? Bondone stared non-plussed quite unused to wisdom come from women, least of all from 'Little Gemma' — 'perhaps his Florentine arrogance was missing a trick'; but was it truth or a convenience, a woman thing, he was unsure taken out of his struggle to make Art to think on people things; visions for him were scenes for pictures, inanimate, simple straight-forward copy-book stuff 'perhaps Little Gemma's got something I haven't seen — the matter of people in what I paint, not just the picture'.

Silence surrounded the little group as two wrestled for the soul of one, impenetrable, unknowable, 'yet surely not un-savable', she thought . She knew Dante's stand offish reputation with women, too arrogant to admit he needed one perched high on his pinnacle of him, yet', she felt, 'deep inside so unsure of what he was, yet did they know the truth of him or was it all a front?' Yet all knew such as those lampoons had not been seen before, they sparkled with more than their malice and bright wit — 'was there not the seeds of greatness there which could be his salvation?' Woman surged through her yet 'Mother' overlaid the turmoil for all had loved Alighieri despite the frictions, as she saw a baby lost upon the way. Then, from deep inside, 'Little Gemma' joined in happy harmony with those surgings to show her something new.

"Come back to mine", she invited, "my folks have gone to our country place and the afternoon draws on so supper will be needed soon — while sofa's beckon after the formality of your father's chairs", she laughed having hatched her plot. 'Win or lose it all', she cheered to herself, 'two men I do not have yet the possibility of saving one and winning the other surely, 'I don't fear my fate that much' so 'I must put it to the touch' — do I really mind how I arrive if joy's abounding?' Dante had never been for her but his saving might be. He, so lost in his misery, was slightly the worse for wine, so was placed between them as she thanked his father with a wink.

The old man watched them go, and wondered. 'Little Gemma' in charge of his angry son with a merry wink, with young Bondone in attendance, could something good lie there?, well at least' he pondered, 'it couldn't be any worse than now it was'. He closed the wall door behind them then retreated through the courtyard to his books — his solace in the turbulence of Florence's iniquitous politics and the naggings of his wife at his son's 'damnations' as she put them. Yet he, a man of letters too, had a feeling for his son's endeavours; though he could never reach them he too felt there was the possibility of greatness there. He wondered as he saw the wink, a very girly wink he had not missed, whether the delicious Miss Donati had seen something in his son which he had not, so chuckled, 'the Donatis were good stuff too not sunk in the cesspit like so many — she would do' he thought. He giggled gleefully at the thought of his high-browed son sprawled across 'The Delicious' with Bondone cheering on, she so virginal yet so clearly up to scruff; 'perhaps a damn good fuck would fix him by emptying the bile from out his soul through his unused cock — what fun, which would prove him human at the least'. 'Mmm', he dreamed, 'Miss Donati chasing me, now there would be a turn-up from the nag-gings' — books seemed a dry retreat as he twirled the thought inside his head, picking up the glasses and the bottle on his way to keep the naggings down.

It was the quiet of the late afternoon so our players progress went un-noticed. The Donati's modest palazzo was not far off so soon they were ensconced — with Dante clearly needing bed. They took him upstairs then undressed him to slip him beneath the gaily quilted covers. "Drink this", she commanded, "the water will flush the wine as I don't do sleepyheads for supper". 'Wow there's a bed', noted Giotto to himself, 'that's some thing, fit three no probs, yippee'? Miss D had other thoughts than beds as turmoil at her vision released juices where none had flowed before, 'now there's happeeness, I wonder how big it gets when it's on show', as thoughts of 'man' suffused her, 'twill do me as appetiser before I feed upon the one I really want but have no sight of yet, still 'tis no matter for it's on the man I love — but I shan't be swayed for now's the time for high ideals, I've set my course, it's a man's salvation not his cock we're after'.

Bondone, though as a Florentine so cock-aware as supplies were had down Cock-of-The Walk where they strutted their stuff ready for action for a bob, was caught by Dante's line and form to wonder if he had the skill to capture it — in paint or stone he wondered as he traipsed downstairs upon a dream, swirling possibilities inside his head; 'better than the face of some damned priest with all those bloody clothes to paint' with he not yet fa-mous enough to afford amanuenses for the graft. 'Clear line', he mused in dream, 'some arts of balance as I flow gorgeous buttock into thigh to flow through calf so serenely down to foot, a torso sketched lightly to show the masses right to set up pectoral perfection, now there's a thought; bugger priests they didn't offer the possibilities of nude — *and* he would only have to please himself — scrumptious so damn convention we'll not have loin-cloths like The Church demands I'll show it all, Man's manhood magnifi-cent, he clutched himself gleefully — when can I begin and can I sell it'?, as he missed his step at the bottom to tumble to the floor.

"Dreaming of a lovely body dear"?, crooned the now tingling Miss Donati, 'now I've seen one I want them both so what the hell, why not'? as she examined the body stretched upon the floor in places she had not bothered with before. 'Florence being Florence it's the thing so if I can please them both while leaving joy behind me there's no bad fling'. "Well indeed I was", he replied as he struggled to his feet trying to do it 'beautifully' before the searching eyes of she who gazed, "but not for the reasons you suppose Miss D, as I can get all that down town if need be; no it was a vision shown me in a way I haven't seen before because down town it's a scuffle in the gutter but I saw a body in its full majesty laid out so I wondered if I could capture it in paint or perhaps even stone — the priests I paint don't do nude you know", as he tried to keep a straight face. "You surprise me Sir", she gurgled with laughter, now splendidly on high, "I thought nude's pre-cisely what they did do behind those fancy robes — who's 'confessing' whom I've always wondered in those boxes". 'Mmm, capture it', she mused, 'but a corpse was no good, if Dante was to be saved he would have to be awake and fit, it would not stand without — even she knew that.

"Ok ducky let's cobble up a decent supper, and you can give me a hand not sit there idly dreaming of lovely bum's in stone or whatever takes your fancy, there's work to do", she smirked joyfully at his discomfiture well aware her's was something else beyond — delectable her own fond em-braces told her. 'Little Gemma' to the world she might choose to be but she was supremely a woman, Man's highest artifice, so had been long aware of where her 'virtues' lay. 'It's been too long', she mused, this 'Little Gemma' thing, it's served its turn' as, having made no enemies the field was hers — but it had been useful too for she knew she had learned the simple truths which should make the journey more success than most of Florence made of it with 'relationships' in'n-out-the-window with much destruction lying for the vultures in the gutters. Not for her she'd decided long ago — but now, despite the surgings, she thought she had the proper meaning of it.

"Mind your fingers with that knife, I want them later", she chuckled delighted with playing the slut to one who would not expect it of her, "I want carrots not bits of finger sauced in blood". He laughed with her enjoying her unaccustomed playfulness quite happy to follow her game now he'd adjusted his horizons — but he knew the 'real' Gemma was still there. Slut he could cope with for a game, to enjoy it like any other healthy male but he respected the values for which he knew she truly stood. "We'll make it a fork job then we can eat it with his nibs in bed, how's that — er with more water not with wine, I want him fit — unfit won't stand", she joyfully took charge. He laughed delighted as possibilities rose on possibilities.

"Giotto dear", she opened out her plan to he whom she knew would be part of it, "I want to blast Dante with some woman to see if we can get through the barrier, break the bars a bit, show him he's human because I'm pretty sure the cock we were mutually admiring could be made to stand then let us see what he makes of it; we've tried all the thinking stuff lets try a bit of lust — a bit of Body to overcome the torments of the Mind — would you mind"?, she asked gently looking her putative mate in the eye. He, not unmindful of her thoughts nor the possibilities of some success took a hand, "Gemma honey, whatever you do has my blessing".

They'd given Dante a good time to surface above the vinous fumes so raised him up, then gave him a plate and fork. "Dress code boys and girls", Miss Tart smirked as she sinuously slid out of everything to slip in bed on one side of Dante, "you're on the other Giotto and no squirming — we're grown up here". Having set her course, while chuckling at her unleashed freedoms, she kept a surreptitious eye on vital kit before it disappeared below the covers, but 'The Kit', deciding all was all, tossed clothes aside then, imagining himself upon a pillar for his painting, posed. "There you are Miss D", he cheered proudly knowing he 'had it', "the works, no messing as I'm not so dumb as you suppose — I've seen 'Little Gemma' born anew but I'm not playing second fiddle to a wordsmith". He twirled before climbing into bed to reclaim his plate. 'Mmm' she thought, 'I can build a life with that, 'twill do me fine once I've made it mine'.

Food was of the essence as the nibbles at Alighieri's had been just that, so stomach's took the prior charge — sizzlings notwithstanding. Dante had become quite human, "you're a very pretty girl Gemma", he complimented thoughtfully quietly discussing her fine salad. She laughed, "hadn't you noticed pretty before Sir Words, or must Florence undress for you to see it"? He had the decency to blush, "you're right dear girl", he acknowledged ruefully, "my head's in the clouds of my own damnation but I haven't the slightest idea yet how to get it out, I fear her loss too much to see my way even with your helping hands".

The Artist, caught up by the twinkling breasts, so much more unleashed than heretofore she'd chosen to display, mused, "could you not make a start by capturing them in words Dante, you can scarify the scandal in the city so could you not turn your art towards the praise of loveliness". "The trouble is", he fretted, "her sort of loveliness's been off-limits for so long there's no longer any art for it". "Then there's your fame", his friend cheered, "go make it to damn the occlusions which have darkened time since the majesties we're being shown here existed in ancient Greece — they knew about bronze bodies we are told, so why not we — sod the bloody chains — how can I serve Popes who call themselves Innocent who murder innocents in far off lands, how can I serve priests who murder Truth when the beauty of Man's body lies before me to inspire — and woman's too", he chuckled bending to kiss a twinkling breast. Gemma gurgled to herself quietly knowing all was well. She decided to try a venture to see which side Dante's arrogance would fall, "what's this Body thing chaps, let a lady see what Man's about".

Dante decided he'd lose more by being coy than he would by showing off so climbed out of bed as Giotto dumped his plate on his accomplice to oblige a lady's pleasure. They posed for her admiration twirling gently. "Swords unsheathed boys", she observed coyly, trying not to gurgle, "you truly honour a lady". Sir Sword giggled aware their audience had her answer, "but how's the line, dear lady, give our wordsmith a lesson with a description of what you see, it might inspire him to out-word you", as he gave what he had what prominence he could, suddenly determined 'to win a lady's favour' against such overt opposition.

The Audience, now totally entranced with the possibilities of the show replied, "I'm no wordsmith Sir, but could you paint it"? The Painter laughed, "that's why I fell down the stairs Gem, I was dreaming I was in my studio with canvas up and brush to hand with Dante, sword on-duty, before me for a try, but the problem Gemma dear is how could I sell such, sword or not, under the Church's eagle eye; should I paint Christ's mother nude, however beautiful, I'd be on the fire in no time with my model with me for 'aiding and abetting'; I paint Francis and St Louis but they are clothed and Francis' Rule's austere specially where Art's concerned — do you know of it?, he may be bashing the degeneracy of priests and Popes but";

You must work without Money and be Poor — "what's poor about pray?, Ok humility and generosity and honesty would do Florence much good but how in hell does one eat — the lilies of the field may not toil nor spin but they get fed gratis and what merit's poverty per-se"?.

You must work without Pleasure and be Chaste — "which", he sizzled irritated, "is just dumb, if work's no pleasure then all you do is duff, just slavery so life's a drudge while rubbish piles around you, did he really mean that"? He leapt on his metaphorical white steed out to slay those who would confront his Spirit's very being, "the very essence of what I want to do is joy, it's the engine of Man's Spirit, it's what makes him worthy to be called Man at all, it's everything of what's best in Him — 'no pleasure' pray what balls is that? — what on earth's he aiming for?", he trailed away thinking. "I'd love to know what he meant by chaste", he readdressed the damnations, "do you feel chaste with barèd breasts for men's delight dear lady of the advancing night"? Barèd Breasts giggled hugely giving them a splendid twirl, "I've always been chaste as I understand it and am no less so now, tits a'twirl or not — yes I wonder what he meant, for chaste's intent".

You must work according to orders and be obedient — "well that's just all the Pope crap in a different guise", he maintained his sizzle, "his rule, do it as I say, what balls, how can Free Thought survive under orders, all those poor Cathari would be as murdered under Francis as they're being under Innocent". "It may be a long way away", he pondered, "beyond our ken, but murder's murder and Free Thought's what built the Greeks they're telling us *which*", he avowed vehemently, "is what's swirling round inside my head because it's not the cock which delights my eye", he advised of his new found vocation, "but what I can make of it to shine the world around me with fresh vision — I'd love to see one of those Greek bronzes they're going on about", he dreamed drifting off into visions of Miss Bum cast in bronze with '*Giotto di Bondone me fecit 1291*' inscribed upon its base.

"How can I paint the lovely you dear Gemma with Francis breathing down my neck"? They both climbed back into bed rearranging so Gemma was in the middle. "It's funny", he reflected thoughtfully, "when I'm painting Francis I love the simplicities of what he says against the gutters of indulgence we live amongst but there has to be a balance which I believe should be made by each of us as we see aright — why should we allow ourselves to be dictated to or why suppose they who do are more wise than we"? "Werl", drawled Dante cynically, "you can't build world domination upon Free Thought which is all Christianity has aimed for since those geezers at Nicea wrote creeds to divide up them's as in from them's as out — Free Thought died there so they're just as bad as the corruptions and conventions we live with here — put a foot wrong in society's clinging code'nd you're done, as I know too well having bust it all my life, so you'll have as much chance of selling nudes to The Church as you would to Florentines despite they're all falling out of their frocks at feast-time", he sneered, "Hypocrisy's the game, dissembling's all so truth lies nowhere so no nudes for you my lad", he raged gently. The Artist lay back in dream because he didn't care what any said, he'd seen what he needed to do, somehow, to leave his testimony of 'how he saw it' to pass beyond; beauty need not be his votive's body but whatever it was it must inspire as it inspired him — 'no more flat priests for me — their whole pompous lives are flat, nothing there despite the posing, I want substance to get a grip on — how dare the buggers cage me, I am me — 3D's the thing'.

Forks were laid happily aside as Dante, grasping a little graciousness to clothe his anger, "thank you Gemma for your delicious dinner and thank you both for bringing me here; I still have no clues but here's better than there while my sword's telling me something I suppose I ought to know". Woman laughed, "perhaps you need a woman to share the journey and the load" — "but a woman would see all the flaws", he paused a moment suddenly seeing a different tack — "Gemma I may be inconsiderate but why should I inflict myself upon a woman"? — "perhaps you might find one who liked it then helped you see the light", suggested 'Mother' quietly then chuckled, "what you were advertising just now would be a considerable temptation to a mutual pilgrimage". "What light, now Beatrice is dead"?, he moaned.

"Snap out of it Dante", High-Art jerked angrily, "make the most of what you've got, is not the lovely Gemma by your side, was it not she who showed you how to use Beatrice's memory as a staff for your journey forward so honour her in Beatrice's stead it might do you good — you might even see some light of which you didn't know", as he placed a surreptitious hand on his love's stomach below the covers for her assurance of his bond.

Replete they snuggled down as the sun slipped below the Palazzo's retaining wall to cast a quieting shadow across our players, each with complexities within, for the journey pregnant laid before them. Gemma, oh cunning 'Little Gemma' had taken her decision clearly, agreed with her putative mate, so did not intend it to slip through another's waiting upon the moment — for the moment she knew was now. She ran her hand down Dante's flank to address what she'd admired before so he should have no doubt of her intention. She might have lit a firecracker. Dante had never done anything gently, he always acted on the spur — now spur he'd had. Flinging himself upon 'the delicious Miss Donati' (with her guiding hand not intending his failure should suppress desire) he set upon her followed by the regulation girly squeal as her girlhood passed away. Giotto did just as Dante's father had supposed so cheered him on assured of his love's intention for he too wanted to see what a 'fuck' could do for Dante's tortured soul. Complex you suppose? Florence had some small merits in that its carnal concupiscence did not set much store by 'Christian' codes of bodily behaviour, if delight should be had then let not rules obscure intent — crudity has merits when rightfully addressed. In our case both our lovers were sure of where they stood and why in which Dante's salvation was the honourable course of the gift of each.

Dante exploded then collapsed — then exploded again but without his 'legs' fell out of bed. "You've cozened me and you say you're friends yet you've exposed me" — "only to yourself Dante", cooed 'Mother' stroking his head from within the bed, "which might tell you something you need to know to help you". "How can lust's feasts satisfy such as I who chide them so in others", he cursed, "I'm above such stuff", Angered at having his walls so publically breached to his friends he flung off downstairs to find a couch below.

Gemma chuckled at the memory, "at least he lives in the world of men, there have been times when I fancied he thought himself a god, but god's don't fuck, even with such godlike pricks as his", she burst out laughing crudely to ease the tension of Dante's leaving. "Oh Gemma what have we done"?, wailed her accomplice distraught at the apparent wreck of their plan. "'Tisn't us dear, it's him", she assured from female wisdom, "we've demolished his deity by proving he's human but he's not up to it yet, self-revelation's not for gods; he's got to 'come down amongst us' to discover his humanity, gods don't do well down here Giotto, they get eaten by rebellious humans — as he's already found but hasn't yet added up", she observed happily with the enormous wisdom of nineteen years. "Come to find humanity Giotto love to forget him for a while, he's got to sort himself *and*", she invited with a wicked giggle, "the style's on me so lie back and stand it up I'm going riding, thrills for Little Gemma for a change".

Humanity smiled enormously then snuggled into her, "will you marry me Miss Donati, impoverished artist with a modest cock; I don't know why I haven't asked you before but I suppose it was the untouchable Little Gemma thing yet I've loved you for a long time for all the reasons I should — *and* what a body"! She guffawed hugely then smiled wickedly again deciding Little Gemma might just as well go out upon a tease, "it's a lady's privilege to try the goods before she buys so stand it for me baby, it's girly fun time". Roaring with laughter at the carnal collapse of her erstwhile self as she set off on that ancient pilgrimage to Banbury Cross they placed side bets on who would reach its citadel first. It happened 'god smiled' upon their fun as arrival was coincident then Miss Donati snuggled across her new found mate still laughing happily.

"I didn't need to try the goods my darling G", she assured fondly, "as I've loved you since I was so high, couldn't you see with your so vaunted vision — you damned artists so bloody blind to what all can see — for all the right reasons too but the sight of Dante's huge tree got me all cock-crazy; let's set Lust back in her rightful place for fun time so wrap those arms around me then we'll settle down to proper snuggle stuff for us, because my lovely man you're mine as however far we travel'n however we choose to share I'll be with you on the way to share the joy and hold your hand — take that as a yes", she burst out laughing at her flight of fancy.

Then she stopped, "but will you love me soiled, are you happy to enter me impure"? she asked. "Oh Gemma Love" he assured sealing her mouth with a kiss, "we planned it so there's no soiling for it was you who did the giving and he the taking — you gave of you for his salvation which is holy stuff so I shall consider you anointed, pure as driven snow for surely gift is a measure of the pure and Dante's still my friend — even when he's not — so what I do for him is sacred, so there does that convince you Gemma mine"? "Coo that's pretty kinky for one who's walking-out on all that anointing and sacred stuff", she observed thoughtfully, "yes we did plan it which I don't regret for a moment". "Yers, size is fun for Lust her satisfaction", she gurgled happily all girly squirmy, "and Dante's cracker I shan't forget, but size is no matter as it's Love's giving which is the test, I've just been there so I know — so never you forget it". The Artist was still catching the bits of these flashing new ideas to make them one, "Gemma Love your gift to Dante was a special beauty 'cause it was of the most inmost woman you yet without any expectation of return — how can you possibly be soiled when your gift was so beautiful — nothing to do with Holy Church's demands", he mused, "what you did was the truth of sacred".

'Yes', he mused, 'sacred was what had always attracted him to his new found lady; nothing showy about her like the florid Florentines, all of a harmony, an inner peace and radiance which clothed everything she was and did, neat and perfect — which was where the gift to Dante had come from'. In its realisation he glowed, so certain now she was 'it' for him exactly because she had given of herself to help save another.

Synaptic assemblies were going on in his head as he lay in her arms, snuggled, 'beauty was so many faceted a glory' he mused in dream snuggling the tangibles with joy, 'but it wasn't just a pretty picture or a fine building or even a twinkling line of verse which made you dance or even a lovely body which had all of you sing because he was discovering the language of beauty was always the same — the gift of the best of us to others. He suddenly saw his cuddles with Gemma weren't wonderful because she had a beautiful body but because they were her gift *of her* to him. He knew what his love had done for Dante was exactly what he wanted to be part of to learn from so he could explode his Art beyond his subject and his skill into another sphere where everyone said 'I like it' to pass on re-freshed. Suddenly even three dimensions weren't enough for him for now he knew he wanted to travel in the fourth — and he knew now it would be his love who would teach him how.

Shining dawns were exploding about him with new light everywhere, "oh Gemma", he cooed, "still my Little Gemma *and* forever, you've just shown me a new beauty, I used to think it was all visuals, all of the line and form and balance I rabbit on about but you've shown me the ultimate beauty as the gift of self as the ultimate love; no allegories about crosses the priests sell us with their sin-saving stuff to cage us but real time gift of you so another might be saved — and not from what they call sin either, just his own unknowing". "Gem Love", he continued apostolically, "it doesn't matter he's still struggling, hasn't seen the light yet, but you gave him the chance from the inside of you". He suffused with a new realisation which spread through him to light him a way forward as he sank gently into Vision — 'the gift of the best he could do is what Art should be so others might see beyond themselves to fresh visions — and bugger the purses of fat priests for no one got any beauty from them anyway', while he knew those daubs were just polishing-persona stuff to arch their pride over others.

"Gemma Love, perhaps your gift thing is what Francis means, that I should give the best of my Art, sort of me free, so others can see what I see to be inspired so go their way the lighter — some of my Vision for them to help them make their journey on the road"? "Never mind the selling Gem", he paused again wrestling with new ideas, "I think's what Francis's saying is just give of your best to light the world". He thought some more while his lady snuggled waiting as 'her man' made beautiful thoughts around them; feeling his Body was pretty special but she was just beginning to see something new herself, a joy in feeling his emergent Mind — now her Mind to which she might add her Body to grow as it seemed to be growing now. "Perhaps that's some of the truth of this rebirth of knowledge thing Simone came back with from Uni at Ravenna", he reflected, "perhaps it's what those old Greeks knew — you just did it because it was good". "Gemma Love we could use that together, a real US thing to show the world". She laughed deliciously at her man on the rampage, "gimme that beautiful body, hunk and quit the theorising, we're where Lady Lust's at play so Body rules because I want yours now Little Gemma's hit the bin".

Snuggled into hunk, playing gently with her new toy, she thought quietly to try to tease out how what she'd done truly stood for surely it had happened on a whim, planned maybe, but a whim sure-footed for all that. "Giotto my love", she began a little journey, "I see my love for you both exists, yet in different forms, which is the truth of it, for my gift to him was of what I could — but my gift to you is me". There was a contemplative silence as this olympic declaration sank in suffused through snuggle's magic potion. "Oh Gemma Love", he assured hanging on tight, "whatever happens, whatever madness comes upon us in the years to come, for I feel them pregnant with possibilities but with crashes too so my gift to you is always me, entire, complete with all its flaws — but always, ever yours to do with as you will — for now I can not see it any other way".

"Gemma love", he assured her devotedly, "you've shown me what's always been your signature — the gift of what you can to those around so you stand beloved by all but, owned by none so you've stood outside the battle, untouched, which is why Florence, even Florence for goodness's sake, considers you a pearl too rare to damage even in its rotten image; you've never taken sides just done what you can for those who've needed it when you can, so I'm vastly proud and humbled you should be giving the innermost you to me". She thought gently for a moment having had what she felt inside her put so starkly, "It's funny Giotto, I've never really thought about it I've just done what seemed to be needed" — "Ah", he noted unusually wisely "that's why Florence has granted you the grace it has because you haven't made a virtue of it — just done what seems right to you". There was a good deal of contemplative snuggle.

High-Art, not unmindful of the fun she'd had with Dante's dangler, while brought face to face with the selfless Love of gift she's shown him, giggled happily with creative inspiration. "I could trawl some of my more discrete friends to find you a biggie for us to share, how so my little nympho — or go buy one in the town, you can see the goods before you buy, as you so rightly put it", he laughed. Miss Donati, with Little Gemma now vanished down the plug gurgled delightedly, " Ooo, yes please, but let's do it one by one dear heart, learn to know each other first, build an US others can't get in between — then go play what games we will — howzzatt"? Snuggle followed. A dreamy Giotto, locked deep in his lady's arms, asked thoughtfully, "what of the child if one there be"? The woman had taken this decision at the birth of the idea, "it matters not", she assured his little doubt, "for genius will be the father either way and who in Florence is ever going to know for Dante will never leak his fall, for is not that the truth of it — but will you mind"?

The Artist chuckled, "I'm happy being genius and since you make me squirmy too let's swamp him out, traditional style, I want to see your eyes, it's eyes which matter when all the Lust is over — so let's try some mission". She giggled supremely happy, 'young handsome and a quick-fire artist too' — her cup ran over as beauty surrounded her all-ways. "Two quickies better than a biggie any day", she burst out laughing as her lover applied his new found Body skills. 'Down-town' was different he was discovering, just a fling for quick release but this totality of Love banned Lust to a lower order which required of him he engage his Mind towards another's being as his lady's message was being made manifest in real time — hands-on. He knew what he needed was to transfer this emergent 'giving' understanding to his brush and fresh emergent chisel he'd been experimenting with to give to what he painted or carved what he was just beginning to learn at Gemma's touch. This wasn't just a 'woman' for his getting this was she for his absolute giving — so it was what she wanted not what pleased him for which mere self-set skill was not enough. 'Yers', he thought, 'mere skill, paint a priest and pocket the purse stuff's yesterday's endeavour because now I've seen the possibilities of the new — what I do hereon I must dedicate outside myself to raise it as high as a pilgrimage would bear it' — so Gemma got the very best he was able.

When snuggle had resumed he asked, "Gem my darling love, will you teach me what pleases you, 'down-town's' all take so I learned nothing of pleasing women there, only myself". "Of course my new found man", she gurgled, yet a novice in such arts, "but you're the visionary, an artist so you say, so apply yourself to fantasy, then enact it, but I'll tell you what might make me hum — but it's a game for two, not one". She picked up a hand to place it where she would, "start here and let's go to sleep on that".

At its appointed hour the Cock arose then crowed, as did another — so they shared. "When shall we announce it honey"?, Bondone asked, "this should give the flaccid a moment's entertainment since we've fixed it for ourselves not had it done by parents". His lady giggled hugely at their taking charge, "oh that's a man thing dear, this is the point where ladies decorously retire as if they had no hand in it — as I feel you have so don't stop", she gurgled deliciously squirming, "I could really get used to this 'man about the house' thing and I'm sure my folks'll cough the loot for a snuggery just to get me off their hands — having spinsters round the house's is a sign of failed parental duty, my Mum'll be delighted so won't ask awkward questions".

They snuggled as the sun began his daily Pilgrimage, he knows where he's going because he's been there — but our lovers had no idea whatever, just a different way of thinking. Mind was appearing above the corrupted Body of Florence's fleshy lusts to fertilise them into dream, to become thereafter the fusion which would spring Man to his creative best for now fired by Mind intertwined in Body as a mutual servo to drive him, if he has the courage, to hang on as the fourth dimension of true pilgrimage which takes him in hand to say 'advance — but you know not where'.

"Do you think we could make Florence Divine", the girly half of new domestic bliss asked thoughtfully — "*and* get paid for it"? enquired the Artist end of the new partnership. "Indeed Sir Artist would I, a woman, propose aught else"?, she started giggling, "there are virtues in being a woman amongst men, specially as untouchable as I because all hope to have a try so confidences abound — feeble beings really, just want their cock's released but in their eagerness to breach my erstwhile hallowed walls I found out the price they're prepared to offer for the building of the new Church they're planning — which should keep the enterprising artist and his lady in cocks-on-the-side for a year or two", she exploded laughing. "But I'm no architect", replied The Limner — "well there's only old Arnolfo", she assured, "yesterday if ever I saw it, anyway you don't need an architect you need a man with a new vision of 'how it ought to be', you can buy a building clerk to make sure it doesn't fall, so it's easy-peasy for the new expanded you", she gurgled egging him on to a venture she knew he could honour with ease.

Downstairs, bursting with new ideas so unclothed Eureka style for haloed in Mind's Light, they dragged Dante off his couch to tell him of the plot their new union had devised. "Why not, Giotto", he replied gaily, "you're the best the city's got and with Gemma here to wheedle them as she did me last night it should be the proverbial 'piece of piss', it's easy to dupe such fools just paint them a fine picture of how it's going to be — with beauty they can't resist writ large all over. Translated too he gurgled, "with lots of grandeur to brush their mealy egos your home'n dry so garn do it, but take Miss Temptation upstairs to keep her happy so honest chaps can get a bit more kip", then froze his eyes re-focused as she changed. "Hang on", he commanded his old imperial self but smiling thoughtfully, "sit down, for I'm no more the intolerable me — I'm changed". He looked at both with new found passion, glowing outwards no longer locked inside, "Gemma dear, impossible I may have been, but not thankless now — you've changed me by showing me I'm not a god sent down to try my fellow man — I needed to be shown that the way you did, brought to my knees, the bile gone out", he chuckled at the memory. "Now I see what Beatrice was, but I refused her, so if I can keep her vision bright I might make the godly shine around her memory for all to see". He sat pensive for a bit assailed with emergent fresh ideas, "mere skill is not enough", he mused on, "I have skill in plenty, the facile stock of fools without it facilitate to greater than itself, so dedication's got to be the energy which fires the vision — to be a mirror of him no more but to show through him a truth". He picked a glass of water off the table by the couch-side to clear his head — to think.

"I don't know if I can do it", he reflected sucking the glass, "for I've only just begun to uncloud my view, but you've shown me how for no longer cursing but giving of the best I may to honour her so others may see the beauty she bore around her; curse the goats I still shall but the lambs must always walk in light — I see my job to try it". He sat on the couch in reverie as his passionate friends watched the translation, then he picked up his translator's hand to kiss it reverently looking deep into her eyes, "I was an arrogant troubled male but your gift to me of you as woman has made me truly Man to go on to honour Woman's central place in Man's estate — will that do"?

Little Miss Donati looked a little overcome by this encomium, then a seraphic smile spread across her face; a smile which would later deck a famous face at the very highest of Renaissance Art, a face which tells us even now of a Mind which knew the secrets of its Body — the smile of woman

knowing she has won life's race. "It will", she cooed pleased beyond measure, "for greater thanks there could not be". "Gemma dear", he cooed so
uncharacteristically, "I'll not forget what you gave of you as Beatrice gave
of her, unstintingly — for both shall be my inspiration". He bent to kiss
her, "there you have my confession — of man saved by woman to ascend
to Man's true estate, with all my love — so take her away Giotto before
temptation overcomes me".

When Dante had finished Gemma laughed deliciously eyeing the two magnificent swords but decided to lower the show from the perilous pillar
upon which it was perched to return to realities, "sorry boys, orgies are off,
he'n me've got work to do, horizons to erect etc", followed by much laughter as Dante, wrapping an arm round Gemma, "at least I've been cured of
the megrims so now I know what I'll be looking for so no loitering by
lonely sedges as hereinafter the birds are going to sing, then sat for a moment in thought, "I have it" , pitching into a heretofore unknown fine
tenor;

> *Go raise yourselves on wings of Art,*
> *To make yourselves Renaissance start,*
> *Abandon shoddy*
> *Meld Mind with Body*
> *That's how to be 'New' clever.*

Our two lovers collapsed laughing, upon which The Architect observed,
"my goodness Gem Dante's seen Damascus Gate, then a scourge now a
blessing, just for a fuck". Miss Donati adopted an admonishing tone while
pursing her lips, trying desperately not to laugh, "ah boy, 'tis the quality
not the width which does it, the best to be had in town delivered from
deep inside me — and don't you forget it". Dante smiled gently at the girl
who had so splendidly made him a man, "she's right Giotto, it's what made
it so Damascene so when you're trawling round town for tools and tits for
your new flights of fancy don't you ever forget the best's to be had at
home — so get upstairs and crack on or I really shall be tempted to try
again". Gemma chuckled thinking 'I made a troubadour on the rampage,
I wonder if I'll end up in the history books as 'The Girl Who set Art on
fire — oooer what fun'.

Our new lovers, now engaged on Life's Pilgrimage, laughing hugely watching conversion occur before their eyes, set off upstairs for a little more snuggle. As they lay thinking about 'what had to be done' they could hear a melodious voice singing;

Banish gloom to Hell's damnation,
Let's start anew with recreation,
Oh twinkle tits
I love the bits,
Let's spread about the pleasure.

Build Light upon the curves of she,
Who will our Inspiration be,
Display the Bust
With uplift Thrust
To shine Art's New endeavour.

'Woman', making a marketing appraisal of 'the goods', noted to Giotto, "bit of a bust fixation there G, is it a man problem 'cause if is'n we're going to conquer world markets we'll need bigger ones than mine — another 'down-town' shopping spree"? she giggled hugely. Her man, overtaken by the delights of Lust, laughed magnificently, "could combine the two to save time as the boss suggested, which should be a real giggle — I'll send you off for the tools'n I'll forage for the tits then we can compare results", followed by orgiastic laughter as Dante set off on freshly minted stanzas. "Blimey we could make him into a troubadour yet", he cheered, "he's got the voice to earn a few bob no trouble, opera next step d'you think love"? — "should blow their minds", laughed his lady as she twiddled her favourite to the canzonæ from below;

Upon the quest of Man made fine,
We need to search at nature's shrine,
Let's see some thigh
To have men sigh,
As Life we fill with Leisure.

At which she collapsed laughing with a fit of girly giggles (thank 'eaven for leetle gurls) "troubadour or what G, I didn't realise it had that effect on men, you'll have to really work on me before I get to the flights of verse" — "ah practice makes perfect girly", her mate laughed. Gemma chuckled, "still if we can't make a success of the Mind'n High-Art bit we could run a private bordello, members only all tastes catered for, tools hired by the inch'n tits by the pound — how about 'Pan's Panacea' for a title, sylvan associations don't you think G, satyrs'n stuff'n you know what satyrs display".

The Creator collapsed helplessly at his new-found mate's imagination "what's the panacea for dear?, I just like to have these things laid out for us simple males". "Maybe quick on the up", she giggled lasciviously, "but a bit slow on the uptake these arty males, Pan's Panacea for Lust's Leanings of course, I may not be in to verse yet but I can manage that — though I fancy the full title might be just a little overt for the purse-lips". Thinking of the singing The Artist mused upon his mate's conversion, "its always the same with these high Art types like him downstairs Gem, dumps or clouds, no grey anywhere — you'll have to keep me out of the dumps bit gal now you've lit the fire if we're going to make a profit". Renaissance-Writer, having composed some more, continued;

> To damn all gods for all of time,
> Let's engage in search sublime,
> Give me some bum
> With curve of tum,
> Immeasurable pleasure.
>
> If Life is going to start afresh,
> Let's with new thought our minds enmesh,
> Pick up new swords
> And play with words,
> Forever and Forever.

"He likes you G", Gemma chuckled overtly, "he spotted the bits I like best" — "yer well", replied her inamorata salaciously, "with one his size he's obviously in the sword admiration game's these artists're always into mirrors, Narcissm knows no bounds with them lot — pond or whatever'll do" — "so that's all right then", they giggled together. "Progress of a sort", mused Creation's Muse, "not bad for an old misogonist, I might return the compliment one day — in stone d'you think Gem"? He thought-on happily flying High-Art's creative wings, "garden ornaments, no drapes, prongs prominent d'you think there'd be a trade"? "Quite an incitement to get a garden his", she gurgled deep in reverie of Dante's sword un-sheathed. The Artist surged on creation's mission, "limited editions, a few journeymen turning them out on a production scale, 'friends & family', erected for cognoscenti, good little money spinner, specially when numbered and signed by the master". His mate, picking up the ball burst out all giggles, "with birds perched on you know what, should keep him in royalties for the genuine Dante model — not bad for alternative employment till the prose hits world markets".

"I have it", he cried jumping up. "This ducky is real Eureka stuff" — "yer well", murmured his mate in crime not having yet got used to the artist rocket mode thing, "*he* rushed down the High Street nude with his gear flailing about so the saying goes'n I don't see you doing that yet, although", she smirked evilly, "anything to turn a buck, parade'n pose to perk up passagiata — Narcissus ducky"?, she enquired.

"Ok girly", he backed up contritely, "I'll modify the pace till you've caught up on the Art thing as there's no volume to be had just me posing, however penile, it's volume makes the money — but it's a real goody", he enthused in full commercial flight as the possibilities of volume grabbed him. "How about 'Bondone's Beautiful Bronzes'"?, he sizzled, "catchy done in that new Italic script which's hit the streets recently — knock out bronzes two a penny, volume stuff with this Lost-wax process old Arnolfo's heard of; where he got it from I can't imagine he being sunk in yesterday's stone so I'll need to quizz the old chap — novelty's the thing Gem", he giggled crazily hanging on to the thing which had got him, "I can see the ads, 'Come to be 'done' at Bondone's', yers, new form of 'adult services' advertisement, miniatures three for the price of two as the Nouveau business card — get some apprentices in for the regular work so erotica to High-Art in one leap with money everywhere as vanity knows no bounds — porn's always been a money-spinner", he careered to a stop with his accomplice more than a little puzzled by the crazed flow of ideas. "Yers", he giggled salaciously, "three for the price of two's easy as its only the main feature which matters with a bit of extra for the smaller chaps — we'll call it artist's licence with extra again for special features'n copies of any tattoos", he chuckled, "you'd be surprised how many of those down-town pros've got tattooed helmets", he fell about laughing on a fine creative high imagining rows of statuettes promoting prominent peni.

"Yers", he mused synapses going ten-to-the-dozen, "'A Figure From Florence', piece of cake with the standard model knocked out in volume courtesy of Cire-perdue, Gemma love — good line for the adventurous tourist", he chuckled imagining the queues, "*and* we'll offer a genuine portrait service, one-day tourist turnaround, stand one day collect the next — "I'll take your word for it Giotto", she agreed a little tentatively hanging on the hurricane while unsure of all the practical techniques. Now well away as 'together' was having a catalytic effect, Gemma climbed out of bed to pose provocatively, "it's teams win G, so it's me for the first original you can keep your peni for later as I'm going to be Beautilicious Bondone's Number One The Bum to Beat The Bust".

Our bard downstairs, now well into the scheme of the thing carolled merrily;

> *If Mind's to truly fertile be,*
> *Then set synapses searching free,*
> *he curve of cheek*
> *that has'em squeek,*
> *For girls'n boys together.*
>
> *Set Man to Body's amity,*
> *To save New World's calamity,*
> *With flaxen hair*
> *And eyes a'flair,*
> *We'll join in joy whenever.*

"I wonder where he's been", chuckled the admiring Artist stroking his lady's dark brunette, "not much of the flaxen hair round here; that's the trouble with High-Art it's always wanting what it can't get, has to bust its gut after the impossible, not the way to happiness at all that angst stuff because it's a hell of a trek down south for flaxen hair where those Scandinavians were marauding — someone who's been said they'd got blue eyes too", he mused happily for a minute, "could be good for the fresco game though, blond hair, blue eyes and burgeoning pink bosoms decked out to give them nature's depth, red tipped to draw the eye to essential features because", he giggled like a little kid again, "flat is yesterday Gem love, the new Bondone Look is going to have painting leap off the page as it vanishes into illimitable distances of depth, that 3D I was on about earlier love, I'll work up a cartoon to see what it looks like — flog a few on those lines to the more lascivious pontiff's I fancy", he gurgled happily captured by flaxen hair swagged across severe Romanesque ceilings in the foreground of majestic scenery you could only have seen outside before (it would be Giotto's creation of dimension and depth which Mr Ruskin recognised as the true beginning of The Renaissance).

Our bard downstairs had really got the bit between his teeth, galloping merrily;

> *If Body's to be enjoyed the best,*
> *Let it be served at Mind's behest,*
> *Avaunt crude Lust*
> *behave with Trust*
> *Let's dance — but mind the seizure.*

> *To keep ourselves quite free of crowds,*
> *We'll set our eyes to pierce the clouds,*
> *with swords'n sheaths —*
> *'Good bye figleaves'*
> *And damn The Cage's pressure.*

"Yers, damn the cage indeed", cheered The Artist off chasing synapses again, "stone's yesterday stuff, ok for those rarified types who like getting dust'n stone chips in those places it shouldn't reach, very itchy I've been there, but volume's it for us Gem; thass the difference between the stone'n bronze thing, Love, we can get quantity *and* quality", he mused concentrating on production's processes to get the cash rolling in. "Small foundry back o't shop", he mused happily imagining the scene, "trainee sculpture blokes knocking out the waxes out front from the models posing for them — *and* Gem", he leapt out of bed to stride about, with his lady now intoxicated by the ideas and the view, "how about this for a whizzer — public viewing for the vain sorts as they're being modelled, the proud as peacocks geezers — come to view the prominent poles" — "I like the cocks", giggled Gemma, "but I hope they're bigger'n peas and it's a good thing you're not rushing down the street like that Eureka bloke, it might have been Ok in ancient Greece but I fancy Florence might flip" — "hush girl keep lust at bay", he chid gleefully, "we're on the wings of cash here, this should sort the sheep from the goats", he mused happily, "and the priests from the posers, better than all the factional family crap so excites everybody's this'll be reality viewing, sort them who have from them who haven't, pierce a few balloons I fancy' n them's 'as it'll be proud to be seen at Bondone's High-Art Emporium waving it about — better than the passagiata any day with no hole in the corner 'over 18' stuff — yers", he sucked his teeth appreciatively, "no end of possibilities".

"Admission to view only", Gemma gurgled deliciously suddenly catching the full force of her man's vision then managing to combine girly-lust with money, "none of the freebie stuff, if we're minting it we charge, not cheap either my lovely, think of the queues of lunch-time chicks keen to case the cocks — solid cash there G, I know the type — yers that'll reverse the age old chick-show bit", she giggled splendidly, "one up for the birds for a change, yummee chicks oggling chaps and paying us for the pleasure — sucks for extra doya think"?, she suggested on a flight, "could be one of those magical money-makers where both are happy to pay", she lay back in mild hysterics rolling with glee as synapses crackled merrily in her now splendidly fizzing head;

"Better than those surreptitious dating agencies the madams run", she mused off after the rabbit, "real girlie-shopping spree stuff — see the goods before you buy, but", she reflected thoughtfully yet hardly able to contain herself laughing, "no feeling the goods unless you've paid, they're not on rails, feeling's my extra thing". Giotto guffawed at the vision of chicks on lunch-time shopping sprees, "yers, 'The Swain Market', hilarious should have the chaps in queues knowing the chicks're on the prowl so ought we to have a separate section for shopping only Gem, that's your scene"? "Mmm", she mused thoughtfully caught by the idea, "Exchange & Mart' we could call it, little annexe on the side, through the shop of course so double takings", she soared away on imaginations's un-pinioned wings, "'Lending Library' service perhaps, 'read your old one come view what's on the shelves' — all the old canards sunk as size secures sales", giggled Gemma now hopelessly lost in orgiastic flights of design.

"Speak for yourself Miss Nympho", giggled her swain, "but at least everyone'll have choice'n you never know the petite might become all the rage" — "'face' painting as an extra", gurgled the Little Lady Lost to Lust hardly able to stop the flow, "you could find out the truth of what your girly-mates really liked". "Um yers", replied her accomplice caught in the little complexities of actual execution, "need a clever miniaturist for face-painting'n tricky if it's already tattooed but could be a swinger for the active chap who's into High-Art — 'spensive though, those miniaturist blokes don't come cheap". "Giotto love", exploded his lady, "if we're going for topsy-turvy you've got about the best — just think of the advertising spiel 'High-Art of The Helmet' you could run it as a show in town".

'Close Contacts of Both Kinds' overtook them as they lay mardling each other's Minds & Bodies sorting out the practical from the merely salacious. "The great thing in the these creation things Gem love", he noted sagely, "is to get the foundation in place then build the frills on top as the years go by, its called 'development', it keeps the image fresh and prices up for the novelty factor, 'new model every year stuff'".

Our Bard clearly enamoured by his having irritated the snobs with his Pizza idea managed to combine the new with the new and some commerce;

> *Flog Bolognese with bum's'n breasts,*
> *To massage cheeks and gorgeous chests,*
> *Oh Pizza fine*
> *Sublimely mine*
> *Let's turn lust into treasure.*

Gemma briskly picking up the commercial possibilities in this verse chuckled thoughtfully, "he's got a cracker there G, I wonder where that came from" — "oh great minds honey", replied Giotto airily, "we could do a deal with the geezer who's cornered the fancy sauce concession, then get the patent from 'im upstairs for that Pizza thing, pay him a little royalty poor old sod — then there'd be people seeping in for a mid-morning 'snak-mit-lust' — *"and"*, she added gleefully, "both sides satisfied as why come to be modelled and flash your kit if there's no one there to leer, theatre's always been a two way deal, no audience no fun'n as we supposed charge both for the pleasure". She sat with the Mona-Lisa smile of earlier, deeply knowing they were on a winner fired by the emergent energies of emancipation freed from the Ages of the Dark for lit by the Love of light — New Knowledge indeed, the light of Love. "Best erotica in town", she reflected, "but we'll need some girls on site to keep the chaps' ends up, ball-massage a nice little chargeable extra", they both collapsed laughing, high as kites on creation's wings. She clutched herself ecstatically imaging being Bondone's No 1 as the toast of the town wandering round sampling the goods to test the quality as the final end of Little Gemma.

A practical girl who knew the ins and outs of the Florentine 'thing' giggled again, "bombproof too G as so many would want to 'be seen at Bondone's' the purse-lip police couldn't touch us — porn on parade by popular plea — pretty good for releasing all those silly repressions and quarrels's you wouldn't go fight a guy you'd stood next to waving your kit would you 'cause bosom mates thereafter — *and*", she added, almost fit to bust, "we could run a surreptitious keep-fit joint in another part of town, 'The Gymnasium'" — "nice one Gem how Greek is that", he giggled like a little kid with a new toy, "no connection with any other place as none of the chaps'll want to be seen all flab'n floppy buttocks, real pecks akimbo stuff, proper tone up service nice'n anonymous".

They collapsed again at the thought of turning the whole damn thing inside out. Giotto still giggling mused, "I wonder how many of those flat priests I paint would be there flashing their kit wanting to join the new in glorious 3D; this should be the best salve this place's ever had, *and* put it on the map as the home of Bondone's — yers", he mused his eyes in the distant future, "Beautiful Florence, Queen of The North". "Yers", he mused on now hooked on the whole mis-en-scène, "waxing service' out front, casting out back with couches sporting aperitifs for a little extra cash honey "? Miss Management observed briskly, "but no credit G, cash only, I've been there, instant fashion'n everyone wants it — cash is king". "It's team's win Gem", he posed, "as I'll need to go off to make with the High-Art, after all we can't build a world-wide reputation on running a porn-bar it's got to be backed by real Designer cred so The Shop will be your affair, for which", he gurgled, "we'll need some top-totty".

He thought for a moment playing with so many new ideas at once, "yers we'll need some careful product placement to get the tourists heading our way but for that you need well publicised iconography — no more of this 'come to Beautiful Florence crap' on the holiday posters it'll be 'Be Done By Bondone — The Only Place to Be Seen' — I'll get the boss to knock out some tempting verses for the posters". *"Then"*, he reflected deliciously cantering into new heavens, "it's going to need a Pope's purse to afford the services of The Great Bondone for their fancy frescoes *but"*, he reflected back into High-Art as his real home, "frescoes with a difference", he carolled eyes ashine, "so begone dull care with its allegories of myths and madonnas, we'll have frescoes with real people in doing real things, enjoying life, yers" he mused on in dream composing on the fly, "fun, real candle at both ends stuff *and* we won't have to go shopping for cock as you'll be able to take your pick of what walks in to pay for the privilege, guinea a minute Gem, we can't lose".

He dreampt-on happily imagining the queues at Bondone's with fawning Popes releasing purse-strings un opened before in such style, "we've got the whole bloody lot of them by the balls Gem". Lady Lust laughed merrily, "I often wondered if those buggers had any balls G, how do you know"? The Limner laughed, "oh some of them get so bored sitting being done they open up to start doing themsleves — a few monsters oddly enough, adds a sort of seraphic expression which I've been known to catch", he noted proudly, "which pleases them so they cough the extra I demand".

"But you can only get the blokes by the balls G", she chased the balls idea relentlessly fascinated by her new toys, "how're you going to get the birds — eh, tell me that 'cause I've always wondered?" "Ok miss clever-arse", he replied gaily, "I'll think about it but meanwhile I'm sure you'll find a way — er hang about, I have it — it's Popes'n priests've got the balls *and* the cash, howzatt gal"?

"Um, yummee", mused his mate, her creative juices on full flow, "'Bolognese with Beautiful Bums', should draw the crowds". Giotto chuckled not, in the general cock-fest, having missed his lady's advertisements of her virtues, "specially if your's is the one on show Big G" — "I wondered when you'd get round to it", she snickered happily. He gurgled in anticipation, "round it surely is, peaches all the way, bootylicious baby — I shall make its proper acquaintance when we have some US time".

"Ok twinkle-bum, work, its iconography time", she chid to get the show on the road, "artwork to accompany the name?, you know the logo stuff the posers sign their daubs with, we gotta do better than them, we need world-wide visibility, er with overtones but not too overt — you're the Arto of our duo". His eyes crossed deliciously as synapses crashed, "crossed swords d'you think my dear, all sorts of connotations if I got the artwork right — tarty but tasteful's the thing", he leered happily "er bald or cowled, what's your fancy dear". Gemma goggled happily for a moment, "we'll need a little research there don't want to get the accent wrong could hold back sales, *but*', she mused intent upon her delicious rear, "how about Sword in the stone, cunningly cleft of course — you could have fun with that". "Ooo yes", he giggled lasciviously, "all sorts of Arthurian elements there — plunge your sword to ride on to fortune with fortune cookies provided with every entry — oh yes Little G we've got a receipt here, a veritable gold mine with a logo for each sex — as their inclinations tend you understand" — "well erotica's always been tops if you can make it acceptable", she giggled happily, "offer them the fantasy they haven't got the imagination to dream for themselves — that's what Art's all about you Artos are always telling us lesser mortals". There was a happy silence as ideas and designs swirled round the artist's head, while decor with arrangements for the 'posing parlour' meandered through madam's mind.

"Oh Gem you've won, you've made us Gods, the Comedy of it and the Divinity too, *because*", he assured with magnificent finality, "he who creates, they're always ramming down our throats, is God". "What larks", he cheered, "the ultimate triumph over priests with the people coming to worship us not them as we turn it all inside out — Us together my Love — Dante had the right of it, it's your womanhood which has made us Man because without you we'd still be at each others' throats, wrangling in the gutter making mess not magic". "Yers", he mused with visions of crawling priests, "Man is God, because Man's the Great Creator, perhaps that's what this New Knowledge thing Simone found in Ravenna's all about, Body's beauty to move Man's Mind so I'd really love to see exactly what those Greeks made of it — but if it is girly I'm with'em all the way, so you'd better go chase whoever holds the purse or we won't have a starter — er best Art forward to get the loot Love's you've shown us how to change men's minds". "Sure thing Sir Artist, different sort of Art, but Art it is", she gurgled supremely happy, "beauty on the rampage for Beauty's ends — cap that Sir painter".

Both fell about laughing as they dressed with vision's celerity then set off upon the day's adventures, Gemma to sort the church commission and Giotto off to case the town for a possible place for Bondone's Beautiful Bronzes, because prompt prosecution is the only way to ensure the life of dreams born in the mists of dawn's erotic surges, which are otherwise apt die in the glare of the mid-day sun — definitely early bird stuff. The wordsmith was finishing his toilette to the words of;

Let's seek High-Art's true exploration
To find Man's proper adoration.
let loving suck
precede a fuck,
With lips on lips
Then labia loved
With mighty sword unsheathed oh,
To drown in Life's true measure.

Drifting down the stairs as our couple left on the wings of dream Giotto shouted up, "don't forget to write it down Dante, can't be having it consigned to the doom of ephemera merely because it came upon a moment — we'll have it run up for sale in the new premises — er we'll tell you later", they laughed as they divided outside the house to go their different ways on Man's ever pressing creative quest.

Reality

The sun began his downward path so siesta was over as movement heralded the second, more joyful, part of the Italian day. A little work then the peacock-preenings of passagiata as the populace perambulated to please the world at large. Mrs Stephen Ralli dozed in half-wake stretching luxuriously — for she had traveled far. "I've dreamed a dream", her lips murmured, "I've met the people, I've seen trauma but I saw the life who saved a soul to make a Spirit who rode on to greatness because I've witnessed the Sacrifice of Self Surmount through Service as Body gave to Mind to spur it as I watched the ancient Struggle between Self and Service Survive Supreme". "They showed me a childlike clarity", she murmured quietly to herself, "which saw through Man's self-focused corruptions to find a greater light which showed me Body come to Mind to make the magic of them intertwined — they showed me beauty born to stand proud in its own majesty as Man's gift to Man so I can now take part in Beauty's Blessing for they showed me of what it's built, Man's gift of the absolute of himself to Man". "They showed me Beauty in some very unexpected places", she sighed stretching ecstatically as a little of her vision floated across her conscious, indeed it was hapeeness. "They showed me how to grow lilies on the dungheaps of lust's licence — I've been and 'seen' so shall we try our hand, a new home perhaps fired by what we've seen today dear"?, as she put out an exploratory hand to join. "They showed me

Love's gift of self to be the truth of Love's Power made manifest magnificently — which I'll not forget for I've been shown Love's bastion as Man's grace — I've been there".

She stopped a moment deep in reverie, eyes shut a long smile upon her beautiful face as she re-visited her erstwhile travels. "I've seen cages crushed to mount creation in Man's Free Will". "I've seen Man made God, *and* I've seen him build more than just a pile of stones — oh yes so much more than just a pile of stones for they showed me the ultimate Truth of Love as they put her in her proper order ranked with Beauty". "I've seen Man reconciled with Man through Art — so I know the truth of Beauty so thus I know what Mr Ruskin encouraged us to come to 'see', because he'd seen it, so finally I know what The Renaissance means for restoring to us what The Greeks gave to the world — which had Art's creation flower forever what they were". A seraphic smile crept across her still dreaming face as she recaptured her magical journey. "I needed to come — to see — then dream; I needed to 'meet the people' as Mr Ruskin told us, for without we get amongst them all is merely academic dust". With a delicious uncurling squirm she woke fully then stretched luxuriously to look her companion squarely in the eye, *"and* I saw erotic re-born exotic as they showed me peni prominent which created Love from Lust — Pandora's Box restored to show its 'gift-to-all' so show me Art ascending everywhere which will stay with me always — so thank-you little guide book 'got up upon a whim' I shan't forget your journey".

Quietly knowing she had 'made the Pilgrimage to Beauty's Blessing' and indeed passed into a new world they packed their kit then wandered off to join the throng which has, since Florence, admired itself amongst itself for knowing it was the birth of beauty's benefice. Mrs Stephen Ralli laughed gently to herself clutching her dream to her still superb bosom, "but I've seen the real passagiata, I wonder if it happens still in some happy cool seclusion waving deliciously in the evening air, but alas Mr Ruskin doesn't tell us, nor Mr Murray either more's the pity".

She mused deliciously admiring the chaps'n chicks parading gaily, 'How I would have loved a session at Bondone's'. Mrs Stephen Ralli, statuesque, prominent and still firm, proud of what she was indeed (her bookplate tells us these) she swirled her vision of standing before the admiring manipulators of wax as their salivation had their moulding adorn her emerging model with majesty for its adoration, as the happy customers of the other sex maintained their poses deliciously at her invitation — 'but would Hove manage such in her fine garden'? She knew 'A Greek thing styled Aphrodite' or some such anonymity would pass unnoticed, but her resplendent as her in her majesty, she doubted it, 'but was it worth the try'? She dreamed of her adorning Hove then smiled to herself deliciously. Giotto would have approved, even if Mr Ruskin might not, but courtesy of him she had 'seen' beyond the curtain of time to know the truth of it. 'Gorgeous Giotto for his understanding of Mankind's truth that Body is an essential spur to Mind' for she had seen The Body is Man's Spirit clothed so shall we not make its admiration fine for we are but half of Man without its adoration? She chuckled hugely at the joke turned inside-out for, did not Holy Church tell us God made it — so surely it be sublime — 'would Hove agree', she giggled as she watched Florence about it's mutual adoration.

Postlude;

'Paradise'? Ah the Paradise Dante sought, do we? Florence had thought so then for she banished 'Hell's Dark Shades' to clothe herself in beauty courtesy of The New Knowledge; indeed as Berenson demonstrates in *'Aesthetics and History in the Visual Arts'* it is to Florence we owe almost all of Western Art for the next five hundred years as her great sons of Art who sprung from the freedom Giotto and Dante bequeathed them from the chains of The Church;

> 'That is what Florence did, a smallish town of money-mongers, not to say usurers, wool-combers, and cloth weavers, with little military force and next to no political authority. Florentizised Italy exerted this diluvial influence upon the entire white man's world at a time when Italy was a 'mere geographical expression'. Armies may, or may not prepare the way. In the long run influence is spread through craftsmen, artisans, architects wood and stone carvers, men of letters, school teachers, singers, dancers, tumblers, clowns, pedlars and fiddlers, as it was spread in late antiquity by Greeks, and then more and more by Syrians, Jews and Copts — the same people who at first contributed so much towards the disintegration of the Hellenic world, and then towards saving Europe from sinking into a dunghill economy and berserker barbarianism.'

Everything was indeed turned inside out — then The Earth ceased to be the centre of it as Holy Church's much vaunted 'knowledge' was proved a fiction as *'Summæ'* bit the dust. Beautiful bodies burgeoned everywhere as Art clothed Pandora's erstwhile vices with angels' wings as Man discovered the beauty which lay within himself by merging Body into Mind to breed new views. The brave vauntings of our heroes would give us Michelangelo's David magnificently unclothed to honour the Greeks whence had sprung the Truth of Man made Magus, to honour his most magnificent creation, himself (did Playboy start here?), but I like to think the founder of it all discovered Life's greatest secret — the Love which gives of its all for others — wrapped in the delicious Miss Donati. It may be a fancy — but the fact's a fact.

Finale — my Fancy Completed

Gentles all, 'tis indeed but a fancy, but 'tis borne upon a fact. The people are, essentially, whom they were, though whom Giotto married I can not find, but does it matter because for what he did he must have had a Gemma. For Dante persuading Giotto to turn architect I have Mr Ruskin to thank and who am I to trade the toss with such as he — Giotto was most certainly in charge of The Duomo which surely he would not have had without 'prentice proof beforehand? Whatever, it is universally acknowledged it was Giotto di Bondone's frescoes in Santa Croce which Mr Ruskin had 'seen' with Dante Alighieri's *'Divine Comedy'* from which sprang The Renaissance in Art from Florence into the wider Italy, two hundred years before The Medici in whose reigns it would peak — but would also perish with them for its fire gone out. Giotto achieved the fame his Gemma knew was in him — clever Little Gemma — because, in Art's first flush true, his paintings portrayed real people, sensuous people with Spirits whom we would love to love as he not only achieved his 3D but his fourth dimension too — I wonder how many of his angels owed their being to the joys of Miss Donati. For the first time in Art Giotto offered us pictures which gave us the chance to travel beyond ourselves into new land we have never seen — which is Art's true measure. I needed an engine to fire that Spirit so chose Miss Donati.

Dante's ghost lives on in his masterwork which honours his love for Beatrice supremely but pillories the times he lived in — not by any means Florence only. It is indeed 'The Divine Comedy' or 'The Vision of Dante' which travels from 'Hell', through 'Purgatory' into 'Paradise'. My 'big' copy, two huge quarto volumes, is copiously engraved by the mid19[th] Century's allegorical master Gustave Doré printed spectacularly, as such should be, in 1903. Dante's Vision was a huge success in his lifetime (sold to jealous cities round about perhaps) to become, like William Tyndale was for English, the creator of a 'new' language which was the fount, in due course through the work of Allesandro Manzoni *(I Promessi Sposi)* of modern Italian.

Mrs Stephen Ralli?; what of her, and who was she?, for she's no fiction either, but; it does not matter as like them she's left us what we need to know — her testimony of how she thought it ought to be to light those who might see it later. Not for her a cheapscate 'bought-out' thing superscribed by hand to crow her 'ownership' but a specially created piece of high design, High Art indeed, to gild yet further what she bought to keep her vision of beauty bright; which came first Florence or the Bookplate, I'd love to know but to honour her mine now faces hers to add to the continuum of Beauty's view down time.

Pride is here, quite rightly, for she announces her style and her abode 'in clear', but did she build 'St Catherine's Lodge' after she had been and 'seen' — I fancy so. Her style as *Mrs. Stephen Ralli?* — the period's convention it may have been but for such as she, an individual of Art's expression at a time when 'emancipation' was the rage, she prefers the announcement of the value of her union for whoever Mr Stephen Ralli may have been she's proud to be with him in life's pilgrimage, united; I deem it the most rightful pride of all in these days when 'together' is branded sin by PC's fractured codes. The period's right for such brave endeavour for surely she of such a plate did not like mere 'Brighton' build for it's not 'Mon Repos' nor 'Dunromin' after all. Such people too, alas long vanished, so none to pay their respects to Beauty now for none now knowing it for look around you to see Britain's blighted land — no more Mr Blake's 'Green & Pleasant Paradise'. I thank her for her lovely bookplate because through her I made this journey to visit the great at the birth of their journey. She has left her signature on time no less than they for she fired one who came after to see as she, which is Art's Artifice achieved, for it is not the size of god we are which matters, but that we be god at all. I thank her fine mortality for she left a little immortality from which I sprang this story — for it's what Man does not what Man is which matters.

Explanation:

Those whose know will recgonise how much I owe to Mr Noel Langley's atmospheric reconstruction of the Dante & Beatrice story '*The Inconstant Moon*' — exquisite, of a style not available in literature today — go find a copy — then 'see'. I make no apology whatever for using Gemma as a foil as Langley does, a master of the story, nor of marrying her to Giotto in the way I have, because the truth (that she, long after, made Dante a fractious wife for coming from within the heart of his enemies) makes no sort of story at all, whereas I think mine does. Nor do I seek to excuse the plays on Dante's Divinity and his masterwork; a childish game I know but fun, and if Johnson's assertion about writing for money's a truth (which for us aspirants it is) then let there be some fun because fun is a form of beauty by raising spirits while beauty sits a self-confessed divinity secure in Man's measure of true worth. Those doubtful of the verity of Bondone's 'tourist attractions' should go shopping in the main street of Delphi, we have a small bronze satyr with one big enough for a coat-hook, no equivocation with the detail either while the painted plates leave no room for equivocation.

Surely Man needs to be taken out of himself, have the lips-un-pursed to free him from convention's pursings — *then* a lovely story to spur him ever upwards, with the interest of his own condition intertwined. It is the secret which storytellers have always known used to be our first concern, alas no more for soaked, like the Florence we have seen in the lusts of us. It is this which songsmiths, bards and troubadours down time have known, that Man needs cheering on, yet with a guiding hand — if he's to prosper. So, I beg to be allowed to join their historic brotherhood — specially in these days of the predominance of The Police State driving Socialism's Cage with the worship of self and fame, which is precisely The Cage of The Dark Ages and the poisons of Medieval Florence which 'Little Gemma' helped to spring — for 'she knew the truths of it'.

Any student of the sublime who wishes to travel The Pilgrimage of 'seeing' should read Ruskin — alas long un-published in his now illiterate native land; but the land to whom we supremely gave our language, America, reads and prints him avidly today from whence you will find him in many gorgeous Victorian bindings as he was published widely, on both sides of the Atlantic. This 'seeing' is no small claim as it was Ruskin's visits to Florence in 1845, aged 26, two years after the meteoric *'Modern Painters'*, (one of the greatest acts of 'seeing' ever) which had him see something utterly neglected since its own day for eclipsed by Raphael, Michel Angelo and the later 'greats' — the truth of those who had blazoned the New Knowledge across art two hundred years before — The Pre-Raphaelites indeed. In 1854 he wrote for The Arundel Society *'Giotto and his works at Padua'*. We might ask ourselves who came first Ruskin or The Pre-Raphaelite brotherhood, formed in 1848 by the young Hunt, Rosetti and Millais for in those three years Ruskin had become a meteorite in the art-world while its founders were all under 25, ripe for the revolution, *'Modern Painters'* had set in motion. To start your pilgrimage try both *'Frondes Agrestes'* which is an independent selection (by a 'Lady of Coniston') of *'Modern Painters'* and the two delightful lectures published as *'Sesame & Lilies'*, which will give you the feel of a great man's Mind, while *The Seven Lamps of Architecture'* should be read by anyone creating anything for its concerns being entirely those of Truth.

My other source is both the study of Dante in my Quarto *'Divine Comedy'* actually titled with its originals of 'Hell' for volume I and 'Purgatory and Paradise' for volume II and the excellent *'The Vision of Dante'* in Frederick Warne's *'Albion Series'* which is the Francis Cary translation.

Specially do I owe Mrs Stephen Ralli the perspicacity to have bought those 'Little' Guide Books upon the impulse (on Hove Parade?), or was she close to the Ruskinian Scene in Victorian London so had them presented to her — but whatever, to be so proud as to attach her splendid bookplate to each of the seven little volumes which I have (set incomplete alas) for it was not merely Ruskin which had me buy (at not inconsiderable cost they being so rare in this single form) but her bookplate which spoke of someone who had not tossed the little books aside, the normal fate of guidebooks, but had treasured them by 'signing' them in such exotic style — a measure of their worth, I thought. I was not deceived for it was the first five pages of **SANTA CROCE** (risen upon my Langley and Dante) which fired this story.

Some time after this story was finished I was completely delighted to find Mrs Stephen Ralli was indeed something — considerable. A Ralli herself she was wife to Stephen, son of Pandias Ralli the founder of the Greek Community in London in Victoria's early reign whose firm Ralli Brothers was the largest trader, of any sort, in late Victorian London. Philanthropist extraordinaire Stephen brought the firm to heights of national importance before his death in 1902. His lady wife died in Brighton in 1922 — something indeed but perhaps his biographer did not distinguish between Brighton and Hove — where was Hove after all!

Aphrodite, January 2010

About the Author

The author behind the Margaret Montrose pseudonym earned his Higher National Diploma (HND) in Mech.Eng. in 1961, then spent ten years in industrial R&D, during which he restored, raced, and rallied the vintage 1920s cars that were his only transport. In 1971 he started his own company, driving his own production machine tools, which he built up to begin manufacturing his own award-winning patented products. Over the next forty years he restored and sailed an iconic 1905 yacht, restored and lived in two Tudor houses, and drove numerous *pro bono* associations, clubs, and campaigns, writing all they stood for. He stood for Parliament on an *Out of EU* ticket, for which he wrote all the material, achieving five times the *UKIP* vote. He started writing seriously in 2001 while building a thousand-book library as a voracious reader across The Classics. He's a folk-dance musician, Bell-Ringer, an absolutely original creator in everything, and a person for whom The Cage is anathema as The High Hills are the only place to be.

For more of Margaret Montrose read *The Golden Path* at

www.thegoldenpath.co.uk

The Golden Path Quintet

by

Margaret Montrose

The Golden Path **is a journey –**
Whose romance lies in travelling through
The Mystic Continuum of Man's Common Humanity
To seek the Spiritual Enlightenment of ancient civilisations,
Which was The Holy Grail of The Templar Knights, to find
The God Within Us.

www.thegoldenpath.co.uk

The Fresh Ink Group

Publishing
Free Memberships
Share & Read Free Stories, Essays, Articles
Free-Story Newsletter
Writing Contests

Books
E-books
Amazon Bookstore

Authors
Editors
Artists
Professionals
Publishing Services
Publisher Resources

Members' Websites
Members' Blogs
Social Media

www.FreshInkGroup.com
Email: info@FreshInkGroup.com
Twitter: @FreshInkGroup
Google+: Fresh Ink Group
Facebook.com/FreshInkGroup
LinkedIn: Fresh Ink Group
About.me/FreshInkGroup

www.ingramcontent.com/pod-product-compliance
Lightning Source LLC
Chambersburg PA
CBHW020051180626
46812CB00006B/2283

9 781936 442287